OBLIVION
a Novel Place to Live

by
Hank Bruce

Copyright Hank Bruce 1999
ISBN   978-0-9797057-0-0
Published by Petals & Pages 2007

Cover photo and design by Tomi Jill Folk

Petals & Pages
860 Polaris Blvd SE
Rio Rancho, NM 87124
petals_pages@msn.com

Dedication

This book is dedicated to the woman I love, my wife, my best friend, and my inspiration, Tomi Jill Folk.

This began as a short story in 1997. Then, with Tomi's encouragement it became a serial with installments created in the early morning hours before she awoke. It was her encouragement, support, patience and above all, her love that made this book possible.

Thank you

A book doesn't just happen, nor is it the efforts of one person sitting alone at the keypad. A book is a reflection of all those we come in contact with, all those who touch our lives in so many ways. It's the everyday people, living everyday lives that provided the inspiration and were the models for the characters who occupy this ghost town called Oblivion. Thank you to all those who make a sense of community possible.

Thanks to the poets and artists, and all those who dare to define today and possess the courage to dream of a tomorrow filled with peace and possibilities. May we all find hope in their vision.

The environmental issues discussed within these pages have been with us for a long time, long before global warming was cool, long before the difficult realities we face today. There have been voices crying out, even when we would not listen. Thank you Al Gore for having the courage to speak, thank you to all those scientists and tinkerers, activists and environmentalists who got their hands dirty seeking solutions. These are the heroes that all of tomorrow's children will appreciate.

The vision of communities based on creativity rather than control, cooperation rather than competition, diversity rather than division is now not only a possibility, it is a reality, and perhaps it is the model for a peaceful tomorrow. Thank you to those daring to dream the redefinition of community.

And, a special thanks to Alvin Rafelito, a visionary who dares to dream of a better world, for sharing his insights and his efforts to create a community built of compassion, cooperation and communication where everyone works, plays and grows together.

Prologue

Empty was the best way to describe this place they once called Oblivion. It was a forgotten community of abandoned memories. The buildings were crumbling, windows vandal broken, roof beams fallen under the weight of too many years. Handmade adobe bricks were gradually, with each infrequent rain, releasing their clay to the valley floor, proving that nature inevitably reclaims her own.

This town had died long ago, as many towns do, from starvation. A community is nourished by its people. It takes men and women thinking, working, learning, worshiping, shopping, eating, playing, laughing, and loving together. Villages also need youth, more than adults; because they are today's promise and tomorrow's hope. Infants, toddlers, school children and teens are all needed by their nurturing community. It's a symbiotic relationship with the future.

The people all left Oblivion. This wasn't a grand exodus. They left gradually, one individual or family at a time, leaving behind fewer neighbors to sustain the businesses not already boarded up. Homes built of dreams were abandoned before they could become realities. The last heartbeat of the community was stilled when the school closed and the post office was moved to the only slightly more thriving community of Juniper Crossing seven miles down the road. This part of New Mexico's high desert country, sitting between the Rockies and the Great Plains, was ruggedly beautiful, uniquely designed by Mother Nature and Father Time.

Part One

Finding Oblivion

SPRING'S LOVE
She comes with gusts of laughter,-
The music as of rills;
With tenderness and sweetness,
The wisdom of the hills.
-Bliss Carman

Chapter One

Belinda's Story

The cell phone rang from her purse across the desk. When she reached for it her elbow tipped the coffee cup, spilling its contents over the sales projection charts she'd just printed. The grandfather clock continued to tick away Belinda's life, one second at a time. Once she had delighted in the rich tones with which it proclaimed the passing of hours. Now, it sounded ominous as it mocked her failure to meet the deadlines, scolded her inability to work faster, reminded her again and again of the pressure that controlled her existence.

She had become a full partner in the advertising agency little more than a year ago. Today it seemed a decade had passed. It began with the need to work through weekends. Then, as her ability to sell high powered campaigns became obvious, more of the work load was on her desk. She, like so many of us, became a victim of her own success. She ate fast food lunches on the run; dinner was a meeting with a client, indigestion was the dessert. Nights were spent in research, preparation, and contract review. Julie, Maddie, and Josh were able to go home to families, find comfort and escape in the security of love. Belinda knew she was a failure in the romance department as well.

1

Now, the only men she had time to meet were clients, and, in spite of the innuendos from competing agencies, that wasn't how she sold advertising.

The phone rang twice more while she re-ran the printout, gulped some coffee, forgot the now cold toast, and changed clothes three times before finding just the right outfit. She stuffed a Granola snack and a candy bar into her briefcase, then raced to the elevator only to wait almost ten minutes in the cold misting rain for a cab. Finally she arrived at the corporate offices of World of Play Inc. with three minutes to get to the fifth floor conference room and set up the Powerpoint presentation. Horns were blowing, people shouting, doors slamming . The crescendo of noise attacked her ears, literally forced her to the wall. She just wanted to scream, to make it all go away, even for just a moment.

The annoying scrape and click of the automated doors announced a means of escape from the street. The outside sounds were held at bay by the muted music of the '60s, murmurs of conversation and the rustle of newspapers being turned to the sports page. As she almost ran to the elevator, she saw Maddie struggling to balance her umbrella, the box full of presentation folders, and a Starbuck's coffee cup.

Maddie should have been here thirty minutes ago. She should have had this all set up, ready for the client's arrival and Belinda's presentation. Anger began to well up within her as she glanced back and forth from the clock on the wall to the elevator door. Her rage was a flame fueled by sleeplessness and exhaustion. Pressure, and the stress it spawned, grew to become the monster in the closet of her mind.

The presentation went well, even though it got underway almost fifteen minutes late. They had to wait for several of the World of Play people to arrive, be seated and conclude their small talk. The biggest ad agency in St. Louis had scored again. A multimedia "School's Out" campaign would hit Saturday morning TV. Magazine ads, grocery and

2

discount chain promo packages, Internet Web pages, and endorsements from actresses who had never had children were all parts of the national program soon to be underway. By June every child would be driving every parent crazy with demands for "Disposa-toy kits." Toys created to be used once or twice, then discarded. What an idea this was. No need to find storage space, no need to fret over loss or damage. These lightweight plastic and paper toys were packaged in plastic bag, and they all sold for under ten dollars, and most of that expense was the cost of advertising.

As the meeting ended, all the men and women clustered around Belinda. For the first time, she noticed they were all wearing the uniforms of their chosen career, grey suits, red ties and that damned ubiquitous cell phone. They shook her hand, grabbed her by the arm, patted her on the back. They fired questions, and bombarded her with suggestions, simply wanted to touch her success as if she were a corporate talisman. Each person present wanted a piece of her, wanted to use her to advance his or her career, satisfy a personal agenda.

She was so tired. Adrenalin had powered her through the hour and thirty minute presentation, but now she was in withdrawal. First, she began to shake; then she was incredibly weak.

One of the World-of-Toys sales managers was suddenly in her face. He grabbed her by the arm and demanded to know, after glancing in the direction of his boss to make certain she was watching, why Belinda hadn't included a cereal box promotion.

She struggled to remain composed as she put down this wanna-be with an explanation that covered a failure in her marketing strategy. "That, we are saving for next year's campaign, along with the Burger-King promo." It was this lie, this damned C. Y. A. lie, that drove her to the realization that she didn't even like herself anymore.

The arrogant bastard had pushed her to the edge. But, as is usually the case, it isn't the big stuff that makes us snap. She picked up a ballpoint pen from the table to make a note. It refused to write. The scream could be heard the length of the hall, all the way to the fifth floor lobby. Belinda held her hands in front of her, clenched her fists, and stared into the eyes of each person in the room, one at a time. The silence was complete. No one moved. She never spoke another word to them. All she did was carefully close her briefcase and hand it to Maddie. Next she slowly disconnected the laptop, carefully closed her briefcase and motioned for Josh. Still without a word, she turned and walked out. She walked out of the building, down the street, past the restaurants, past the office complexes. She continued to walk until her legs would carry her no further.

This was a part of St. Louis she had never seen before. It smelled different. The people didn't wear suits and ties. No one was carrying a laptop. There were accents in the speech she heard, the music that escaped windows was different. She glanced at her reflection in a storefront window. The rage returned. She had to get out of this damned uniform, this "dressed for success" business suit. Across the corner was a Goodwill Thrift Store. For less than ten dollars she had a pair of slightly used jeans and a Mickey Mouse sweatshirt, along with jogging shoes endorsed by no athlete, abandoning the heels and hose. They seemed to appreciate the donation of the business suit, and she certainly wanted no part of it, not ever again.

She stood in the doorway and looked up at the gray sky. The drizzle of rain had stopped. There was the hint of a sun beyond the clouds. Energy returned once she was free of the burden of corporate fashion. She began to walk again. This time the steps were lighter, her burden was lighter.

She was standing beside Ronnie's Used Bicycle Shop. The elderly man who ran the shop patiently explained the differences among the bikes he had available. He gave her a can of Coca-Cola while she tried the blue and green ten-speed that seemed to invite her to escape on its back. She paid the fifty dollars cash and thanked Ronnie for letting her buy her freedom.

4

She was going to return to her apartment but passed another thrift store on the way and stopped. There she bought another pair of jeans, several tee shirts, a raincoat, sweatsuit and a backpack. She laughed to herself about how shocked her associates would be to see her wearing recycled clothes. Then she realized they'd never see her again. This realization, this germination of an idea within her mind brought a broad smile. The K-Mart on Hyde street was where she filled her backpack with snack foods when she realized she was never going to return to her apartment. It was in the other direction. It was in her past.

By seven that evening she was enjoying a dinner at a Day's Inn twenty miles west of St. Louis, twenty miles and an eternity from Disposa-Toys. She slept well that night.

Belinda was a lonely traveler on this journey we call life. She was also a poet. True, she didn't know it, not yet. As with all creative arts, poetry wouldn't be work as much as a state of being for her. As is the case with many adults, she had not yet found herself. Only recently had she become aware of the fact that she was even searching. In her mind she was, at best, in retreat from a life that wasn't bad, simply not what she was anymore; at worst, she was the consummate failure. It took courage to pack all of her life, or at least all that she deemed necessary, and leave on a bicycle for she had no idea where. She had possessed not only a job but a career, and she ran from it. She was so successful that a work week of seventy or eighty hours was the norm. She was good at devising ways to convince people that they should add to the clutter of their lives with money they didn't have. Now, this no longer had meaning to her. She wasn't certain that life itself had much meaning at this point in time. Belinda was one of those people who had lived with intensity, with fire. Then it seemed to her that smoldering coals were all that was left. Now these embers were being fed and new flames were being born.

It had been almost three weeks since she left the apartment and that meaningless existence centered on work, the career that had vampire-like drained her soul. In the days cycling along the highways and country lanes, chasing the sun into the west, Life was becoming a reality for her. She had encountered the beauty of what others called weeds: daisies forming a lace of petals along the roadside, dandelions with their powder puffs of gold and seedheads glowing silver in the sunshine, Indian paintbrush with its flares of red marching up the hillsides and down the road cuts. She had seen rabbits, owls, lizards, horned toads, several fox, a skunk, deer, and the more domestic views of sheep and cattle. She had heard multitudes of birds, magpies, ravens, and jays. This morning coyotes greeted the fading moon from the distance of several hills, but that lonely voice had carried clearly and it spoke a powerful message to her. While she paused along a little traveled highway for breakfast, hummingbirds visited penstemons so close to her that she heard the faint hum of their wings.

Without understanding what was happening, she was beginning to turn these sights into visions, then mentally wrapping the visions in words. The words formed songs in her head. It didn't even dawn on her that she was answering the coyote's mournful howl, the mockingbird's blissful trill, even the conversations between ewes and lambs. She was feeling the terrain as it changed under her feet; rock, clay, sand, bare soil and soft grass all soothed her soul through contact. Often now, the shoes were tucked in the bike's basket as she sought this primal connection with the earth. It was so different from the feel of concrete, tile, and carpet. The soil seemed alive, and she seemed alive with it; perhaps she was drawing life from it.

Belinda tasted wild berries, something she had, all of her life, been afraid to even think of doing. After all, Mother had so often warned her about such dangers as poison fruit, strangers, and new ideas. This afternoon she had gathered a plastic bag full of strawberries, sweet wild strawberries. She cracked the shells of some peanuts, and shared them with a friendly stellar jay. She was beginning to take her meals less in restaurants or diners, and more along the road. Twice, she

6

even slept out in the open, under the forever blue-black sky, lighted more beautifully than Christmas by billions of stars, more stars than she had ever seen under the city nights. Even though she had cash and bank accounts that would afford her a comfortable, even luxurious motel room, she liked the scents carried on the night breezes. Moist earth and sweet herbs, junipers and night flowers satisfied the soul far better than the artificial atmosphere produced by roaring air conditioners. Her legs and arms strengthened, her skin tanned. She earned a sense of self confidence that her life in the city, work in the office, never afforded her.

It was on the twenty-first day of this journey that she decided to leave the paved highway and follow an abandoned road, now being reclaimed by gramma grass and golden wildflowers of spring. In her now playful mind, this was the yellow brick road, and she was Dorothy.

The sign post was broken and lay forgotten in the arms of a sprawling cholla cactus. The fading letters read "OBLIVION" and the arrow now pointed skyward. She held the weathered piece of wood in her hand and smiled with anticipation. Belinda didn't know if this was some joke, or if there really was a town named Oblivion. She was hoping to discover a forgotten ghost town. Her new found sense of adventure drove her forward.

She had rounded the hill and began the descent into the valley before she saw it. She had to stop and etch the picture of these decaying buildings into her mind. Words danced in her imagination, words of sadness, words of past joys. She closed her eyes and heard the cries of infants, the shouts of children, the murmurs of life itself.

There is a distinctive and perverse beauty in a town devoid of its humanity. Such a place is filled with mysteries. To some, coming upon such a discovery, the question is one of plunder and salvage, "What can I take from this place?" These are the unfortunate people who lack the ability to build and create for themselves.

For others, there is an almost overwhelming loneliness. These are the people who know the terror of being alone, live with it, perhaps face it daily.

Others see the abandoned structures, and contemplate the events that forced those people to seek their lives and futures in the vast somewhere else. Belinda could feel the pain of these people in leaving what they knew, deserting their dreams, uprooting their families. Were they facing an undefined future with desperation and fear, or were they eagerly anticipating the change, the new opportunities? Such an act can be either courageous or cowardly, depending on the motivation.

A fortunate few are intrigued by the process of change. Perhaps they can relate their life to that of the ghost town. They see a beauty in the way nature, with quiet confidence, reclaims its own with nature's trinity; wind, the breath of Mother Earth; water, the life blood of all existence; and the sun, the source of all. The sun holds the promise of life, illuminates and warms the earth, defines the cycles of existence, and, most importantly, encourages plants, from simple fungi and lichens, to grasses, shrubs and trees. These plants are the workhorses of nature. The earth mother uses them to clothe while they consume, repair and rebuild. Asphalt, tin cans, buildings of wood and adobe all fall to the green leaf, the most powerful force on earth. And a new community is born.

"It's the way the flowers run wild, the way the colors splash against the open doorways, the way the vines rejoice in another hill to climb. Even if that hill is a decomposing house," he spoke as he stood and slapped the dust from his faded jeans.

She was startled by the presence of another human being, and righted her bike, ready to flee. She could find no words to respond, yet curiosity held her to the spot. The voice behind her sounded gentle.

"Didn't mean to startle you. I just thought you were taken with the way the afternoon sun was throwing shadows and halos." He adjusted his baseball cap, and fumbled with the sketching pencils held

8

in his hand. Finally, he simply dropped them to the ground, stepped forward and extended his hand in greeting.

Suspicion tightened her grip on the handlebars, but she found her eyes drawn to his. As he stepped closer, she could see into his soul through his bright brown eyes. Soft lines curved from their corners. There were also lines from his mouth and cracked lips that broke up into a multitude of past smiles. This man's history was recorded on his face. She was reading this story and saw pain, courage, joy, sorrow, and hope. She also saw the loneliness, but most of all, she saw a sensitive soul; so sensitive that they communicated without words. In these few moments, their hearts were engaged in a most intimate conversation.

He was in the dappled shade of a juniper, but the sketch pad rested against a sandstone rock, glowing in the sunshine. She was intrigued that the work was illuminated, but the creator remained in the shadows. She smiled again when she saw the well-worn holster on his belt. It contained not a weapon, but a handful of pencils, blending stumps, and a couple of shading brushes. A worn and frayed blue bandana was tucked into his belt. A plastic grocery bag rested against a clump of gramma grass, revealing a cheese sandwich, a pack of Oreos, a battered old army surplus canteen, and a well-used Mickey Mouse Thermos. A small digital camera completed the catalog of his existence on this hillside.

He motioned for her to climb the few steps that separated them, and again extended a hand. When she felt his grip, she felt safe, comfortable, and happy. His smile broadened and a joy, unknown before, swept over him. Images from the photo album of his past flashed through his mind, but they were discarded as the present overwhelmed him. Career failure, his inability to be what everyone else wanted him to be, times of loss and loneliness were washed away in this flash flood of happiness.

"Do you come to Oblivion often?" he asked, then apologized for his breech of etiquette. "My name is Ben. I'm a half-assed artist and

9

part-time gardener, farm hand, odd jobber down in Juniper Crossing." Shame at the failure to own a successful life drove the smile from his face halfway through his introduction.

Belinda introduced herself, and apologized for her appearance. She felt waves of guilt over her abandoned career course, and reluctance to be what was considered a responsible adult.

"No, I've never been to Oblivion before; yet, there's something about it. Like, somehow I'm a part of this town." Her thoughts were flashing from empty life to empty town. The analogy was a simple one.

"You must be a poet," his smile broadened at this perception.

"No," she fumbled for words, "office, business, that kind of stuff," was all she could force herself to disclose. She pushed the wisp of brown hair from her eyes and tightened her lips to hold back any more words that might escape.

"Yes, you're a poet; for you to see the beauty in the decay of a building, you have to be either a poet or an artist, . . . and . . . I'm the . . . a . . . artist." It was as though he was struggling to identify himself.

They shared an uncomfortable laugh, neither willing to open their past to the other. The town became a safe subject to discuss. They climbed down the hillside hand in hand, and soon stood at the edge of Oblivion. Almost all the buildings were hopeless ruins, crumbled shells of their past glory. They entered the doorway of the first structure, a blacksmith shop/garage. All the tools had been hauled away, most of the scrap iron had even been gathered. The adobe bricks had eroded into talus slopes of red clay, but the sandstone of the forge had held its own against the elements and vandals. With a little repair to the chimney, and the removal of the swallow's nests, it would even now hold the comfort and warmth of fire. The vigas that had once held the roof lay on the floor and across the heavy oak work table. The mechanical bones of an ancient auto and whiskey bottles were all that remained to speak of the former residents.

10

Several homes lined the street. Built of wood, they were skeletons of framework. Siding and roofing lay on the ground, felled by wind, weather, and age. Mamma Nature had, here and there, used the domesticated members of her family to heal the wounds humanity had inflicted. Roses had gone wild. They rambled over fallen timbers, shattered glass, and lost dreams. One of the houses even had roses reaching out of the windows into the sunlight. All the windows were now devoid of glass. Doors had been stripped from their frames, and hauled away by previous visitors.

Ben pointed out that even within these deserted structures, the decay was not as severe as first glance would imply. The framework was still sound, even if the siding shell was being shed, like a snake sheds its skin to gain a new one, bright, and supple, and better than before. The wallpaper had peeled from the walls and lay in shredded piles, where the Great Recycler had used it to provide warmth and shelter to kangaroo rats and deer mice. The tile that gave the floor substance held true, providing a dependable base for whatever future claimed this town.

They roamed through the shops, and an old doctor's office. One of the more substantial buildings was the bank, where time had collapsed the teller's cages into a prison for unclaimed boxes of mortgage papers and bank memos. These were the remains of debts that had been paid not with dollars, but with souls. Now, the debts were being held prisoner, and the souls were free. The police station was stripped clean; even the stove pipe had been stolen.

Few of the buildings in Oblivion still retained their doors or the security of a roof. The most structurally sound building was the jail. It was built of sandstone, with bars cemented into the walls for windows. The jailer's office still retained its oak paneling, now weather stained, while the four cells continued to hold their cots behind iron bars. In one of these cells there was a battered and dust-filled tin wash basin and pair of boots, now occupied by mice and spiders. The solid roof timbers still held the clay tile without complaint.

Belinda was startled by the rustle of life. Birds had nests in the rafters, swallows built their homes on the secure walls, lizards and horned toads sunned themselves on the window sills, and bats gathered in one corner of the ceiling. Buffalo gourd and unicorn vines found their support on the bars and paid for their place in the sun with green leaves proudly supporting their first bright flowers of spring. From the bars of one window, they watched a roadrunner pursue a small snake, and a family of quail seek their dinner of sunflower seed and wild rose hips.

"Strange, isn't it," he spoke while standing behind her, with his arms about her waist, an embrace that neither realized was happening, "that the most secure building in the community is the one designed to restrain its members."

They laughed, joked and took childlike delight in each shared discovery, every bright flower, all the golden rays of sunshine. They spoke barely a word about their yesterdays, nor did they contemplate any tomorrows. For now, they were content with the joys of today. As the shadows lengthened and the sun turned orange more than yellow, they sat in the doorway of the jail. They shared the coffee from his thermos, his cheese sandwich and the one she had bought in the Jiffy-Mart that morning. They watched a woodpecker seek his fortune along the fallen timbers of Jacob Baur's Saloon and Dance Hall. This was the largest building in the community, obviously the center of social life, when there had been a social life in this now empty town.

Ben pointed to something rustling through the briars climbing toward their glory along the side of what had, in the days when people occupied Oblivion, been Martinez's Mercantile Emporium. Today it would be called a convenience store. The round eared, white-footed mouse came out from under the leaves and studied them with its nose. The owl appeared, on silent wings from unseen obscurity, and the grocery continued to provide sustenance for Oblivion's residents.

12

The owl stood on its stilt legs, looking like an out-of-proportion clown, smaller than it really was. It held its head sideways, trying to study both the mouse struggling in its beak, and the visitors it apparently felt obligated to entertain. Finally, the mouse was dropped, as the burrowing owl chose to satisfy its curiosity before it filled its belly. It took several steps toward them. There's a comic incongruity in an owl on stilt like-legs walking toward you in the middle of the afternoon. Owls are supposed to symbolize wisdom and intrigue, witchcraft and the secrets of darkness. They are, after all, supposed to be creatures of the night. But here was proof of nature's sense of humor. So much so, that Belinda laughed. Her spontaneous response broke the magic of the moment. The little burrowing owl wasn't curious enough to overcome his instinctive fear of being laughed at. He took flight.

They explored more of the town, found grass growing in the long abandoned adobe brick forms carelessly piled at the side of a clay pit. They found several battered enameled tin cups, a pot, several broken farming tools, pages of a newspaper from 1912, the year New Mexico became a state. They came up the back street to a barn and a corral that was in surprisingly good shape. There was a watering trough and a hand pump. The trough was dry and filled with sand, seeds, leaves, and flakes of mica; windborne silt, but not pollution, as much as potential life. All that was needed was to add water, and life sustaining green would appear.

Ben worked the pump while she used the broken shovel to remove the accumulated silt, but nothing came. The sweat of exertion now soaked his shirt and dropped from his face to moisten the soil. Large wet patches appeared under her arms, as both the back and the front of her shirt darkened. He thought he could hear a gurgle deep in the well. A hint, a promise perhaps, but not yet a reality. They looked at each other, not sure why it was that they wanted the water, why they needed the water.

"It sounds like this old pump needs to be primed." This was the first he had removed his cap. He looked older in the setting sun. Older with the silver claiming its dominance over the browner hair of youth. It was like snow that first dusts the hillside before claiming it totally. Yet, when the snow wins, it provides first the purity of the moment, then, the sustaining water of life.

"I think I can hear water down there somewhere," Belinda responded as she leaned closer. "What do you mean, prime?"

"You have to pour some water down this pipe to create the suction that lets the pump pull the water that's deep inside."

"Sounds like a Catch-22 to me. If we didn't need water, we wouldn't be playing with this pump to begin with."

He looked at her, wiped his sweaty palms on his jeans, and took her hands in his. "Why are we doing this?"

She pulled him closer, wrapped his arms around her, and kissed him lightly on his salty cheek. She didn't answer his question. She simply took his hand and led him back toward the blacksmith's shop. "I have a water bottle is on my bike. Will that work?"

His canteen was half full, her water bottle, slightly less. To use this to prime the pump was risky. It very likely wasn't enough. Even if it was, the water from the well might not be potable. He pointed out that they were in the middle of nowhere, literally in Oblivion. Being without water is very much a matter of life and death in this arid terrain. It was with reservation and a lot of self doubt, that they sacrificed their remaining water to hope. It was a gamble, and it was also an act of faith.

She emptied his canteen, while he plied the pump handle. They could hear their water trickling down the old pipe, but he couldn't feel the subtle change in pressure that would announce their success. He became almost fanatical, cursing under his breath and driving the handle up and down, faster and faster, while his breath became shorter, almost gasping.

14

She wanted him to stop. She grasped his arm, fearful of what failure would do to him, but also understanding that he already owned the failure. Finding the water, bringing it forth, sharing the effort and the victory was the only way to erase it. She whispered a silent prayer that he would know this small success, as she unscrewed the cap from her bottle, and emptied it down the pipe.

Nothing! Nothing at all changed. The pain in the pit of her stomach was for him. Then she heard, from deep underground, a change in the pitch of the gurgle. He felt the increase in pressure on the pump handle. His strokes became more deliberate. He raised the handle's arc as high as possible, and drove down as the orgasmic gush of water splashed into the wooden trough.

They laughed. The salt of joyful tears mated with the sweat as they took turns at the pump, so each could drink the cool, fresh liquid. It was pure, and so was their joy. They splashed each other, and both felt a happiness they hadn't known before.

It wouldn't have been a matter of life and death, this sacrifice of their water. Juniper Springs was only seven miles down the road. That was where Ben currently lived. He had a little one room apartment there, a part time job, and a half empty life he could easily have returned to. The failure to fill the trough would have been only one more addition to his catalog of failures. Belinda could have gotten back on her bike, and ridden out of Oblivion, into her undefined future. Instead, they celebrated.

Dusk is only a brief interlude between daylight and dark in the high dry air of New Mexico. They took this opportunity to carry all their possessions into the jail, the most substantial building still standing. They hadn't spoken of this approaching night. He felt different, since they had shared the sacrifice and success at the water pump. He watched Belinda as she opened her sleeping bag. His soul was wrapped in a warmth and glow he hadn't known for years. What he felt, he dared not hope for, yet he had already risked failure at the

15

pump. He gathered twigs and scrap wood and built a fire in the street. While it was not yet completely dark, the night chill was beginning to descend.

He felt his salt-crusted shirt, and smelled the day's sweat on his body. He gathered some of the wood under his arm, and told her of his intention to wash up at the trough.

She busied herself with the sorting of her few possessions, mostly jeans and tee shirts for traveling. She felt something, but couldn't force it to the front of her mind. When she pictured Ben, smiles claimed her lips and eyes. She felt a safety with him she hadn't known before. She reminded herself that he was an unemployed artist, a relic of the sixties, flower power and free love. But perhaps, just possibly, his quest for beauty was more right than her empty career had been. Perhaps there was something she could learn from this strange man she knew nothing of. It was curiosity that led her steps as she gathered her soap, towel, and washcloth.

He had removed his shirt and washed his hair, face and arms. Then he glanced around, added a few pieces of wood to the second small fire, leaned against the trough, and eased his feet from his boots and socks. She stopped, and stood watching in the shadows. She saw poetry in the broad back and shoulders that could carry an artist's burden.

She gasped as he loosened his belt buckle and unzipped his jeans. He pulled himself free of all clothing, and stood naked before the water trough. She felt uncomfortable feelings, as she debated whether or not she should offer the towel and soap. She hadn't expected him to be nude. She didn't know if she was ready for this. Yet, she was driven by something other than reason as she called to him.

He turned, startled, then instantly embarrassed. He had been splashing water on his chest and stomach. In the reddish glow of the fire, his body glistened. He reached for his shirt and held it in front of him, as she extended her hand to him, the one containing the soap. Her

16

apology was awkward, and ended in a giggle. He dropped the shirt to the ground, as he accepted the soap and washcloth. His shyness was being overcome by other feelings, emotions his body felt and reacted upon.

"Oh! What the hell," she laughed as she laid the towel on the edge of the trough and pulled her tee shirt over her head. Her liberated breasts were beautiful in the firelight, soft, smooth, comforting, and inviting. He wanted to touch, but dared not. She washed his back, savoring the feel of his skin, the warmth and gentle strength within. He washed her hair, then spread the soapy water over her back. They giggled away their embarrassment as they helped each other into the tank for a proper bath. After the day had been washed from their bodies and discoveries made, they stepped out and dried each other. Then, they washed their clothes in the bath water, and rinsed them under a fresh flow from the pump.

They gathered their clothes, and put out the fire. He draped the towel over her shivering shoulders, then, hand in hand they walked through the darkness toward the fire in front of the jail. She had dry clothes; he didn't. She lent him her jacket, and laughed out loud every time he bent over, exposing his buttocks. He stacked some pieces of lumber to make a drying rack by the fire and hung his clothes for morning. They had a light snack of crackers and canned tuna. The last of his Oreos provided an acceptable dessert.

They sat in the doorway of the jail talking, while a symphony of night creatures serenaded. Neither spoke of themselves. Rather, they discussed Oblivion, pondered the people that must have lived here, what the future of such a place could be, or, if this village was like many people, who seemed to be possessed of no real future. Finally, he spoke of art, and his drive to create, capture beauty, and make statements. She began to talk of the images and words that had gone through her mind on her journey of discovery. Without realizing it, at some point in the evening, they stopped saying "I" and began saying "we."

It was time to sleep, and a delicate question arose. There was one sleeping bag, and his only clothes were still wet. She'd had lovers before, but this was somehow different. This man possessed something none of the others had. There was an inner wisdom and understanding; a depth and dimension; a willingness to question. He didn't try to impress her with talk of money, cars, power and possession; this, she had never encountered before. There was a part of her that wanted to surrender herself body and soul to this man. Yet, there was a voice inside that said, "You don't know him, he hasn't spoken to you of his past. You don't even know if there's someone else, somewhere else."

He felt waves of desire throughout the evening, and worried that in the pursuit of his instinctive lust, he would cause harm to this tender lady. He didn't know her, not really. She couldn't find the courage to make an invitation, and he lacked the confidence to ask. Finally, inaction made their decision for them. He took the little flashlight she had in her backpack, and cleaned out one of the cells. Then he borrowed her sweatshirt as a sheet, and wrapped himself as tightly as he could in her jacket.

She tried again to ask him to join her in the sleeping bag, but the words would not form on her tongue. Sometime during the night, he walked past her to add wood to the fire, and climb into his almost dry jeans and shirt. He paused, studied her sleeping so peacefully in the open, under the stars. Then he then returned to the cell and slept alone.

She was awakened by the first rays of the dawning sun, a flowing river of light, washing away the darkness, and bringing a flood of hope in the door. She smiled in her half-awake thoughts of Ben. Her jacket and sweatshirt were neatly folded and lying in the doorway. She called, but there was no answer. She pulled on her socks and shoes, combed her hair with her fingers, and stood in the doorway. There were birds, lizards, a turtle of some sort, and the burrowing owl from yesterday; but Ben wasn't there. His bag and sketch pad were gone.

The tears came against her will. Soon, they were accompanied by great sobs, anguished sobs from the heart, a heart that had dared to let itself feel. Then, between the tears, she saw the bouquet of flowers. Yellow goatsbeard and poppies, coral shades of globe mallow and violet scorpionweed, blue sage, and a sprig of juniper greeted her from the battered blue enamel coffee cup. It sat on a sheet from his sketch pad. This was a pencil study of her sleeping in the doorway of the jail, surrounded by flowers, birds, and animals. A hummingbird courted a mountain penstemon while a coyote looked in the door. A fox, several chipmunks, and a burrowing owl watched from the side, and a pair of doves sat on the railing.

She clutched the drawing to her breast, and felt new waves of emotion. It was when she looked at it a second time that she saw in the corner, under the paw of the coyote, in the most minute of script, the words "I love you, Ben."

Chapter Two

Ben's night had been agonizingly long. Sleep came only in broken pieces; shattered nightmare visits from the past, and dreams from a future he was afraid to face. He was torn between a desire for this mysterious lady asleep in the outer room, and fear that a new relationship would only result in new pain. Several times he awoke with a sense of suffocation; a half awake terror at the sight of the moonlit bars on the windows. Even with the door open, he felt that he was being held prisoner.

Indistinct sounds invaded his mind. Several times he thought he had heard faint footsteps, the clink of a tin cup, muted tones of men snoring. Sounds touching his mind came from some great distance in time or space. He hummed softly to make these noises go away. But when he closed his eyes again, they were back. They were suggestions of activity that could be felt, more than heard. Was this the life of the past forever imprisoned within the walls?

He thought again of Belinda as he sat on the hard wooden bunk. Was she a future he would never know, or was his future being held prisoner by a past he could neither change nor escape?

Finally, he pulled on his boots, gathered his pad and pencils and left the cell, even though he couldn't set his life free. He walked past her, sleeping peacefully in the sleeping bag. Her hair spread softly over her face. He knelt to give her a kiss, started to brush the hair back from her cheek, then withdrew his hand and stood. He stared at her for several minutes. Tears of emotion escaped the corners of his eyes.

The fire warmed his hands and illuminated the sketch pad while he plied the pencils with a passion his art had rarely known. He studied the form in the doorway, the doorway itself, then drew images from his memory. His hands and mind were in perfect sync with his heart. He shaded, darkened lines, softened and accented features, created depth, employed every technique he knew. The result was truly a work of art, but more than that, it was a work of love.

The sun was hinting its arrival while he made the last corrections, added the last lines, used up the last ounce of his creative soul, and included the fullest measure of love he was capable of giving. His regret was that it was all in black and white, when he knew how much delight she had taken in the colors of this ghost of a town. In the first light of the almost dawn, he gathered a handful of wild flowers and placed them on the drawing. Then, he heard the voices in his head again, along with morning sounds of coffee cups, faint shouts and fainter laughter. These were sounds of happiness, and he had to escape. He studied her sleeping form for several minutes, almost kissed her again, then turned and ran. He ran harder than he had ever run before. Out of Oblivion, down the yellow flowered road, and onto the paved highway leading to Juniper Crossing. His lungs were aching, his legs throbbed with pain, but he couldn't stop running. Finally, he stumbled and fell. He could go no farther. Each gasp brought intense pain to his chest. He was dizzy; his vision was blurred. He heard the early morning calls of the raven. Then, his mind faded into its own oblivion.

"Hey! Hey, Man! You been drinkin' again?"

He could feel his body being shaken. Voices were floating in the air above him. His eyes focused on the smiling, concerned face of Carlos Chavez.

"Don't smell no booze," the voice behind him said. "He may be having a heart attack or somethin'. Be careful with him." This was Domingo, Carlos' older brother. "Ben. Ben, can you hear me?" He was fumbling with Ben's wrist, trying to find a pulse.

After a drink from Carlos' two liter bottle of Pepsi, Ben convinced the brothers he was, at least physically, OK. They offered him a ride into Saturday morning farmers' market at Juniper Crossing, and during the fifteen minutes it took them to reach the parking lot, he never stopped talking about Belinda and the time they spent together in this forgotten town. They let him out at the entrance to the long row of stalls where the farmers, local craftsmen, and Indians brought the products of their labor to sell.

Normally Ben took great delight in visiting the stalls that displayed the variety of cultures and the characters that define the humanity of New Mexico. He was usually mesmerized by the laughter, sounds of vendors hawking their produce and products, voices speaking in English, Spanish, Navajo, Pueblo dialects and the music that was so spontaneous. His mind would swim in the aromas of chiles, fresh bread from the Picarus Pueblo, Stanley Crawford's garlic and fresh herbs, hay bales, live rabbits and chickens, dogs in need of a bath and the honest sweat of working people.

His artist's eyes should have been fascinated and stimulated by the colors, bright and bold, in constant motion, ever changing, like a kaleidoscope, in the always present sun. But not today. Today every lady bore Belinda's face, walked like her, smiled like her. He didn't hear the joy of the marketplace, he smelled only her perfume as it had come to his senses the day before. The color of the place was, to his eyes today, as black and white as his sketch to her had been.

"Man! You better go back and marry that gal," Domingo advised with a wink.

"Yeah! You really got it bad, Ben," Carlos added as he handed the artist the remaining half bottle of Pepsi.

"How," Ben thought, "How do I dare let her know how I feel? How would I find her again? Surely, she's not going to stay in Oblivion."

They wandered past the stalls and tables, watching as young lovers and old couples strolled past, wrapped in each other's love at best; companionship, at the least. Ben felt more alone than he had ever felt before. His mind could place Belinda at his side, but his hand couldn't feel the warmth of her hand, his lips couldn't feel the warmth of her lips. He strolled past the booths and tables, not really seeing

22

anything but the images of Belinda in his mind.

He passed a battered card table where some bearded and besotted vagabond of an artist had set out his work for the edification of a small town market. Here was another refuge from the age of Aquarius, the time when innocent idealism let an entire generation to dare dream a better world. A time of youth when they actually thought they could make a difference. Ben felt a kinship with this casualty of the great culture wars. His mind recalled his campus friends who had turned against the prophets of peace and hope for a better tomorrow, to follow the profits of greed for a richer today. To Ben, this crushed soul before them may have been defeated by his society, but he had never surrendered; for that he deserved respect.

Ben studied the renderings of barns and missions done in acrylics. They failed as art, much as the artist had failed at life. The spirit of those buildings was more imprisoned than captured. His artist's soul was insulted by this derelicts's watercolor landscapes that replaced the depth and enchantment of the land with ineffective splashes of misplaced color. Yet, he grudgingly admired the courage this derelict possessed, the guts to let his talent stand naked before the world.

Ben knew his work was better. He cursed his reluctance to publicly display the art he had created. The room he occupied at the back of Sam McGiven's Realty office was filled with true expressions of the soul. The moods of people, the beauty of flowers, the charm of wild and domesticated animals, the dynamics of mountain and desert, and the spirit of the land were to be found in his work. He understood that good art comes not from the skill of the hands, but the perceptions of the soul. Yet, he always found his work inferior, unworthy, not quite good enough. Just as in living he was inferior, never quite good enough, unworthy of love.

"Hey! Hey! Ben," the voice was coming at him from behind a waving newspaper. "Look at this, man. They're sellin' your town."

23

Ben stared at Carlos, struggling to comprehend what was being said, "What town?"

"Oblivion, Man. That pile of rubble where you screwed that gal of yours. It's being sold at some kinda government auction. Look here. It's in the paper."

"I didn't screw her," he was immediately defensive and secretly regretful.

"The hell with her. The town's what I'm tellin' you about, Amigo. The state's sellin' the whole damn town." Carlos put the page in Ben's hands, and wet the pencil lead with his lips. "Here." He circled a couple lines in the middle of a page of property being sold at auction.

The state's intention was to return more than a hundred thousand acres to the tax rolls, and that included a parcel listed in the smallest print possible. It was Property #301 and all the notice said was "two hundred and seventy-two acres comprising the prior community of Oblivion."

Compared to the vast tracts, timbered mountainsides, and prime sites for development, or those with mining potential, this forgotten and abandoned community of Oblivion was vastly overshadowed.

"Carlos, I ain't got money. How the hell could I make a bid. Why would I want to?"

"Amigo, you buy this place, then you spend your life painting pretty pictures of it."

"Yeah! Ben," Domingo added to his brother's sales pitch. "You fix up one of them buildings, out there. Marry this Belinda of yours. She can write her poetry and make tortillas y frijoles, or whatever it is you Gringos eat," he delighted in teasing Ben, as only good friends can, "while you do your art thing and fix up those buildings."

"My brother, he's right." Carlos was tag teaming Ben now. "You give her a town, she'll give you lots of ninos. You'll be 'El Patron'."

24

"I never did anything like this before. I don't even know how to bid in a government sale." Ben protested, but Carlos waved him off with a smile. "Besides, I ain't got no money."

"Man, I seen your room. It's so fulla paintings, you can't even walk to the bed without stepping on at least one. You can sell some of that stuff and make several hundred dollars, I betcha."

Ben started to protest, but Domingo joined in again, "Look at this," he pointed at the canvases leaning against the card table, then at the wannabe artist who was scowling at them while he clutched his Jim Beam. "Don't mean to run down your pictures. I'd guess you're maybe just a beginner at it, no? Now, Ben, here," he pointed at the embarrassed figure standing beside him. "Now, Ben's been doin' this a long time, and he's got it down right. We're just tryin' to talk him into lettin' folks have a chance to buy some 'a his stuff. Don't you think that's a good idea?"

Carlos motioned to a young couple strolling past, who had shown some interest in the crude art on display. "Hey! You like to see some really good stuff? Yes?"

The artist's neck was reddening with anger. He threw down his sweet-smelling hand wrapped smoke. Without a word, he began to gather his paintings and load them back into the battered 60's vintage VW van. Ben started to apologize, but the Chavez brothers stepped between the two artists and maintained a constant chatter with both. Carlos even helped the poor vagabond pack up, while Domingo offered to haul Ben's art out to the now empty booth. It was almost impossible to argue with those two Chicanos.

Soon Carlos was on his way to Ben's one room apartment, to get a load of "good art stuff." Ben and Domingo were using magic markers to design a sign for "Premier showing by a world famous local artist." Again, Ben's protests were totally ineffective. As people walked past, Domingo would grab them by the arm, and suggest that they stick around for a few minutes and see some great, museum quality art. "Free Showing!" he kept saying. "As good as Georgia O'Keefe and R. C. Gorman."

By the time Carlos returned, at least twenty people were waiting and munching on the apples Domingo had distributed. Carlos began to pull landscapes from the bed of the pickup. As he held each one above his head so all could see, Domingo would say something about the landscape.

"Ben, he knew a cowboy that used to roam that hillside. Ahh! Such a tragic story of lost love and a desperate life. That cowboy's soul is a part of each brush stroke."

"I kissed my first girlfriend under that juniper." He informed the audience with a wink.

"A shootout that claimed the lives of two men took place behind that barn. It's not common knowledge, but two of the notches on Billy-the-Kid's gun came from that gunfight."

Carlos held above his head for all to see a large canvas done in bright oils. "Any student of history knows that in this canyon a small group of Navajo held off a band of drunken cowboys for two days, till they sobered up and went home."

The crowd was growing with each canvas that appeared. Carlos pulled from the bed of the truck a painting of a fox, and began his spiel, "Pueblo legends tells us how the fox could disappear at will, symbolized cunning, and . . ."

This brought the desired effect. A lady wearing pink straw cowgirl hat and more silver than the average Navajo could work in a lifetime waved her arm, "Are you going to sell these?" Before Carlos could answer she added, "I want the fox."

"How much for that one?" a fellow in scuffed boots and faded jeans called out, pointing to the same canvas.

Ben started to protest, but Carlos held up one finger to call for some time to confer. He thought twenty-five dollars would be a better deal than what they sold that stuff for over at the K-Mart in Santa Fe.

True, it was a used frame that Ben had pulled from someone's trash, but there was a certain comfort in a frame that was worn, chipped, bore the marks of time and survived, much like some of those doing the bidding.

"Hundred bucks and I'll take it." The cowboy was digging into his wallet.

"Wait a minute," an obscenely obese lady called from under the shade of her feathered hat. "I'll give $150 for it."

"You can't. I said a hundred, and that's what I got right here." He was waving the money in his hand.

"Please," Ben called, "This ain't worth . . . "

Carlos whistled in disbelief, but immediately grasped the kind of market he was dealing with. He began treating the paintings with considerably more respect.

Domingo interrupted, "Ain't worth fightn' over. Lady, how would ya like to have this magnificent owl. You know, the owl symbolizes wisdom, and it seems it would be appropriate for you. You certainly seem like a very wise lady to me." The wink was what did it. She smiled. And opened her tote bag of a purse.

Carlos held up the 16 x 20 canvas of a burrowing owl, with two owlets peering from their burrow. She handed him the $150, and seized the canvas before anyone else had a chance to bid. Doming was working a deal with an old cowboy for the landscape of Valle Grande, the great ancient volcanic caldera. They finally agreed on a figure of $200.

By two-thirty, most of the shoppers had either run out of money, or lost their enthusiasm for the open air market in the heat of the afternoon. Carlos had gone foraging among the food booths, and returned with three bowls of "buffalo chili" and a loaf of horno baked bread. Ben counted the money between spoons of a chili that definitely was not the high water mark of culinary art.

"Hey! You hafta get that bid in by four o'clock this afternoon." Domingo was reading the paper while finishing off the can of warm beer he had procured from somewhere in the bowels of the pickup.

Carlos was rearranging the litter and clutter in the bed of the truck, and came up with two more cans of warm beer. "Now, how much money you got?"

Ben carefully counted the cash again, not quite trusting his math the first time through. "One thousand nine hundred and sixty dollars. Wow! This is more cash than I've ever held in my hand at one time in my whole life."

"Come on. Put that stuff back in your pocket. We gotta get you to the courthouse."

The county seat, Las Vegas, was twenty miles away, and it was now three-thirty. Carlos was almost demonic behind the wheel. Curves, potholes, even cattle on the road were only minor inconveniences. Sometimes he was on the pavement; sometimes the tires crunched over sagebrush and saltbush. At one point, he took a shortcut down an arroyo, and saved about two miles while jarring Ben until pain claimed every ounce of his body.

Shortly after they regained the pavement, Carlos got the speed up to sixty-five. Unfortunately, Officer Manny Martinez had just slid his bulk behind the wheel, after relieving himself against a scrub juniper at the side of the road. Ben saw the flashing blue light in the rear view mirror. So did Carlos, and he immediately pushed the gas pedal to the floor.

"It's that son-of-a-bitch, Martinez. Let's see if he can keep up." Carlos was grinning as he engaged in a race. The adrenalin was surging.

Manny was able to stay with them, and the siren screamed an alert to anyone unfortunate to be on the highway ahead. They screeched into the courthouse parking lot, and stopped in front of the "no parking" sign at the bottom of the steps.

Manny pulled up behind them, blocking any escape. He was wheezing when he climbed out of the patrol car. He was also pissed, and his gun was drawn.

Domingo put on his broadest smile, while Carlos offered a handshake, "Gracias, Amigo. We never would have made it in time without your help. Sure was great to have a police escort. Only shouldn't you have been in front?"

These brothers knew that kindly confusion was the best way to disarm any opposition, and they were well aware of the fact that Manny was relatively easy to confuse. The patrolman's brow furrowed, as he tried in vain to understand. He holstered his gun, then pulled out his ticket pad and his ball point pen.

"You were speeding. You endangered the lives of others," he stammered, "you were goin' over 80 miles per hour."

"Manny, that can't be. You know this old truck won't go no mor'n 60. Besides, that piece a junk the county gives you would fall apart if you got it up to 70." Carlos began the debate.

"Later, why don't you two meet out on the old air strip at the Benton ranch and prove who drives the worst piece of junk? Right now we got to help our compadre here," Domingo put his hand on Ben's shoulder, "he has to get to the courthouse before four o'clock."

"Si, Manny. Ben, here, he's goin' to buy himself a whole damn town."

This was more than Manny could take. He shook his head and mumbled something about how glad he was to be of service, as he put his pad back in his hip pocket and made a hurried retreat toward his patrol car.

"Thanks agin for the escort, Amigo." Carlos beamed a victorious smile, and extended his hand once more.

The bids had to be filed at the tax collector's office. They just reached the door as the wall clock began to chime four times. Carlos pushed Ben up to the counter, while Domingo called to the pleasantly

29

plump daughter of Arty Sandoval. He couldn't remember her name, but neatly sidestepped that little detail, as he explained their reason for being there. She got the form out of the drawer, while Carlos spun the hand back to 3:50 on the clock. He then turned and smiled to the clerk. "See. We still got ten minutes."

Domingo continued to flirt with her while she guided Ben through the maze of forms. Then, she pulled a large white envelope from the drawer, and asked Ben for the bid money. He didn't realize that the money or statement of collateral had to accompany the bid, and wasn't certain yet just how much of his cash from the sale of the art work he should put into the bid.

Domingo patted her hand, and made some comment about how lucky the tax collector was to have such a beautiful flower blooming in this office. She blushed, and looked down at the floor. "By the way, Ms. Sandoval, just between us, how have the bids been running on that pile of rubble they call Oblivion?"

She told them was that there were only two other sealed bids on that piece of property, and was about to pull them out of the locked box when Vidalia Shoat, the tax collector herself, came in the door, studied the clock, then her watch. After a moment of hesitation, she reset her watch and warned everyone on both sides of the counter that time for bids was almost up. Ben hesitated for only a moment, long enough for the image of Belinda to appear in his mind, before he put every dollar he had in the envelope.

Carlos had gone out to the pickup for a smoke, and was looking at one of the few remaining works left from their impromptu art auction. It was a small pen and ink sketch of a coyote pup watching a mouse. The softest of watercolor shadings gave the work almost a glow. Carlos was studying the picture so intently, that he didn't see the bicycle pull up beside him. The lady was so drawn to the sketch, she didn't bother with the kickstand, but let the bike fall.

"Is that for sale?" she asked from behind him.

30

He spun around and held up his hand, while he started his spiel about the local artist who had a great love of nature and . . .

"I think I know who did this. You don't need to tell me about him." She pulled two twenties and a ten from her wallet, and handed them to him. Before he could grasp what had happened, she had wrapped it in her raincoat, and gently placed it in the basket of her bike.

He shouted, "Muchas gracias, senorita." But she was already on her way down the street, heading into the bright afternoon sun.

Carlos ran into the courthouse and burst through the tax office door, just as the clock began to chime four, for the second time.

"Here! Here! I just sold another one." He handed the fifty dollars to Ben, who, without thinking, added it to the one thousand nine hundred and sixty already in the envelope.

Vidalia took the packet from his hand. "All bids have to be in by four p.m. The commissioners will be here in a few minutes to review them. If you care to wait about an hour, we will be posting the property awards."

Chapter Three

Carlos left Ben and Domingo sitting on the tailgate of the pickup. They were joking about what Ben would do with Oblivion if he did win the auction. As Ben's friends, they both knew he had a great deal of affection for the town. First from an artist's perspective; he saw great messages in the decay of human endeavor, and the undaunted reclamation of her own by Mother Nature. They also understood that there were now deep personal feelings attached to buildings. Feelings that echoed his personal emptiness, his private loneliness.

He knew he wasn't here just because he didn't know how to say "no" to the Chavez brothers; his mind was focused on Belinda. He could picture her, sleeping in the doorway of the jail, standing beside him in the shade of the juniper as they gazed down on the town, and bathing with him in the water tank.

"Hey! Ben! Where you at?" Dom laughed and slapped the artist's knee, "Man, you got it bad."

Ben smiled weakly, "I was just thinking. What would happen if I did buy the town?"

"Sure beats buyin' the farm," he joked again.

"That old town's dead. It's falling apart. Just like me."

Domingo laughed out loud. "Don't think like an old man. You just learned today, you're really an artist. Man, you just hit your stride. You're gonna give this senorita of yours a whole damn town and you're gonna fill it full of ninos. You watch. You gonna have folks flockin' to Oblivion. You gonna be El Patron."

"Yeah, Ben." Carlos came up behind them offering cans of Dr. Pepper and Hostess Twinkies. "You're famous now. That gringo gal on the bike that bought your coyote, she said she knew the artist already."

"That was HER!" Ben jumped down from the tailgate, "You saw her. Where did she go?"   He pointed down the street, toward what passed for the low end shopping district of Las Vegas, a K-Mart, a run down Albertsons, and several other shops in a strip mall where grass and cactus were growing through the cracks in the parking lot pavement. Ben took off at a run, leaving the Chavez brothers laughing and shaking their heads. It was with a combination of drive and desperation that he checked each bike, bike rack, store front and alleyway. He was gasping for air, lungs aching when he got to the other end of town. He had found neither Belinda nor her bike. He stood, staring at the only highway out of Las Vegas, a dusty road, devoid of traffic. The late afternoon sun turned the tears on his cheeks golden. He didn't even bother to dry his eyes. The loneliness was soul-crushing, a burden that bent his back and made his feet so heavy he could barely put one in front of the other.

He stared into the setting sun, as it cast long shadows. Shadows that became ghosts of the day before. These gray images spoke to him in whispers. They told him he was a fool. He had known happiness, and he had run from it. Then the shadows laughed at him, and they wouldn't stop, even when he screamed.

He didn't see Carlos approach. He didn't even feel the friend's arm on his shoulder. He accepted the can of Dr. Pepper without conscious effort. He was thankful that the shadows had quit their torment. He could hear Carlos babbling, as they turned and started back toward the courthouse, but nothing registered. He saw Belinda's face in his mind, his hands were touching her hair, he saw his lips gently kissing her cheek. He could almost see her smile, but the tears clouded his vision. He was angry with his own cowardice, his own insecurity, his own surrender to fear. Twice he stumbled on the broken pavement of the WPA vintage sidewalk before Carlos slapped him hard across the face and shoved him down onto the concrete park bench.

"Listen to me! Damn you, Ben. Listen to me!" His hand was raised and ready to slap his friend a second time, "You fool. You bought Oblivion!"

Jose's Café seemed like a good place to pause in her retreat from Oblivion, and Ben. She took the piece of art inside with her and found the most secluded table.

There were tears in her eyes as she carefully unwrapped the pen and ink sketch of the coyote. Her fingers traced each line. Her eyes absorbed every subtle shading. Gradually, as she studied the work of art, the animal's face became the face of Ben. Finally, she was inside the work of art herself. The words poured forth without effort. In flowing script, she wrote a poem about Ben, his art and the nature of coyotes. She began comparing the much maligned canine, the trickster of Indian legend, to the Fates of the ancient Greeks. Her writing was out of her control as the coyote turned into a muse, both inspiring her words and mocking her cowardice in the face of love.

The waitress interrupted her with a glass of water and a menu customized with food stains and splatters. She settled on the $1.95 bowl of chili and a cup of coffee. Her mind kept returning to the empty town. Yet, Oblivion wasn't empty. That's where Ben had spent the night with her. The tears flowed into her chili as she struggled to understand why he had left.

The coyote in the painting asked her in silent whispers, "Why did he run from you?"

Before she could respond to his ridicule he asked her, "Was it your flaw, or was it his?" She studied the innocent looking face of the coyote in the painting for several moments before she answered with a question of her own. "Should I have invited him to my sleeping bag? Should we have made love?"

He winked at her, then retreated into the two dimensional world of paint and ink once more.

34

Images formed a collage in her mind: of him standing nude before her in the twilight by the water tank, of him sitting by the fire wrapped in nothing more than her sweatshirt, of him sleeping in the jail cell. She could see them standing on the hillside. He was holding her hand as they looked down on the town bathed in the glow of the afternoon sun, awash in the glow of their own new found feelings. Why had he run from her? What had she done wrong?

The unanswered questions were like knives thrust deep into her soul. She consumed half the bowl of chili and left a five-dollar bill on the table. She dried her eyes on the sleeve of her sweatshirt as she wrapped again the two drawings she had acquired in this day of joy, pain and confusion. Then she peddled the bike as fast as she could, hoping that distance would relieve the pain in her soul. It didn't work.

When Carlos and Ben returned to the courthouse, there were dozens of people milling around the steps. Rita Sandoval was taping the list of auction bids and winners on the door. Domingo, was smiling broadly and motioning for them to hurry.

He grabbed Ben by the arm and literally dragged him up the steps. There had been three bids on the defunct town of Oblivion. Courtney Dobson had bid $1000 with the hope of turning it into a wildlife haven. Cal Benton, of Benton Enterprises, had put in a bid of $2000 and was in a state of rage because he had lost. Ben's bid of $2010 made him the owner of a town called Oblivion.

Most of the folks on the courthouse steps were interested in the timber, minerals or grazing rights, or access to water to be found on the larger parcels. As the winners were formally acknowledged, speculators brought out their checkbooks, and the same piece of property was bought and sold several times. One strip of barren land, where rumor had put great deposits of silver and turquoise, had gone for two hundred and fifty thousand in the auction. The winner was offered two million. He didn't hesitate a minute. He had walked the land and knew scrub juniper and cholla were all that was to be found there. He lived comfortably by mining the greed and stupidity of others. His career was based on his ability to plant rumors and reap a harvest of greed.

Courtney had Ben by the arm before he got to the top of the steps. "I just wanted to congratulate you on the acquisition of Oblivion," she purred at him as she brushed the silver hair from her grandmotherly face. "I was wondering if we could perhaps have dinner and discuss your plans for that charming little haven."

Ben looked deeply into her face, blinked and saw the smile of a grey fox. Through her thick bifocals her aging eyes had the depth and magnitude of an owl's. At some inner depth he knew she possessed a spiritual connection with nature. Perhaps she was one of those who he had read about, someone that could pass between the two worlds, the human and the wild. He also sensed that she was not as much a creature of the present as she was of the past and the future. Her smile was benign, but within was great strength. That kind of strength that lies somewhere between warrior goddess and universal grandmother.

"Are you the one that just bought that tumble-down pile of ruins they call Oblivion?" The tense voice spoke from behind Ben. Then he felt the hand, heavy on his shoulder. His artistic sense felt the negative aura. He could also read it in the eyes of the lady beside him.

"I'm Cal Benton. I own the land beside that town and would sure like to add that little worthless piece of empty desert to it." His smile wasn't intentionally mocking, but he couldn't hide the sense of superiority his checkbook gave him. He was accustomed to buying and selling people, as well as property.

Ben stepped back, and studied Cal. Courtney's hands clutched Ben's arm tightly. He could feel energy and courage flowing into him through her. "If Oblivion is that worthless, why are you so desperate to own it?"

Cal waved his checkbook, "Look here! I'll give you thirty thousand dollars right now for that pile of rubble and firewood." His face was reddening with rage.

36

A raven called from the elm. Courtney smiled. Ben turned and started down the steps.

"Fifty thousand!"

Carlos smiled this time, "He don't understand, does he, amigo? You can spend the money and it' gone, but if you can build the town, it gives you life."

" Don't give into him, he's dinero loco, money crazy. He don't know how an artist thinks." Domingo added.

Ben had no intention of selling Oblivion, even though he had no idea what it was he had just bought, or what he was going to do with it. He was just doing what felt right.

Courtney kissed him on the cheek, "Belinda will be proud of you." She turned and started to walk away, then reached into her pocket and removed a crumpled fifty dollar bill. "Take your friends to dinner. Then return to your town."

The sun was behind the mountains now. The brief southwestern dusk was tucking all the trees and creatures of the day into bed and covering them with a blanket of twilight. The creatures of night were awakening. The raven took to wing with one last call. It was answered in the distance by an owl.

"That Courtney is sure one strange lady," Domingo commented as the trio entered Anita's Cantina.

"Yeah," Carlos added, "She worked with Robbie Madrogone, when he ran for governor. She helped form the Green Party. Then she gave up on politics. Said she had a better way."

"Es loco en la cabeza," Domingo added.

"But, how did she know about Belinda?" Ben pondered out loud.

It was almost eleven when the pickup rattled into Oblivion, and Ben removed the two cardboard boxes that held his unsold art and a bag of groceries from the bed of the truck. He started toward the jail. True, it was the most secure building in Oblivion, but that security confined, restricted, limited. Security was, in many ways, a prison. With his flashlight he began to explore the other buildings. His sense of the town was totally different now that he owned it. He was possessive; he felt responsible. An inner sense told him that now he was obligated to protect it as well.

The little Catholic church was almost directly across the street from the jail. Part of the roof was gone, the windows had all been broken out, the bell had fallen from its moorings and crashed through the floor. But this was the building he was drawn toward. Ben stood in the doorway. Toward the front, in the light of the flashlight a rose was in bloom. A vine had crawled in the window and sought the light that streamed in from the heavens through the hole in the roof. Ben spread his blankets on the floor under the flower and slept well. In his dreams he relived the night before.

Belinda was trying to escape Oblivion, Las Vegas, and the heartache of Ben's retreat as she followed the setting sun. She was exhausted when she finally stopped for a drink. The small open space between two hills seemed to be a secure place to spend the night. She found a comfortable spot down the slope from the road and started a small fire. With the flames she could feel secure and enjoy a cup of coffee. While the fire began to release its warmth and light she set the two works of art so that they were illuminated. She thought she was staring at them, but she was actually looking deeply within herself. Logic told her that Ben was still in the little community of Juniper Crossing. That she could find him, if she wanted to. What was this swirling blend of emotions that she was feeling? She had been in love before, but it had never worked. Had she spent too much of herself on her career? Was she afraid of the soul freedom that Ben possessed? She looked again at the pictures, flames dancing across them, giving them a life of their own.

38

She poured the coffee and reminded herself that it was Ben who had run from her. She heard the night sounds, distant coyotes conversing, owls, the orchestra of insects, the hiss of a wildcat and lonesome moaning of the wind as it climbed the hillsides. She shivered and pulled a sweatshirt around her shoulders. She could hear the roar of motorcycles in the distance, but she didn't hear the footsteps behind her.

"It's going to be a cold night." The voice spoke, "A cold and lonely night."

As she turned, she seized her canister of hot pepper spray. Fear made her tremble. At first she couldn't speak. Then, as her eyes focused on the little grey haired lady with the grandmotherly eyeglasses, she started to laugh.

"Belinda, you are in danger if you remain here. You have someone who will protect you, if only you will give him a chance." She stretched out her hand and brushed the fire across the stones and clay, destroying the flames without any apparent harm to herself. "No need to advertise your presence."

"Who are you?" was all Belinda could say.

"My name is Courtney Dobson. I'm called by some a naturalist/environmentalist. I like to think of myself as an activist. Others call me crazy, but isn't everyone? Tonight, I'm here to help a friend, two friends."

A small owl glided silently into the juniper.

"We haven't much time. Put your bike in the trunk of my car. I'll gather your pictures. He's a great artist, isn't he?"

They were barely on the road before the herd of motorcycles descended. They were on both sides of the car, and soon two of the bikers were in front of them. When they stopped, Courtney had no choice but to stop also, or run over them. She couldn't do that. One of the bikers was searching the edge of the road for a rock he could use to break the windows. Several of the others were shouting, laughing and making vulgar comments. The one with the bandana tied on his head stood on the hood of the car and urinated on the windshield. They began rocking the car, then the one who had been looking for something he could use to break the windows returned with the tool he had been seeking. It was without warning that the lightening flashed. The thunder was deafening. The rain was a deluge, frightening in its force, devastating in its effect.

"Rain always washes away the filth," Courtney said as she drove over one of the cycles and sped down the road toward Oblivion.

They hadn't gone a mile before the rain was over. Belinda gazed at the sky filled with stars, more stars than she had ever seen before, and tried to understand the source of the rain. They spoke little as they continued past the county seat and on through Juniper Crossing. Courtney stopped at the cholla holding the sign for Oblivion. "This is as far as I can take you. The rest of this journey is yours alone. Much has happened that you don't know about, and you have much to learn about yourself." Courtney handed Belinda the sketches, "Cherish these as a beginning. Remember that all art is a journey, not a destination. Understand also that life itself is an art, and you are the artist, painting your own destiny."

"What is it I'm supposed to do?" Belinda was in tears. This old lady was the only person she could turn to.

"That isn't a single question, but a multitude of them, a lifetime of them, and the answers lie in here." She responded, pointing to Belinda's heart. "You can go down the paved road to cities yet unvisited, or you can take the rutted lane to Oblivion."

40

Chapter Four

Belinda stood by the edge of the road and watched the car disappear into the distance. She carefully lifted the sign from the arms of the cholla cactus and positioned it so that the arrow pointed down the weed filled ruts. Then, she righted the bike and followed the arrow. She was certain that it was right to be there, but she also felt that Ben wouldn't be in Oblivion. He was probably in Juniper Crossing. She needed some solitude, some space, some time to think, to find her direction. The old lady had said, "Much has happened, that you don't know about." What did she mean? Belinda was trying to understand, not just what Courtney had said, but who this gray-haired old lady was. Was she a witch of some sort? Perhaps she was just a crazy old woman, escaped from some institution. Yet, she seemed to know Ben.

Each question begat another; soon it was so overwhelming that she had to stop and look again at the sketches. In the moonlight they seemed to take on a glow, to again become almost living things that spoke to her. The picture of her sleeping was calling her back to Oblivion. The birds and animals beckoned. She could even hear their calls. In the night breeze she could grasp the scent of roses mingled with the sage and creosote, the juniper and chamisa.

The coyote in the second picture looked up at her and smiled. Then she heard the cry from the distance. The lonesome call of a single coyote. She gathered her belongings again and continued in the only direction she could go. She paused on the hillside where she had first met both the town and the artist. Oblivion looked so different in the moonlight. Now it seemed somehow to be alive. Shadows moved in the cloudless night, and a warmth drew her from the hillside to the town itself. She walked her bike from the shop at the edge of town to the doorway of the jail.

It wasn't rational, but she felt that she wasn't alone. There were faint sounds that could be mistaken for footsteps, voices whispering in the night, children coughing, dogs barking; all so far in the distance that they were felt more than heard. For a brief moment, she heard drums. She wasn't fearful, not apprehensive, but rather comforted by the non-existent presence. She felt safe in the arms of this town. She unwrapped a Nutri-Bar and set about opening her sleeping bag on the floor of the jailer's office. It somehow didn't seem right tonight. She pulled it out onto the street and sat finishing her snack. She was trying to decide whether she wanted to start a small fire where they had built one the night before, when she thought she heard someone snoring.

This was a clear, distinct sound, heard by the ears, not the mind. It was coming from the church across the street. Her first instinct was to retreat to the security of the jail, but curiosity overpowered the fear. With a flashlight in one hand and pepper spray in the other, she cautiously approached the house of worship.

From the doorway she could see the shower of moonlight bathing Ben, while above his head hung a rose. It was a picture of such serene beauty, she wished for a moment that she could paint it. Then she returned to her backpack and removed the pad and pencil. She retreated to the back of the church and sat cross-legged in the doorway while she created a poem; words of a love yet unexplored, a life yet unlived.

After it was completed, she slipped the sneakers from her feet and walked silently to the sleeping figure. The page from the notepad was speared on a thorn from the rose; to be held until he awoke. As she turned to leave, the thorn lost its grip on the poem. It drifted down on a soft breeze to rest on his cheek. He turned, and through half opened eyes saw her, framed by the doorway. "Dreams can be powerful things," he thought as the vision of her vanished. He rolled over and felt the paper. He held it up to the moonlight and began to read her words of love, and hope, and joy. He read the lines of insecurity, fear, discovery and loss. He was inside the words. He was the words. What

42

was written was from the heart, her heart, but it was from his soul as well.

He couldn't understand how she could be here. He was afraid to go out into the street. Afraid she wasn't really there. If she had been, had she run, like he did? He sat on the edge of one of the remaining pews and shouted, "BELINDA, I LOVE YOU. WHERE ARE YOU?"

She had been trembling since leaving the poem. Now she heard his cry. She turned and ran up the steps of the old church, up the aisle and into his arms. They hugged and kissed. Few words were spoken, but few were needed. They made love on the church floor, and slept well in the comfort of each others arms.

Belinda was awakened by a rose petal falling on her face. She could smell coffee. She pulled on his plaid shirt and went to the doorway. He smiled up at her from the stone fire ring he had made, and offered a chocolate chip cookie. She crossed the street to stand before him, wearing only his unbuttoned shirt in the crisp morning air. They had a cup of coffee and several more cookies before returning to the blankets on the church floor. They again explored and enjoyed each other.

When they awoke the second time, they raced to the water tank and splashed and played with the innocent abandon of small children. They washed each other's hair, teased and reveled in their love for each other. After an hour or more of this, they dried each other and raced nude to the church and their clean clothes. It wasn't until they were watching a roadrunner, racing clown-like from bush to bush, that Ben told Belinda about the auction. It was as he was telling her just how close the bid was, that he realized that her purchase of the coyote sketch was what made the difference. They laughed at what both agreed must be their destiny. They spent the rest of the afternoon examining every building. They agreed that the first building to be repaired was going to be the small stone and adobe at the end of the street. It had a secure roof and good fireplace, for comfort. In earlier days it had been a restaurant. The large windows would be ideal for an artist's studio.

It was assumed, without any comment from either of them, that this was to be their town, their life together, their love to grow and make fruitful. It may have been because each was too insecure to say anything to the other, or perhaps, with the awareness of the depth of their love, it was simply not necessary.

It was late in the afternoon when Belinda pointed to the dust cloud up the road beyond the hill where they had met. Her first fear was the bikers from the night before. She started to tell Ben about them, but he told her not to worry. It was only a minute or two before the old pickup rattled to a stop in front of them. Carlos jumped from the ancient vehicle and waved to Ben. Then he took Belinda's hand, and with a courtly bow, kissed it.

He turned to Ben and winked, "See. I tol' you. Buy the town, you gonna be happy. I betcha you got a nino in the oven already."

Domingo scolded Carlos, nodded, and greeted the couple. "We brought you some food and the rest of your stuff. We got some news, too."

While they carried the second-hand double bed, purchased at Goodwill to replace Ben's old cot, into their new home and put it together, there were jokes and laughter that became delightfully risque. Ben was embarrassed by his friends, but Belinda was comfortable with their genuine friendship. She enjoyed the company of real people. She helped them carry in boxes of art and books, while the brothers placed Ben's old table and four chairs, none of which matched, by the window that would catch the morning sun. He was ashamed of the furniture that reflected his poverty; she reveled in its sincerity. Into the small dwelling the four carried a battered old dresser, a tattered sofa, a wooden rocking chair, and several oil lamps. They joked about the lack of electricity, while Carlos brought in a can of lamp oil. The brothers kept up a constant chatter as the empty restaurant gradually became a home. Joyful ghosts of the past lived in the walls, and during the brief moments of silence, Ben could hear other sounds, other voices from the past, pleased that new occupants, new life, had come to Oblivion.

"Cal Benton, he ain't gonna to give up. He's appealing to the state for the right to seize control of the water rights." Carlos told them.

"It seems that rights that haven't been renewed for so many years are up for grabs." Dom explained. "He's got thirty days to convince the state that Oblivion doesn't really exist."

"That means we have to prove it does," Belinda was ready to fight.

"How can he claim it doesn't exist? It's even on the maps." Ben was trying to grasp what this was all about.

"To have a town, ya gotta have people." Domingo was getting worked up now, "A town's gotta have a gas station, someplace to eat, a school . . ."

"Yeah, and a town's gotta have kids, and adults, to use these places. They say you got thirty days to fill Oblivion with enough people to make it a town."

The four finally unloaded the entire stock of Ben's worldly possessions, then shared the beers and a bag of Doritos Carlos had brought along for the celebration.

It was Belinda who posed the question, "How are you going to get people to move into a town like this?"

Ben thought first of turning Oblivion into something like an artist colony, as they had done at Madrid. Then, he thought of his past, and suggested the homeless families he had seen in Santa Fe. "They might want to come here and fix these places up, grow some vegetables, and such."

Carlos was concerned with the kind of people they would be. Druggies, winos, wackos, and worse were found on the streets. "Some hard workin' Chicano farm hands. That's what you need."

45

"Yes," Belinda asked, "How do we pick the people for our town? Could we make it something like a retreat for people who need to escape from the stress and pressure of the business world?"

Thoughts, ideas, fears and possibilities from each of these four were shared and explored for the rest of the day as they set about bringing life to Oblivion.

By nightfall the kitchen was as functional as possible without running water or electricity. A makeshift bedroom had been set up, and windows measured for glass. Ben had made another pot of coffee and was just about to pour a round for the four of them, when the otherworldly call of an owl invaded the building. It was a sound that was both threatening and reassuring. The brothers looked at each other, but spoke not a word. Belinda's mind raced to the sounds of the night before, and the face of the old lady. They heard the approach of a vehicle and gathered at the open doorway. Courtney Dobson waved to them from the car; a wide smile of victory was spread across her face. She was dressed in jeans, a yellow plaid shirt with a black vest and black felt lady Stetson. Whatever it was she had in the briefcase, she was obviously very proud of it.

"If you fellas can get these groceries out of the trunk, the young lady and I will set a most unique table for you." She was winking at Belinda. She walked past Ben and patted him on the backside, whispering something that made him blush.

While Carlos unpacked the groceries, Domingo continued his struggle to secure the door that swung on bent and twisted hinges. Belinda and Courtney conferred at the table. Papers were spread in little piles that soon claimed part of the floor as well. Soon they were placing an assortment of foods on the papers. Glasses of water, little loaves of bread, slices of what looked like ham, a bowl containing a cheese spread with an array of herbs around the rim, and a brown bag filled with jewelry and trinkets occupied the table. Belinda had a bag

46

full of objects that she was setting on the books and papers stacked on the floor. First was a package of light bulbs. A roll of toilet paper crowned another pile of documents, while a children's book of animal stories topped the last one.

Courtney motioned for them to be seated. First she suggested that they each build a sandwich with the bread, ham, and herbed cheese.

"This is agriculture," she said as they consumed their meal. "Our state, in fact, all humanity, civilization itself, exists because of this industry. It is an enterprise that can either replenish or deplete the land." She picked up the stack of papers that had been under the bread, "This is research data on underused grains like quinoa and millet, recently discovered and long forgotten vegetables. She put a paper sack on the table and removed what looked like weeds. "Amaranth, purslane and lambsquarters are incredibly nutritious, but we ignore them because they are native and common."

She slammed her hand on the stack of papers again, "There are literally millions of dollars in research money available, as well as jobs for those able to do this work."

Belinda, with her business background was eager to crunch numbers, but held back and offered the explanation of what they were eating, "The bread is a combination of quinoa and amaranth flour; the ham is a vegetable substitute. No pigs died for our dinner tonight."

Courtney held up her glass and proclaimed, "Water. As you know, this is a critical factor in the southwest, but it is also a matter of growing concern for the rest of the country and the entire world. We have much to learn about water use. Even if we think of ourselves as land creatures, our lives depend on this liquid. Your life doesn't require oil, but it cannot exist without water. Which do you think is more valuable?"

Domingo interrupted, "That's why Cal Benton's gonna beat Ben here outa his town."

Belinda again entered the conversation, "Courtney has bought us time with the water rights issue. Today, she applied to the state to declare this a research center for the study of ethnobotany and paleobotany, sustainable agriculture and the sociology of community-wise water use. The University of New Mexico, the stae of New Mexico and the agencies will review these proposals. They will probably reject them, but nothing can be done to deny Ben's, or Oblivion's, rights until they decide whether or not they have the funds. Then, we go into the court system where we have some powerful friends in the environmental movement, and they have some very good lawyers."

"Until that time, we have to develop a minimum population base and establish a municipal water supply." Courtney was almost lecturing now.

Ben interrupted, "How do we do that? We don't have any people."

Carlos was pleased with himself that he had an answer. "Jimmy Carter can help us. He has this program, I read about it in the papers. I think they call it Habitat for Humanity. Here's habitats. Maybe he can get us some humanity?"

Belinda knew someone who had been involved in the Habitat program and offered to call her the next day.

Next Courtney held up the bag of jewelry, "This represents mining and manufacturing, the twin industrial engines of this nation. Not only do many in these industries rape and plunder the land for the resources, they pollute the air and the water in the manufacturing process, especially uranium mining."

Domingo entered the discussion, "But people, they gotta make a livin'. We can't just stop mining and making things."

"True," Courtney responded, "but we can show industry cleaner, and even cheaper, ways of doing things. All of the items in this bag are recycled products. They are making 2 x 4's from recycled milk jugs;

roofing, roadbeds, even ball point pens, from recycled tires. The bag is made of recycled paper."

Carlos caught on to the concept quickly, "If we could set up a recycle business of some sort in Oblivion, we could make jobs, and people could live here."

Belinda added some thoughts of her own, "Beyond recycling, the future vitality of American industry could very well lie in the development of environmentally friendly ways for people to exist. With yesterday's wisdom and today's imagination we can create survival for tomorrow's children."

Ben sat silently through most of this. Finally, he had to share some of the thoughts that were troubling him. "Every town I see has poverty, street gangs, crime, stinking garbage , and too much noise. I came out here so I could think, and find inspiration. Now you want to turn my town into something just as bad as those."

Belinda wrapped her arms around Ben. "No, Don't you see? We are talking about making a small community that works together to avoid these problems. The future of our earth depends on how we solve these problems, how we respond to the dangers of global warming."

Ben shook his head and watched the rest of the presentation in silence. Courtney held up the light bulbs, then a grant proposal for solar energy research. It would be possible, she explained, for them to actually produce enough energy in this sunny climate to sell the surplus and make a profit with absolutely no pollution or even consumption of natural resources.

Domingo whistled, "Think, man. We spend most of our time working to pay for the energy we use. If energy is free, what do we do with all that new time?"

Sewage was another topic of the conversation. It also got a negative response from Ben.   "Small towns can use settlement ponds to produce a composted sludge useful as a fertilizer on the crop fields. This can replenish the land used by the agricultural community. But, here is an outline for a research project that turns sewage into bricks that can be used for fuel. This eliminates any danger from disease. There are many options that need to be explored. If we are to survive we have to find new answers to some very old problems," Courtney explained.

Belinda and Courtney both held up books for the others to see. Belinda began with a children's book, "The Miracle of the Moringa Tree" then a text titled "Global Gardening."

"It's not only possible for people and nature to work together in harmony, it's the ultimate necessity." With this Courtney held up a thick manuscript. "I have devoted years to the research of this subject. The findings are all right here. IT CAN BE DONE!"

"Incidently," Belinda added, "This book was printed on paper made from recycled plastic, cheaper to produce and recycle than paper."

Ben was beginning to grasp what the presentation was all about. He understood that they wanted him to turn Oblivion into some sort of model community that demonstrated social harmony, environmental common sense, and experimental solutions to the problems facing all of humanity. He understood the nobility of such an endeavor, but was skeptical of their ability to accomplish much.

They talked long into the night about the need for business in their community, defined by Belinda as a convenient middleman in the flow of goods and services from source to consumer. Courtney expressed her concern that many in the eco-activist community viewed business as the enemy. Her argument was that they were in reality the means to be used in achieving this enlightened balance.

They also discussed the need for all people to be a part of something greater than themselves. It was agreed that there was a need to cooperate with each other if there was to be a future, but that one of the greatest needs was to be in harmony with nature rather than at war with her.

50

Finally Ben rose and spoke to the group. "I am the owner of this town, but that didn't happen through my efforts." He turned to the Chavez brothers, "It was your idea, and you made it happen." Next he turned to Belinda, "Because you had an appreciation of my art, you made the winning bid possible." Then he looked into the eyes of the old lady, "You have, in one day, developed a program that may enable us to keep this town. It seems to me that what is happening is no accident. I don't understand the forces at work here, but I don't think any of us could stop it, even if we tried."

Courtney leaned back in her chair, a benign smile formed, complimenting her knowing eyes.

Belinda took his hand, "Don't you see, Ben? You are an artist, and this town is your canvas. This community can be a monumental work of art."

"Only if we do it together." His eyes were almost pleading as he studied her face, trying to read her feelings. His expression echoed the apprehension in his words.

"Was that a proposal?"

Laughter filled the room. Finally, Courtney gathered some of her papers and prepared to leave. "There will be a team of graduate students here tomorrow to plot an array of solar collectors and windmills. Some more of my friends will be contacting you about potential projects that can make this a viable community."

Ben stopped her at the doorway, "I think we have the potential to change the concept of a village. Perhaps we can attract, like a magnet school, a mix of people that share a common goal. Can it be that in the future, communities will be selective and homogenous, rather that the vegetable soup of humanity we have today?"

The owl's call was ominous, a clear warning coming from the remote darkness.

Courtney, shook her head, "The most successful ecosystem is the one that is most diverse. Beware that you don't limit your little society.

The more you exclude, the greater the loss. When you eliminate variety, you create monotony. Animals that evolve specialized lifestyles that limit their ability to change, are the ones known only from their bones. Diversity of thoughts and actions, that is the vitality, the essence of life."

"But, shouldn't we allow only productive, working residents?"

Courtney shook her head again, "Ben, Ben, by the standards of many, you would not be considered productive, nor would I. Because Carlos has an accent, because Belinda is a woman, they would be considered unworthy by some standards."

Courtney departed, the Chavez brothers drove off into the night, and Belinda and Ben were left to make plans, dream dreams of a future neither could yet envision. It's a heavy responsibility, creating your own town, creating tomorrow. Ben was almost overwhelmed with the prospects, and the problems.

The first flares of morning's radiance crowned the crest of the mountains east of Oblivion. Hope and optimism rode these dawning rays. The negative thoughts Ben experienced the night before had made for a fitful sleep. The comforting warmth of Belinda's presence hadn't given him the peace of mind that would let him rest. Now, sunbeams streamed through the windows, turning to gold the flecks of dust that floated through the rays. " Maybe" replaced "impossible" in Ben's mind.

Ben lay on the bed, smiling at her sleeping form beside him. He watched her bare breast rhythmically rise and fall with her breathing. His hand gently rested on her hair, then traced the outline of her cheek, paused momentarily on her shoulder, then softly cupped a breast in the palm of his hand. He had known women before, but he had never known love. For the first time in his life he felt complete, almost confident.

He sat on the edge of the bed for several minutes. The challenge of establishing a town was something for which an artist is totally unsuited . "A town has to be run like a business," he whispered to himself, "and what do I know about business?"

He felt her hand on his back. Her touch was magical. "Perhaps, just perhaps, the problem is that we think a community is a business." Her arms wrapped around him while her fingers gently played with the hair on his chest. "Could it be that you might create, with that mind of an artist, something better? Couldn't we create a better community if we viewed it as a work of art?"

He felt her breasts against his back, as her hands found his increasing desire. While they gave each other the pleasure of passion, the sounds of canyon winds carried, along with the morning chatter of birds, the distant sounds of clinking tin pots, cackles of chickens and the meow of a cat. They could feel the music of a once vital community, the ghosts trapped within the walls of the buildings, hungry for companionship. The energy of their love gave strength to the past and made time a valley one could walk through, in any direction, rather than a one way street where mistakes and failings could never be righted. "Love is the power that can right wrongs, free us all from our imprisoning pasts," was the message they both felt, although, neither said a word.

Belinda dozed lightly while Ben dressed and took a couple plastic gallon jugs to the pump so they would have water for coffee. She rolled over and felt the empty space on the bed that still held the warmth of his body. She thought back to their first night spent in the jail, and how they both felt secure there. Then the joy of discovery when she found him sleeping in the church; how, in the heavenly moonlight, they felt liberated, freed from their past. She surveyed her surroundings now. A building designed to feed people; was it now feeding their souls?

She awoke with a sense of purpose, a whole new set of dreams. Dreams that swirled around Ben. She had never known an artist before.

He was so different. All the other men she had known, both friends and lovers, were focused on success, measured in dollars. These men were mental children, engaged in childish posturing, competing with each other for meaningless goals. Ben was so different. He was capable of looking inside the soul to mirror emotions, of expressing a concern for life in its greatest sense, of seeking joy in a flower, of finding pleasure in the discovery of a fossil eons old, or a stone polished by centuries of running water. She sat on the edge of the bed and, with her new found talent. She painted with words the beauty that was now in her heart.

"The Circle of Yesterday's Tomorrows" flowed easily from her pen, as if unseen fingers helped her hands record thoughts that were more than hers alone.

The last lines were on the journey from mind to hand when she looked at the golden dust dancing in the sunbeam streaming through the window. Her eyes refused to accept the image before her. The first instinct was a wave of fear, to be expected when one discovers that her solitude has been violated. Momentary emotions soon gave way to natural curiosity. She approached with caution, but the instinct to cuddle a small creature is much stronger than the initial fear she had felt. She gently patted the sleeping yellow kitten. It yawned and began to purr. By the time Ben returned with the water, she was feeding it bits of the bread left from the night before.

"We have to call him Sunshine," she announced as Ben stood in the doorway smiling.

He set the jugs of water on the floor and reached for his sketch pad. Within minutes he had captured her likeness, sitting nude on the rumpled bedding, holding the kitten in her lap. He drew the sunbeam flowing across her face and breast to illuminate the feline. With a skill born of love, a skill greater than he knew that he possessed; warmth, hope and happiness were captured in her eyes and smile. The trusting kitten provided the focus for her expression of the gentleness and caring that resides within the soul of us all, just waiting to be set free.

54

Chapter Five

The ancient, battered and abused Jeep emerged from the cloud of dust and came to a halt at the edge of Oblivion. It must have been mechanical inertia that caused it to lurch forward and continue to sputter even after the rotund driver had made his exit and firmly planted both feet on the ground.

He spotted Belinda and Ben by the corner of the building that had once served as a general store. With a grand gesture and wave of the Coors can in his hand he introduced himself, "Chad Van Metter, at your service." He pulled a battered briefcase from the back of the vehicle and started toward them.

Ben was struggling with an arm load of trash. It was with reserved courtesy that he dropped what he was carrying and extended a hand in greeting. Over Chad's shoulder he saw a pathologically thin young lady climb down and begin to pull boxes and bags from the back of the Jeep. While Chad babbled away about the buildings, energy resources, beneficial climate and more, Ben's eyes were focused on the growing mountain of camping gear, books, junk food and cases of beer.

"Hey! Can you boys help me with the bikes?" she called from the back of the vehicle.

Belinda had held back, witnessing the process of greeting that was taking place before her. Now she came forward and stood beside Ben. She studied the young lady, dressed in shorts that were little more than a belt, and a cut-off tee shirt so stained and faded that it's original color and logo were indecipherable. As the dust settled to reveal the visitor's face, Belinda was forced to the unkind thought that this was about the ugliest person she had ever seen. Stringy rust colored hair was pulled back into an off-center pony-tail. Her eyes were hiding behind the thickest glasses imaginable, and the length of her face brought to Belinda's mind a horse's head.

Chad turned, "Frog, that can wait, come on over and meet these folks. You need to put them at ease. I think we scare them a little bit."

Ben was shocked that this crude individual before them would use such an insulting nickname. He was trying to read the young man, but sunglasses concealed the eyes that could tell him so much. Yet, the smile appeared genuine. The clothing was well used, obviously frayed and stained by hard work. Chad's boots were scuffed, nicked, worn at both toe and heel. These were the boots of someone who spent time climbing the hills, hiking the trails, walking the deserts. These were not the dress boots of some wannabe cowboy. Whatever Chad was, he was sincere about it.

Ben's first impression was that this was some macho character, someone that he might have to protect Belinda from, someone who might even be a threat to Oblivion.

But, the smile argued against any such threat, "Damn, I wish he'd take off those sunglasses," Ben thought as Frog joined her companion. He directed his attention toward her. Age would indicate graduate student; the backpack she held spoke in faded and worn letters of the University of New Mexico. Her clothes certainly weren't the high point of fashion. Then he noticed her necklace. It was made of various seeds, some carved, some polished, others simply strung between small pieces of turquoise. This small accessory somehow linked her to him. It was a key that unlocked the door to her soul and revealed a kindred sensitive spirit. It told him she was of the earth, she possessed the sensitive nature of an artist, even if she wasn't one. Regardless of her physical appearance, her soul was possessed of great beauty.

"What brings you to Oblivion?" Belinda finally asked.

"Didn't Courtney tell you we were coming?"

"Are you the students she said would design a solar energy collector, or whatever you call it?" Ben was beginning to relax. The complexity of owning his own village was already beginning to overwhelm him. He was almost ready to accept them, and was thankful for reinforcements.

Frog offered them each a cold beer from the ice chest, "This will be the first time we have had the opportunity to start from scratch. As you build your community, we can make natural energy work in the real world." There was the enthusiasm of a visionary in her voice.

"We'll be taking some measurements, working on some preliminary designs, and, in the next couple days Dr. Taggartt will be on site herself." Chad was becoming increasingly excited as he gazed from the buildings to the expanse of sunlit valley, to the rugged beauty of the canyon walls. "God, what a place to harvest the sun and the wind!"

Soon the four were walking through the town and onto the land beyond.

"How far does your property go?" Chad asked as they stepped over a rusted barb wire fence, falling from weathered posts.

Ben had to admit that he had no idea how much of the ruggedly beautiful valley before them was a part of Oblivion.

"This open space will be a beautiful site for the array, and the backup wind collectors can go against the canyon talus to harvest the canyon winds." Chad was again making grand gestures with beer can in hand. This was a different person that the one who emerged from the Jeep. He was now speaking with the voice of a Baptist preacher at a revival meeting. He was selling something for which he had a true passion. He obviously possessed an absolute confidence in the future of renewable energy, and his own ability to make this project work.

Ben liked people with passion, he could understand them. He was that way with his art. A friendship was forming with this student/scientist/engineer.

Belinda was intrigued by Frog, and wanted to know more about her and the apparently free spirit she possessed. This was something Belinda was just now learning. After years of doing what everyone else expected of her, she was beginning to understand that she had a life of her own, a worth of her own. She didn't have to be judged by her career, her bank account, her possessions. While she was discovering the talent she had with words and images, she still lacked the confidence to identify herself by that skill.

Frog had been reluctant to engage in this project with Chad. She didn't want to see him used again by some greedy insensitive business type that would consume Chad's mind, his talent, his strength, then discard the empty shell. She loved Chad completely, and couldn't bear to see his energy drained by corporate vampires, to see his ideas raped by people possessed with the demons of profit lust. After talking with Belinda she was feeling somewhat better, and was soon eager to be a part of the planning.

Chad had no talent for judging people. He accepted everyone, could talk with anyone, would share his ideas freely with all who expressed interest. Instructors had stolen his work, businesses had made great profits because of his talents, but he was never angry or bitter about it. He was pleased if he could make the world a little more aware of the environmental issues that would influence all life for centuries to come. Although he knew nothing of art, he was beginning to feel a certain kinship with this artist that was walking beside him.

It was Chad who spotted the coyote studying them from the shade of a scrub juniper, but none of them saw the man on the hillside, watching their movements intently with the binoculars. Marker flags were placed at various locations along the valley, potential sites for solar collectors. Frog explained that one of the concepts they were working on was the use of the space under and around the collectors as agricultural land. "I have been thinking that the land could be carved up into garden plots that each family living in the town could use to produce their own food, flowers and peace of mind."

Belinda thought it was a beautiful idea and easily pictured the bright futuristic metallic monsters holding erect their solar panels.

58

Surrounding these she could see green gardens and bright flowers, tended by parents and children as an expression of family and community. It was becoming easier to look into the future of her mind and see images of peace and harmony.

Chad was exploring ideas with Ben while they continued their first tour of the land that was now their responsibility. "If we can combine the concept of sane consumption with the harnessing of solar energy, we can eliminate so many of the problems that plague the world today."

Frog continued Chad's discourse. "We can rediscover our connection with the land, because we will be freed from the need to devote more than a third of our existence to jobs that produce more pollution and global degradation than they do the goods we want and need."

"When I was in business, I created elaborate advertising campaigns designed to convince people to buy things they didn't need with money they didn't have. What you seem to be suggesting is going to run into heavy opposition from the advertising people. Keep in mind that more money is spent to advertise many products, like toys and breakfast cereal, than is used to produce them. Advertising is the engine of industry. The field of advertising is where the truly creative people in the business community reside, not product design or production." Belinda wasn't trying to be negative, but she felt their idealism needed to be tempered with a touch of reality.

"All I'm suggesting," Chad continued his discourse, "is that there is the possibility that we can achieve a state of equilibrium with the forces of nature and the needs of our cultures. The early hunter-gatherer ancestors expended approximately three hours a day on the work of survival. Today both husband and wife labor eight hours or more away from the home and family. Progress since the industrial revolution is what has broken up the family unit, shattered the sense of community and isolated the individual."

Ben could follow this argument. He knew that traditionally the family pulled together, as a team working the family farm, building their homes, running the family business, raising their children by their example, not day care surrogates and baby sitters. Culture wasn't transferred from generation to generation by the virtual reality, or, perhaps it was the virtual unreality, of TV. The computer was well on its way to changing the way human beings communicate, shop and work. He also understood that yesterday's answers do not always match tomorrow's questions.

Belinda knew first hand the frustration and exhaustion that comes from the treadmill of contemporary life. She had known burn out, as the pace of life became faster and faster, the demands greater and greater. She could not only grasp what these two dreamers were saying, she eagerly embraced the opportunity to enrich her life by simplifying it. She viewed the problem as one of lifestyle obesity. The solution was to work off the excess weight.

The stroll along the base of the canyon wall gave them great discoveries of wild flowers in bloom, chipmunks and field mice at play, several jack rabbits, a sleepy pair of elf owls nesting in a cholla, the beauty of Apache plume with its white flowers and feathery seeds. Ben playfully stroked Belinda's cheek with the soft stalks of gramma grass, picked up several quartz crystals he called desert diamonds, and a sheet of mica large enough to serve as a mirror. Belinda thought he was joking when he told her that, in earlier times, sheets of mica had been used as a window panes.

Chad was on his knees picking up rust colored stones from an ant hill when Frog pointed to the trail of dust on the road leading into Oblivion. He continued the lecture about how ants will carry these garnets in their rough from underground and throw them out onto the ant hills where college students can find them, and sell them for beer money. No one was listening to him though. Ben was already marching back toward his town. Belinda and Frog were close behind.

60

The scene before Ben, as he stood at the edge of Oblivion, was unreal. It was like something out of a Disney animated movie. The dust had barely settled around the line of pick ups, well worn cars and several vans, but already there was a ballet of activity.

Men and women were pulling lumber and bundles of shingles from the trucks and piling them in front of several of the buildings. Panes of glass were set, with exaggerated care, near the waiting frames. Their labor and sweat would re-establish the structure of this town.

Others were sweeping, pulling weeds, filling wheelbarrows with trash, litter and the accumulated garbage of neglect, discussing the colors of paint that would brighten the weathered structures. Their voices and plans were turning the abandoned houses into homes.

Children of various sizes were pulling tumbleweeds from fences, foundations, steps and sidewalks; making a great pile in the open area behind the jail. Their laughter was granting the village its life again.

The confusion and activity was given voice by laughter, shouts and incessant chatter, all to the loud Tejano music emanating from the radio of one of the trucks. The rhythmic tap of hammers provided percussive accompaniment. The sheer joy of these people, the joy of positive activity, was contagious; it filled the air like a heady fragrance. But, it bewildered Ben. He could only gaze in mute astonishment as several children raced up to him and handed him a rake. One of the girls smiled and told him, "Papa says everyone gotta work."

Carlos removed his hat and wiped the sweat from his forehead as he approached. "I told you, Amigo, Oblivion would have people." The breadth of his smile and the sparkle in his dark brown eyes spoke volumes of great satisfaction. "I didn't even have to call Jimmy Carter. I found lots of hard working Chicanos. They ain't got money, but they got good hands and strong backs."

"How am I going to pay for all this?" Ben was trying to estimate the cost of these truck loads of building materials.

"You don't gotta." Domingo joined the conversation. He was waving a piece of blue plastic in Ben's face. "Courtney, she gave me her charge card. She tol' us to get whatever we needed. So we did. You don't gotta worry, Boss."

The town itself seemed to be pleased with all the activity on its behalf. The naked and neglected roof rafters seemed to sag less, sand polished floor boards seemed to straighten in preparation of the expected traffic. The siding seemed eager to have weather-loosened nails re-driven, and receive renewal in a coat of paint. Carlos led Ben through the mass of people, introducing everyone with a smile and comment on their special talent.

Grandma Rosa was from Acoma Pueblo. She made the best tamales and apple pies in all of Nuevo Mexico. She was a gray haired grandmother whose children and grandchildren had all moved to cities she could no longer name. She lived alone, her arthritic hands labored over her bread and pies while she warmed away the pain with the hot oven. Her pies had become her life, her art. Unfortunately they didn't pay her rent, so for the past four months she called the streets home. Through her tears she continued to pray for the health and happiness of the family that had abandoned her. She had no idea what Domingo was telling her as he helped her into his truck and threw the bundle of bowls and pans, her tools, into the back of the pickup. Now she was cleaning out an ancient horno while she was humming in tune with the pervasive music. This beehive shaped outdoor oven had survived the years of abandonment well. She was joyful in the knowledge that she would be serving bread baked in this horno by supper time.

Inez y Luis Diez were growers of herbs and vegetables. They had owned an adobe home and two acres in Santa Fe but as the Californios came and the property taxes increased to match the meteoric rise in property values they lost everything they owned. They had been living in the Gunthers' garage while working as maid and gardener, nanny and chauffeur. For over a year they had worked seven days a week for room and board. To them this empty town was prayers answered. Carlos had told them there were free homes and lots of room for a garden. Luis saw visions of himself in the farmers' market selling the best produce and the finest herbs. Inez was skeptical and held back. She didn't want to leave the security of the Gunthers. She had known too much poverty, too little music, too little joy. Now they dutifully bowed before Ben and called him "El Patron." Embarrassed, he shook their hands and welcomed them to Oblivion. Inez was still suspicious. She clutched tightly the velvet pouch in her pocket. That pouch contained her rosary beads, her comfort.

When Luis pointed to the rich soil behind a weathered adobe house and had visions of gardens there, Inez grumbled, "There's no electricity in this town. At least in the garage we had electricity, and running water." For some the future is viewed as a dream, for others it is feared as a nightmare.

Porfirio Robello was a plumber's helper. A hard worker with skill learned from experience. He asked Carlos for a chance to come to Oblivion, an opportunity for a new beginning for him and his friend Vincente. While they never came right out and said it, the rumors flowed through Juniper Crossing that they were gay. Carlos shrugged his shoulders when they asked if this would be a problem in Oblivion. He told him two strong young backs were welcome in this town. Besides, there wouldn't be time to worry about such an insignificant issue; there was much work to do, and too few hands.

The introductions continued as Belinda, Chad and Frog caught up. Soon they were all engaged in the beehive of activity.

Counting los ninos y ninas there were twenty-eight people in Oblivion. Twenty-eight people that chose to share their hope for something better. Twenty-eight people who had faith in the future, or had lost faith in the present. They were all so focused on their efforts that no one saw the young man who stood in the shade of the pinon pine at the edge of the town and watched them for more than an hour.

The cleanup continued all afternoon, until the sun shone red from the crest of the mountains to the west. It was with exhaustion and satisfaction that a halt was called to the day's activity. Bowls of chili con vaca, stacks of tortillas and bread from Grandma Rosa's oven, filled the impromptu table built of a sheet of plywood and two sawhorses. Children ran a relay of potatoes roasted in the open flames that consumed the trash and accumulation of neglect. The streets were clean, windows and doors were being repaired or new ones installed, roofs had been replaced, even flowers had been planted. There was life in Oblivion. There was joy and happiness in Oblivion.

The evening meal was followed by a few relaxing beers. Guitars, accordions and a trumpet were soon put to use as an informal Mariachi band began to play and the children danced in the light of the flames and the joy of hard work. Frog and Chad pitched their tent and brought more beer to the group. Frog also brought her guitar and caused a great deal of laughter as she vainly struggled to keep up with the music in progress.

The fiesta broke up about ten o'clock as weary eyes closed and the vision held jointly by these people was replaced with dreams. Soon minds and bodies were sprawled on blankets in the beds of the pickups, tents, floors of once empty buildings, now bustling with life.

Ben and Belinda had retired to their bed, but sleep proved an elusive prey. By midnight they were again dressed and hand in hand began their stroll. In the moonlight Oblivion was no longer a ghost town; it was a living community that was only asleep. They could feel the magic in the air. An aura of excitement radiated not only from the people, but the very buildings themselves. In the sounds of passion that escaped the doorways and tent flaps, the whispered plans for tomorrow, the giggles of small children, was the energy of rebirth. Every one of the twenty-eight had known fear, despair, hopelessness or pain. Instinctively, Ben and Belinda knew these were the people that could make Oblivion alive. As they rebuilt Oblivion, they were rebuilding

64

themselves. They could never escape their past, but they could climb on its shoulders and see farther than they had ever seen before. Oblivion was giving them sufficient hope to envision a future.

Ben was looking out over the valley, trying to place in his mind the shadowed outlines of the structures that would follow the sun's journey across the sky, mechanical sunflowers that would satisfy the hunger for energy that the people of Oblivion would have. It was troubling to him that these families had come to Oblivion without an invitation, had staked out claims to houses without asking, and begun repairs without his input. What would he do if one of them got hurt. Could he be sued? He had never owned property before and now he owned a whole damned town. In the shadows of the night, the joy of the day's vitality was being replaced with fear and insecurity, self doubt and heavy weight of responsibility.

Belinda could feel the retreat of his excitement and sensed the need to talk seriously. She led him to the cottonwoods that held their counsel behind the water tank. Under the ancient branches was security. The smell of life was carried in the air under these sylvan giants. The promise of life was voiced in the gentle rustle of the leaves. To the campasinos, the cottonwood was "alamo," a tree whose bark and leaves could reduce fever and heal wounds. Instinctively they sought this grove as a healing place for Ben's troubled mind.

They talked for over an hour of how to house these families. Some had been introduced as homeless; the Montoya family was soon to lose the little house they occupied in Juniper Crossing. There was no place else for them to go. They had, without asking, begun to repair the crumbling adobe at the north side of Oblivion. It had, in the town's previous life, been a pasture and pig pen. Ben understood that they planned on putting the rich soil to good use. They could, through wise stewardship of the small plot behind them, support their family with ease.

The widow, Grandma Rosa, had no skills beyond baking. She had chosen the smallest of the houses. It was also one of the ones most in need of major repair. How could Ben object to this? The Indian family, Danny and Salli Sanchez and their son, were camping beside the former stable and pasture. Danny had six sheep and hoped to increase his flock in the warm spring sun. Ben felt a certain kinship with them. After all, they were artists as well. Danny worked silver with a fine and true hand. Salli put her soul into her pottery with the gentle touch of fingers that had known much of the hard life. Their son, Colo, a child of fourteen, displayed a sensitivity and interest in nature that would lead him to be an environmentalist, and an artist in his own right. This was a good family that retained links to the Pojaque pueblo, but could never return to the old ways. Danny had a drinking problem. He had to escape the streets of Santa Fe if he was to crawl out of the bottle. Oblivion was his last hope.

Then there was Dirty Maria, a perpetual student who rarely bathed. She was a woman of almost obscene proportions, body, mind and soul wounded and scared by a life of abuse, failure and drugs. Yet, she was possessed of the rare talents of a true teacher. Even with her bulk she had labored hard, cleaning the building that had once been a school. She had talked briefly with Belinda and Frog about the need for a library. Her suggestion was that the school be not only a place of learning but a library, art gallery and museum, a fountain of living knowledge that would serve the whole community. Earlier in the evening she had sat by the fire with the children, told several stories about animals, then the tales of Native American and Hispanic heroes of the area. Of all the people who had come to Oblivion, she alone had a sense of place, an understanding of what had led them all to this town. She understood that it was a unique moment when all their separate paths converged. To her, this was a cosmic destiny.

She hinted to Belinda that forces were driving them that could not be denied. "Why else would all these failed bodies and wounded souls dedicate themselves to an undefined purpose in a town inhabited only by the ghosts of the past?"

Belinda had seen each of these people become something more as hope and cooperation in the pursuit of a common goal united their efforts. For her, committees were the only cooperative ventures, and even they were composed of conflicting personalities, each set on advancing his or her own career. As Ben surrendered to his exhaustion and slept with his head in her lap, she struggled in her mind to understand just what a sense of community could mean. Would it require surrender of the competitive instincts? How do you get this diverse group of personalities to live, work, and play together without conflict? In the darkness, when one's vision is limited, when the existence of buildings, trees, mountains are only silhouettes, it is easier to feel the demons of doubt, to fear the unseen details.

She looked skyward. On this clear night, she could see forever. She could see uncountable millions of stars, masses of energy; points of light and hope so far away. Were the dreams of these people, of all humankind, equally distant and unobtainable? These thoughts invited waves of doubt, shivers of despair. She leaned back against the tree and slept. In the branches above, an owl (keeper of truth) stood watch. The rabbit (personification of fear) approached the sleeping couple, seeking the tender spring blades of gramma grass. On silent wings the truth brought death to fear. Ben and Belinda spent the rest of the night sleeping in the security of the tree.

Chapter Six

They were awakened by the sounds of laughter and splashing water. Some of the children were washing in the tank, while others were pumping buckets full and carrying them to the families already at work. Domingo walked out of the brush bordering the dry stream bed where he had relieved himself. He spotted the sleeping couple and, with an embarrassed look on his face, apologized for wakening them. Together they walked toward the town's center and the smell of eggs, bacon and chiles.

In the dawn all the demons were gone and hope again reigned. The truck radio was tuned to the morning news. The usual drone of international intrigue, political scandals, drunken brawls, teen violence and traffic tie-ups was polluting the sound of the wind and the song of the birds.

"Terrible way to start the day. Isn't it?" Ben said, as he reached through the window of the truck and silenced the offending broadcast.

Breakfast was an informal affair, consumed amidst the confusion of motion and fragments of conversation. Ben noticed that two of the trucks were gone, that Chad and Frog were already at the edge of town, charting the flow of sunlight and placing more red and blue marker flags. He was just draining the last of his coffee from the blue tin cup when a white Bronco with the official looking logo cautiously entered Oblivion and came to a stop near the community breakfast table. All activity came to a halt and a blanket of silence fell over the crowd. Even the children knew enough to fear anyone who looked official. The uniformed officer of the county Department of Health and Sanitation opened his briefcase on the hood and removed some papers.

"Who's in charge here?" He asked as he removed his sunglasses and shuffled some of the papers before finding the ones he needed.

Ben stepped forward and acknowledged his ownership of the now populated community.

"I need to examine your sanitary facilities."

Ben was flustered. There had only been people here for one day. This was something he hadn't had time to even think about yet. He stuttered an ineffective answer and looked around for help. These people were all used to having their plans shattered by someone in uniform. The homeless ones were used to being told to move on, those who rented were accustomed to being evicted. Officials brought warrants for the arrest of their teens, documents that said they couldn't have their children any more, threats and orders they couldn't comprehend. These people understood that they were doomed to fail one more time.

"I have a complaint about a bunch of derelicts and winos living here without running water and sanitary facilities. I can't permit occupancy if you don't meet the minimum standards." He paused, surveyed the crestfallen crowd and apologetically added, "It's for your own health and safety."

Porfirio, the plumber, stepped forward, spat on the ground, almost hitting the officer's shoes, "Who complained?"

"I can't reveal that information. All I can tell you is that without proper sanitary facilities you cannot remain here."

"Have you ever been to Coyote Creek Park?" Porfirio was nervous, but he was being driven by anger now.

"Yes. Coyote Creek is one of our popular state parks."

"I can camp there for a week if I buy a permit from the state. Right?"

"Well, yes, but . . ."

"You got running water there now?"

"No, but that's a natural area, designed for family camping. There are no buildings there."

"Si. That is just my point. If I'm there and I want to take a shit, I go behind the rocks and then bury the mess. Isn't that right? Isn't that what it says in your park use booklet?"

Carlos entered the debate, "I been to Coyote Creek too. They got trees there. Some of these houses are built from wood that was once a tree. You got a lot of rocks in that park. What you think that jail is made from? You got mud there too. Some of these buildings are built from the earth. That's what adobe is. This is only a more refined nature than you got in your park, NO?"

He wasn't prepared for this kind of argument. He left the warrant to vacate and retreated to the security of his vehicle. On the way out he almost ran head on into a flatbed truck and a convoy of assorted pickups, jeeps and cars.

Dr. Taggart was out of the passenger seat of the flatbed almost before it stopped. She looked like a female version of Albert Einstein; an elderly lady with an electrifying personality and a head of white hair totally lacking in discipline. Chad unstrapped a bike from the truck and wheeled it over to her, along with a small black briefcase and her trademark cholla stem cane.

She grasped Ben's hand warmly and gave him a light kiss on the cheek, Belinda got a hug with her kiss. "We have much to do," she said with a smile. "Is there one of these buildings we can use as an office?"

Ben was leading her toward a house at the north end of Oblivion, near the area Chad had been measuring and plotting, but she stopped them at the jail. "This will do nicely," she said as she stepped through the doorway. Soon she was waving with her cane, directing the flow of equipment, computers and papers.

On the truck were two port-a-johns and several gasoline powered generators. One of the pickups contained surveying and GPS equipment, plot maps and water rights documentation. Her dynamic personality and slightly befuddled appearance were an immediate hit with everyone in Oblivion. In a matter of minutes she erased the dark cloud that had descended with the arrival of the sanitation officer.

Cal Benton sat in the small cramped office that served as the command post for his mining and financial empire. He controlled over one hundred and forty thousand acres, but held deed to less than three hundred. He lived in an imaginary world of his own creation. He was Ben Cartwright and this was the his Bonanza. He had grazing rights on federal lands to the north and west, mining and logging rights on the reservation lands to the east and south of his property.

His problem was a common one in arid climates. To run the mining, to grow the cattle, took water. He had hired an engineer to find him new sources of this liquid that was in many ways more valuable than oil. In the early morning light he was reading again the report that had cost him twelve thousand dollars and given him only bad news.

He picked up the phone and called his two sons. Derritt was thirty years old and possessed by a violent temper. Landreth was four years older, calmer but totally without any sense of compassion. Life was business to him. Well educated, capable of moving with ease from the saddle to the boardroom, he was the heir apparent to the empire; and he knew it. Derritt was only a rock in the road to his future.

Cal wouldn't call Brandy, the youngest of his three children and the only disappointment in his family. She was weak; not physically, not intellectually, but in the way she seemed to lack ambition, drive, the competitive spirit. Derritt claimed it was because she was female, "She just ain't got the balls for it, Daddy," was the phrase he used. Ever since Cal's wife and the mother of the trio surrendered to cancer,

Brandy had run the household, kept the office organized and waged a never ending campaign against the alcohol that was becoming more and more a part of the life of Cal and her brothers. The conflict with Derritt had twice reached the physical stage. Cal was angry with her for "rilin' the boy so much."

71

The boys had never married. There was no need for that. They had the money to buy whatever was necessary to satisfy their needs. That was exactly what Derritt was doing when the phone rang. Marquitta had been a frequent guest in this huge log and stone house. She had shared Cal's and Landreth's beds in the past. She understood some of the dynamics of this family and her instincts told her to cultivate the relationship with Landreth, not Derritt. Landreth would destroy both his brother and his father in order to gain control of the "empire." Marquitta intended to be by his side when it happened. She was not sorry that Derritt had been interrupted. He was a selfish lover. In truth, none of these men was capable of love. This knowledge was a tool she could use against them all, when the time came.

Cal spread the geologic survey maps on the desk while Landreth poured them all a cup of coffee. Derritt had studied geology and knew where the conversation was going before a word was spoken. He knew where the water was.

Cal traced the red lines that marked their property boundaries. "The stream bed belongs to that ghost town. Had we been able to buy that valley we could pump that water to our land on the other side of the canyon. Boys, the days when we could just dig a ditch to get water are over." His voice was rising as he continued, stabbing the map with his stubby finger, "The water's here, we are here, and we need that water."

Landreth, eager to seize leadership in the discussion, leaned forward and drew a big circle around the one hundred and twenty-seven acres that held their ambition at bay. "All we need to do is scare them out of that cluster of shacks."

Derritt, still angry from being interrupted, pulled a shotgun from the rack, "I'll scare the livin' shit out of 'em."

Cal took the weapon from him and motioned for them to sit down. "Look. They got a couple dozen uneducated Chicanos down there and a handful of moonbeams. We don't need a gun to make them run."

"Once they learn the power they got with those water rights, it's going to be a lot harder to get them to move out." Landreth was stalling for time while he struggled to put his ideas into words. He did this by slowly pouring some Jim Beam into each of the coffee cups. "We own enough judges, county commissioners and state senators. Can't we use them and keep our hands clean?"

"I called the boys in the sanitation department," Cal explained. "They won't do much, but at least we can tighten the cinch on them folks. Make 'em uncomfortable. I'm still ahead of ya, boys. This afternoon, Landreth, you are going to Santa Fe to file claim for assumption of water rights. I cleared the path for you. It will be prior dated so that the application predates the decision by the state to sell the property. Take these checks with you. These aren't bribes. They're campaign contributions. We are doing our patriotic duty; supporting the democratic process."

Derritt was feeling left out, as he often did these days. Cal sensed this and assigned him the task of surveillance. He would continue to watch the activity, as he had yesterday, from a distance.

The day was off to a good positive start. Plans were in place, and there was little that could be done to stop them. As they walked out of the office into the crisp morning air, a lone raven flew from the tree near the door to a post on the corral fence. Derritt retrieved the shotgun and took careful aim. The post was in splinters but the raven flew off without the loss of a feather.

Chapter Seven

Derritt spent almost an hour in the concrete block supply shed at the entrance to Benton Mines. This building was, in effect, an arsenal containing enough explosive materials to level a mountain, and Derritt was knowledgeable in their use. It was a matter of deciding just what he wanted to carry with him. Finally, a dozen small sticks of dynamite were carefully placed in the backpack. He selected the appropriate blasting caps and a coil of lightweight fuse. He didn't know if he would use them or not, but he wanted to be prepared.

The anger was building inside him again. He was angry with his brother, so obviously the favored son; his father, who had little confidence in him; and all the scum in Oblivion that had robbed him of his water. Most of his anger was directed toward that damn artist that had brought so much shame to his family. They were the laughing stock of Juniper Crossing, and, he was certain, the jokes about the Bentons being beaten by some stupid artist had reached Santa Fe by now. He returned to the house, opened his desk drawer and removed the black leather holster. The classic Colt 45 fit in his hand well. This was a link to the west of yesterday, when men could control their own destiny; when real men didn't hide behind their lawyer's briefcases, like his brother did. The weapon gave him the power to solve all the problems that plagued him. It made him better than his brother. He paused, then walked to the bar. He removed a bottle of Seagrams and tucked it in his pack, with the explosives.

It was as he was leaving that he saw Cal and Marquitta embracing. The anger welled within him again. His hand felt the solid power of the gun. It seemed to force his hand to move as it slid free of the leather. He was a volcano about to erupt. Trembling with rage, he overcame the temper of the moment, vowing to have revenge when he no longer needed either of them.

His mind was screaming at him, "Coward! Coward!" The Colt was telling him, "If you won't do something, I will."

By the time he reached his Blazer, the gun was in his hand again. It was raising his arm. It was taking aim. It was recoiling from the 45 caliber explosions as the trigger kept pulling his finger, again and again, until the cylinder was empty, and the rage was spent. Three bullets had carried his frustration through the side of Cal's Lincoln. Three more had planted his hate in the porch post and door of their house. Freed of these demon emotions, he drove off. Cal stood in the doorway, watching, lines of sadness aging his face.

The drive to Oblivion took about twenty minutes. He parked behind a sandstone outcrop along the canyon wall and hiked the talus until he reached the point where the junipers and pinon marched over the eroding slope of sandstone. This is where he sat when he had watched them a couple days ago, as Ben's companions stuck red flags in the valley floor that should have been his.

He studied the buildings, watched the activity. These were not the kind of people that the Bentons wanted for neighbors. Breeding all those kids, just to get the welfare checks. Lazy, thieving Chicanos, only good for stoop labor; that's all they were. Then it dawned on him. A smile of respect crossed his face with the realization. That's what that cagy old artist was doing. He was using these damned Spics to rebuild the town; then he'd run them off, make it safe for White folks, and make a bundle when he sold it. Perhaps Ben was a more worthy adversary than they thought. That's when he finally made the decision to blow up one of the buildings. In his mind this would be the way he could hurt Ben the most.

With his binoculars he studied each building. He watched Dirty Maria and a flock of children bustling around the old school and thought perhaps this was the best building to erase. He hated that woman. Maybe he would try to time an explosion so that she would be inside. She was a mongrel, half Black, half some Indian tribe from Canada.

She had spent a lifetime in various colleges; never did a real day's work in her life. Yet she had always done the dirtiest of jobs; cleanliness and fresh clothes were sometimes lacking in her lifestyle. She had pulled winos out of the gutter, and tried to washed away their hopelessness. Their stench she wore like a badge. She had cared for the infants of illegal farm hands; taught the children about their proud heritage along with the ability to read. She led desperate Native Americans back to the harmony of their traditions. She had worked suicide intervention in the alleys of Omaha, Tucson and Albuquerque. To Derritt, she was a trouble maker, stirring up scum labor. She was someone he could easily hate.

The Vietnamese family from Tucumcari was already carrying boxes of food and assorted goods into what was again becoming a convenience store. Chan Ton, his wife Lau, and their three children had worked everything from garlic fields to flea markets to keep food on the table. Derritt could remember when they came to the region. It was one of those damn government resettlement programs that subjected good hard working Americans to Oriental vermin. They might make a good target too.

Within his mind, so filled with hate and rage, each building contained a reason to be blown apart; each was occupied by people who have no right to live. The old jail was another target he liked. It was near where everyone was gathered, the stone walls could make an impressive explosion.

With the patience of a snake waiting for its prey to come close enough to destroy, Derritt waited, all day long. Through the heat of the afternoon, into the long shadows of evening, he waited, and drained the bottle at his side.

It wasn't until they were all gathered in the middle of the street, around the plywood dinner table listening to that damned Chicano music, that he was moved to action. By staying within the deepening shadows he was able to reach the edge of the old school without being

76

seen. The assorted houses and storefronts provided cover as he reached the center of the town.

The jail became the objective because that's where that lunatic professor, Dr. Taggartt, had set up shop. He had watched the students and their mentor roaming the valley, and guessed that solar energy was the objective. The intellect and intensity with which the absent-minded scholar focused on a subject was well known to him. After all, he had studied under her when he was a student. Memories of her being so mesmerized by something she was reading that lunches were untouched, appointments missed, notes lost. He almost laughed out loud at these visions from the past. Mind pictures of her unkempt hair and ill-fitting clothing, of how she was so stupid she sometimes forgot where she had parked her bike, flashed before him. She was a laughable little old lady. It would be fun to see her reaction when all her gadgets became shrapnel.

The bonfire was the focus of all the tired, but hope-filled occupants of Oblivion. Dr. Taggartt and Chad were trying unsuccessfully to dance to the mariachi music. Derritt paused to watch for a few minutes before he slipped around the corner and into the jail. When he spotted the raven roosting under the overhang a shiver raced down his back. His first impulse was to reach for his revolver. Then, he smiled at the thought of those black feathers settling, one by one, on the rubble, after the explosives had done their work.

Because this was the building closest to the fire and the people, some of them were going to get hurt. That should scare them off and put an end to this problem. Daddy could play patty-cake with his lawyers, Landreth could spend his time jerking the chains of the politicians they owned, but Derritt was going to take action. Derritt was going to level this town. After these folks scattered it would be fun watching the rest of these buildings explode in the night and become suitable for little more than rattlesnake housing.

As a small child Derritt had played cowboys and Indians in this abandoned town. The jail had been one of his favorite buildings, but it looked so different now. Unless eyes sought the moonlight shining through the barred windows it no longer had the feel of a jail. Folding chairs and tables filled the small office. There were stacks of papers and books on the floor. Scientific equipment and laptops claimed the tables. Maps and charts hung where wanted posters, gun racks and bare walls had once reigned. The change disoriented him for a moment or two. Then he entered the first of the cells, now used for equipment storage. He wrapped two sticks of the dynamite together, set the cap and wedged it under the cot that was now covered with GPS gadgets, assorted gauges and meters. Since this was the first charge, he cut a long fuse, uncoiled it and held it in place with several books. He ignited it and hurried to set the next explosive.

He entered the second cell, obviously used as the sleeping quarters for the addled scholar. He placed the charge in the suitcase that held her clothing. The fuse was placed and ready. He thought he heard the raucous squawk of the raven in the distance, or was it inside his head, in his own imagination? It was as he was reaching into his pocket for the lighter that he heard the iron grated door squeak and squeal behind him. He turned and watched as, unaided by human hands, it slowly swung toward the frame. He leaped forward and grasped the bars. Unfortunately, he was off balance. Rather than halting the door's movement, he hastened it. It was his hands that drove the solid iron into a union with the waiting frame. He heard the clank of the lock. It was when he tried to force the door open that the lock pin fell into place. In that instant he knew the terror of prison walls.

His response was immediate. It was fear and anger that drove the anguished scream. The horrible sound of terror was heard by the group outside. It was a haunting sound that halted all speech and movement. Instinctively, the families drew together, gaining security from each

78

other while they sought the source of the screams. His hands beat on the door, breaking knuckles and coating the bars with blood.

Ben and Carlos were the first to enter the jail. It was impossible to understand Derritt's incoherent ravings. Ben immediately began a search for keys. Carlos was trying to calm Derritt while he tried to understand why he was in this cell, but his attempts met with nothing more than increased rantings. Finally, exhausted, he fell to the floor, defeated by his own hatred. It was then that Carlos saw the fuse on the floor and understood what was happening.

"BOMB! BOMB!" he shouted as he stumbled down the steps. The crowd panicked and retreated to the other end of the Oblivion. Dr. Taggartt had some important papers she needed to retrieve before anything happened. Cane in hand, she entered the jail, calmly walked into the first cell and reached for the files. She smelled the smoke from the burning fuse, then spotted it under the cot. She knelt down on her hands and knees to observe closer. Her curiosity held her immobile for several seconds, then, with her cane she deftly hooked the parcel and fuse, now only inches long, and pulled it toward her. With a "Tisk, tisk," she threw the fuse behind her and looked over at the moaning figure in the next cell. Blood had run from his hands down his arms. His shirt was torn and covered with his vomit.

She walked out into the street, "Chad, Frog. This man needs help."

Then she returned to the cell and scolded Derritt, "You shouldn't have slammed this door so hard. I'm not certain that I can get it open."

The latch released with no difficulty to give the door its freedom. It easily swung back against the wall, liberating the man within. The most curious were returning to the jail now. Dirty Maria saw the blood and immediately turned her bulk to the task of finding water and bandages. Within minutes Derritt was sitting by the fire. Maria and Inez were cleansing the wounds and a hot cup of coffee was sitting beside him.

Ben, Belinda and several of the others were standing beyond the fire's illumination. It was inconceivable to him that anyone would use violence to oppose what they were doing in Oblivion. Belinda was concerned that there was no system in place for law enforcement within their town. "Perhaps, control is necessary in order for a society to function."

Domingo nodded agreement and left the discussion to drive into Juniper Crossing. There he could phone the sheriff. He worried about the repercussions of arresting the son of Cal Benton, but it would have to be done. Ben couldn't understand why Derritt had been locked in the jail cell. His mind was still refusing to believe the obvious, that this neighbor had attempted to destroy this building.

In the darkness, all their thoughts were speculation, devoid of the light of knowledge and understanding. Minds began imagining the worst. Safety and security had been assaulted. Ben felt responsible for the people assembled in Oblivion. Carlos wanted to post armed guards. No one would sleep well tonight. The myth of cooperative humanity had been exploded, even though the bomb had been defused.

As the conversation drifted from what had happened to why, Belinda offered the thought that Cal Benton simply couldn't bear to lose. Ben had won. Had the father had sent the son?

Chad suggested that it was more than that. From his understanding of geology, there had to be sub-surface water. Frog explained that the plant growth along the dry stream bed indicated that when the rains came, it was a viable waterway. A dam at the upper end of the canyon, and wells in the lower valley could be a valuable water source.

Ben was born to the Southwest and understand the value of water rights. A lawyer friend down in Albuquerque even made a good living from waging legal battles over this liquid. He suggested, as the discussion of the night's events reached the rerun stage, the fear and anger had begun to wane, that they talk with Derritt himself. Inez had wrapped healing poultices on his wounded hands. They had even found a clean shirt for him. A tea brewed from the cottonwood bark had eased the pain. Someone had fixed him a plate of beans with a side of soft flour tortillas. He couldn't use his hands to eat so several of the children delighted in taking turns spoon feeding him.

Some of the men were in favor of giving him a good beating and dumping him at the doorway of the Benton house. The coil of fuse in his hip pocket was a reminder. They grumbled about the care and compassion shown this obvious enemy. Ben and Belinda sat beside the younger Benton and engaged in a strained conversation with him. First they expressed concern over his self-imposed injuries, then gradually began to ask questions about why he was in the jail? Why he had set the explosives?

He offered very little in the way of explanation. At one point he demanded the return of his gun. As the pain began to increase again, he became more belligerent. The anger wrapped itself around the fear he felt, and when Inez approached with a second cup of the soothing tea, he spat at her and knocked the cup from her hand.

When the deputy sheriff arrived, Ben felt relieved. A system of law and protection did exist. This presence relieved him of the need to deal with the problem. Deputy Lyle Forrest approached the group by the fire and nodded, "Now, just tell me what's going on here."

Ben started to explain that Derritt had set explosives. When Lyle recognized the hot-headed son of local power pathetically wrapped and bandaged, sitting before him he whistled and shook his head. The younger Benton, seized the opportunity. "They locked me in the jail with a bomb! Look! They busted my hands."

Deputy Forrest then sat down beside Derritt. "I'm going to need to take a statement from the victim. I would appreciate it if you folks would give us a little privacy here. OK?"

The crowd obediently stepped back, but Ben and Belinda were confused about just who was being viewed as the victim. Lyle wrote pages of statement from Derritt, then stood and walked toward Ben.

"What you folks did to this man can't go unpunished," he said as he spoke into the radio strapped to his shoulder. "I'm going to have to take you in, Ben. I'm calling now for some cars to evacuate this place and get this poor boy some medical attention."

"I don't think you understand what happened here," Ben stammered as Lyle pulled his hands behind his back and snapped the cuffs over his wrists.

"You can't take a fine, upstanding citizen, a pillar of the community, lock him up with a bomb, and expect to get away with it!" The door of the patrol car was opened and Ben was shoved inside.

Chapter Eight

Cal was waiting when Deputy Forrest pulled into the parking lot. He met them on the steps of the sheriff's office. "Go easy on this boy, Lyle. He ain't done nothin' wrong."

Lyle was too puzzled to respond, but stood before the elder Benton, gripped by fear and unable to look up into his eyes.

"Where's my boy?"

"Ambulance was taking him to the clinic in Las Vegas."

"He ok?"

"Will be."

Cal's attention was then directed toward Ben, "Mister, you robbed me of something I wanted real bad. I hate your guts. But I've pieced together in my mind what must have happened in that sorry excuse for a town. I want you to know I didn't send Derritt to blow up Oblivion or bring harm to any of those people." He extended his hand, then became awkwardly embarrassed when he realized Ben was handcuffed. "Get those damned things off him, Lyle."

Benton removed his hat and opened the door to his Lincoln. "I don't want any trouble. Lyle, call off your boys and let the rabble in that ghost town be. Ya hear what I'm sayin'?"

The deputy nodded and almost tripped on his way up the steps to radio this order to the officers already on their way to Oblivion.

"One more thing. Lock Derritt up for a couple days. It'll do him some good."

"Am I free to go now?" Ben asked.

Cal spoke for the deputy, "Ben, I'm gonna make a deal with ya. You go back to that heap of shit you call Oblivion without filing any charges against my boy, and I promise ya nobody's gonna get hurt." He extended his hand, "Deal?"

Ben was an artist; his sensitivity gave him the ability to read people. What he saw in Cal confused him. Instinct told him they were adversaries, yet he could sense the aura of a man with vision, dreams, misguided perhaps, but still dreams. Mostly though, tonight, he could see stress in the elder Benton's face, a fear that he was losing control. Ben suddenly felt a wave of sympathy and grasped the offered hand. Something had aged this man today.

"One of these days, Ben. One of these days, I still plan on having Oblivion." Cal spoke, but the absolute determination was gone.

Ben understood that Cal's current adversary was generational. Derritt was the wound Cal now carried, not the loss of pride Ben had caused. The image flashed in his mind of a young wolf challenging its elder for domination of the pack. It was a painting he would create as soon as possible. Perhaps he would do it as a gift to Cal, and as a warning.

Cal had started to pull away, then stopped and motioned for Ben. "How you going to get back?"

Ben shrugged. Without another word, Cal pushed open the passenger door.

For the second time this night Derritt heard the soul-shattering clank of solid steel. This time there was no fight left. He sat on the corner of the cot and wept. Sleep came fitfully, between bouts with anger, hate and cries for revenge. He vowed that he would get even with Ben, Belinda, the scientists, students, and families of Oblivion. But his mind was, with deafening shouts of rage, telling him his father must be punished. Asleep, he saw his father's face laughing at him on freedom's side of the door. He had always been held prisoner by this man. "No more!" shouted the voice inside his head. His mind drew pictures of Cal and Marquitta together. The old man had lost the right to mount this woman. He grasped the bars with his broken hands and roared. He pounded his head against the door until consciousness was gone and he sank into a pool of his own blood.

84

Belinda was arguing with the three deputies, who were confused as to why they were there and just what they were to do with the crying children, students threatening lawsuits and a little old lady shaking a cane at them and delivering what seemed like a lecture on energy sources and the threat of global warming. They hadn't been prepared for this at the police academy. They were better prepared to deal with the half dozen men waving shovels, hammers and two-by-fours while shouting their choicest insults in Spanish, English and several other languages.

It was with great relief that Deputy Lopez accepted the radio message that they were to leave Oblivion's occupants where they were and return to the sheriff's office. Even after they were in their cars and turning around, Dr. Taggart continued her discourse on energy consumption while invectives continued to be hurled from the other side of the street.

Courtney's car came to a stop just as the last of the patrol cars cleared the hill and disappeared.

She laughed as she came toward the confusion. Each of the new residents was trying to tell her what was happening. She only smiled, "Are you always going to get into this much trouble if I leave you alone for a couple days?"

Inez offered her a cup of herbal tea as an owl glided into the sparse branches of a desert willow blooming at the corner of the church. She calmed their concerns about Ben, then let them take her on a guided tour of the jail, the site of the night's excitement. She pointed to the little fluff of yellow kitten curled in a ball behind the cell door. At the sound of their voices it stretched and stood, rubbing against the door, starting it on its journey toward the frame. The second time it had made this journey tonight.

Courtney laughed loudly, then offered an explanation to them, "When you are in harmony with the great forces, strange, and wonderful, things can happen."

She bent over and picked up the kitten. "It's good to have a little sunbeam in the middle of a difficult night."

"Now," she turned toward Dr. Taggartt, "How is the energy project coming?"

They were engaged in a discussion of the combination of solar and wind power with the need for water, when Cal's Lincoln eased into the edge Oblivion. Ben waved a sincere thanks and walked toward the group. His arrival in that car would require some explanations.

All Courtney would say on the subject was, "Beware. Doesn't the farmer always fatten the hog before butchering?"

The stress of the night before was cleansed by the morning light. Before everyone gathered for breakfast and made plans for how to best use the day's gift of hours, Ben was already at his easel. The rough forms of two wolves circling, youth relentless in its challenge to maturity, greed threatened by its own offspring. The rocks, large but worn by eons of existence provided the solid footing, symbolic of the universal past. Yet, it was clear that this permanence of tradition was an uneven floor, requiring constant awareness and attention. But, to focus on the rocks meant the adversaries would have to stop looking forward.

The cottonwoods that framed the left edge of the sketch were coming into leaf. This Ben chose as the symbol of regeneration, life always being reborn. The twisted, tortured branches of the juniper behind the senior wolf represented the strength and courage to face every new day; the evergreen tree was the will to live. The cactus that framed the right side of this work of art suggested that each must seek his own means of survival. The flowers, daisies, penstemon, poppies and other spring blooms were being trampled under the feet of the young wolf as he focused only on his enemy. He was now unable to see the world around him. He was in too much self-imposed danger to even glance at the refreshing, renewing beauty. The sky contained gathering clouds in the west and rays of sunshine, pillars of light, tying heaven and earth into one single work of art. The background was sketched lightly, containing another male wolf, while a female with angry eyes watched from the side of the painting. In the trees he placed the forms of the raven (totem of knowledge) and an owl (totem of truth). A hummingbird (totemic messenger of God) flitted into the sketch at one of the penstemon near the challenged leader. On the edge of the bluff, in the shadows of the storm clouds, sat a coyote (the observer) watching the conflict and smiling at the foolishness of life.

While Porfirio put together a crew to dig ditches for water lines, Belinda worked with several of the instructors from the Sangre de Christo Technical Institute. Through a contact Courtney had engineered, crews of students were being made available to install wiring, insulation, plumbing, as well as masonry and carpentry work. This would be a symbiotic relationship. The students would get much needed experience and scholastic credit; the town would be made habitable. Materials were made available through donations Courtney had arranged, with the understanding that these people would have homes where they could raise their families and be a part of what was becoming an eco-social experiment.

The families were, at first, distrustful, feeling that they were no longer needed. As the planning continued it became obvious to them that these students weren't replacing them; rather, it was going to be a joint learning experience for them all. By the time Courtney returned they were eager to have these Vo-Tec students working in their town. They were becoming possessive. They had a tremendous amount of pride in Oblivion. The events of last night that had drawn them together, turned some of the unbounded enthusiasm into defensive caution.

The noon hour brought the first of the trucks bearing the equipment needed to erect the windmills that would bring running water to each home and business. This was one of the projects that Chad and Frog had been planning. Windmills had traditionally posed a threat to birds in flight but these were a radical new design that would be as visible to wildlife as trees. The gasoline powered generators had brought light, power for the construction tools, and refrigeration. These windmills would pull water from deep beneath the sand and clay, and they would also drive electrical generators, eliminating the need for a combustion engine with its constant pollution.

Dr. Taggartt was lecturing a new contingent of UNM students under the cottonwoods. "First we capture the wind. With that energy we can put aside the gas powered generators that give us more pollution than electricity. The wind will give us the means to harvest the sun."

The students were possessed by the enthusiasm of missionaries. They felt that they could make a difference in the way humanity and nature functioned together. They sensed that what they did in the next few months would affect the way people all over the world lived in the future.

"It is a heady thing to be present at the birth of a revolution," Belinda commented as Courtney accompanied her on the stroll along the dry arroyo.

They walked along in silence for some time. Belinda paused and reached down to pick up an arrowhead that lay exposed in the sand. The piece of obsidian was turned over in her hand, then passed on to her companion. "Isn't it sad that an implement of war, death and destruction is what survived to mark this past culture?"

"You misunderstand what is cradled in your hand," Courtney sounded more serious than usual, "Most arrowheads were employed to harvest food. This was humankind's false teeth used to bring down prey and defend the family."

Belinda still clung to the mental image of barbaric Indians raiding wagon trains, plundering homesteads. An education derived from the entertainment industry, that long ago abandoned truth in its pursuit of profit. She had, less than two months ago been a warrior herself, a member of her corporate tribe. She had assumed, until she escaped that all-consuming life style, that existence centered on the duality of attack and defense. It was inconceivable to her that a "primitive" way of life could be less aggressive, less war-like than her corporate culture.

"Did you know that in the southwest, scientists, hikers and farmers have found many times more potsherds than they have arrowheads and spear points? Much more of the time allotted these people was spent farming, harvesting, manufacturing, building, singing, dancing, honoring their deities, and doing their art, than was spent on war and violence." Courtney's voice was reflecting a growing anger. "Ours is the most destructive time the world has ever known. In our pursuit of material comfort and irrational acquisition, we have destroyed our most valuable possessions. How do we explain to our children that an automobile was more important to us than air pure enough to sustain life, gold was more precious than the soul healing mountains, a side of Brazilian beef was more valuable than a climate controlling rain forest, a barrel of oil was worth more than the all the fish in the sea? When we spend more money on guns than books, is it any wonder we need more jails than schools?"

Belinda was uncomfortable having her image of the world questioned, her sense of superiority challenged, even though she had done just that when she walked out of the office and away from those demands. She was becoming just a bit irritated with this aging know-it-all. Unfortunately, she was ill prepared to engage in an intellectual debate on the lifestyles of other cultures, past or present. Still, deep within a consciousness she could not articulate, was a sense that there existed the possibility for something better. In the headwaters of her awareness was the knowledge that humanity could neither return to a past that existed only in fragmented collective memories , nor could it endure in its present state.

"The future is the most precious gift we all possess; the choice is ours whether to make it a safe nest for our children, or an ensnaring web," was all she could offer to the conversation. Her mind was struggling in the direction of hope, of what can be.

Courtney wasn't certain that Belinda understood what she was saying but she knew that she was planting the seeds of wisdom, and that Belinda was a fertile field. "When we speak of human nature, that is exactly what we mean. As human beings we are a part OF the natural world. All that we call civilization is only an extended nest, that, in many ways, is less efficient than an ant hill or beehive. We eat the same food and drink the same water as the rest of the life that makes this such an interesting planet to occupy. The fact that our needs are the same often puts us at odds with our fellow inhabitants. If you look at the natural world you will see that the most successful plants and animals are the ones that are the most cooperative, most willing to adapt, and best suited to change. It's no different with people."

It was late that afternoon when Landreth finally picked up the phone and arranged for the release of his younger brother. He also made certain that there would be no record of his ill spent night in the county jail. The older brother had been only partially successful in his passage through the labyrinth of the state house. At almost every office, some UNM research grant application, a variance requested by one of the radical environmental groups, or a directive from one agency or another was already on the desk. He had spent thousands of dollars and had only sympathetic nods and empty promises to show for his efforts. The decision was made on the drive back that the most effective attack would have to be against the university. That's where all the road blocks were coming from. It was ridiculous. The sale of a derelict old town, a lifeless jumble of empty buildings, was becoming a challenge to his whole existence. Those academic dreamers were turning it into a socio-scientific experimental lab. He was confused as to how this was happening, but it was clear that it had to be stopped.

90

On his cell phone he had already dictated a letter to the UNM president's office. It was a blunt reminder of where the administrative salaries came from, and how some members of the state house might want to examine very closely how every penny of the university's budget was spent. He kept the phone busy during the entire drive home. Calls were made to business associates, rallying them to a cause, the defense of their control over events and people. Local building materials suppliers were cautioned not to sell the stuff of construction to this "commune" if they intended to keep the Benton Enterprises business.

When Cal returned, late that night, Landreth was in no mood to hear about Derritt's problems. He also, for the first time, noticed just how old his father looked. It wasn't with any sense of compassion toward the elder Benton that he suggested that Cal concentrate on the timber sale coming up on the Jemez Pueblo lands. He told Cal to leave Oblivion in his hands, and also suggested that he could take care of his hot-headed younger brother. After the third shot of whiskey Cal agreed and went off to bed. Landreth sent Marquitta to provide some comfort for the old man. He would be certain to sleep well and rise late tomorrow morning. This would give Landreth enough time to do what he needed to do to gain possession of Oblivion's water rights.

Chapter Nine

Courtney and Belinda walked to the remains of what had been, in earlier days, a blacksmith shop, then a mechanic's garage. Now it was being prepared to assume a new role as the energy center for Oblivion. This first week of Oblivion's rebirth had already borne the fruits of the combined mental and physical laboring. Every family had hot water available in the form of a makeshift solar water heater. These had been made from a fifty-five gallon drums, sheets of aluminum and cheap plastic fresnal lens. It was an invention of some medical missionaries laboring in a region of Africa where there was simply no spare fuel for fires to heat and purify the most precious liquid.

Residential solar collectors were now in place on several of the rooftops, eliminating the need to run the gas powered generators for such mundane necessities as refrigeration. The new occupants had, in less than a week, established a cooperative community, where each was eager to be a part of the research projects, anxious to try the new ideas, ready to become the future.

Bartlett Breaman was the newest addition to this community. He was a Black man of imposing stature. His 6'6" frame carried his three hundred and twenty pounds with ease. The heavy salt and pepper beard gave extra dimension to the benign, grandfatherly face. He was on loan from PNM where he was respected as one of their most competent site engineers. His mission was to design the means by which the energy Dr. Taggartt's team harvested was to be converted into a form that could not only be used by Oblivion's occupants, but transported to PNM's customers as well. The sale of the hoped for surplus energy would be a source of income for the residents. For that reason, Bart Breaman was showered with attention and assistance. It took less than a day for him to decide his family needed to join him in this "ghost town filled with dreamin'."

92

Porferio Robello and his partner, Vincente had been working closely the past two days with Bonita Montoya and her staff from Environmental Solutions Inc., a new generation engineering firm, dedicated to finding the means to return human waste to the environment by a safe, non-polluting means. Plans were being discussed for safe water recovery, solar composting, solid waste conversion into fuel bricks and more. Vo-Tec students were already installing plumbing, laying the pipes for water and sewers. Paint, glass and caring hands were creating a new Oblivion. After the workday was complete, in the brief hours before sunset, native herbs, penstemon, desert four-o'clocks, chamisa, cacti and sages were carefully lifted and planted along porches and foundations.

Research grants, student projects, hope, and hard work were putting together the physical, structural aspect of Oblivion. It was almost as if the town itself had called together all these diverse forces. It was sensed by several of the "New Oblivions," as they called themselves, that the town itself was a living organism. That the community of souls present expanded far beyond the small numbers of those employed today in building their dreams. The winding stream that separates superstition and faith was crossed and recrossed many times as these people discussed their good fortune in being drawn to this place, and as they talked in hushed tones of the tragedy averted the night before by a cell door imprisoning the evil that was in their midst.

What Courtney had tried to initiate in her discussion with Belinda was that Oblivion could become more than just an experimental showcase for earth friendly technology. Here was an opportunity to try new ways that the members of society could work together, solve their problems and be a complimentary part of the natural world. Courtney didn't see a vision of a handful of people desperately escaping their present dismal existence in some soul purifying back-to-nature retreat. She saw all of humanity growing toward a future where cooperation replaced competition, where the spirit could flourish and grow, where harmony could replace conflict and the joy of art and reason could be the bounty reaped by all.

She left Belinda and sought a comfortable retreat in the shade of the cottonwoods. It was there that Ben spotted her, tapping away on her laptop while talking to a raven. He saw a hawk swoop from the sky to rest on her shoulder while a coyote sought counsel at her feet. His mind couldn't accept the scene before him. The sense was that he was intruding on a private and personal moment. He hurried away, but the image of ageless wisdom and today's technology surrounding a lady, who was in some sense timeless, swirled in the confused clouds of his mind. He hurried away, not yet ready to deal with these amorphous realities.

Landreth had marshaled his forces while on the return to Santa Fe. When he arrived at the Office of Archives and Historical Documents, Monty Themaine was waiting for him, wearing the satisfied smile of a job well done. Monty was a mole who lived in the dark musty catacombs of the state's records. It was his job to serve as the undertaker, burying the paper corpses of the body politic. He was pathetically servile, and pathologically obedient to the need for acceptance.

Landreth greeted Monty with solid handshake and a broad smile as he handed him a bottle of Calvert Smooth with a hundred dollar bill wrapped around it.

They went to the table where the old leather bound book lay open to an official document from King Charles of Spain, dated 1652. It decreed the grant of a large tract of land to a loyal and faithful servant of the crown, one Benedito Alvarez Lopez. The old Spanish land grants had mostly been overturned when the New Mexico territory became a part of the United States. But this one had never been brought before the courts. In recent years several claims arising from these historical deeds had been decided favorably. He was certain the Benton family

94

had enough clout to make this one serve his purposes.

Landreth smiled as he remembered the night several weeks ago when, in the after glow of a very satisfying liaison with Marquitta, she told him she was the heir to the land the Bentons called home and thousands of acres that extended beyond the county lines. He studied the grant and the accompanying map carefully.

"YES!" He shouted. "Yes. This does cover all the property now owned by that damned artist, and the range land between Oblivion and Juniper Crossing."

The map was poorly drawn but clearly marked the boundaries of mountains and canyon rims. This document proved prior ownership. Land grant claims that had not been reviewed were still open to legal action by the heirs of the grantees. That's what Sid, Landreth's attorney, had told him before he called Monty this morning.

Copies were made and notations recorded. Then Landreth was on his way to meet with Sid. The plan was falling together, thanks to that little bitch of a whore, Marquitta.

In less than an hour Sid was on his way to deposit the ten thousand dollar check. Once the money was safely in the bank he would begin to prepare the petition to the court for a priori water rights on behalf of Marquitta Lopez. Sid doubted that there would be any way the courts would put the rights in Ms. Lopez' hands, but this would definitely forestall activity in the little community that so obsessed Landreth. He was also fairly certain that he could secure the water rights for the Bentons with little trouble, since there had been no agricultural activity in the last two decades. All that was needed was a prior claim. Even if the court decided in favor of Marquita, Landeth was comfortable in the knowledge that he owned her. He could make her do what ever he wanted.

Calmut Benton had been mellowed by the whiskey and pleasure of Marquitta's company. In spite of the humiliation Derritt had caused him, and the humbling act of driving Ben back to the town that was becoming his obsession, he had slept well. His eyes were responding to the early morning sun streaming in the windows of his room while his body was awakening to the warmth of Marquitta's soft flesh next to him. Her long dark hair washed his face with pleasant memories. Memories his manhood was recalling as well. She rolled over to face him and the first smile of morning was turned into a kiss. She actually enjoyed the company of the elder Benton, especially in the morning when he didn't view lovemaking with such determination, or perhaps it was desperation. She took much of her pleasure from the knowledge that each time one of them surrendered their bodies to her, she increased her control, both over the men and what they owned.

Cal slept peacefully while Marquitta showered, plied the makeup artfully, and pulled on the tight jeans that abandoned all pretense at subtlety. She went down to the kitchen and poured herself a cup of coffee, then began the search for Landreth. He was usually in his office, but when she found it empty she went to his room. Perhaps, she thought, he might be in the mood for a little something. When she found his bed empty, she walked out into the courtyard. His little red MG was gone. She settled behind the wheel of her BMW to do some shopping. She smiled as she watched the big rambling house become smaller and smaller in her rear view mirror as she headed down the long tree lined drive. Some day, some way, that would be hers.

It was almost eleven when Cal pulled himself to a sitting position on the edge of the bed. Several strands of long black hair were all that remained of the woman's presence. The contentment that his body had known twice in the past night had already faded. His mind was organizing the day, determining priorities, assigning tasks. Derritt would have to come home, but Cal had to smile at the thought that his hot-headed offspring must have been humbled by the experience. Derritt was a problem Cal felt he could handle.

As the warm pulsing spray of the shower eased the aches and pains of age, his thoughts turned to Landreth. He knew Landreth wanted him out of action this morning. He knew his boy had a plan to seize Oblivion. He had decided the night before that he would see if this dog could hunt. He had been ready, in the face of his defeat last night, to let Landreth assume more of the power the family held. Now, in the morning light, the old man wasn't as ready to let go of any control.

This morning he wanted both his sons on short leashes. He had a plan, too. While he sat at the kitchen table waiting for Chi to prepare his breakfast burritos, he worked the phone. He had once referred to the telephone as the ultimate weapon. One can kill an opponent with the phone and never see the blood. It was also a universal tool. It was a shovel that could dig up dirt. Today it would build a fence. It would deliver Oblivion and let him keep his promise that no one would get hurt.

The independent survey company that Benton Enterprises used assured him that they would be ready for his crew and their equipment before noon. Cal knew that a small finger of Benton land was crossed by by the road that lead to Oblivion. Another phone call assured him that when they had purchased that little bit of hillside, there were no right-of-way easements in the deed. The road to Oblivion was over Benton land. Between sips of coffee he gave the orders for some of the earth movers from the mining operation and crews to be moved into position.

Cal didn't own the land bordering Oblivion on the north. The federal government did, and it was under the control of the Bureau of Land Management. Cal leased this property for a few dollars a year. In theory he was to graze cattle on it, but no more than a few strays had nibbled that grass in over a decade. The lease was held by the Bentons mostly so no one else would gain control of the land and access to the water that lay beneath Oblivion.

As he wiped the last vestiges of the red chiles from his lips and chin, he turned his attention to his younger son. Derritt was a problem he didn't want to face. He almost wished he could just keep him in the county jail for a while, but he couldn't do that to his son. The news of a Benton behind bars would bring the press in like a plague. Cal knew how the public would respond to the scientific and social experiments that were blossoming in Oblivion. He also knew the damage bad publicity could do and wanted to avoid the stench of scandal.

Chapter Ten

The hard physical labor of the morning had soaked the shirts of the men and women eager to make truly livable the homes they now occupied. Ben and Belinda had been painting in one of the houses that had not yet become home for any family. They felt optimism for the future reflected in the new brightness. The fresh pastel colors seemed to make the building smile with hope as well. It was time for a pause in their efforts. They playfully kissed and laughed at the paint they were both wearing. On the street there was a curious blend of Selena's Tejano sound and Itzhak Perlman's interpretation of Shostokovich's Second Violin Concerto.

They used the opportunity the break in the painting afforded to check the progress being made in more mundane but necessary community needs, like the sewer and water lines. One of the stone buildings had been raided years ago by someone seeking the beautiful sandstone for their own purposes. All that was left was a foundation and part of a back corner. They stood at this remnant of a once proud house that was becoming the depository of the community's garbage. Across the dusty street a hungry ditch-witch was eating its way from a house wall to what would be a well when the windmill was completed.

Flies and hornets circled the growing mountain of plastic bags as the contents ripened in the hot sun. Dr. Elisa Montoya, an environmental ethics expert from UNM, and Chad joined in the conversation. She explained, "Humans are the dirtiest animals on earth. Our consumption and waste production have made possible the pandemic spread of disease, the destruction of our own habitats and even the loss of valuable species. Handling sewage is the easiest of our waste challenges, and we already possess the knowledge and tools necessary to deal properly with this problem."

"Think about it. We can not only control, but also, by following the example of nature, completely recycle human waste." Chad was as enthusiastic about someone else's ideas as he was his own. "She has been showing me what reusing our dirty water can mean to crop potential in this valley."

Belinda had put together an advertising program several years ago for the city of Milwaukee. It was promoting an item called "Milorganite," a processed sewage sludge, dried and packaged for use as a lawn fertilizer. She contributed this information to the group.

Ben had noticed that the first efforts made by Inez and her husband had been in their garden. It was the creation of a compost pile. They actively sought the corn husks from everyone's tamales, the rinds of the melons and the vegetable parings as raw material for the creation of new soil. Ben suggested that this might become a community wide enterprise. Dr. Montoya informed him that many communities already had yard waste composting programs that provided free of charge a valuable garden soil conditioner. She then went on to explain that a soil scientist in Los Lunas had developed a method of using nature's own soil organisms to produce humus from the accumulated botanic waste of human communities. She then went on to describe how this scientist was now working to perfect ways to use these same organisms to break down some of our most toxic waste into bio-useful compounds.

"In the future we will all be held accountable for the waste we produce, but today we simply leave the problem for our grandchildren to deal with," Chad added.

Dr. Montoya then pointed in the direction of the garbage. "This is our biggest problem."

"There are many items recycled already, like soft drink cans, glass bottles and newspapers," Belinda replied defensively.

"True, but less than two percent of our waste is currently reused, and for most of it, we simply can't find a economical second use."

Chad fielded Belinda's comment. "What makes this such a difficult problem is that it requires a change in the way we conduct our lives. It's our pursuit of a false sense of safety and security that is as much at fault as any innate laziness of our species."

Ben asked for an explanation and was given numerous examples, like multiple packaging and single use products.

"Most of our convenience cannot be converted into compost," Courtney added as she sought their companionship and the shade. "Yet, we spend our valuable hours of labor to buy all this convenience, which, in truth, makes it all quite an inconvenience."

Dr. Montoya added, "For most of our culture, we have lost contact with the earth, with our instinctive connection with all life. Our insatiable hunger to win, possess, acquire material possessions is all a substitute for the need to be a part of nature itself."

"When our culture declared war on nature we, in reality, declared war on ourselves." Courtney was shaking with anger as she spoke. "And I assure you there can be no victory in defeating yourself."

Their conversation was interrupted by an ill defined noise in the distance.

The clouds of dust rolling over the hill drew their attention. The roar of heavy equipment followed the advancing wall of dust. The sound, the sight, tied Ben's stomach in knots. The instinct for defense proved victorious over his dislike of confrontation as he marched resolutely toward the source of this new threat. As they reached the crest of the hill, it became obvious what was happening. A surveying team was driving stakes across the narrow entrance to their valley. Eight earth movers, borrowed from one of the Benton mining operations, were lined up along the roadway, roaring their mechanical challenge to the people soon to be trapped in Oblivion.

Courtney left the group and climbed to the crest of the hill. Ben and Belinda watched as she sat among a bright profusion of spring flowers, golden yellow, pink and blue. Wild ancestors of the marigold and zinnia, sages, daisies and sunflowers, morning glories and more made this section of the canyon's mouth a kaleidoscope of color as they marked the march of the seasons. But the dust was beginning to descend on them, clothing the blooms in a red-tan cloak. Within a few minutes the wind reversed its direction. The cleansing breeze revealed the colors of life again, but the dark choking air was now swirling around the surveyors.

The mechanical roar was being answered by a faint hum. As the wind pushed the dust back toward the machines and the men these machines were using to guide them, a new cloud followed. This one was darker and seemed to be born from the sky itself as minute specks of energy converged into a force. The hum soon became a ominous buzz that filled the air and invaded the senses. Then, as the sky turned black with this expanding cloud, the buzz became a roar to answer the motors that had begun to push a wall of dirt up to the line of the surveyor's stakes. The edge of this dark cloud hit the six man crew at the transits and siting poles first. Their valuable equipment was discarded and abandoned as they fled to their vehicles. Those that stumbled and fell, were covered by the edge of the cloud and rose screaming in terror.

It took only seconds for the cloud to hit the operators of the hungry machines. The horror of millions of angry bees descending from the sky was too much for these men as well. In their attempts to escape, some machines were turned off, some engines were left at idle, and two were left in motion. Tracks and wheels drove the mechanical greed into the side of the canyon wall, where one fell over onto the other, exploded and burned, turning both to scrap iron and silence.

As quickly as it had formed, the swarms of bees dissipated. They all returned to their more benign pursuit of gentle flowers and their sweet nectar. Courtney knelt and carefully selected a sprig of sage, a poppy and a spring daisy; tucked the mini bouquet in her hair. Then she returned to Ben and Belinda. They had cowered in the grass as the bees massed overhead. Now they were trembling with relief.

"Where did they all come from?" Ben asked.

Courtney smiled her most grandmotherly smile, "They were defending the flowers that grow on these hillsides. The blossoms give them life, you know." Then she walked off, followed by butterflies and bright indigo buntings, chattering finches and a pair of Stellers jays.

It was by the weapon Cal valued so highly, that the word of this, his second defeat, reached him. The phone on the desk was ringing literally minutes after the swarm had dispersed. The cell phone in the surveyor's truck had been used to convey the terror of the men held prisoner inside. The fact that they had received a few bee stings and ran like a bunch of cowards angered Cal. Then they described the destruction of over a hundred thousand dollars worth of heavy equipment. This threw him into an uncontrollable rage. Brandy was listening on the other side of the office door. In a way she couldn't understand, she was almost pleased that her father and brothers were encountering failures in this undeclared war against a ghost town.

This shadow of a town now boasted a population of forty plus thirty-two temporary residents whose ranks included students, scientists, visionaries and dreamers. All of these people of Oblivion could best be viewed as artists painting the canvas of the future. Each of these people brought a unique talent, a willingness to work and a shared dream. Every last one of these men, women and children stood with Ben and Belinda as they watched the flames consume the engines of destruction that had been aimed at them. Knees were bent and prayers directed heavenward. With the last gasp of exhausted flame, while the metal still glowed red hot, they all turned and walked quietly back to Oblivion. While they rejoiced at their victory, the second within twenty-four hours, they knew that this would only strengthen the resolve of the Bentons. Their dreams were most likely doomed to failure, but they all knew that they had to continue, to try; to do all that they could. Surrender would be far worse than defeat.

Ben and Belinda discussed the resources they had. Definitely intellect was one of their weapons. The University of New Mexico, a goodly segment of the scientific community, the vast power of the environmentalists and the governmental agencies all carried some weight. Belinda suggested that perhaps the most powerful arms in their arsenal belonged to a little old lady that talked to the animals.

There were some muttering among the Chicanos that perhaps a bruha was in their midst. A witch was not always bad, but always to be feared. Many of the curanderas were witches; perhaps that is why those who are healers are also distrusted. The same power that can bring health can also take it away. It was well known that only one connected with the spirit world could call all the bees together as they had witnessed. While some were fearful of bruhas, others were clutching their rosaries and offering prayers God and the saints.

"Gracias, Madre de Dios, Gracias, por los milagros."

The students and scientists were also moved by the sight of tons of steel, equipment capable of moving mountains, halted in their tracks by a tiny insect. Frog wanted to talk with Courtney, but couldn't find her. She seemed to have simply disappeared among the rocks and junipers of the canyon wall.

Chad and several of the other students were trying to understand what had happened. Amid the jokes was the uncomfortable knowledge that they had no explanation for what they had seen.

One of the energy specialists offered his speculation, "Vibrations caused by the eight earth movers stirred all the bees in their nests. They simply attacked what they saw as a threat."

Dr. Taggartt waved her cane at the students, "As a scientist, I'm wise enough to know that the lesson here is clear to all of us." She smiled and walked on. Chad, Frog and several of the others pressed their mentor for an explanation. She stared at them for a moment then replied with a smile, "It's simple. Don't mess with Mother Nature."

The forty residents returned to their town, but not to their labors. The old church was now the focus of their attention. Several had spent their evenings sweeping the floors, and clearing away the broken glass from the windows, righting the few pews left, and dusting the several santos and retablos overlooked by looters. Now the students, engineers, scholars, and the rest were swarming over the structure. The bell that had called the faithful together so many years ago had fallen from the braces in the steeple, and crashed through the floorboards to the earth beneath. It still lay where it had landed. Chan Ton and Chad were soon on the roof calling for the needed tools and materials to make the bell's tower once again sound and stable. Sagging beams, bent by loneliness as much as by their age, were strengthened and straightened.

Chad pointed to the dove's nest and care was taken not to disturb the occupants or their eggs. It was Chan Ton that was the first to notice the faint ringing sound. It was audible only to the soul, but his Buddhist sensitivity felt this message from another faith. It was as if the sounds had been trapped in the wood, just waiting for someone to hear them.

While they made the steeple ready, Ben, Belinda and Bartlett pulled the bell free of the crushed floor boards and washed away the dust, grime and neglect to reveal the beauty beneath. A rope was located; within an hour, the piece of iron was returned to its former glory.

The activity around the church was so intense that an observer could not have avoided drawing the mental image of an ant hill. In fact that is exactly what the old man was thinking as he sat cross legged in the dust of the street. It was strange that no one noticed this solitary figure. His grey hair flowed down below his shoulders in graceful waves that implied they were sometimes worn in braids. The sweatband was an old blue bandana, salt crusted. Tucked in the side of this band were several eagle and hawk feathers. The shirt he wore was faded

105

plaidwith the sleeves rolled up to reveal a large silver bracelet with huge nuggets of turquoise mounted on it. The shirt's tail hung down over his tattered and frayed jeans while around his waist was a silver concho belt. His bare feet held the calluses of many miles. By his side was a canvas bag, across his lap was a wooden flute and in his hands rested a Bible.

His face was rugged, darkly tanned to the color and texture of old leather. Lines were eroded deep into the cheeks, forming the channels for tears; but there were also lines marking smiles past and future. As he watched the bustle of activity, the lips pulled the face into a gentle and reflective curve that hinted at laughter, spoke contentment. The eyes were closed in prayer when the dove flew from the steeple to land on his shoulder, to preen and groom the feathers in his headband. Chan Ton followed the bird's flight and saw a monk of his faith seated in meditation. The bird's fluttering wings drew Frog's attention. She saw a Rabbi she had known in her youth.

The old man began to chant softly, so quietly that it was easily heard above the chaos of chatter and construction. The Catholics saw a devout priest, Belinda saw a mystic of great peace and went to sit near him to read his thoughts and bask in his serenity. Ben also was drawn to this Indian by the sense that the harmony of the universe was reflected in his ancient eyes.

He slowly rose to his feet, closed the book, and tucked it in the bag with many others. He spoke not a word, but put the flute to his lips and played a gentle, not mournful, call to hope. He walked toward the church. With measured steps he walked toward the people. As he moved through the crowd, many claimed later that they could hear the beat of drums, distant but unmistakable. Some heard the drums of Africa, others ears captured the sound of oriental percussion. Amed, one of the Vo-tec students, heard the desert sounds of his ancestry, Dr. Taggartt saw the beauty of an ancient Hebrew temple, an image evoked

106

by the joyful drums of a festival. For each of the seventy-two people present, different images were forming before the mind's eye.

They all followed him into the church and up the aisle. He knelt before the altar and tucked the flute into his belt. He retrieved an old wooden chair that someone had been standing on while cleaning the window frames. Then he sat, facing them.

"Thank you," were the words he uttered first. Then with a gesture he motioned for them to all be seated. Some found the pews that were left, the rest sat on the floor.

"I have been watching you, from the hills. It is good that you have also made this house ready. He pointed to two of the children seated before him. "Would you two be so kind as to ring the bell for the first time?"

After a brief glance at their parents, they raced to the rope. The sound was pure, clean and glorious to their ears. Hope was being proclaimed throughout the community, and on to the edges of Oblivion. The ringing echoed against the canyon walls and carried beyond. The sound waves, born in the expression of joy, began their cosmic journey.

"The words we utter, and the notes of our music, are like the coo of a dove and the cry of a cougar. Once uttered, they are ours no longer. They belong to the universe. They become the echo of all life. When you drop a pebble in the ocean it makes ripples that reach distant shores. So it is with ideas, dreams, messages of good will. What we all say and do ripples forever to affect and influence in some small way whoever and whatever they touch."

He reached down and pulled from his canvas bag a bouquet of beautiful wildflowers, "Each of these is different, each has a charm of its own, but by uniting with the others the beauty is not only added, it is multiplied. As you build your village here, don't lose sight of the knowledge that each person possesses talent and beauty, but it is together that you will make a work of art."

107

He pulled the flute from his belt and played for several minutes. "If you don't object, I will stay with you awhile." he said, as he stood and started toward the door. "It was the wisdom of my ancestors," he spoke as he paused at the hole in the floor where the bell had been, "that humanity escaped from the underworld to the world of light through the sipapu. In our places of worship and meditation, this was a focus for our thoughts. It serves as a reminder. No matter how trying the times, the light was still better than the darkness. I am pleased that your church has a sipapu."

He stood at the doorway for a moment. "It is also good that the door faces east. The direction of morning light." He took a small leather pouch from his belt, opened it, and removed a pinch of the pale yellow powder it contained. He opened his fingers and blew the dust into the air. "Corn pollen. For good luck." he said with a smile, as he walked down the steps and into the street.

"I'll meet you here tomorrow with the morning light." he called over his shoulder as he walked between the buildings and on toward the canyon wall. The sound of the flute continued to soothe their minds and comfort their souls long after he was out of sight.

Calmut Benton was in the middle of a heated argument with Derritt when the pain in his chest forced him to his chair. In that moment of silence, that interlude where neither Benton was shouting abuse or hatred, he heard the faint and distant peal of church bells. Memories of youth pushed and shoved the anger to the side as they seized control of his mind. He could still see Derritt raving. He could feel the rage that surrounded his son as he held the large chunk of gold ore in his hand. It was the bells he heard as the rock paperweight crashed down against the side of his head. Even when consciousness departed to haul away the pain, he could feel the ringing of the bells.

Derritt threw the paperweight at his father's chest as a last parting shot. The blow told the heart to start pumping again. Cal was

108

on the floor, blood flowing from the side of his head. Blood was filling his eyes, washing away his vision as Brandy entered the room. Derritt saw her standing beside the doorway. His rage drove him. His broken fists found her face. As she fell he viciously kicked her in the side and abdomen as he fled the room and his father. The pain in his hands was so bad he couldn't turn the doorknob. He slammed his shoulder against the wood and glass. Splinters, like daggers, were driven deeply into his arm and side while slivers of glass slashed his face and back. His anger followed him, a shadow that clung like shackles to his heels and would not release the man who had spawned it.

Brandy managed to call for help. Within half an hour, Cal was on his way by helicopter to the Good Samaritan Hospital in Sante Fe. He would lose his right eye, but would live to come to terms with both his son and his Oblivion.

Chapter Eleven

The night was haunted by harsh winds that howled and moaned as they made their journey through Oblivion. Belinda slept fitfully, clutching the small kitten to her breast. She found comfort in its soft innocence; it found security in her warmth and protective arms. The events of the day held claim to Ben's mind. Belinda had twice tried to initiate the comfort of love-making. Twice Ben failed to respond, either mentally or physically. This rejection hurt her deeply, and it was this pain that denied her sleep as much as the wind.

Ben was frustrated by his inability to answer the call of Belinda's body against his. He couldn't shake the images of Cal from his mind. A promise had been made and broken, yet something, at some level he couldn't understand, told him his adversary was paying a terrible price. He had tried to sleep, but the drive to complete the painting of the wolves for Cal drove him to the easel. The colors flowed as the acrylic paints gave texture and life to the animals engaged in the competition for power. The watercolor wash he had used for the sky and rocks provided depth and almost forced the wolves to leap from the canvas into the eye of the viewer. Drops of red paint dripped onto the head of the challenged leader. In Ben's attempt to erase the error, he accidently filled the one eye with the blood red paint. The decision was made to leave it as a wound that somehow seemed to belong in the picture.

The male in the background was limping. Ben hadn't realized this when he started the sketch and wasn't certain when the wound to this wolf's paw had occurred. It was with a drive he rarely felt that he plied the colors. He felt several times that this had ceased to be his painting, that he was only a tool being used by some force, a power he could sense but not define. By the time he was finished, there was no energy left. He sat on his chair, nude except for the robe that had fallen from his shoulders. He lacked even the strength to return to the comfort of their bed. He slept the sleep of exhaustion.

Belinda found him sitting before the finally completed work of art. She sat on the floor in front of him. In the wavering light of a candle she studied his sleeping form, the first lines, hinting at age, increased the depth and dimension of his eyes. The gentle smile, the dabs of paint on his chin, the tussled hair framing his face; all the bits and pieces of the man she loved. He wasn't handsome. She knew that, but he was lovable.

She smiled at the modest muscles of his arms, not the rippling biceps of a well conditioned athlete, but arms that could hold her warm and secure with love. Her smile broadened as her eyes traced the soft folds of his robe across the arm of the chair revealing his recumbent maleness. The lines of his legs, lightly crossed at the ankles, angular shaped feet, and the long toes completed the journey her eyes had taken over the body of the man she loved.

This was the first time she had even actually watched him as he slept, watched the rhythm of life as he breathed, watched the slight movements of his fingers as a mind freed from the reality of wakefulness turned to other pursuits. She was intrigued by the fact that asleep her lover was quite active. Smiles crossed and recrossed his face, his eyes moved under the cover of their lids, there was even movement within the protective nest of his loins.

Finally, she could restrain herself no longer. Loosening her robe, she leaned over his sleeping form, giving him gentle kisses while the warmth of her body caressed his. His arms wrapped around her as they again found great comfort in each other's love.

The wind continued to howl through the valley and up the canyon walls, carrying with it a chill, not uncommon for the spring season. There was also a promise, perhaps threat would be a better term, of rain to follow. Ominous is the name of a night wind. Sleep was a stranger

111

to most of Oblivion's own this night. Countless candles were lit, and many rosaries felt the warmth of trembling hands. Those living in tents felt the most insecure. Dr. Taggartt hosted many of her students in the jail. Others clustered in the church. Chad and Frog had intended to endure the coming storm in their tent, but soon rethought that decision. They gathered a few of their current possessions and ran through the first warning drops of the deluge to come, seeking shelter with Ben and Belinda.

The pounding on the door awoke Ben. By the time he found his robe, the full force of the storm had hit. Chad and Frog were drenched. Belinda quickly gathered blankets for the uninvited but welcome guests. Ben stood by the open door watching the violence of the storm, feeling the roar of the driving rain, watching the awesomely beautiful flashes of lightening. These explosions of electricity came so fast and frequent that the town was illuminated. Ben could see other people huddled in their doorways witnessing the dynamic display of nature's force and power. The deluge continued for over an hour, answering the prayers of those who had called for rain.

Twenty-one men, women and children huddled in the church while the wind carried such force that the bell was ringing. It wasn't until the storm began to subside, that the old Indian was spotted lying motionless at the base of the altar. Several of the more superstitious were fearful of death and refused to approach. Inez, the reluctant resident, the sceptic, the healer who would grow herbs, held her cross to her lips and knelt before the figure. He seemed so small, so still; but Inez could hear the distant tones of a flute as she bent and touched the cross to his forehead.

His eyes fluttered and a smile covered his face. The gentle folks massed behind Inez gasped at the movement, the presence of life when they thought it was absent. Some thought they were witnessing a miracle, others feared a ghost was in their midst. Inez helped the old man to his feet.

112

"I apologize if I startled you," he said as he straightened his hair. "You didn't think I was stupid enough to stay outside in weather like this, did you?"

Laughter started slowly but soon rippled through the families and individuals gathered there. More candles were lit, aas each uttered prayers that answered their own needs. He pulled a small pouch from his canvas bag and poured its contents into a bowl. "This is the secret my people kept for many years. A small handful of these seeds will give you the energy to travel many trails, survive many trials."

Inez knew what these black grains were, but she was prepared to keep the secret with him. This old man was in the purest sense a teacher. He could not help but explain to every one as they cautiously sampled the specks and enjoyed their nut-like flavor. "This is the seeds of a sage we call "chia." You White people make pets of them and sell them in the K-Mart." He laughed at the idea of little terra-cotta animals growing heads of chia hair. Soon everyone was engaged in comfortable laughter again.

Dawn, after a torrential rain, does not come softly on cat's feet, but roars into existence, leaping over mountain tops with a blinding brilliance. All the sins of nature's past days are washed away by the scouring water. The air itself is cleansed, and life shines with renewed enthusiasm. This is the Sunday morning that greeted Oblivion, clean, pure, filled with hope.

"Father," Inez spoke as she handed the ancient Indian a cup of breakfast tea, "Will you speak to these people today?" In her eyes he was a priest.

He sipped the hot liquid slowly and declined to answer for many minutes. She feared that she had offended him and sought the means to make amends. He pulled a small bottle from his bag and held it to his lips. As the honey slowly flowed into his mouth, he began to smile. Years melted from his face. She handed him a tortilla and a small bowl of diced chiles, onions, tomatoes and cilantro.

113

The old man tore a small bit from the bread and dipped it in the delicious pico de gallo.

"Let all of us enjoy your gift," he smiled at Inez again, then motioned toward the people who had spent the night in the safety of the church, calling them to come forward.

Courtney's face was the first image he saw. Derritt was having trouble focusing his eyes. First he thought her thick glasses were the eyes of an owl, then he thought her nose was the beak of a hawk. When she spoke, he heard the roar of a mountain lion. As her hand tore the door of the truck open, he felt the claws of a bear. He could remember the pain in his hands from striking his father and sister, but did not understand the source of the blood and agony that surrounded his back and shoulder. He could remember the thunder and lightening that followed him into the valley that held Oblivion, but he couldn't recall why he had come there. He had known when the rain hit. He had been parked in the arroyo and tried to get out. But the clay had become mud, too deep to give traction. The wall of water roared at him, announcing its victory. His scream was lost in the voice of the wind and water. When one seeks to be alone, all cries for help are unheard, and might as well be unspoken. Even after he lost consciousness, the truck continued to roll and tumble. It had become a toy bobbing in the newborn river of the flash flood.

His Dodge Ram truck came to rest against a rude and defiant clump of salt cedar. He knew nothing of this. All he knew was that he was being carried to the water trough that was the life blood of Oblivion. The old lady did nothing to wash the blood from his face and head, provided no comfort for his bruised arms and legs. All he understood was that now she was gone and he could not stand. His body was a bag of pain. That was the way he was when they found him, rolled in a fetal position, hands over his face, whimpering incoherently. It was Frog who first spotted him and called for help.

114

The old man left the church for a pre-dawn stroll and gathered several items as he walked. The broken shell of a jay's egg, a piece of ancient pottery, a wedge shaped chunk of Spanish stoneware, and the handle from a blue delft china cup all found their way into his canvas bag. As the first hint of sunrise lightened the eastern sky, he picked up a small lump of bluish-green copper ore and the opening bud of a wild rambling rose. Soon he had a fistful of flowers and twigs. He retrieved a discarded, sun blued bottle, and filled it with water to make an impromptu vase for them. He returned to the church with this bag of treasures, just as the first true rays found their way through the window and door to illuminate the altar.

Without a word he spread the contents of his bag on the table. Then, he removed a heavy gold chain from his pocket and laid it with the rest. He walked to the door and made the offering of corn pollen to the morning sun. The bell rang softly in the strength of a morning breeze. All the citizens and friends of Oblivion directed their steps toward the building that seemed to glow in the morning light. It appeared so much cleaner and stronger after the night's great deluge.

Frog, Chad and Inez cleansed the wounds and washed away the blood and mud that had been the night's mark on Derritt. His hands were so painful he couldn't hold the cup of soothing tea Inez offered. Frog helped him with the drink. Soon the body set the pain, agony and torment free. Inez claimed she could see it floating from him, vaporizing into the atmosphere. Chad helped him to his feet and they all found their way to the church. Derritt tried to turn away, but his feet refused to do as he commanded them. They found a place on the floor near the sipapu the bell had made.

The Indian sat on the same chair he had chosen the night before and welcomed them all with a benign, grandfatherly smile. Finally, several minutes after all had been seated, he began to talk with them.

"All the earth is older than time, and the father of time," he began, "The flowers bloomed before man was here to smile at them.

The deer and the bison roamed the grassland before we sought their flesh. The squash and the bean knew their seasons before we were here to cultivate them. The trees provided shelter eons before we rested in their shade."

"Some places were chosen, not by you or me, as places of healing, like Chimayo or your Lourdes in France. Others were places of dreaming, places of peace and hope. Philadelphia was such a place, and so is this." He stood and walked behind the alter, to the items he had collected on his walk through the town.

He held up the shell of the jay's egg in his right hand, "This is the always hope, the forever goal. Youth for each of us is wasted the first time we get to experience it. In our children we see it a second time and are a bit wiser. We now know a little of what youth is, but must work too hard to enjoy it. The wisdom of the Great Mystery is far stronger than ours, therefore we are given another chance at youth. You call them grandchildren, and grand they are, because you are finally wise enough to live your youth this third time. If you are blessed, you will get another chance at youth, and each time you are wiser still. This is the way it is with your villages too."

"A community is a living thing, just like you, and once it sees its youth, like you it can be reborn many times. This place you call Oblivion was a home to those before my people, when they were once young. Thousands of years ago, they, like the owl and the coyote, found life good in this valley. They hunted, ate, made children and buried their dead here. They knew love and joy, fear and pain." He was silent for some time and starred at Derritt; his eyes penetrated the body and studied the soul.

"Before the first people, before my people, were the bird people, the fur people, and the finned people of the lakes. They knew all that you know, and much that you need to know.

"This has always been a place of dreams." He held up for all to see, the curved piece of pottery with black markings on it. "My people

116

dreamed of happy families with much music, beautiful pots and fields of corn, squash and beans. Then all the trees were gone, and drought told the corn not to grow. Then the Spaniards came with their dreams." This time he showed the occupants of Oblivion the Spanish stoneware. "They wanted a peaceful valley where they could watch their sheep and enjoy their fruit trees and gardens. But they had too many sheep and the grass was soon gone. Others dreamed dreams of valueless things." He held up the gold chain. "For this they would kill each other, destroy the land itself, cut wounds in their Earth Mother so deep that she bled to death." He threw the chain on the floor in front of them.

Only Derritt reached out for the gold, with the pain in his arm, and a hand he could hardly command, he grabbed the chain. A satisfied smile crossed his lips; but couldn't overcome the pain in his eyes.

"Fools know little of value." The old Indian picked up the whiskey bottle. "All wise peoples seek beauty. It is the food of the soul. Don't you think God, or whatever you choose to call the Great Mystery, loves beauty? Otherwise, why would there be so many flowers, birds, deer, mountains and children? Aren't these more beautiful than that chain? A flower will never choke you like that gold chain will." The warning was direct. The strength of the old man's eyes frightened Derritt as he clutched the precious metal to his chest.

He handed the flowers one by one to the people seated before him. There were just enough for every man, women and child, except Derritt. He had chosen his own beauty.

The old Indian held the bottle filled with water high in the air. "This is value," he spoke as he poured the water into his hand. "Water is life. To deny any person water is to deny life itself.

"When the Anglos came to this valley with their dreams," he now held the blue Delft cup handle up for all to see. He had traced the history of this valley in the pottery found in its refuse. "they first brought their cattle and grazed them on the short grass until it was all gone. The stone foundation, where you are now piling the refuse of your lives, was the ranch house where men and women whose names are now forgotten lived and worked their dreams.

"Later, more Anglos came with dreams of copper and other metals. They laid bare the skin of their mother to steal her flesh. Then their dreams turned sour, and they left the Oblivion you came to know as a ghost town. Don't let your dreams spoil with the rot of greed. Please, first cooperate with each other, then cooperate with the forces that can help you. You can have a life of harmony, if only you are willing to be a part of the whole. Don't let this be the marker of your tenure here." He held a Styrofoam cup above his head, and with a hint of anger, crushed it in his ancient hand.

With that he put his flute to his lips and slowly walked toward the door. Again, many claimed they could hear drums; some said they could feel the presence of others in their midst.

Derritt spat as the old Indian walked past. Without a thank you to those who had helped him, he painfully rose to his unsteady feet and began the long and difficult walk to he didn't know where.

Chapter Twelve

Landreth stroked Marquita's hair and smiled at her sleeping form. He often took her to his cabin north of the Cochiti Pueblo forest lands, above the dam. The view from the mountainside was relaxing, there were no telephones, computers or FAX machines; no brother or father panting after his woman. In fact, the most serious interruption they encountered was the chatter of jays or, on occasion, the harsh protests of a magpie.

She was not asleep, but concentrated on keeping her eyes closed and maintaining a slow rhythmic breathing. She wished he would stop playing with her hair. She could feel his body readying itself for her again, knew that next his hands would find her breasts. While he was far more gentle than his brother, he still lacked the natural understanding that made his father's love making almost enjoyable. She wished he would go to the kitchen and put on some coffee.

The flames from last night were rekindling within Landreth. Every inch of Marquita's body was erotic territory; his to explore. He took great comfort in the fact that he owned this woman. Then anger welled within him as images of Marquita in Cal's arms filled his mind. This anger served as a tonic to his lust. His hands forced her over onto her back and she made a fateful mistake.

She blinked her eyes to feign waking and in the moment of confusion, smiled and whispered with practiced coyness, "What is it you want, Derritt?"

In all the years she had been lover for all the men of this family, she had never before made the mistake of using the wrong name.

Landreth's anger turned immediately to rage. He slapped her hard across the face. His left hand seized her hair and pulled her upright on the bed. His right hand became a fist that no longer belonged to him as it pounded her. Bones splintered and blood flowed freely from the broken teeth and the heavy sensuous lips. Again and again the fist struck.

Later she insisted that she could hear church bells and a flute playing, but it was Brandy shouting in the doorway that Landreth heard. Actually, it wasn't her screams that made him stop, it was the small, clicking sound of a hammer being pulled into position, readying itself for the job for which the gun was made, creating the horror of suffering and death.

Marquita pulled the sheet over her nude form and held the pillow to her mouth. She was trying to comprehend what was happening, but her mind was working in slow motion. The pain felt as if it belonged to someone else. Drums were beating the heartbeat of time as her body surrendered to the comforting arms of the dream people. Mist swirled before her eyes and she saw the campfires surrounded by the horses and wagons of an entrada. Soon she felt herself being carried under the protective arches of the portico as the Dona and other mujeres washed her pain away.

Landreth's eyes focused first on what he had done to his mistress; then shifted to the heavy old colt revolver Brandy held. His mind was trying to shift away from its rage; rage about realities he didn't want to acknowledge. He knew she was the family whore, but it was knowledge he didn't want to know. At some level, he did truly love her, at least, as much as he was capable of love. He was appalled by the evidence of his awesome, and uncontrollable, anger. The fury spawned by this woman's flaunting of the fact that she was sleeping in his brother's bed was forced to retreat before the immediate threat to his life.

"You disgust me." Brandy spat at her brother. "This whole family disgusts me."

She pointed the gun at his chest; but they were both distracted by Marquita. Her body fell from the bed onto the heavy buffalo hide rug.

Landreth tied his flannel shirt around his waist, to hide his nakedness, before kneeling to offer assistance to the lover he had just beaten. His analytical mind had explored his sister's possible actions and decided that she couldn't pull the trigger. But, what was she yelling about their father and Derritt? It was a difficult journey for his mind; from rage, to fear, and now, comprehension.

Why would Derritt try to kill Dad? Why was his sister bruised and bandaged? He turned from the unconscious Marquita to sort out whatever it was Brandy was ranting about. He sat on the corner of the bed and motioned her to the chair. Instead, she knelt beside Marquita as she tried to explain the events of the night before; that Derritt was missing, and Cal was in a hospital in Santa Fe. While he went to the kitchen for some ice and cold compresses, Brandy started to dress the unfortunate mistress. The sight of the open wounds and the smell of the blood made her vomit.

Marquita could smell the smoke of the pinon burning in the fireplace of the old hacienda. She felt the comfort of prayers and poultices, tasted the bitterness of a cup of steaming osha-root tea. Now the hushed tones in Spanish were becoming mingled with angry Anglo voices. She tried to open her eyes, but they were blood filled and swollen almost shut. Vision was difficult, as though a dark cloud had descended over her. When she tried to speak, pain shot through her jaws. She could still taste the bitter tea, but the fragrance of pinon burning was gone; replaced with the odors of fear, anger and hatred. She tried to force her mind back to the better place; it refused to cooperate. It insisted that she live in the now.

Landreth carried her to Brandy's car; even tried to make her comfortable in the back seat. "Five thousand dollars, Marquita, and I promise this will never happen again."

"You'd better get dressed and meet us at the Juniper Crossings clinic," Brandy was struggling to control her rage now. "There's going to be a lot of explaining to do." She got behind the wheel, then as the engine started, she made one last comment to her departing brother, "All

I can tell you is that I will try to keep our family name clean, but I don't know why."

Cal had expected a phone call from Derritt. He had insisted on leaving the hospital, although the pain in his head wouldn't stop. The eye was damaged beyond repair and he felt so exhausted. "That's the worst of it." he told the nurse, "I'm so damned weak I don't think I can stand."

But he tried. That's when the second dagger of chest pain hit him. He gasped for breath as he fell against the bed, on his way to the cold tile floor. The struggle was futile. It now felt like an elephant was standing on his chest. Breathing was almost impossible. The last thing he could remember was the chill he felt from his sweat soaked shirt. That wetness bothered him more than the pain and torment that gripped his chest and made his neck and arms numb. He simply closed his eyes and drifted into his own personal oblivion.

A spontaneous community picnic was underway in Oblivion. The Chavez brothers had made a run to Juniper Crossing for the basic foods of a cookout: hot dogs, hamburger, chicken wings and ribs. They returned with information more interesting than the food; news that had to be shared with Ben and Belinda.

The tamales were steaming. Chad and Frog were making a pot of chili with a solar oven that consisted of a complex series of reflectors and lenses arranged with mathematical precision on a discarded satellite TV dish. Dr. Taggartt was putting the finishing touches on the blintzes, when Domingo jumped from the truck and began his harried search for Ben.

Because he seemed so troubled after the comments by the old Indian, Belinda had talked Ben into a stroll out to the arroyo, to see the effects of last night's storm. The coffee colored water continued to flow as the canyon walls were drained of their precious liquid. Trees had

122

been uprooted by the force of the rampaging water. They had tumbled and floated down the once dry riverbed. They came to rest against the body of a dead Dodge Ram truck, almost buried in the mud and debris. This defunct vehicle and the trees piled against it trapped the brush, garbage and rocks to form a dam. A lake was forming behind the cottonwoods by the watering trough.

Ben had been reluctant to go to the meeting in the church, but was drawn by the innate curiosity of an artist. He wanted to know more about this old Indian. During the lecture on the history of the valley, Ben had been sketching. It wasn't until they had started on their walk that Belinda took the pad from his hands and leafed through it. The first page was a series of studies of the old man. Within the lines of the face were hints at the various cultures he had discussed. The second sketch showed the broken eggshell, in a bird's nest, that in faint lines took on the form of the valley and its canyon walls. Inside the shell were the pieces of pottery from the three cultures. The last of the three drawings was of Courtney holding a rose bud, about to open. Beside her stood the bent figure of the Indian, leaning on a gnarled mountain mahogany walking stick. He was holding in his open hand a dead and dried apple with a seed sprouting from it. In front of them was a globe shaped pot with warm steam rising from it, enveloping them all in its vapors.

She wanted to ask him what it meant, but instead she held her silence and began to put the words of a poem together in her head. "Life swirling in the teacup of time."

Ben was troubled by what the Indian had said. It struck him as a warning of some sort. He continued to be preoccupied by the uncomfortable feeling that he wasn't in control of Oblivion; but then, he had never intended to own a town, anyway. The Chicanos called him "El Patron," but they were doing what they wanted with whatever buildings they chose. Porfirio was installing sewers, drain fields and water lines, without any consultation. The scientists and engineers seemed to view him as a convenient means to their ends. They had

123

chosen where to dig wells and install windmills to draw the water to the surface without the courtesy of a project review. The system of water delivery was remarkably simple to him. Wind drove the blades that pulled the water from underground into a holding tank. When the desired quantity was in the tank, a float valve released the pumping mechanism and engaged a generator that converted the relentless energy of the wind into electricity. This energy was in turn stored in a series of batteries that already provided light and power to three or four families. He understood that this was good, but it bothered him that he had not been involved in either the design or the creation of this prototype free energy system.

Twice he had seen great threats to the town's existence thwarted, but it was through no defensive effort of his. He felt powerless and overwhelmed, a pawn in someone else's chess game. That was it, not even a rook or a knight, but only a pawn. He was a game piece that could only move forward in time, never back. Yet, if in this cosmic chess game there were pawns, there must be knights, rooks and bishops, too.

He tried to explain this to Belinda, but when she looked into his eyes she saw the flame of creativity, the depth of soul possessed only by an artist. "Rejoice, Ben, that you are given the opportunity to be the artist you know you can be, do the good that you can do, and receive the recognition you deserve."

"Please understand. I don't even feel that my art is my own anymore. It seems like the pencil and brush are directed by something I can't control."

They sat on some sandstone at the edge of the arroyo. She rubbed his neck and back with gentle loving hands, trying to relieve some of the tension that was tying the man she loved in knots. "Did that old Indian say something that bothered you?"

"He speaks of the permanence of change, the perpetual recurrence of discord, the common thread of greed. I am only an artist. I can't understand these things. Damn it, Belinda, I don't want to understand these things."

"Ben, we have no choice."

Their discourse was interrupted by the appearance of Domingo. "Thank God. I've found you," he gasped for air. It had been a long run from the center of Oblivion, to the resting place they had found.

"Calmut Benton is in the hospital!" Were the first words he could force from his tortured lungs. After another gasp he added, "Derritt tried to kill him."

Ben and Belinda fired questions at him so fast he couldn't answer. The meaning behind Ben's painting from the night before was clear now.

"That's not all, amigos. That whole damn family fell apart. Derritt beat up his sister."

Belinda was still trying to understand how all this could happen. Ben was asking how badly Cal had been hurt.

Domingo continued the chronicle of events. "Brandy went to the cabin, where Landreth was screwin' his whore, to tell him about his daddy," he paused again for breath, then apologized for his language. "When Brandy got there he was beatin' on his . . .ah. . . girlfriend. They tell me that when she got to the clinic at Juniper Crossing, her face looked like hamburger."

Neither Ben nor Belinda could follow what Domingo was telling them. It all seemed to unreal. How could the most powerful family in the county destroy itself in one night?

Ben decided immediately, that he needed to visit Cal in the hospital. He needed to take him the painting. If he had done it sooner, he might have saved his adversary some agony. Why had he hesitated to do the painting? He had known it had to be done, but didn't comprehend why. He'd had no understanding of what force was driving him; just that he had to do it. Why did he wait so long to put the paint to the canvas? Ben didn't want to be engaged in a struggle for control of Oblivion. He would rather, somehow, make peace with Cal. He didn't want anyone to get hurt, not even self declared enemies.

Courtney was waiting for them when they got back to main street. "I see the windmills are being assembled, solar panels and solar water heaters are appearing on rooftops, and solar collectors are waiting to sprout like aluminum trees from the valley floor." While she spoke, she stroked a mountain lion cub that sat on the bench beside her, much to the amusement of the children gathered around.

Chad was spreading blueprints across the table, but she was more interested in the tamales steaming on the plate Benito Alvarez proudly placed before her.

"That's nice, Chad. Keep up the good work." She said as she dismissed his efforts and turned toward Ben. "So, you want to enter the lion's den?"

"What do you mean?"

"Weren't you going to ask me to drive you into Santa Fe to visit old man Benton?"

They all enjoyed a festive lunch. Most of the residents were gleeful about the rumors of Benton troubles. Some were fearful that there would be revenge. Others assumed that the time had come for the Benton family to reap their dark harvest. There was music and an informal softball game. Ben had hit a home run and Belinda, playing right field, made two great plays that saved the day for the "Blue Bandanas." The Blues beat the Greens by a score of 5 to 4. Then it was siesta time. Belinda wrapped the painting for Ben, kissed him goodbye and waved as he and Courtney left for Santa Fe.

During the hour and a half drive to the hospital, Courtney never stopped talking about the significance of what was happening in Oblivion. She explained again that the way Oblivion handled such

126

problems as energy production, waste disposal and cooperative resource use could spell success or failure for the future of not only humankind, but of the earth itself. "I can't let us continue on the present course," she told him as they pulled into the hospital parking lot, "There are so many lessons to be learned, and through half a million years humanity has learned less than the butterfly."

Ben carried the painting into the lobby while Courtney left to visit a friend who lobbied at the state house. The smell of the hospital made him uncomfortable. Ben knew that these were supposed to be healing places, but they subjected their patients to artificially sterile rooms, without green plants and their energy giving oxygen and life force. They kept family and friends at bay, while subjecting the infirm and injured to nonstop TV with its raucous used car commercials, or the gadgetry of a science fiction movie, with its beeps, whirrs, and thumps. "Why couldn't they instead provide them with music that would soothe and heal the soul?" he thought out loud as he rode the elevator. They plastered WARNING signs on the walls instead of art. "How could such a place heal?"

Cal was in a VIP private room near the cardiac unit. Ben was first told he couldn't visit; then, that he could have ten minutes to deliver the gift. When he entered the room, there were two lawyers and a business associate talking in hushed tones; no family, no friends, just attorneys wearing three piece suits, the uniform of that occupation. Ben felt out of place, and out classed, with his plaid shirt and blue jeans.

When Cal saw him in the doorway, a look of fear joined the pain on his face. This was quickly erased by a weak smile. Cal understood the art and etiquette of conflict. He, too, would have called on a wounded adversary. He motioned for the three piece suits to leave the room. An oxygen tube was at his nose to feed his lungs, IV's dripped unnamed solutions into his arm, while wires tied him to monitors at the nurses' station. A private nurse stood in the corner, an almost invisible servant, waiting to do her master's bidding.

The first greeting was awkward for both, but there was a strange and natural communication that energized the atmosphere between them. Ben handed the canvas to his adversary. Cal accepted with a puzzled look, but he was too weak to remove the wrapping. He asked Ben to do it for him. When he saw the wolves circling, and the wounds on the leader of the pack, he understood. He looked first at the painting, then at Ben. As he fully grasped the message, tears escaped the corners of his eyes; the first tears Calmut could remember shedding. Ben wiped them from Cal's face.

Without thinking, Ben pointed to the wolf behind the leader, "Beware of that one. He can destroy you." Ben was shocked at his own words, and wasn't sure what he meant, or why he had said it.

Cal asked the nurse to hang the painting on the wall across from the foot of the bed. He wanted it to be a constant reminder, a warning. Not a word was spoken about Oblivion. This wasn't the time.

A team of nurses entered the room with more needles. They descended on the body of Calmut like a swarm of sterile vampires, drawing blood with artificial fangs. Ben was again disturbed that they spoke among themselves, as though their patient wasn't a living, breathing human being, not a fellow traveler on this earthly road; rather, as a mechanical object on a medical assembly line. They discussed dates, dinner plans, hospital gossip and movies while they filled vials with blood and clipboards with paperwork. They poured a rainbow assortment of pills down his throat, and pumped other liquids into his body with a varied assortment of hypodermic syringes.

"You're going to have to leave now," his private nurse told Ben, "He's going to sleep for awhile."

Two floors below, a team of doctors was working against time to repair broken jaws, loose teeth and battered tissue. Marquita could remember arriving at the clinic in Juniper Crossing. There they did

128

what trauma care they could, then sent her on to Santa Fe. The pain killers had done their job. She recalled nothing of the ambulance ride. All she could recall were childhood days when she and her friends would escape the sounds and smells of home and explore the buildings in the ghost town in the canyon. She could smell the clean air with its hint of juniper and chamisa. As the ambulance bounced over rough roads, she was watching tumble weeds roll down the street and come to rest between the buildings.

Her mind giggled at the games she and Ernesto played in the back room of the empty town's boarding house. They were games of discovery as they both grew from childhood into something not yet adult. She missed Ernesto, his smile, his playfulness, the sheer joy with which they sang, splashed in the water trough at the end of the town, and made sweet discoveries as they shared their bodies. In her dream world where there was no pain, she missed Ernesto. The tears she shed were real. The EMT gently wiped them from her swollen eyes. He didn't understand their origin, and gave her another shot of morphine.

This pushed her into a deeper sleep. The tears were replaced with a faint smile, as Ernesto came back to her. He was fifteen. He held her hand as they cautiously entered the old church. Together they righted the benches, blew the dust from the santos, and returned them to their niches. Her mind was caught in the swirling time, riding through the fog. She and Ernesto stood outside the window and watched as people of all colors and accents painted, repaired and brought to life the old church. Her mind led her on a journey through the town of Oblivion, and into the valley where families were tending gardens under the gleam of great mechanical monsters with giant mirrors drawing the sunlight like a magnet to the valley. She and Ernesto walked to the lake behind the town, a lake that formed at the end of the arroyo. Trees surrounded it, and water plants marched out into it. Plastic panels with fiber pads extended out over the surface. More plants and flowers grew on these panels. She and Ernesto were wading in the water that lapped at the willows and cottonwoods. She felt free. Time swirled, without direction.

They made love in the shade of these trees. When she awoke, she was in a hospital bed. Strangers were making her head and face hurt as they probed, twisted and pushed on her wounded flesh. She wanted to slip back into Oblivion, retreat from this reality into the better one she had just left. They wouldn't let her. Much pain is involved in healing, and they were helping her to heal. Again there were tears. She was too tired to fight the pain; she only had enough strength to miss Ernesto.

She could hear all the doctors, nurses, technicians and attendants. She wanted to tell them it was all right. She tried to tell them her mother would be home soon. Madre would know what to do for her. They wouldn't listen to her. She felt herself being wheeled into surgery.

Chapter Thirteen

Belinda had spent the early afternoon pondering the various directions that were possible with this resurrected town. She understood the sense of powerlessness that Ben felt, but, unlike his discomfort with this lack of control, she was exhilarated. It was with a heady sense of harmony that she watched Oblivion being reborn. She was inspired by the sense of mission that drove the dreamers, the engineers, the scientists, all the new residents. Even the children were caught up in the optimistic joy that accompanies the challenge of a new way of life, each tomorrow filled with sunshine and possibilities.

She watched the old Indian slowly climb the steep west wall of the canyon, toward the sunset that would soon bathe the entire valley in its golden glow, like a blanket of softest fabric that would keep their souls safe for the night ahead. He had shared their community lunch with them, and later visited with Courtney for a few minutes before she left with Ben. After their departure, he sat at the edge of Oblivion, lit a small fire of juniper twigs, inhaled the pungent, purifying smoke, and began a chant. Many of the children left the games they were playing, and came to watch this strange old man. Belinda, herself, was drawn to him. They all sat in a semi-circle around the small fire, inhaled the smoke, too, and felt comfort.

"Yours will not be an easy task," he spoke to Belinda without opening his eyes.

The ever present breeze, a river of air, a current of life and energy, blew against her. She felt a chill as her hair tried vainly to follow the wind. She wanted to respond, but could not.

"You have come so far in your life journey. Yet you have only taken the first steps. You are still a toddler, seeking both the freedom and the responsibility that comes with knowing your destiny." He continued to speak, eyes closed, almost asleep. He lifted his arm and made a broad sweeping gesture. "You will find your true harmony when you tell the stories."

There was silence for several minutes. Then the children began to whisper among themselves.

The ancient, arthritic hand now pointed to children, "They will find their harmony when they hear your stories."

He spread the glowing coals with his hand, freeing smoke and sparks to follow the wind on its perpetual journey. He stood, and, with his bare feet, ground the smoldering embers into the sand. He put his flute to his lips and followed the smoke through the valley.

"He's quite the mystic. Isn't he?" The voice came from behind her. She turned and saw the tall, bearded gentleman. He wore a denim jacket. The wind had thrown his green tie over his shoulder to give him a casual appearance, despite the semi-formal clothes. She guessed that he was middle aged, based on the wire-rimmed glasses and the greying of the uncombed hair in need of a trim. He seemed comfortably self-assured and wore a relaxed smile.

Before she could respond he continued, "I'm sorry. Let me introduce myself." He switched the briefcase from his right hand to the left, and offered a handshake. "I'm Larry Scott, reporter for the Albuquerque Journal and adjunct instructor at UNM. Some folks at the university suggested that I do a feature on what you are developing here. It sounds so exciting, being on the cutting edge of new technologies and changing lifestyles."

Belinda liked this man. She felt comfortable with him, and spoke eagerly of what was happening. She took him on a tour of the town, outlining each of the plans, introducing him to many of the people, giving him the stories of how they had become a part of this community. After the brief exploration of Oblivion, they walked out to the arroyo, visited the lake forming there, then on to the sites for the solar collectors. While they sat on a sandstone shelf at the base of the canyon

132

wall's talus, she briefly outlined the difficulty they'd had with the Bentons. She even mentioned the painting Ben was in the process of delivering.

Larry wrote furiously in the notepad, gleaning all the names and events. She led him to the two burned out carcasses of earth movers. They both laughed when they noticed the buffalo gourd vines that were already reaching for the sun over the charred steel. The rain had caused life to burst forth with unbridled energy. Wildflowers were offering their buds to the sun, pocket gophers, packrats, and chipmunks were building nests within the deceased machinery. Birds were exploring the potential, while bluetailed lizards basked in the sun. A swarm of bees was laying claim to a sheltered area behind the radiator.

"Mother Nature wastes no time in reclaiming what is her own, does she?" Larry laughed. "You know, this might be the real story here."

Belinda's mind was back on the old Indian, and what he had said to her. What was it she was supposed to do? What was this about stories?

They sat in the shade of the junipers. For over an hour, they simply looked down on the town. The reporter was intrigued by the way such a diverse group of people could work and play so well together. Larry shot many digital photos, talked with her again about Ben, and finally asked to see some of his art. She led him back past the church to the little house she shared with Ben. There were several wildlife oils, the coyote she had purchased, the sketch of her asleep in the doorway of the jail, a couple of watercolor studies of wildflowers by the arroyo, and the sketches he had done that morning in the church. Shyly, she revealed the sketch of her and Sunbeam. Larry was fascinated by these, and took more photos before he left.

Belinda's mind wandered, and she followed it, climbing to the top of the canyon wall. Then she sat, watching the bowl of life below. The western part of the valley was federal land, part of the Santa Fe National Forest, leased by the Bentons. The northern end of the canyon was property owned by the Bentons. It was as she was marveling at the rich green color that had burst into being almost overnight, that she noticed what the violent storm had done. The course of the feeder stream that had flowed onto the Benton ranch had been changed. The north end of the canyon now drained into the arroyo that flowed through Oblivion. This was the source of the lake forming by the cottonwoods. The small stream had its beginnings in a seep on the public lands along the far canyon wall. It was a dependable source, water always flowed from it. Even from across the valley this spring was easily spotted because it gave life. Lush greens of willows, grasses and brush marked the water source. Now, this water, the source of life, no longer flowed toward the Bentons.

Wishing Ben were there to share the new discovery, she ran back to Oblivion. Carlos and Domingo were the first people she met. Between gasps for breath, she announced the source of the lake. Carlos immediately named it Lake Hope, because it assured Oblivion's future.

After Ben and Courtney returned, all discussion centered on the lake. To everyone's surprise, Ben was troubled by the change in water flow. "Cal Benton has to have water for his cattle, for his family. It isn't right to deny anyone water." He stared at each in turn, " Is it?"

Belinda understood what Ben was saying, and the joy she felt over her discovery now faded. When Ben described Cal in the hospital, so weak, so alone that it was lawyers who visited, not family, not friends, she was ready to take everyone in Oblivion to the far end of the canyon with shovels and picks and return the water to its former course.

Courtney was the one who raised the objection. "Don't be too quick to undo what nature has done. Let Mother Nature be your partner, even when you're dealing with the Bentons."

It was late that night, while Ben and Belinda were relaxing in each other's arms, that she told him of the strange things the old Indian had said. It was almost as an afterthought, that she mentioned the visit from the reporter. She couldn't even remember his name.

Sleep came on the gray-blue clouds of night. Belinda was in the valley, but it was much different. The sky was pink, dogs were greeting the dawn with a cacophony of yelps and howls. As she saw the last of the coyotes call to the fleeing night, a great trumpeting sound came from the mouth of the canyon. She watched from behind a pine as the mammoth entered the valley, tested the air with her trunk, eyes too weak to see any potential danger. Her massive head moved from side to side, seeking the scent of great cats or wolves or humans. Once satisfied, she trumpeted again, and was soon joined by a calf. It barely reached above her knee. She stood seven feet at the shoulder, twelve feet to the tussled reddish topknot. They walked through a colorful meadow of tall grasses and wild flowers, lilies, spring daisies, lobelia and more.

This wasn't the high desert of Oblivion's time, but Belinda knew this was the same valley. A great flowing stream coursed through its center, oaks, pines, sycamores and beeches lined the waterway and gave shade. Other mammoths followed the lead cow into the fertile valley, while the great bull positioned himself at the canyon's entrance, trumpeting a challenge to any creature daring to threaten his family.

Belinda saw these huge animals express all the emotions one would expect of humans; caring for their young, even assisting an injured and aging cow on her journey to the life sustaining water. Two youngsters were arguing over who was going to wallow in the mud first. Others were preparing to defend their territory if necessary. A young cow was coyly nuzzling the loins of a mature bull with her trunk, and another was tasting and rejecting a tall grass for the more succulent flowers nearby. Her dream mind was weaving these images into a story; a story about how the mammoth family lived in harmony.

135

Then the wind came and hugged her in its arms. She was twisting and spinning, now faster and faster. When the dizzying ballet ended, there were people in the valley. The images were hazy, but she could see that it was a hot afternoon. Naked children were playing near the water. Adults were also lounging near the stream. As the haze cleared, she could see more details. Their skin was dark, the hair was black and hung loosely down the back, or was tied in a ponytail. Few of these adults wore clothing; only a few skirts or loincloths of animal skins were in evidence. Several were wading out into the water with baskets woven from willow stems. She watched as they deftly scooped their baskets into the stream, and threw the trapped fish to shore, all in one smooth motion. Others were chipping pieces of flint, making knives and scrapers, the tools of their civilization. One of the women was collecting herbs, while another was painting designs on her body. She noticed that most of these people were wearing necklaces. Many had earrings and bracelets of woven cord, stones and bone. Several of the children were throwing a stick for a small grey and black dog to catch. In the shade of a huge beech tree, an old man was teaching a youth how to play the flute. Another was tightening the sinews that held a skin stretched over a hollowed section of log. She could even see the designs painted on this drum: birds and bison, fish and flowers.

Something told her that there was a story here, too; a story about how through time, little really changes. Before she was ready to leave these people, her mind drew her through a gossamer screen into another era in the valley. Here, the people were making pottery, and cutting the trees to make room for the cornfields. She saw the coyote on the hillside again. It was laughing. The stream was smaller, the grass shorter.

The trees evaporated, as she floated over the valley. Something inside her mind told her that here again were stories she had to tell: a tale of the pottery maker, a legend of the corn mother.

Then the winds of time spun around her once more. Through a veil, she could see the strange men carrying helmets of steel, driving

136

carts drawn by horses. She knew this was the first she had seen horses during this dream journey. She could hear these men speaking Spanish, but it was different than the speech of her friends in Oblivion; yet, she knew this too was Oblivion. These explorers of the valley came seeking riches, and left with empty hearts. She knew they had missed the true wealth of the valley. There has always been a warmth, comfort, special energy here. What gold could match the first rays of the morning sun, as they bathed the canyon floor in life-giving light? She understood that these, too, were stories for her to tell; stories of the disappointment that is the constant companion of greed. She had no understanding of what was to be told, or of how to do it, but she knew this was her mission. She was comfortable in that knowledge.

She saw the passage of owls and elk. Wild horses and herds of sheep moved through the valley. With each image that flashed before her, the stream became narrower, the grass more sparse. Cacti and juniper replaced the lush trees and delicate lilies. Pieces of pottery and bits of Spanish stoneware, along with tin cups and bone china, washed to the surface of the clay and sandstone. Mexican sheep herders, Anglo cowboys and treasure seekers of all types crossed and re-crossed the stage. These shadows of Oblivion past were illuminated in Belinda's mind, and she began to build stories around them.

These were stories that told all who would listen, that there is the potential for good within each and every one of us, that all life can live in harmony, that life is a grand adventure, that with each dawn, God smiles on us all.

Sleep is the gift that frees the mind, if only we are willing to give it the opportunity. Belinda was in an almost trance-like sleep. Her mind went on a great journey of discovery, and it returned with a roadmap for her life to follow.

Ben saw visions of Courtney and Calmut. It was a titanic struggle between the irresistible force and the immovable object. He had gained respect for the Elder Benton, almost a warmth, definitely an understanding.

"Once you know the first name of your enemy, it becomes difficult to hate. Peace will be possible only when each of us knows, and understands, our enemies; for then we have made them friends. We have opened our minds to them. That's the true victory." The voice spoke in Ben's ear. He saw Courtney in the shadowed closet of his mind. She was speaking, but what he saw were images to be painted. The Bentons were walking toward the sunset. Calmut carried a large bag over his shoulder. Derritt was in a wheelchair, being pushed by his brother. The shirt on the elder brother was torn and bloody. Chains hung from his neck and shackles hobbled his steps. Coins were falling from his pocket into the dust, and drops of blood splattered the ground. Ben felt an overwhelming sadness in this vision. In his dream, he asked Courtney if it was the future he was seeing.

"The future doesn't belong to me. None of us owns the future, but we can make the trails that others will follow. All of us are single cells of the global organism."

With this he watched her raise her arms in a circle. In the middle of the circle were children sitting at Belinda's feet. Then Oblivion was as he had once known it. Empty, devoid, even of dreams. Gradually, through a haze, it changed, constantly moving from what it was today, to what it could become tomorrow.

At some inner level, he also understood his role. He knew, with a profound knowledge, that he was the dreamer. He didn't need to control events; he couldn't, even if he wanted to. He was to reflect what could be. He was an artist who could see the possibilities, not the engineer who would realize them. His art was to be no more than a road sign pointing the way to a future better than its past.

He knew he must paint the soul at peace with itself, the earth reaching for its own harmony. He dreamed many dreams, but he would remember very little when he awoke.

Chapter Fourteen

Marquita spent the night in agony. She was alone after the surgery that gave her a new face, wired her jaw in place, and put the jigsaw puzzle of broken bones back together. The doctors gave her powerful drugs to fight the pain, but what they did was interrupt the communication between the suffering in her body and the understanding in her mind. The greatest agony came from the aloneness. There was no loved one to hold her hand.

Through her bandaged eyes she saw horrible, huge black ants biting ands pinching her face. That must be what was causing the pain. She could hear the growls of mad dogs as they tore at her jaw. Silent screams were heard in her mind, but no sound escaped her lips.

Nurses charted that she was resting comfortably while her body, mind and soul wrestled with demons she couldn't identify. Sometime during the long night, she could feel the three Benton men making love with her. She could hear them laughing at her. She felt humiliated. She tried to seek comfort in death, but her body fought her mind and won. Tears soaked the bloody bandages. With the first morning light, the drugs began to release their hold on her. Then the sobbing began. The bandages held her eyes shut, but she could feel the warmth of dawn across her face. She thought she was blind. She tried, but couldn't move her jaws to speak. The terror came when she discovered she couldn't even lift her hand to feel the bandages, to determine what was left of her face.

The bed shook with her sobs. She moaned as the pain finally connected with the brain. The blows were felt again. The memory was not accurate. She felt Landreth's anger, but saw Derritt in the doorway with the gun, not Brandy. In order to explain the pain in her shoulder and back, her mind drew a picture of Derritt's gun firing. She saw herself floating from the bed to the floor. Then to a pickup truck that somehow became an ambulance.

She could hear talking, but voices, when you can't see the source, are a special kind of terror. She tried to scream, to call for her mother, to plead for help from Ernesto; but all that escaped the wire and gauze was a moan. The nurses looked at each other. The RN nodded, and in minutes returned with the morphine. Marquita was returned to the midnight world of drug induced horror. The ants came again, she heard the growl of an unseen dog, and smelled the stench of a gun after its orgasm. She whimpered a hopeless cry, then surrendered herself to the Bentons, one more time. The white clad angels of mercy smiled at each other, pleased that they had relieved her pain.

Calmut Benton was pissed. First, because he hated to be confined to a bed. The eye that hid behind the bandages felt red-hot stabs of pain each time he moved his head or blinked his good eye. He feared the loss of the eye, but already pictured himself with a patch. Brandy, standing at his side, was another source of irritation. She had told him about Landreth and Marquita. He had to now rethink his family. He was too tired, too weak, too old, to handle the boys now, and he didn't like his options.

She also discussed the nosey reporter that had spent most of the night in the hospital asking questions. Unfortunately, he was also getting some answers. He didn't want the publicity that he knew would explode in the media. He hoped that Landreth had taken steps to keep the family whore quiet.

He felt weak, incredibly weak. It was an effort to lift the glass of orange juice to his lips. The anger had consumed all of the meager reserves of strength he had. Nothing remained to fight with, no weapons with which to defend himself, except Brandy. She was all the family he had left. She still stood by his side; and now he was forced to trust her.

He had her send an enormous bouquet of flowers to Marquita's room, discussed briefly the details of a mining lease he had negotiated with the Taos Pueblo governor, and asked her to visit Oblivion, to see what was going on. Brief naps were the interludes between topics in their conversation. Thinking required more strength than he had at the moment. He now feared both of his sons. In one of his sleep times, he saw an old Indian shaking his fist at him. He was saying something that Cal couldn't understand. He struggled to hear. All he could make out was something like, "When you father ambition, you carry greed on your back forever."

Brandy was angry with her father, but still assumed the role of devoted daughter. She would stand beside him in the coming battle with her brothers. Cal seemed to fear violence from Derritt less than he did some threat he couldn't define, from Landreth. She talked briefly with the private nurse about his condition, recovery time and general needs for the next day; then left. She would do as he had asked, but she also had some places to go, some people to rally to her side. She would show them all that she could play the game, too. And this time, she knew she was going to win. After all, she was making the rules.

She ordered the flowers, and wrote a lengthy note of condescending best wishes. She didn't want Marquita to think any stupid whore was going to be able to control the Bentons. It was important that this little bitch understand that Brandy had just taken over the family.

While driving to the law offices of Scrum and Montoya, Brandy defined in her mind her role in the family. Calmut had built the empire with incredibly hard work. But now, he was too old, too weak, to hold it together. Derritt had expanded and defended it with brute force. This reliance on physical solutions had possibly destroyed him and definitely damaged the family. He was now a threat to be eliminated. Landreth had used bribery, blackmail, and guiltless deception to establish respect for the family in the community and state. He had to pay off too many people now. He was a family liability.

Because the scandals and recent failures would make business difficult within the state she was already putting together a plan that would take the Benton power far beyond the confines of New Mexico. From the ashes of the last few days, from the monumental and self-destructive actions of her family, she would create "Phoenix Enterprises." She would show them how to build an empire, and she would do it with charm, cunning and her ability to tell people exactly what they wanted to hear.

It was late in the afternoon before Brandy drove over the bridge that served as the gateway to the Benton estate. She noticed that there was no water in the small stream bed that gave life to the ranch, but thought little of it at the time. She was preoccupied with a sincere fear of Derritt. So strong was her fear, that she kept the small German pistol in her lap when it wasn't reassuringly close by in the leather bag that hung from her shoulder. She drove completely around the house and the out buildings, before parking behind the salt cedar at the side entrance. Neither of the brothers was home. This would give her time to find some of Cal's papers and get them out of the house.

She was sitting behind Cal's desk when Chi Lai brought the coffee pot and some chocolate cookies. Chi Lai had been with the family for two decades, and had watched the Benton children grow up. She had survived by knowing how to be invisibly present. Years ago Cal had hired her husband, and then advanced him the money for the rest of the family's journey to America, an indebtedness that made them all virtual slaves. Their two children had grown up on the Benton ranch, played with the Bentons as children, experienced prejudice from them, and accepted it. She remembered the shame of being cornered in the kitchen by a teenage Derritt, of feeling his crude hands and body pinning her to the wall. Other visions of the past raced forward. She couldn't count the times she had been led to young Landreth's bedroom.

They held her family's green cards, so there was little she could do, except satisfy their lusts. She recalled other shames, like the times she held her tongue silent when her son, Lee, told her how Brandy as a child had ordered him to undress so she could play with his "little boy thing." Her husband had died in service to this family. Bin, the older son, found peace when he met death in a drunken brawl. Lee was her bright shining light. He had escaped, and was now an engineer working in Arizona.

No reason to swallow the angry words that remained, other than that it had been so long. She was nothing more than an old woman, who, after 24 years, was still in a foreign land.

She had heard them all talking about this town with a strange name. "Oblivion" is what she thought they called it. She had no idea where it was, but she felt somehow drawn to it. Finally, after pulling together all the courage she could find, she returned to the office and stood before Brandy.

"Yes, Chi. Did you want something?"

"Miss Brandy, Ma'am. You know I have never asked for favors, but I was wondering, Ma'am, would you take me to this place you were talking about?" She paused, and for the first time in years, did not bow her head. She stared into Brandy's eyes. Stared so deeply that Brandy felt the quiet power that this old Korean possessed, and it made her uncomfortable. Finally she broke the gaze, "You know. That place you call Oblivion."

Brandy laughed, explained that she had to visit this town full of radicals herself, then suggested that Chi pack them a picnic dinner they could eat on the way. Chi was dismissed with a wave of the hand. Brandy returned to the desk drawer and removed several envelopes and a file folder. One of the first steps she would have to take would be to gain control of the bank accounts. Attorney Scrum had outlined the mechanics of this. He also suggested that she arrange a warrant for Landreth's arrest. A brief phone conversation with the sheriff set the process in motion. While it was certainly true that he would post bail, the media coverage would damage him seriously. By the time Chi returned, Brandy's briefcase was packed.

As they approached the bridge, it finally registered with Brandy that there was no water. She immediately grasped the consequences of this. Cattle can't live without the water. The estate couldn't continue to exist without this stream bed. Besides, it was HER water. Without hesitation, she left the driveway and eased the pickup into the upland scrub that lined the empty waterway.

When she saw the point where the course changed and directed the flow toward Oblivion, she immediately assumed that the residents had deliberately robbed the Bentons of their water. Anger had grown into irrational, uncontrollable rage by the time they arrived at their destination.

Courtney , Ben and Belinda were sitting under the shade of the lightening scarred cottonwood at the corner of what had been a blacksmith's shop, bicycle shop, then gas station. The roof had been replaced, and the structure now served as a garage for machine assembly. Courtney knew Brandy, and seemed to have been expecting this kind of entrance. Her benign smile drove Brandy's rage to new heights. She couldn't speak, she could only scream and shout.

Chi sought refuge behind the corner of the building, where she met the old Indian. He was sitting cross-legged on the ground, watching puffs of smoke, like imperfect rings, escape from his pipe.

"Looks like the whole damn family's loco," he said with a smile as he offered her the pipe.   Chi looked into this man's eyes, and saw the Buddhist priest that had given her and her brother lessons so many years ago. She watched the smoke; and her mind could smell the incense from the temple. He handed her his flute, and she played a calming tune that she heard in the long ago time of youth.

Chi was in the temple yard, now, with her family and friends. The children were doing a dance. Chi joined in, and began to weave and

144

turn while the priest chanted the song of inner peace. The Old One began the slow steady beat on the small drum. The flute and drum together made the music of the soul. It was the calming heartbeat of universal life; measured beats that let the soul take charge, and permit the mind to accept peace. The voice of the instrument released the mind from the body, as was the role of the flute player with the desert people. The swirling smoke, powerful drum beats, and calming notes from the flute created harmony with the body, mind and soul.

The harmony spread like a fog around the building and surrounded Brandy. Courtney smiled, while Ben and Belinda tried to understand what was happening. Brandy felt the music with her soul, but her mind forced her body to resist, to fight. Still, the rage slowly gave way to a need to understand what was happening. She gazed intently at each of the buildings. The cottonwoods seemed to her, for the first time in her life, to be living things, filled with energy. She knew she was drawing strength from the trees, the people standing before her, and the music that was now inside her. She felt a sadness. The loss of control over herself, or at least her defiant, aggressive self, was a truly emotional loss.

What was happening was more than knowledge feeding a hungry mind. As the seed that germinates, or the chick that fights its way free of the security of an egg, she was exhausted from the struggle yet overwhelmed by the light. She stood on the brink of awareness within the spirit, of a great and undefined truth, and the loss of an old way of thinking, and acting.

She studied the remodeled buildings with their solar panels, water tanks, earth banked against walls, experimental intensive gardening plots using water retaining cells for each plant, orchards of young trees, windmills. There was so much that she couldn't understand. This didn't look like any community she had ever seen before. As the flute continued, against her will, she began to follow the music. She was given a warm and friendly greeting from everyone she met, in a variety of languages. She felt so safe, so loved; a feeling she had not known before, a feeling she didn't know existed, a feeling she didn't know how to handle.

Chi continued to dance as she played the flute. First, she saw images of the distant past of her youth, then is was yesterday. As she continued, the yesterdays of youth swirled like the smoke and became now. She could see her old master telling her, as he prepared the flute, "This music is the voice of the soul, because it is made from the breath of life." Her aging feet reclaimed their youth as they moved to the Indian's drum beat. She filled Oblivion with her captivating music. She danced down the wide street. All of the residents of the community, over a hundred now, followed this old flute player, back bent by years, but possessed of a soul still fed by her youth.

As Chi led the people down the street toward the church, the old Indian leaned against the adobe wall and stared deep into Ben's eyes. "It's a fine work of art you're putting on this canvas."

Ben started to protest, but a wave of the old man's hand silenced him. "You are troubled by the fact that you aren't in control of the events that are happening here. You are bewildered by the people and their activity. Think on this. How would you change it?"

Ben searched his mind for answers, but was given little time to respond.

"Is it so difficult for you to understand that you are living in harmony? The Great Love has given you Belinda with which to share your life, the talent you need to do your soul's work, and surrounded all this with great friends, grand beauty and dynamic challenges. What more is it you want?" There was almost a hint of anger in his voice, but it was soon arrested with a smile.

When Ben looked toward the crowd, it was almost at the church. When he glanced back at the Indian, he was gone. All that remained was a thin wisp of pipe smoke where he had been standing. Ben felt uncomfortable alone where he would have to contemplate what had been said. He hurried to join the crowd.

The flute played softer and softer as Chi entered the building. She paused at the hole in the floor where the bell had fallen, then continued up the aisle. The old Indian was sitting on the folding chair in front of the altar, reading a phone book. She knelt and placed the wooden instrument at his feet. The residents filled the seats and found spaces on the floor. Brandy stood just inside the door, almost a captive, between Courtney and Belinda. She studied the humanity before her, and was intrigued that Blacks, Chicanos, Anglos, Orientals and Native Americans, all sat here together. She could hear whispers in many languages. She saw farmers, laborers, scientists, teachers, artists and poets. Somehow, there was a sense of universal community. Somehow, they all seemed to be working together. She wanted to know who was in charge here, and how the control was exercised.

"It is time to ask many questions," the Indian spoke as he closed the book and handed it to Chi. "I have been reading the book that lists all the people," he paused and smiled and gazed into the eyes of each of those present, "and none of us residing here in Oblivion is to be found there."

All eyes turned toward the rafters as a dove fluttered upward on its way to the steeple. The old man smiled again, as he too, followed this flight. "It is good." he spoke softly enough that all could hear. "We follow the wings of the Creator's symbol of peace. This is what the future must hold for all humanity. There are only two alternatives." He removed from his pouch, a chunk of petrified wood, a trilobite, a piece of ivory from a mammoth tusk, and a sliver of dinosaur bone. Each, in turn, was held up for all to see. "All was once life, and it is no more. If you are to join them, it will be by your own hands. Don't waste time blaming your neighbors, or demons of the darkness, or the Great Mystery." He passed the fossils around the assemblage.

147

"You have all come here for different reasons, but none of you came for greed. You came to be a part of a dream." He pointed toward Chad and Frog.

"You came to find harmony in teaching the young people the love that is in your heart." This time he pointed to Dirty Maria.

He made reference to each of the people; man, woman and child who was in the building. Every one brought a special talent, skill, insight or ability that was valuable to them all. At last he came to Brandy. He paused, thought deeply in a silence that became oppressive in the single room of this old church. Finally he stood, and walked through the gathering to her.

She almost trembled in fear as he neared. He was so close she could smell his age, the breath foul with tobacco, the pungent herbs that filled his medicine bag, the juniper needles that clung to his shirt. He untied the gourd from his waist, and held it before her. She knew she was outnumbered in this den of her enemies. She would have fled if there had been an escape, but there was none.

"You have shared with these people your most important possession. For this act of love, we ask you to accept Oblivion as your community, and we ask that you let us share our timeless love with you." He pulled the plug from the gourd and held it above her head. "You give us life when you share your water. For this gift your reward will be great."

After he emptied the gourd over her head, all came forward and embraced her. She had never known such affection, and was overwhelmed by it. It made her uncomfortable. All came forward, that was, except Chi. She sat by the altar pondering how the meanest spirit among them could be deserving of such gifts of love. Then she heard a voice say, "Forgiving your enemy makes you both victorious." The old Indian helped her to her feet and with his benign smile urged her to forgive the past and fill the future with love. Then she, too, approached Brandy and embraced her, but, this time, as an equal. They both

148

understood that for one brief moment, all were equals, all gave and received love, and it was good.

Brandy was not yet ready to accept all this. Like her brother Derritt, her anger and distrust forced itself to the surface like the bubbling lava of a volcano. This flow of molten hatred pushed the sense of love away and renewed her defiance. She spat in the old Indian's face as she screamed, "You stole my water. I didn't give it to you."

The shockwave rippled through the crowd and found a home in the old walls. Some were angry, others pained by the rebuke of their friendship. Ben started to form scolding words of response, but she didn't give him the time to speak. She turned, pushed Courtney aside, almost knocking her to the floor, and was gone.

Her parting comment was, "My name is in the phone book. I matter." She continued to mutter as she strode toward her vehicle, "A town filled with weirdos, every one of them a figment of their own imaginations; and they stole my water." As she drove away, in the bright late afternoon sun, an owl flew past the windshield. Ravens followed the pick-up as it bounced its way back to the false security that was the Benton ranch.

Derritt was waiting on the porch when she got there. His anger was palpable in the air between them. A wave of pity for her brother washed over her, and for a moment she could again hear the faint ringing of church bells. He was so wounded, so tortured by his own greed. Then he cursed at her and threw the whiskey bottle at her, hitting the vehicle instead. She felt for the security that lived in her purse. The gun felt comfortable in her hand. It gave her confidence, made her as strong as her brothers. She kept her eyes on Derritt as she walked the twenty yards to the porch steps. Her heart was pounding hard, responding to the adrenalin that told her she must either fight or flee. Her soul was looking for another answer, but her mind was telling her there were no more options.

Her hand gripped the metal so tightly it took the warmth from her. That heat gave it life. It seemed to pulse. The gun became a living thing, using her as a tool to carry out its purpose, its reason for existence.

Derritt stood and held onto the railing with his bandaged hands. Wounded by his own rage, he faced his sister. Then he saw her gun. The tiny weapon pulled her arm up from her side as it sought its target. It was while the hammer was being pulled into position that she heard the bells again, and felt the soothing aura of love that had almost smothered her in Oblivion. She regained control of the metal, aimed it at a cloud and discharged its power.

She didn't see Landreth as he followed her steps. Too late she became aware of his presence. He grabbed her arm and tore the gun from her. Disarmed, she crumbled to the ground and sat sobbing.

"What did you do with Daddy's papers?" Derritt had worked his way down the steps and now stood over her. Anger spawned a new wave of rage that left him shaking, made speech difficult.

She whimpered and shook her head as she muttered over and over, "no, please, no."

The steel toed boot came toward her. She closed her eyes, already feeling the pain. After the kick to her stomach, she barely felt the second blow to her head. It must be happening to someone else. Now, she saw nothing more than velvet darkness. Her body floated ever so slowly back toward the sparse grass and coarse sand. She heard again the flute. This time the tone was deep, sonorous, mournful. She didn't see Derritt and Landreth struggling, didn't hear Derritt's scream as his broken hand pounded into his brother's chest with such force it knocked him to the ground. She didn't feel the weight of Landreth as he fell across her legs.

When she returned to the world of awareness, the pain from her side and head made her vomit. It wasn't until she tried to stand that she discovered the broken ankle.

Courtney was sitting on the railing, stirring a cup of tea. Brandy couldn't understand, first where she was; second, why this enviro-freak was sitting there smiling at her.

"A few sips of this should help." Courtney said as she knelt and offered the cup. Ravens called from the trees. "You'd be a lot safer in Oblivion."

Brandy's vision blurred, but the tea did drive the pain away. Sleep was a friend that now comforted her and wrapped her in soft clouds that absorbed all the hurt that was controlling her body and mind.

Landreth watched from the window as the crazy lady and the old Indian loaded his sister into the pick-up and drove away. He couldn't deal with them now. Derritt moaned in agony, the rope was tight on his wrists, making his hands feel like separate, unattached bundles of pain. One arm was secured to each side of the massive oak bed. His wounded and re-broken hands hurt with an intensity that drove all ability to reason from his mind. The urine that soaked his jeans was now cold and uncomfortable. The knowledge of what his brother could do, and the fear that he not only could, but would, paralyzed Derritt's thoughts. This was the greatest fear he had ever known.

Landreth laughed and opened another Coors, "Are ya getting thirsty, huh, brother?" He splashed some across Derritt's face and laughed. "I need you out of the way while I do what's gotta be done to save Benton Enterprises." Then he left the room.

Derritt knew he had to escape; there was only one way. His legs weren't tied. If he could get his toe around the lamp cord, he could pull it over onto the head of the bed and perhaps burn the nylon rope loose.

151

It took over an hour of exhausting maneuvering before he got the cord wrapped around his toe and pulled the lamp onto the pillow beside his head. The synthetic fiber of the pillowcase melted onto his neck and the back of his head, but the rope did char and weaken. Finally, one broken hand was loose. Then with fingers he couldn't control, he struggled to free the other wrist. While he was doing this, the bedding burst into flames. By the time he got to the door, the flames were roaring their own rage, seeking to satisfy their own lust.

Derritt fled his home and his brother. Fear and pain gave him the strength to find the empty stream bed, and follow its path to the safety of the seep and its sheltering trees. His memory refused to record anything beyond the flames.

Chapter Fifteen

The twilight walk gave Ben and Belinda time to be alone, time to reflect, time to love. Belinda had written a poem for Ben. A few short verses of dreams and visions, a story of love, and the joy of love when there is a harmony between two people. She knew that Ben had no grand vision for Oblivion; she also knew that destiny can, for a time be evaded, but never avoided. She had traded a life of material successes for a future that seemed without direction. Now she was beginning to understand that there was a direction, a purpose to her life, a reason for living. She now grasped what the old Indian had said about harmony and her stories. She was now beginning to feel as comfortable with herself as she did with Ben.

Ben had spread the jacket on the rock and opened the paper bag that held their sandwiches. She sat and read to him, first the love poem. This brought tears to Ben's eyes. They kissed gently as they enjoyed a lengthy embrace.

Then Belinda turned pages in her notebook and read to him *Tales of Oblivion*. It began with:

Creatures mammoth huge and field mouse small,
Rainbows of flowers beautiful, and green trees tall.
Warm, soft and gentle, the whispering breezes of spring,
Carrying far the joyful songs the feather people sing.
To Oblivion's canyon, valley, meadow and mountain,
To the cool, fresh, clean water; that life sustaining fountain
In the days of centuries past, long before the tribes came;
They visited this place under Oblivion's sun, not to claim,
But to share, under the protective arms of the Great Love.
To live their destiny with earth below and sky above.

The days were lengthening. It was almost eight, but the red sun still sat on the top of the canyon wall. It was as Ben tried to picture in his mind the Oblivion of which she spoke, that his eyes roamed the walls and saw the great black cloud of smoke. It spread its gray ugly form over the wall of the canyon, creating the appearance of a rampaging forest fire.

They ran back to Oblivion and alerted all the residents. Some gathered shovels and tools and ran to change the course of the water back to Benton Creek, while the rest drove as fast as possible to the Benton ranch. By the time they reached the house, the flames were dancing their obscene dance on the roof. The fire truck from Juniper Crossing arrived at the same time. It was Ben and Belinda that found Landreth, unconscious, on the floor of the office. He had a bandana over his face and clutched a briefcase to his bruised chest. They dragged him to the yard and tried to find Brandy and Derritt, but were forced to surrender to the heat and smoke.

Landreth was rushed to the hospital. The people of Oblivion watched in sadness and horror as the flames consumed the home of the family that had shown them all so much hatred.

Chi sat under the tamarisk at the corner of the bridge and wept. The tears were for the loss of her past, and the collapse of the family she knew. She also understood that her future was now in Oblivion.

Belinda and Ben walked down to the now reborn stream and began to follow its path back to the seep. As they walked in the almost darkness of early night, they removed their shoes to cool their feet. At a shallow pool in the water's course, they stripped to wash the smoke, grime and smell of the home destroyed from their bodies. They stood in the almost waist deep muddy water and embraced without a word. In silence they satisfied their bodies' need, each for the other. Disaster, even that of your enemies, is painful. So painful that only love can heal the wounds. They sat by the edge of the small waterway for a long time watching the dying flames shooting great volleys of sparks into the air, only to relax into a glow just below the horizon. Images raced through Ben's mind of tragedy, lying just below the horizon for so many. For a moment he pondered if this was a part of his destiny. Even while holding Belinda in his arms, he shivered. Still, they spoke not a word.

The spring of Oblivion ended that night in late May. The seeds had all been planted. It was now time to tend the crops through the long summer.

Part Two
Benton's Folly

The gnat that sings his summer song
Poison gets from slander's tongue,
The poison of the snake and newt
Is the seat of Envy's foot.
The poison of the honey-bee
Is the artist's jealousy.
William Blake, *Auguries of Innocence*

Chapter Sixteen

The seeds of a violent spring had been sown on the sparse New Mexico landscape. Calmut Benton's seed was bearing a bitter crop. Landreth was a fruit of deceit and arrogance, buying temporary friends while selling dwindling influence. Derritt was a harvest of uncontrollable anger and hatred. Brandy was a beguiling and cunning poisonous apple. All four of the Bentons had suffered for their excesses. Calmut had almost destroyed himself with overwork and a dedication to greed. He was now a powerless shadow of himself, too ill to even comprehend what was happening.

Landreth would, in the months ahead, reap the harvest of revenge that he had nurtured so well. He would find that his duplicity and bribes were not enough to hold friends of convenience. Truth would confront him during summer storms in the courtrooms and back rooms of New Mexico.

Derritt had been reduced to little more than a deranged lunatic, so crippled by his pain and hatred that all reason had deserted him. He would begin the heat of the summer as a hermit, festering with hate, living in filth, existing by stealth.

Brandy would find herself a prisoner of her own worst fears, nurtured by people she couldn't understand. Separated from her family, she would know soul destructive depression.

Belinda had taken great risks in leaving the secure, yet smothering, world of office cubicles and client lunches. She had, in a moment of emotional desperation, traded security for discovery, and in the process found love and herself. She was the windborne seed of the dandelion, floating on the breezes, glistening in the sunshine, coming to rest in Oblivion; there to finally sprout and grow into something she never dreamed, using talents she didn't know she possessed. She would be a bountiful harvest, sweet in its season.

Ben had been a simple artist, creating beauty between the odd jobs needed to maintain a meager, and often empty, life. Fate gave him a great gift; a gift he was not yet certain how to handle. His was a spring of bewilderment, confusion, and, love. He wanted to be a part of the town that was forming under his watchful eyes, but couldn't find his role. His wish was to be the perfect lover for Belinda, but he wasn't certain how. Still, he basked in the sunshine of friends old and new, and gloried in the rainbow of people and ideas that surrounded him. He knew greater happiness than he had ever experienced before, but also greater stress. He was not a fighter, but was forced to defend his town, his friends, his responsibilities. He had sown seeds of hope, and was now nurturing a crop of ideas. His art was changing, as he was changing, thanks to Belinda's love.

The Old Indian and Courtney had spent the spring sowing the seeds of the hardiest, yet most tender species. Love, a perennial that can withstand the most vicious of seasons, was the most plentiful seed. Second was cooperation, a gentle plant often falling victim to the weeds

157

of greed and competition. Gentleness was perhaps the strongest of the seeds they planted, for gentleness could defeat wrath, turn coarse anger into nurturing mulch, and transform a landscape of hatred into fields of peace. They also gathered seeds from the rainbows of summer rains, and with them grew mountainsides of majestic beauty, filling the valley with color and joy. They also visited the mists of time and collected moments, the seeds of minutes and hours. These they planted with great care to grow into a forest of fog where one could find cosmic peace and insight into each being's place in the ultimate order we call chaos. All of these flowers, nurtured in this valley, combined to produce harmony, for any willing to open their hearts to it, and most did.

Dirty Maria worked all summer tending her seeds of knowledge, and saw them flourish in the minds of not only the children, but all the residents of Oblivion. Each shared his or her wisdom and experience with the others. The earth itself was her textbook, the sun her students' reading lamp, Oblivion was the laboratory. For Dirty Maria this was a glorious time, the place for which her life had been preparation.

Frog and Chad reveled in the opportunity to plant the seeds of their dreams. Their energy was intense as they explored ideas, shoveled earth against walls to make insulation, helped make adobe bricks, built windmills and dug cisterns.

The Benton estate had been reduced to ashes and charred remains. Their empire was now little more than fragmented rubble as the family turned on itself. Calmut was too weak to stand without help. When one of his attorneys brought him the news of the fire, he wept, then became angry at his tears and weakness. The attorney was on the way down the hall when Ben and Belinda stopped at the nurse's station to inquire about his health. Belinda held a large bouquet of wildflowers and cards from everyone in Oblivion.

Ben entered the room first, grasped the old man's hand and wiped the tears from his face, a simple act of kindness that confused Calmut.

158

The flowers held by Belinda, as she stood in the doorway, brought a puzzled smile to his face. He motioned for her to come to the side of the bed. She placed the bouquet on his stand and gave him the bag containing almost two hundred cards, notes and letters. Some were from the children, crayon pictures with happy words of youth. Others were simple caring words written on the backs of photographs, some in English, others in Spanish. There was a three-page letter from Chi. The old Indian had sent a small medicine bag filled with corn pollen and herbs. It was tied with a thong that held an ancient wolf's fang.

Calmut grasped Belinda's hand between his and without thinking, brought it to his lips. He was then embarrassed by his action and turned toward Ben. "I don't understand. What is all this?" He motioned toward the cards that now covered his bed.

"Whenever anyone has suffered a loss, it is only right that the neighbors express their concern and offer condolences." Ben explained.

Calmut turned to Belinda, still holding her hand in his, "Why are you here? After all we have done to you . . ." He could only shake his head, to speak further would only bring more tears, and these could not be shed in the presence of adversaries.

"The people of Oblivion want you to know we are willing to assist in any way possible to rebuild your home." Ben was looking for a way to approach the subject of the sons and daughter, but Calmut leaned back and waved his hand.

"My children have hurt me far worse than you have." He was struggling to express the thoughts that now poisoned his soul.

Belinda responded, "That's why we must end the conflict. Together we can create a new world that will be better for all of us."

Calmut shook his head and gave a benign smile, "You are so innocent, so filled with idealism. Be careful, my child. Reality will destroy you." He tried to say more but was too weak.

During their return to Oblivion, Ben and Belinda discussed the two views of humanity. They were both of the conviction that people

159

are basically good, that altruism is not only a noble, but instinctive virtue. Still, they were troubled by the knowledge that many bad and evil acts had been committed. They discussed the dichotomies of love and hate, greed and generosity, wisdom and ignorance, trust and suspicion.

"If there isn't evil within us all, then how could Derritt have done some of the things he did? How could Brandy have reacted in the church the way she did? How could Landreth have beaten Marquita?" Ben posed questions for which he knew they lacked the answers. He knew that these acts were balanced, perhaps overwhelmed, by what was happening in Oblivion.

The drive back to their town took them through the glorious hill country of north central New Mexico. The cholla continued their display of purple blooms, while beavertail opuntias created flashes of cherry Popsicle red across the roadside. Desert willow shrubs were beginning to greet the sun with their lavender blooms, while white candelabras of yucca bloom reached toward the blue sky. The Maximilian sunflowers were starting to dot the lower valley areas, while the sages and creosote bush surrendered their fragrance to the enchantment.

They entered Oblivion's valley, but didn't return to the town itself. They needed some time to themselves and followed the talus slope beyond the garden of mechanical leaves collecting the sun's rays, on past the rhythmic thump and whirr of the windmills that spun in the forever breezes that danced up the sandstone wall.

Ben stopped near an arroyo where several junipers had provided enough shade for seeds of the unicorn vine to sprout and grow. The yellow and purple flowers splashed across the red sandstone and clay as the vine rambled on its joyful journey in the sun.

"These beautiful and unusual flowers become the horned seed pods that some call devil's claws." Ben commented as he picked one of the flowers and tucked it behind Belinda's ear.

160

Belinda was overwhelmed with the beauty in miniature that surrounded her. Tiny flowers, unseen from the road dotted the dry stream bed. Stone, rocks and an assortment of lizards all added their own charm.

"The Indians used to eat these fruits before they got ripe," Ben broke the spell the landscape had over her. "The flowers are the best part, though."

They sat in the shade of the rugged old evergreen and embraced. They both needed this shared solitude. They slept in each other's arms and awoke to the chorus of jays and desert wrens.

Words were flowing in Belinda's mind while Ben was seeing images on canvas. In the blossom of the buffalo gourd he saw a face of the past, within the waving stalks of gramma grass he caught a glimpse of great beasts and could hear the trumpeting of the woolly mammoth. It was as he spied the broken, wind worn pieces of ancient pottery, that he heard the flute, then chants, carried on the ever whispering desert winds.

They spent the rest of the afternoon in this spiritual oasis of inspiration. Belinda worked on her poems of Oblivion past, while Ben studied the dry streambed and sketched a picture of the ancient ones bathing and dipping their fish baskets into the water. He could smell the smoke of their fires as the fish were cured for these people's tomorrows. A decayed and crumbling piece of harness and a stray chunk of iron pyrite were spotted in the sand. These spoke to Ben in Spanish of the ones come to seek wealth. He heard them speak words of anger, words of frustration, words of lost faith. In the gleam of the pyrite he could see the faces of those who whored after the gold and prostituted themselves to their own greed. For these men of despair he heard no music, no songs of joy. These people weren't happy with themselves.

When Belinda pointed out the sheep on the distant hillside, Ben heard idle conversation, comments of reflection, the caring words of shepherds and the distant music of their guitars. He could see them

161

roaming the valley looking for their strays, and hear their joy when the wanderers were found.

Belinda strolled among the chollas as she searched for the words. The wood that she almost stepped on was more than just a fallen branch. She knelt and turned it over. It was a crudely carved santo, an effigy in homage to an unknown saint. Weather and time had worn the image, softened the lines, blurred the distinction between the work of nature and humanity. When she brought it to Ben he cradled it gently, like a great treasure. He could hear the whispered prayers and smell the waxy smoke of candles. This would have a new home in Oblivion's church, but for now it was a sketch and a poem. Both artist and poet felt the inspiration and their work was a perfect compliment. She described a hopeful prayer to the saint that this must represent, San Ysidro, patron of the farmers. She wrote of the campesinos kneeling in thanks as the rain fell on the fields of corn and beans. She heard their voices in her mind as her pen created the beauty of words. Verses expressed the farmers' hopes and fears, the soul satisfying labor and the excitement of the harvest. The last lines were of a harvest feast where all the campesinos gathered and took food to neighbors who had not fared as well.

He sketched with flair and drive. The border of the drawing was a black pencil sketch design of leaves, ears of corn, squash blossoms, chiles and beans. The strokes were bolder, less precise but more dynamic. The focal point of the drawing was done in colored pencils and showed San Ignatio holding the basket as the family harvested their crops. This image was completed with another black and white image, this time in hazy fog-like strokes of the pencil. This part of the work showed the family sharing their harvest with others.

It was a technique he had never used before, this creation of three dimensions by contrasting color with the black and white. The effect was one of great depth that permitted him to tell a more complete story.

162

His art illuminated her poetry. Her words gave meaning to his drawings.

The coyote sat in the shade of the junipers and watched them. He smiled. The Great Mystery had given him the gift of a great task, to show humanity the folly of its ways. In this way it was hoped that the peoples would again find their harmony. He knew that within the circles of time harmony had been found and lost many times. Coyote knew the difficulty of guiding those for which he was not a totem. He laughed at the thought of the people despising him because he was their reflection in the mirror. They called him "the Trickster," considered him a lazy fool, overwhelmed by gluttony and greed, but he knew that when they saw him, they were looking at themselves. He smiled once more at the late afternoon sun, then turned and walked to the place where the canyon wall meets the sky.

It was Belinda who spotted the old Indian climbing the steep slope in the distance. She was embarrassed with the thought that he must have been present during their love-making. Still, she was comforted that he was near. At some level, she was almost pleased with the thought that he might have been a witness to their passion. Ben was pleased with the images he had produced. He wondered if there was a link between the creative energy they had expressed and the physical joy they had experienced.

Late afternoon in the high desert country of New Mexico is the golden part of the day. The sun's rays change in intensity; shadows take on their own life. Birds and animals begin their foraging with new vigor. Feathered choruses greet the evening with almost as much enthusiasm as they welcomed the dawn. Perhaps it is the change that is exhilarating. The flowers of the day fold and begin to close, while the fragrant blooms of the night release their olfactory lures, beacons for moths, bats and the other creatures of the night.

As they returned to Oblivion, Belinda matched the drawings with her poetry and was pleased with the way they went together. The town was its joyful bustle again. Children were at play or tending the gardens behind the school. The reporter that she had talked with several weeks ago was sitting on one of the benches in front of the library. The building had, in the days when Oblivion was a thriving town of mines and commerce, been a bank. By accident, it had now become a depository for something of far greater value than money. The Chavez brothers had tried to help by gathering all the varied reference materials used by the students and scientists. The bank was empty and required little work to make it weather sound. Since the brothers frequently relaxed with a good book, it was only natural that works of fiction soon found a home on the makeshift shelves as well. Chi naturally assumed the role of librarian, because she was possessed of great organizational skills and viewed the printed word with something akin to reverence.

Belinda's introduction to the reporter was awkward, she couldn't remember his name. He helped her out of the social embarrassment by launching into a stream of complimentary comments about Ben's art work.

They sat in the shade of the cottonwood and shared their afternoon's words and drawings.

"This is great," Larry commented, "This should be published."

Neither of them had thought of being in print. They weren't sure what that meant. Larry explained some of the mechanics of the publishing industry to them and offered to contact some friends he had in Santa Fe and Albuquerque. The evening was spent preparing a sampling of the lengthy manuscript and making copies of the art work.

In the distance they could hear Coyote howling. From the elm trees outside was the lonely call of an owl, lonely and haunting, yet filled with life and hope.

It was almost midnight when Courtney knocked at the door. She greeted them with gleeful look of one who knows a secret and desperately wants to share it. She held out a bottle of wine and a bag that held cheeses and a loaf of horno bread, and assorted fruits.

"Tonight we celebrate." She declared as she swept past them and began to set the table with her bounty. "First, congratulations on the anticipated publication of your first book." She then turned toward Larry, "Thanks for giving them a little boost in that endeavor. Now, may I see this literary masterpiece?"

Larry didn't understand how she knew about the Oblivion epic, but was given little time to think about it.

She studied each line of the poetry, traced every pencil stroke with her fingers. Her eyes sparkled with pleasure as she literally absorbed the work. She finally leaned back, a smile on her face like that of a proud parent, "It's good. Very good," she said.

Then she went to the table. "This wine was produced at an experimental organic winery west of Taos, made in the finest Spanish tradition by Manuel y Theresa Molenez. These cheeses are from Gene and Laura Murchenson down in Tijeras Canyon. They keep their own goats and a jersey cow for the cream. The bread is from the Cochiti Pueblo. It was baked by students struggling to learn their legacy by living it. These are all links to cultures past. They are all a part of the culture present. They are also the seeds for the culture of the future. Your "Oblivion Epoch" is the gossamer fabric upon which all people, all time, is printed." She spoke with an intensity and a zeal as she filled the glasses.

"Let us all drink to Oblivion," the voice called from the open doorway.

They all turned. The old Indian stood in the shadows outside the door, just beyond the light of the lamp that hung over the table. Like so much of our existence, they could sense his presence, they knew he was there, but they couldn't distinguish him clearly.

165

Larry was intrigued by this old man and cataloged in his mind the questions he wanted to ask, but tonight he was a participant, not a reporter standing on the sidelines. For the first time in his life, he felt like he was more than a spectator. It was a revelation to him that this is a reporter's curse, to be a perpetual audience, never one of the actors on the stage. Why did he feel different in the presence of these people? Why did he feel that Oblivion was his destiny, too? Why, in the presence of Courtney and the Indian did he feel a flow of energy, and an enlightenment?

They shared the food and drink of an enchanted past as they talked of an exciting future.

"Time occasionally presents us with grains of opportunities," the Indian began.

"And nature takes those seeds and grows the future." Courtney concluded. "That's what we are dealing with here," she was now standing in the doorway gazing into the darkness, "an opportunity to reunite the fire people with the earth people, an opportunity to work together rather than in opposition with all the energy and force of nature."

"But first, don't we have to learn how to work with each other?" Ben asked.

The old Indian laughed, "Yes, my friend. We have no choice."

"This is an experiment. You will not be creating utopia here. You will establish a living laboratory. There will be challenges and failures. But there will also be great potentials." Courtney leaned against the door frame and suddenly looked very tired.

"The Great Mystery doesn't lead you by the hand as though you were blind, but rather shows you trails you might choose to take. The people collectively decide their destiny." The Indian spoke as he took Courtney by the hand.

Larry shared another glass of the wine with Ben and Belinda, then secured the notes, poems and sketches that would become a

166

manuscript in his briefcase and departed for Albuquerque. In the morning, he would visit old friends with powerful minds, the anthropologist, Frank Hibben, and Rudolpho Anaya, one of the best writers New Mexico had ever produced.

Belinda was exhausted. First from the mental effort the afternoon's writing had taken, then from the entertaining at late hours. She pulled off her shoes and rolled back on the bed. She was asleep before she could do more than unbutton her shirt. Sunbeam, the kitten curled up against her. Ben undressed and prepared to join them, then noticed the sunflowers she had picked earlier, still lying on the table. They were wilting. Their beauty ebbing away. He trimmed the stems, washed the now empty wine bottle and filled it with water. The rustic brown and tan label complimented the gold of the flowers as they regained their vigor and stood tall and firm in the impromptu vase. He reached for his sketch pad.

In his old style, filled with detail, shading that gave dimension to every line and life to the subject, he drew his love, Sunbeam and the wine bottle with its bouquet. He drew her floating, as was the vase of flowers, floating over the arroyo where they had spent the afternoon. In the upper right corner was a hummingbird, courting the flowers of a penstemon. He was pleased with this work, technically it had great depth. Details were revealed in the fine lines, strokes of the pencil used as a brush. This gave intensity, but it was his passion that gave the piece of art its life. The creative process is sometimes almost orgasmic in its intensity. Ben had, in his long years alone, thought that his art drained his sexual energy, gave the frustration of solitude an outlet. Now, he understood that neither art nor love was a hunger to be satisfied like an empty stomach is sated by a Macdonald's hamburger. Both were passions that needed to be shared and experienced. One fed the other. Belinda, by her presence, made him a better artist. His art, by its existence, made him a better lover. He hoped he provided for her in a similar way.

As he placed the drawing on the easel, she rolled over and opened her eyes. She liked to watch him working late at night, in part because he often did his art in the nude. Sometimes she would pretend to be asleep while she watched, because she respected his passion for the creative acts of an artist. She was intrigued by this creative process and had been watching him as he sketched. As she studied his comfortable shoulders and the gentle hands that captured moods, thoughts as well as images of a poem formed in her mind. She wanted to write it down, but denied herself the passionate need to write because she didn't want to interrupt his art. Finally, she saw that he was finished. He stood and turned to face her. His passion wasn't spent, his art had fed his love for her. She studied him with sparkling eyes. Her smile was an invitation. As they embraced, lines she could not write came into her mind.

Chapter Seventeen

Dawn came early, but Ben and Belinda missed it. Mid-morning found Ben filling the coffee pot and preparing some fresh fruit while Belinda sat on the bed with her notepad. She was putting on paper the poem that had formed in her mind the night before. These were some of the most erotic lines she had ever conceived. She blushed as she reread her own words, then added lines about love in the morning, sharing coffee in the nude while serenaded by birds outside the window.

The knock at the door startled them both. There was an urgency to it. The sound was grating on the nerves, incessant and demanding. Ben grabbed his robe. Trembling with the expectation of bad news, he turned the knob. Before him stood a middle-aged man in a three piece suit, a rare commodity in the high desert country. His hair was graying and clipped short, he carried a bulging briefcase and a sober expression. He studied Ben from head to toe, including the egg turner in his hand.

"Ahem. Are you . . .ahh . . . the owner . . . of this community?" he spoke with some doubt in his voice. Ben nodded, then as an afterthought invited the gentleman in for a cup of coffee and a mid-morning breakfast.

He cautiously stepped inside the door and surveyed the room. Art supplies, assorted drawings, watercolors and oils in various stages of progress lay about the room. Belinda's journals, notepads, flowers, curiosities and mementoes of Oblivion filled the spaces between the canvases. He wrinkled his nose as Ben retreated to the kitchen, and the now charcoal encrusted eggs that would have been breakfast. Belinda entered the room tying her robe and trying to put some order into her rather disheveled hair.

"Wanton hedonism," the visitor muttered to himself as he fumbled for a card. "Murdock Hivers, certified community planner, at your service."

When Ben asked what a community planner does, Murdock rolled his eyes and muttered to himself, "What have I gotten myself into?" He then tried to explain that a private community with over two hundred residents needed to have a governmental structure, organization, control. "Running a town can be a very profitable enterprise for you," he began his pitch as he opened his briefcase and removed a shiny black three ring binder filled with charts, financial statements, sample charters and an organizational flow chart. "No offense, but I can see from the haphazard way things are handled here that you really need my help. I've taken the liberty of doing some research . . ."

"Why?" Ben asked, folding his arms across his chest.

"Well, look around you. How do you collect the rent from all these people? Most of them look like they can't even afford to pay rent. I saw a couple of hippy freaks shoveling dirt against the walls of a house when I came into town. You know that's going to lower property values. Don't you?"

Belinda rose to this insult, "Frog and Chad aren't hippy freaks. They happen to be two of the nicest people we know. They are hard working dreamers. They have more ideas before breakfast that most people have in a lifetime." She was standing, her voice was becoming shrill. Ghosts from her business past were swirling inside her head. She had been a victim of this type in her past life and was not about to let it happen again. With every ounce of her energy she would battle the accountants and managers who make dollars the bottom line and view people as an expendable commodity. Ben was a babe in the woods with the Philistines that lived to control, were driven by greed, and gloried in their own sanctimonious self-righteousness. He had no concept of what this man meant to accomplish.

"I took some notes while I walked around this morning and there are some serious concerns that we need to address. You own this

170

community and no one knows if you even have any insurance. What would you do if someone got hurt?"

"We all take care of each other here," the voice from the open door calmly explained. The old Indian had that benign smile on his face and a sparkle in his eye that implied that he was up to something. "Besides that, I offer corn pollen to the rising sun every morning. I do that and every one stays healthy. Corn pollen is good insurance, and it's cheap too." He went to the kitchen and filled a mug with coffee. "When you worry that something will go wrong, you send a message that you want something to go wrong. We all get what we expect from life. When you live in Oblivion, you expect to be happy. We live in harmony here. This is nothing new, in fact it's a return to my peoples' traditional values."

"You have to have control over these people."

Ben had been quiet, but he now pointed the coffee spoon at Murdock, "Almost every day after we are done working, we gather at the church and discuss what we are going to do next, what good things happened today, and the children tell us adults what they learned. Everyone shares their experiences, dreams and concerns. This is all we need. This is what Dirty Maria calls democracy, and it certainly seems to work for us."

"You have to comply with building codes, statutes, laws."

Courtney entered in time to field this comment. "We have laws. Laws of nature, Newton even found some of them under an apple tree." She smiled at her joke but Murdock missed it. "These people are trying to learn to live by the universal laws of love and cooperation. Do you have something better to offer?"

"A private community is a business. To be successful, the rules have to be written and a system established to enforce them."

Belinda fielded this comment, "Would you consider Great Britain successful?"

"What do you mean?' was all he could muster as a response.

She explained, "Common law is the basis for British society. That was a method of functioning that was commonly agreed upon, based on fairness and the social needs of the time, not a set of edicts handed down by some power hungry control freak.

He saw that this argument was going nowhere so he sought to redirect it, "What about the children. The state requires schooling and qualified teachers. Of course you will establish a private school. That will require tuition fees and you . . ."

Before he could finish his sentence Ben was up again slashing the air with the spoon to make his point. "Dirty Maria runs our school and the children of Oblivion already get the best education pssible. She holds four bachelor's degrees, one each in English, education, anthropology and biology. Her minors include Spanish, history, philosophy and Native American studies. No one pays rent in Oblivion because they all contribute to the community. There are forty-six children here, and all the parents take part in their children's education. This is possible because each of these people has something to offer, something from their culture to share. There are more scientists per square foot here than in Los Alamos. The computers in the school receive Internet classes from the University of New Mexico. These children are daily exposed to some of the best minds in America. We have no discipline problems, there are no drugs in Maria's school, nor are there any failures. Do you know why?"

Murdock stuttered, but Ben gave him no time to formulate a response.

"I'll tell you why. It's because Oblivion's school is based on love, not control. The teachers are the parents. Everyone takes care of these children. This is a village in the purest sense of the word, and it really does takes a village to raise a child. Look out the window." He pointed at a group of children tending a series of raised beds under the watchful eye of Grandma Rosa, while three others were recording

172

readings from gauges on the windmills. Dirty Maria was showing another group of them the difference between two similar wildflowers. "Now, if you will excuse me, I have an art class to teach." With that he grabbed his portfolio and stormed out the door, still wearing nothing more than his robe.

Murdock shuffled his papers, "I could make him rich. If only he'd listen, I could make him rich."

"He's already rich," Belinda replied as she put his briefcase on the table, "He has a wealth of talent, the richness of a super creative mind, the bounty of wonderful friends and gems beyond value in the form of dreams. You wouldn't know how to begin to measure his wealth. Every day he invests himself in every one of the people here, and they in turn invest their trust, friendship and love in him. You don't buy and sell love, you nurture it. You don't pay for cooperation, you invest yourself in it. You don't force people to do your bidding, you encourage them to do the right thing. This is Ben, and he is the wealthiest person I know." She sat down, exhausted.

Courtney smiled at the old Indian, "I think she's got it."

"Yep. Unfortunately, Murdock, you probably never will. Don't blame yourself entirely. It's the way you were taught as a child. You see, we put most of a child's learning in his head, not by what school teachers lecture, not even what parents say, but by what parents do. A child is a sponge, it soaks up attitudes, fears, values. Like a caterpillar it feeds constantly, only children feed on information, knowledge and wisdom, not leaves. When they become teenagers, they spin a cocoon for themselves and metamorphose into an adult. They begin to act just like they were taught by their parents. Sometimes we get mighty upset when we look into our grown children's eyes and realize we are looking into a mirror."

"You're all a bunch of looneys," Murdock muttered over his shoulder as he sought the door. Then he turned, to deliver his final argument. "With a well planned ad campaign, we could bring thousands of people to this valley. Think about it. We could lure all sorts of light industry, create jobs, draw Wal-Marts, build shopping malls. With some of the novel ideas you have here, we could become a major tourist destination complete with motels, golf courses. I've got friends that for a percentage will even. . . ."

Belinda saw the ghosts of her past standing beside Murdock. She saw the spirit of uncontrollable greed in the business community that drove it to always increase sales. The specter of human resources, a euphemism for people who viewed their fellow employees as disposable machines, leered from over Murdock's shoulder. Clinking his chains of coins was a phantom accountant hideously obsessed with profits, at any cost. The apparition of an ad man danced at Murdock's side, excited that he had talked thousands of people into spending money they didn't have for things they didn't need. A shadow of a quality control technician gave a ghastly giggle, unable to hide her glee at the corporate deception. Yet it was in the name, wasn't it? She controlled the quality of the products they manufactured. She understood the company's true objective was to control quality; if it was too good, it would last too long. Then the market would lose the replacement sale. These ghastly visions of her past weaved and floated around the unfortunate Mr. Murdock Hivers. Belinda was suddenly overwhelmed with sympathy for him. She understood that he was their prisoner. She knew instinctively that he lacked the strength or courage to escape their gossamer bonds, their ethereal net. Because she had been in the grasp of these demons, she understood. She would try to explain to him what Oblivion was, but she knew he wouldn't understand.

She approached him with her hand extended and a smile on her face. His ghostly keepers halted their gyrations, giggles and mockery. Quality Control stuck out her tongue, Greed made an obscene gesture, then they became still. Several of them began to fade. All semblance of glee left their grotesque faces, to be replaced with apprehension and fear.

174

Murdock felt the prodding of his spectral companions and absorbed the fear they generated. Yet when he took her hand, he felt the warmth of comfort. There was a calm confidence in her eyes that began to melt his tension. He thought that his mind caught glimpses of movement around her. Glowing ever so slightly were feelings; that was the only way his mind could comprehend them, feelings of compassion, joy, and a kind of happiness that was beyond his understanding.

"Mr. Hivers, everyone else is leaving to go about their day's activities. Would you have a quiet cup of coffee while I dress, and perhaps I can show you what Oblivion is really about." She gave him no time to reply, but turned toward the kitchen.

He sat at the table, unable to do anything else. He looked at her hair, no longer wantonly disheveled, but expressing a freedom that surrounded this woman, or perhaps, emanated from within her. He turned toward the sketches and paintings that lay about the room. They ceased to be clutter, and became the pages in a story he wished he could read. He knew how to invest in art, how to buy and sell it, but now he understood that he knew nothing of the messages of art itself. He felt ashamed of his ignorance.

When he examined a series of pencil sketches of the individual buildings of Oblivion, he was overwhelmed with the sense that the structures were living organisms with feelings, fears and joys. He thought for a moment that he could hear bells when he picked up the sketch of the old church.

She returned wearing a paint spattered yellow tee shirt and faded jeans. Around her neck was a squash blossom necklace. Her wrist sported a silver and turquoise bracelet, but the greatest adornment was her smile. It radiated a contentment, a harmony, that he was unaccustomed to. The women he worked with were all climbing ladders. They all wore the mask of troubled ambition, afraid to look down, yet unsure of what lay ahead. He knew from his own experience that climbing ladders was accompanied by a pathological fear of falling.

This could become a paranoia so powerful that it would drive people to willfully use and injure others for the sake of another rung. Yet, when that rung was gained, it only meant there was another one to go. If you could climb your entire life and never lose your grip, you got to the top and realized you had been climbing down. You were not in the sunshine, but in a deep, dark pit, a hole from which there was no escape. 'Why, why do I think these thoughts when I look into her face?' He asked himself.

"Because I'm free of the forces that hold you so tightly," Belinda answered with her understanding smile. She again extended her hand, "Let's take a walk."

The sun was warm and bright, bathing everything in its life giving energy. It gave light and life to the adobe buildings with terraced garden walls, the brightly painted frame houses, the old church gleaming white and the school surrounded by children and adults actively exchanging ideas and facts, the building blocks of knowledge. The community was alive, the buildings had vitality. Flashes of light reflected from the solar collectors as several of the people tended their gardens beneath. Scientists and laborers worked side by side at the expanding Lake Hope. They were laying irrigation lines, and planning islands of agriculture that would float over the surface, controlling the evaporation loss and extending the crop potential. Aquaculturists were working with freshwater biologists to introduce a balanced ecosystem into the lake. An aquatic ecosystem could be created that would keep the water clean, provide a harvest of fish and aquatic plants that were edible. Lake Hope could become the lifeblood of the valley.

Murdock was at first appalled by the apparent confusion and seeming lack of direction, but he soon realized that this chaos was in reality poetry in motion, harmony in action. These people he had referred to as human weeds were laboring not for money, but for a dream. He heard music ranging from Vivaldi to Selena. The people were singing in Spanish, English, Korean, Tai, and Japanese, but above all the voices he could hear a flute. It was more than an awareness, it was a sensuous veil that enticed him toward its source. He was drawn from the bustle and joy of the community toward the hillsides, where windmills thumped and whirred a rhythm of their own. He could see a wisp of smoke rising from a pile of rocks and scrub juniper. He wasn't lured against his will, for it was his will to follow the music, something he had never done before.

Belinda smiled as she followed him. His dress shoes slipped repeatedly on the uneven ground, but each time he stumbled, he sought the music with greater drive. He didn't see the coyote as it sat silently smiling at his struggle. Belinda was puzzled when it simply disappeared. It hadn't turned and fled, it just evaporated. Where it had been there was a turquoise ring, like the one the old Indian wore. She picked it up and put it in her pocket.

Behind the rocks, at the source of the smoke sat the Indian, eyes closed, playing the flute like a skillful fisherman with a net. Murdock sat by the fire, inhaled the smoke and tried to speak. Belinda saw the ghosts and demons that had plagued him earlier. They had shrunk, and almost melted into the healing juniper smoke.

The flute was laid aside as the old man placed a small drum between his knees. He tapped lightly, coaxing a resonance not unlike the flute's in tone from the tightly stretched hide. "Welcome to my fire. I asked you to come so that we might talk." The palm of his hand struck the drum as punctuation.

Murdock was struggling to control the situation, because control was all he knew. Life to him was a matter of being controlled or being in control. The swirling pariahs grew larger as he began to resist the music.

The old Indian turned to Belinda, "By my carelessness you have learned something this morning. But, it is knowledge you would have acquired in due time anyway." The smile was so benign, so without threat, so like the coyote's. He held out his hand, "Thank you for returning my ring."

He stared deeply into Murdock's eyes while his fingertips tapped their message on the drum. He was reading this man's soul. Belinda wondered if he too, could see the ghosts that were trying to hide Murdock's face, vainly attempting to cover the eyes and shield the ears from the slow rhythm of the percussion.

"I have lived long and know much of time." The drum beats were heavier now. "It is time for Oblivion. You do not yet understand this, perhaps you never will. I want you to leave this valley with one thought, and it is simply that," now his fists beat a rapid staccato, "you are loved, even when you fall under the power of greed, and fear and ignorance, you are a part of the Great Mystery. You must have felt the care and warmth these people extend to one another as you walked through our valley. Your hungry soul must have been fed by the peace that flows through Oblivion. Understand as you leave us today," again the drum's tempo increased, "that love is the lifeblood of the spirit, just as water is the life blood of the body. Your soul is dying from this thirst."

Without another word he put the drum in his bag, gathered his flute, and as he stood, put it to his lips. He turned and walked among the large rocks and boulders that dotted the talus slope. This time the song of the flute didn't beckon. It led their steps back toward the community.

As they neared the gardens that Rosita Gonzales tended, the sound of the flute disappeared. The phantoms of Murdock's life rallied.

Chapter Eighteen

Marquita could feel the warm afternoon sun shining on her eyes, but could not see it through the bandages that concealed her face, held her jaw in place, and protected her injuries. The pains, awesome in their presence, were being held at bay. She knew they were lurking out there, somewhere in the warm darkness. Her brain struggled with the chemicals that had driven the pain into retreat, for those same chemicals played with her mind. Mixing yesterday with tomorrow, but always avoiding today. Always stepping around the present, because that's where the hurt was.

During the hours when her eyes could sense the darkness of night, she could feel Ernesto lying next to her. She felt the warmth of his breath against her neck. The rhythm of his heartbeat was a drum in her head. Or, perhaps, it was her own heart. The warmth of his body comforted her. Her mind knew his love. Then he was gone, and she was in her mother's arms. Now she was a little girl, crying. Madre was rocking her, rocking with the rhythm of another heartbeat, in the chair her abuelo had made. She could hear the nuns talking in their hushed tones. "I am now in the safety of the convent of the Sisters of St. Joseph." Her mind told her, as they pulled their blanket of love over her.

The nurses were injecting the chemicals that would keep her alive, would keep the demons of pain away, but would accomplish this by confusing her mind, leading it through labyrinths from which there was no escape. She could hear them talking about her face, how it would never return to the beauty she had once possessed, but, also how she could sue and never want for anything again. As the one nurse injected the scheduled morphine, she commented to her companions, "She's already out, but this will sure send her into oblivion."

179

As they left the room, she could feel her Ernesto take her by the hand. She could see again, and he was more handsome than ever. For a moment, she stood aside and watched herself. She was pleased when he ran his big hands through her long black hair. When she tried to see her face, all that was visible was a blurred haze, but she knew she was smiling. They were walking along the arroyo, as they had done so many times in her youth, their youth. That time when discovery was so agonizingly sweet. They came to the old water tank behind the crumbling ghost town. Ernesto removed his shirt and worked the pump handle. She studied the way his young muscles labored as he filled the tank with cool, life giving water. Muscles of his back and the arms in rhythm together. Those of his stomach and legs stretched and relaxed with each motion. He was a community of parts all working together. The sweat dripped from his dark hair, ran in rivulets down his back and chest. As they stripped and began to play in the water, the abandoned buildings took on life. They straightened; color returned, and the sounds of vitality could be heard.

While passion ruled their existence, hundreds of people came out of the buildings and gathered around them. The joy of youth was replaced with the sense of shame and guilt that had become the constant companions of her adulthood. As she wept, Ernesto gathered his clothes and abandoned her. She reached for her grandmother, but Abuela's chair was empty. She ran naked to the sisters, but they waved accusing fingers at her as they guarded the door to the convent. Finally, the Benton family, gathered her up and took her home. There she paid in pain and shame for her comfort and shelter. For a time, she had even deluded herself into believing that love was being shared, but she knew better. She knew now that love was a fiction she read about in romance novels. In reality, it didn't exist.

Days and nights weaved a tapestry of time in Marquita's life as she wandered in and out of wakefulness. Bright colors splashed in random patterns as her mind fought to control itself. The bandages had

180

freed her face days before her mind was able to escape the drugs that had been both its faithful friend and worst enemy. Vases of flowers filled the room, lined the windowsills, stood in rows along the floor, each with a card from Calmut Benton or Brandy. As her mind cleared, she began to hate the entire Benton family, not Landreth alone. Her heart pumped this poison of hate through her mind and soul. She despised Derritt for his brutality, Calmut was loathed, not only because he used her when his need for a woman was strong, but because he let her be abused by his sons. The most venomous acrimony was aimed at Brandy, for she above all the rest should have understood, and she did nothing.

When the morning sun finally gave her enough strength, she ordered all the flowers removed. As the aides carried them out, she vowed that she would have revenge, revenge against the entire family. It was later that same day that the gentleman in the business suit knocked at her door.

"Marquita Lopez?" he asked as he sat the heavy briefcase on the floor.

She acknowledged with difficulty through the brace that held her healing jaw in place.

"Bueno," he said as he sat on the corner of her bed and opened his case. "I am Donald Aragon. I am an attorney with the Land Grant Foundation in Santa Fe."

Marquita knew that when the New Mexico Territory was seized from Mexico, the grants were to have been reviewed by the courts and honored as legal deeds. She had learned in school that most of the Hispanic land holders didn't understand the American court system and legally, though not always morally, lost their homes, ranches, and livelihood. She remembered the stories her abuelo had told of how they were heirs to the greatest land grant of them all. She remembered the jokes her father made about it as well.

"It seems that you are a legitimate heir to a large parcel of land that we would like to test in the state courts."

She pressed him for details and he presented her with a folder of papers, photo copies of grants, deeds, transfers, claims and tax records for a parcel of land that included all of the Benton property, the canyon that contained Oblivion, and hill country beyond that was a part of the Santa Fe National Forest. This was the area where the Bentons held the mining rights and grazed most of their cattle.

"Because this has been federal land, the issue of property taxes is nonexistent. The community of Oblivion was originally deeded to a member of your family, before the land grant hearings in the 1840's. The Benton ranch was also a part of this sale of property. These sales were recorded in proper fashion at the old temporary courthouse that was the Kit Carson Ranch. These documents and hundreds of others have been literally stored in a closet in an annex building for over a hundred years. There are only two deed transfers missing."

"What does all this mean?"

"This means that you, as far as I can determine, are the sole heir to virtually everything in the western half of San Miguel County." He paused and studied her face. He reached out and gently touched her bruised and swollen cheek, put his hand on her shoulder as if to impart some of his strength to her. "This will not be an easy fight. Understand that the Bentons will not easily accept this claim. I think we can present a strong case, even with the missing pieces to the puzzle, but this will be a tough legal battle."

"I know the Bentons." Through the pain in a broken and wired jaw she spoke with an almost frightening determination. "I know what they deserve."

The young lawyer literally saw the sparks ignite in her eyes and watched a smile agonizingly form across her lips. "I remember mi Abuelo talking of these grants, showing them to me. But I thought they

182

were meaningless pieces of paper. They were so old and stained, so old they crumble when we tried to read them."

"You have seen the missing documents?" He was so excited by this revelation that he grabbed her by the shoulders and kissed her.

It was an exquisite mixture of pain and pleasure. He was so gentle, yet possessed by the flames of enthusiasm. She studied his face, looked long into his eyes, searching for some knowledge of this man. She whispered to herself, "He must know me, know what I am, and yet he did not back away as if I was vermin."

For a moment her mind put Ernesto at the foot of her bed, but, when he began to protest, she waved him away and took Don Aragon's hand in hers. She knew who he was. She had read about him in the Harlequin Historical Romances. He was a knight in shining armor, defender of her virtue. Her mind saw before her a champion, her El Cid.

She tried to describe the old papers she had seen while on her grandfather's knee. She told him about the blue and green stamps that were at the bottom. How she wanted to play with them and was told that they were what made this an official paper of the government of Los Estados Unidos. She remembered her Abuelo telling her, "Some day when I have some money I will take these to Santa Fe. Then we will live like los patrones of the past." She also remembered that they buried his dreams with him on a cold January afternoon. Tears formed in her eyes for her abuelo y abuela, then for her madre y padre.

He tenderly captured the tears in the corner of a tissue and kissed her forehead. In the hour he spent with her, they discussed the violence that had brought her to the hospital, where she could go when she was ready to leave this medical sanctuary, and lastly, where these documents she remembered from her childhood were today.

It was agreed that she would stay with his sister. There she would be safe. It wasn't until he was at the doorway, that she remembered the old wooden chest.

183

"That had to be where he put all his papers." She muttered through her artificially clenched teeth. "He had this old wooden chest with the Virgin of Guadalupe and roses carved on it. It was about this big." She held her hands about a foot apart. "That's were he kept all the old photos, medallions, his Santos. In that box were his past and future, all the symbols of his hopes and dreams."

Don returned to her bed. "Where is that chest?"

"I don't know!" she sobbed.

But she did know. It was a week later, while she sat in Abrieta Aragon's living room sipping licorice tea through a straw, that the picture flashed into her mind. It was almost like a vision. Her padre had wanted to bury it with the old man. To him the box of dreams was what made his father unhappy, discontented, "Dreamers always walk with their eyes on the clouds and step in the cowshit underfoot." He would tell his children, "It's better to be sure in your step than think of things that cannot be." In his mind the old man was an abysmal failure.

"Madre rescued the box and kept in our pantry until my father came home drunk one night. It had been a bad day at the pottery where he worked. He was filled with anger. He found the box while looking for her kitchen money. I was a teenager at this time and was . . .ah . . . seeing a fella named Ernesto. I was so frightened of my father that I grabbed the box and ran. Ernesto and I went to the old ghost town in the canyon. At the end of that canyon there is a cave behind a waterfall."

Now she couldn't look into his eyes. Her hands involuntarily rubbed her knees, as she saw before her the priest, Father Andy, an ancient man who, if he had ever known the fire of a youthful body, had long ago forgotten the nature of those flames. She bowed her head in contrition as she confessed.

Don Aragon laughed and held her close to him. "Don't tell me of your misspent youth, and I won't horrify you with stories of mine."

184

Abrieta laughed in confirmation, "And he could tell you some tales, too."

Derritt was now crumbling, both physically and mentally. The burns on his scalp and shoulder were infected. His legs were too weak to carry him any further. The bandages of his hands could not concealed the stench of his festering wounds. His clothes smelled of filth, smoke, urine and sweat. He had to retreat to this cave. It would be a defensible haven. Landreth was following him. He knew it. He could see the glowing eyes of his brother, first behind the juniper, then hiding in the branches of the desert willow. There he was ahead. Lying in the darkness, waiting like a rattlesnake, ready to strike.

He held the revolver with both hands and fired until the cylinder was empty. The pain from the recoil was so intense it drove him to his knees. A mocking laugh arose in his throat and was set free into the night air, only to be answered by distant night sounds. He looked up and saw his brother standing before him, now twelve feet tall and wearing a hideous mask. Struggling with his uncooperative legs, he finally stood and lunged forward, pulling the trigger of the empty gun as fast as he could. In his mind, he head the roar of the phantom shots, and he saw the blood spurt from the bullet holes in his brother. He laughed again as he stumbled through the still standing corpse.

Beyond this stream bed was a small waterfall, and behind it was a cave. He didn't know whether this was a retreat where he could heal, or a quiet place to die. He remembered the cave from his childhood. He knew he would be safe from Landreth here. His mind told him he had just killed his brother, but he knew that Landreth would return. Big brother always returned to do terrible things to him, to hurt him, to laugh at him. Also from the cave he could watch the growing community of Oblivion, and formulate a plan to destroy it. It had to be destroyed. Daddy wanted to make it all gone. Derritt knew that if he could get rid of the town Daddy would be proud of him. He sat at the entrance to the grotto, the thin flow from the waterfall splashing on his face. The water mixed with his tears as he screamed, "Daddy, why don't you love me?"

When he awoke, the water was still splashing on his face. He could see his father and brother laughing at him as he came down the steps of that house in Santa Fe. It was the house of Margaret Fitch, Madam Fitch. The whore was tying her robe and throwing his shoes after him as he descended the steps. "He is only a little boy, too little to be a man. He es muy pequeno!" she screamed so that all could hear.

He crawled inside the cave, because they couldn't follow him there. It was a rule that only he knew this place. Sure enough, they shrugged their shoulders and turned to walk away. He raised his revolver and pulled the trigger until his fingers ached. The ooze and blood from his wounds dripped from the butt of the useless weapon. The silent bullets all found their mark, and as the father and brother walked down the stream bed, holes appeared in their backs. Blood again spurted in great arching streams. Derritt smiled and muttered to himself, "I can kill you two any time I want to."

The afternoon sun woke him, but the weakness and pain were too great to permit movement. He turned his head away from the bright light that almost blinded him, and studied his sanctuary. He remembered the first time he had been in this hiding place. He had followed a couple of teenage spics. He waited outside until he was certain they were making love. Even now he smiled as his mind projected them onto the floor in front of him. There she was, Marquita, with that long black hair and those teen ripe breasts. He could remember the look on her face when she saw him. The kid was too involved in what he was doing to know what hit him. Derritt remembered the blow from his fist to the small of the Spic's back. Again he could see the agony and pain that drove the lad to roll against the wall of the cave and moan in helplessness. Now he could clearly see the terrified face of Marquita as he lowered himself onto her, how she

186

struggled when he tried to kiss her. For that he had to teach her a lesson.

Now he studied the primeval room. It had been shelter to so many. Traces of woven baskets and sandals were half buried in the dirt, pottery from several different ages had been discarded among the rocks that lined the dark walls. There were shepherd's blankets, cigarette butts, whiskey bottles and beer cans. From his prone position, he could even see a wooden box of some sort tucked back under the sandstone at the far end of the elongated grotto. He thought he would have to find out what was in it, but was interrupted by his brother. He reached for his gun and fired until Landreth collapsed again; until they both fell to the floor of the cavern and the game was over.

Chapter Nineteen

It had been a quiet week in Oblivion. After the reluctant departure of Murdock Hivers, Ben and Belinda quickly fell back into their rhythm of work and life. There were so many people in Oblivion now that it was difficult to find quiet time to ply their arts. They planned early to take the materials they needed to write and sketch and retreat to the far end of the valley. They packed a picnic lunch and a bottle of wine. The hike was a pleasant one, with frequent pauses to study the flowers and rocks, examine a piece of pottery, or watch some of the varied wildlife of the high desert country. They both thoroughly enjoyed this solitude, this uninterrupted time with each other.

Ben felt a moral dilemma was developing. He loved Belinda deeply, and felt the need to formalize their relationship. Twice he had almost asked her to marry him. Twice he faltered as he found himself unworthy. The fact was that while he owned a town, he was living off the generosity of others, plus the infrequent sale of a painting. "What," he asked himself, "do I have to offer her?"

He also felt that his was a bad example to the children in the community. He had even overheard some of the comments the gossips were wont to make. This troubled him as much as his poverty.

Belinda was also torn. She understood that to be an artist was to possess a free spirit. Thus she had no right to expect Ben to do any more than love her the way he did now. Still, she longed for some permanence in their relationship. She had seen the way some of the other single women, and several of the married ones, too, looked at him. She could read their eyes. She had asked for this little outing, hoping to find the opportunity to propose to him. Now she was afraid. Afraid that he might say "no." Then the dream would burst like a soap bubble. She feared losing him more than anything else, even life itself.

She was also afraid he might say "yes." She had been

independent her whole life and wasn't certain what turning their love into a marriage would do to her. She couldn't feel owned. She refused to be a possession. Her former career had done that. Still, she wanted to be assured that Ben was always going to be a part of her life. She needed to know that.

They both fumbled with their words that afternoon. Both felt awkward, uncomfortable. This disquietude was partly because, as they struggled with their deepening love, they were also struggling to assume more traditional roles, believing that each had more traditional expectations of the other. They were both uncomfortable with the past and unsure of the future. Ben, in an attempt to relieve the tension, suggested that they visit the waterfall at the end of the canyon. It was small, as far as waterfalls go, but still filled with peace and beauty.

They approached with care because the rocks were wet and slippery. Ben thought the grass, lush because of the abundant water, looked packed down, as if something had walked through it to get closer to the cooling stream of water that cascaded down the rock wall. Belinda noticed an odor, not unlike the winos she had encountered in St. Louis. The odor became almost a stench as they felt the cooling spray.

Ben was the first to notice that the waterfall concealed a cave. It was too dark to see clearly, but he could distinguish some pottery within the play of sun and shadow that filtered through the cascading water. Taking Belinda by the hand, they stepped through the water. The sun was in its afternoon retreat toward the canyon wall. It illuminated the inside of the grotto.

Belinda gasped. She clutched Ben's arm, and pointed at the hand hanging limply over the rocks. Ben approached with caution. When he reached Derritt, his first thought was that the young Benton was dead. When he rolled Derritt over, the pathetic shell of a madman raised the empty gun one more time. His hand silently worked the trigger until finally, with tears streaming down his cheeks, he cried, "Play fair. I killed you. Drop dead. Daddy said you have to."

He crumpled into a sobbing heap. Ben pulled him into the light, while Belinda moistened one of the napkins in the pure spring water and wiped the grime and vomit from his face. Ben unwrapped the filthy bandages that covered his hands. The burns on his back and neck had festered. Blood and pus had dried, bonding his clothes to his flesh. They had to literally cut the shirt from his back. Ben then removed the rest of Derritt's clothes and carried him to the pool at the base of the waterfall. The cool water revived him, but his ranting remained incoherent. He kept cursing his brother and calling for Daddy.

Belinda started a small fire and burned the infected bandages and Derritt's filthy clothes. Ben gagged as he attempted to clean the wounds. The infection had devoured the flesh in several places on Derritt's hands, so badly that bone was visible. The burned scalp was a mass of infection, while the skin was gone completely from his shoulder. As he sat in the water, Belinda brought him a glass of the wine. His hands held so much agony that he couldn't grasp it. Ben put the cup to his lips. Next Belinda offered a few morsels of cheese and a piece of bread.

While Ben pulled Derritt's naked body from the pool and placed him on the grass to dry in the warm afternoon sun, Belinda explored the grotto. She found a wooden box and carried it out into the sunlight. The religious carvings intrigued her and told her that this was someone's treasure, something to be treated with respect. She tried to open it but the clasp was rusted tight. Ben took the blanket they had spread for their picnic and wrapped it around Derritt. Belinda gathered the wooden chest and the picnic basket, while Ben hefted the young Benton over his shoulder.

Derritt moaned in his sleep, called for his Daddy, cursed his brother, and made vulgar comments about someone named Marquita. At several points in the return to Oblivion, he began to struggle violently. Ben would put him down and begin to walk away. Derritt would then scream, "Don't leave me alone, Daddy. I'll be good."

190

Ben was exhausted by the time they returned to the edge of town. The old Indian was the first to greet them and offer assistance. Bandages were replaced, and clothes were found that would fit, before he was taken to the clinic at Juniper Crossing. From there, he was taken to Santa Fe Memorial Hospital where a week later, because of gangrene, his right hand was amputated, as were two fingers on his left.

Don Aragon led Marquita by the hand as they approached the waterfall. Dark memories cascaded over her as they entered the cavern. A gentle kiss destroyed the ghosts. Marquita, by returning to the cave, had defeated one of her personal demons. Still, her emotions were almost out of control as she knelt down and reached under the rock for her abuelo's wooden chest. It wasn't there. Don sat with her and held her in his arms. As they rested, she wept quietly on his shoulder. She couldn't understand where the box had gone. She couldn't understand where she had gone.

Belinda had removed the small wooden chest from the picnic hamper that evening. While Ben strolled down to the lake with the Chavez brothers, she carefully cleared away the dust and dirt to reveal an exquisite carving in relief. The Virgin de Guadalupe was so detailed that smile lines creased her face. Each petal of the roses she held was clear and distinct. She understood the great love that had gone into the creation of this icon. With a small pocket knife she scraped the rust free of the iron hasp and the small padlock, then with a screwdriver she broke the lock.

She had expected no jewelry, money or precious metals. She instinctively knew that it would contain riches far greater than that. The first papers were baptismal certificates for three children, and death certificates for two. Under them were some photos of a rural Hispanic family, dressed in their ill fitting formal Sunday clothes. There were several papers that appeared to be property deeds, and an article from

191

a Spanish language newspaper. It was so fragile, crumbling with age, that she dared not try to read it. In the bottom of the box were religious medals and medallions, candles, several rosaries, and a wood and silver crucifix. She spread the story of someone's life on the kitchen table, tried to organize the pieces of this puzzle chronologically, attempted to put together the existence of people she didn't know.

Without thinking, she reached for her notepad and wrote a poem to the children in the photos. She described los ninos as candles bringing light to the lives of their parents. Other lines spoke of the quiet rural faith that sustained this family, gave it hope and comforted its losses. She assumed that the deeds were for farmland, and saw visions of a family clearing the acquias, tending the fields, harvesting the crops. She also felt a kinship with these people, felt they were the ones for whom Oblivion existed.

The photo of one of the children, a charming little girl of about ten, with sparkling eyes and long black pigtails, fell to the floor. When Belinda picked it up, it begged for lines in her poem. Her mind pulled a name from the mental mists, a beautifully lyric name she had heard Derritt speak, Marquita. She dedicated her poem to this little girl, whose real name was unknown. Lines flowed as Marquita spoke to Belinda's mind of all her childhood hopes and dreams. Finally she was finished and titled it "Marquita's Dream."

While spring is a season of excitement and new challenges, a time when optimism rules the mind, body, and soul, summer is a time of routine. This is as much a pattern of the weather as of the people. After the joyous beginnings, the threats of violence from the Bentons, the thrill of creating something new, the daunting task of unsought responsibility, Ben was also falling into a routine. This was a rhythm that permitted his artistic soul to have expression, his love for Belinda to nurture itself, and still accept the accidental role of el patron.

Ben devoted early morning to his art. Then, as was the duty of everyone in the community, he spent some time at the school, or helping with one of the many experimental projects that the community had devised. Lunch with Belinda, and usually several other Oblivion residents, at Las Golandrinas Cafe was a time of light discussion about what was happening in the town. The heat of the day was accepted as quiet time by most of the people. It was a natural rhythm to nap, read or spend an hour fishing in the shade of the cottonwoods. As the temperature began to moderate, activity began anew, with a positive attitude. Work would continue until the sun fell from the canyon rim. Then there was a gathering at the church where the day's events were discussed, following this was a festive evening of music, games and friendly discussion.

The sense of purpose that brought the scientists and dreamers to this community continued to sustain them as they saw some of their ideas fail and others succeed. Dr. Taggertt had set up an information center in one of the old houses. This served as a welcome center for statesmen, environmentalists, the curious, and those unable to dedicate their minds and bodies to this community of the future, but willing to help with funding for the ideas showcased here. Students of all ages, elementary to graduate level, were eager to explain the exhibits and conduct tours of the valley. Computers gave them instant contact with the powerful, the curious and the obscure. These people hadn't turned their backs on the rest of the world as they sought security in some idealized past. They were racing into the future, but it was a future filled with hope, ideas and ideals. Oblivion had become far more than an accidental community; but it was not a prototype of some idealized utopian future. It existed as a working village expressing faith in its people, and a growing confidence that dreams can be the blueprints for a better tomorrow.

The residents were not all scientists boasting degrees like the military sports its medals. Many of the people who made Oblivion work were the hopeless and homeless of New Mexico. In Oblivion they found their dreams, too. They were thriving on a sense of belonging to something great. They regained the ability to dream, plan, grow. They rediscovered hope, and it was a treasure greater than gold. There was pride in themselves that was evident in the way they worked, played, and eagerly sought to learn. Mid-summer found the creation of an adult school in the library. The afternoon siesta time was often spent meeting together to learn. For some of those who made Oblivion a reality, formal childhood education hadn't been an option. They now pursued literacy as a noble quest. Each shared her or his knowledge with the others, studies in philosophy, thermo-dynamics, herbal healing, guitar, family planning and healthy cooking filled the hot afternoon hours. They weren't there to get a degree, for there was no formal credit given. They came to learn because that was a thirst within each of them that had to be quenched.

The old Indian had explained it to them one evening as they watched several of the former street people entering the library. "A hunger for knowledge had been rekindled, for within every child is that overpowering need to know. The journey toward adulthood supplants this with an unnatural thirst for money and the material possessions that become a heavy burden. Sometimes the weight of having becomes so great that the soul dies of exhaustion, simply from carrying the load. When we make our possessions knowledge, it isn't a burden at all, but rather a balloon that lifts us above the mire and muck of ignorance and fear. This is something that the mind can easily carry. In fact, wisdom and knowledge strengthen the mind, body and soul, so that all burdens are easier to shoulder. Then, if we can learn to live in harmony, there is no burden too heavy."

Courtney often quoted a wise and loving lady named Wilhelmina that she had once known, "The thoughts of people are more valuable than money. When two people exchange dollar bills, each still has only one dollar. When they exchange an idea, each then has two ideas."

Ben had, to a degree, come to terms with the role of el patron, but there was still stress, as questions, minor disputes, and major issues all found their way to him. Often all he wanted to do was paint, to hide somewhere and ply the pencil and the brush, his tools. In early morning there was little interruption, but he found himself more and more hurrying to finish a creative thought before there was a knock at the door, before there was a meeting to attend. This pressure resulted in a loss of detail in his work. Broad strokes replaced fine lines. Detail gave way to suggestion. This troubled him. He worried that he was losing his artistic ability. It was while he sat at the easel one morning creating a contrast between the ancient cottonwood and the solar tower that Belinda came up behind him. She set the cup of coffee beside him, then pulled the robe down from his shoulders. With soft gentle strokes her hands roamed the tense muscles of his neck and back. Love radiated from her fingers. Love soothed the anger he didn't even know was building within him. She bent down and kissed his neck. The warmth of her lips, the warmth of her love flowed to his hands. The strokes of the brush were freer, more dynamic.

Belinda studied the work for a long silent moment. "In your early work I could see each leaf in the trees on your canvas. Now you force me to see them in my mind." She paused to form her next sentence, "Now you make me more than a spectator looking at your painting. You force me to become a participant in your art."

Ben heard this as a criticism. There was the pain of a wounded soul. He stood with head bowed, the robe fell to the floor. Art was his world, and now he stood naked before his world, ashamed of his failure to create well.

Belinda embraced him and tried to explain that it was a compliment, but he couldn't hear her words. Tears of failure found their course down his cheek to the corner of his mouth. It was the pounding on the door that finally broke the mood of despair. While Belinda answered the knock, Ben retrieved his robe.

It was Chad, bursting with enthusiasm about the success of one of his solar conversion projects. As was his habit, he studied the work in progress. A long whistle escaped his lips.

"This is good." He said. "I don't know art, but I like the way you blend the colors to stimulate the mind." After a pause he added, "My mind isn't as much stimulated as it is liberated. Here you let me see what my mind can see, more than what your mind sees. Am I making any sense, Ben?"

At this Belinda started laughing, while Ben forced a smile. She kissed Chad on the cheek and turned to Ben again, "See, isn't this what I told you?"

Ben still felt that his art had lost something, that he had lost something. Through forced smiles, he shared coffee with them, then dressed. With sketch pad and pencils, he left Oblivion and climbed the long trail to the canyon rim.

It was from this vantage point that he hoped to gain some perspective, to find whatever it was that was missing from his soul.

"Harmony," the coyote said.

Ben saw the creature sitting on the rocks to his left, and his mind heard the word "harmony," But he couldn't believe the beast had spoken to him. The thought entered his mind, that he might be going crazy. He looked around for another source for the word he knew he had heard. When his eyes returned to the rock, the coyote was gone. He sat and looked down on his town. All he ever wanted was to be an artist. He had no desire to be a landowner, he had no drive to be a social experimenter, or a cutting edge environmentalist. This was all an accident. He threw his head back and screamed. A loud, long, from the

196

heart, from the soul type scream escaped his lips. Finally he fell back against the rough sandstone, exhausted.

"Sometimes that helps. Sometimes it doesn't." The voice behind him said.

Ben turned and saw the old Indian sitting calmly smoking his pipe and tightening the thongs on his drum.

"Harmony is the word. Think on it while I get this thing fixed." He opened his Swiss army knife and continued his labors with the leather.

From this vantage point he could see all of Oblivion, the slowly expanding Lake Hope, the arrays of solar collectors, the windmills and solar towers, greenhouses and artificial islands, garden plots and ant-like people scurrying about their nest. He could look far to the north and see the sunlight reflecting from the waterfall, and this made him sad because of Derritt. The burden of anger had given this young man a terrible handicap. He could barely see the charred remains of the Benton estate, and felt sadness for the self proclaimed enemy of Oblivion, Calmut Benton. How horrible it must be to see your life's work destroyed. He wondered about Brandy. He hadn't seen her since that evening when she spat at the old Indian in the church.

"She's being taken care of, just fine. You don't need to worry about her." He looked up from his drum, "There, I think that does it. Now let's talk."

"Can you read my mind?" Ben asked, not certain whether he had spoken his thoughts aloud or not.

"Sometimes it ain't easy." the old man replied. "But let's talk about you. Your problem is that possession is weighing you down. You can have help if you want it. It's waiting for you."

"You mean Murdock Hivers?"

The Indian laughed, "He is what you Anglos call 'an ass-hole.' He has no understanding of what Oblivion is about. Think on this.

Some cannot know peace until they have experienced war, cannot feel love until they have suffered hate."

Rings of smoke rose from his pipe and he smiled. "This isn't easy to do. The tobacco has to be burning evenly around the edge of the bowl and breath has to be even, with just enough force." He blew another series of smoke rings and smiled broadly, then began tapping lightly on the drum with his finger tips. It produced a sound that could be felt better than heard.

The cry of a hawk distracted Ben. When he turned, the Indian was gone, but he thought he could still hear the drum. The beat had been captured by his mind, and it soothed him. Solitude and the height of the canyon rim combined to give him a broader view, a better perspective. The soul freeing beat of the drum that continued to resonate in his mind, coupled with the warmth of the afternoon sun all contributed to the sense of freedom that swept over him. This calm liberation of his soul found its way gradually to his fingers.

The early afternoon had been spent producing several poor sketches of the valley. This was the first time Ben had tried to capture the entire community, and the magnitude of it overwhelmed him.

The voice inside his head spoke to him, "When you walk though a town, you see individuals, you pass the buildings one at a time, you see the trees one on one. From the distance, it all blends into a oneness." Ben discovered a truth on the last sketch he tried. Oblivion became a unit, a single entity unified in purpose. Within this unity he saw his harmony. The pencils pulled his hand across the paper as he relaxed. He didn't even realize he was whistling. Sketch after sketch formed under his hand. As the sun touched the west rim and cast long shadows across the valley, he drew with a fury. His mind and hand were racing with each other, but neither could keep pace with the freedom his soul felt.

He returned exhausted, but excited by the work he had done. Belinda studied the sketches, but was almost afraid to comment on them. Instead, she sat them on the easel and seated herself before it with her notepad. While Ben washed and ate, she wrote. The lines flowed from her pen with a rhythm that was the music of her soul. For hours she continued to write, page after page of verse and commentary. It was almost midnight when she finally dropped the pen to the floor. She was spent, drained by the creative experience.

Ben had been wise enough not to interrupt her train of inspiration. He walked the perimeters of Oblivion, strolled the lake front, then sat in the doorway of the jail for over an hour trying to understand what it was the Indian had been talking about. He knew he was most at peace when he was creating his art. He understood that Belinda was his love, but art was his true passion. To share his love and express his passion was all he wanted of life. Oblivion had brought him greater love than he had even known, and it had given him the freedom to truly live the life of an artist. It also gave him a heavy burden, great responsibilities. The idea didn't burst forth in a flash of light. It germinated like a cottonwood seed along a fertile bank. Tonight all that became certain to him was that there was a solution that would answer the needs of all.

He returned home to find Belinda asleep at the table. The pen had dropped to the floor. He picked her up and carried her to bed. As he undressed her, she almost awoke, but the creative effort had so depleted her physically, mentally and emotionally that he couldn't rouse her from her dreams. He took the bottle of lotion from the shelf and warmed some in his hands. As she slept, he spread the soothing cream over her feet, gently rubbing the ankles and arches, pulling the exhaustion from her. This was a pleasant exercise for Ben as well. Giving love is its own great comfort. He fell asleep in the chair, and awoke there in the morning.

Chapter Twenty

Larry returned with great news that afternoon. The University of New Mexico was now deeply and irreversibly involved in the environmental research of the "Oblivion Project" as it was called. The UNM Press was eager to also become a part of this unique experiment by publishing their book of art and poetry. But there was even more good news. The Jonson Gallery on campus wanted to do a single artist showing of Ben's work.

While he was sipping some iced tea, he glanced at the sketchpad and Belinda's writing from the night before. It was a broad smile that consumed his face. "Is this the beginning of your second book?" he asked.

Larry enjoyed the company of these two. In some way, they were kindred spirits. Perhaps it was because they were possessed by a creative drive. He was also envious of their freedom to act on those drives. He was laden with responsibilities, work assignments, and students that demanded much from him. He would dream of abandoning all this to live and labor in Oblivion. It was the sense of living life as a spectator that bothered him the most. The last two years had seen him work sporadically on a novel. He wasn't certain whether it was really writing, or if it was therapy. Whatever it was that he was searching for, he was making the long journey to Oblivion more and more often.

He had been reading the words she had written and studying the mood of Ben's sketches. When he paused in the reading to enter into the conversation, as he placed the pad on the table, his eyes were drawn to another pad that had another poem on it. The name is what first drew his attention. Across the top of the page, in bold letters was "Marquita's Dream." While he was researching a story on the Benton family, a difficult story that seemed to be going nowhere, he had talked to a severely beaten lady named Marquita in the hospital. She had rambled on about revenge and constantly quoted and cited a multitude of romance novels. At first she seemed to be living on the other side of reality. Then Larry discovered she really did have some sort of claim to a vast land grant. At least part of her story was true.

Belinda saw him reading the poem. "That's a curious little mystery. We discovered this old wooden box the day we found Derritt at the waterfall." She placed the chest on the table and opened it.

As they examined each item, photo and paper, Larry became convinced that this was somehow linked to the women he had met in Santa Fe. He soon returned from his car with his notes. The last name was Lopez, same as the one on the baptismal certificate.

"I'd like to meet her." Belinda's voice carried a sense of excitement. "She should have this poem. I had no idea . . ." She had heard about Landreth's violent beating of a girlfriend, but hadn't connected the dots. Now she wasn't certain how to handle the news. She wanted to help, but didn't know how.

Calmut had been released from the hospital into the care of one of his lawyers. An apartment had been rented in Santa Fe, and a nurse had been retained as a live-in caregiver. The old man struggled with his limited capacity to function. He reluctantly began to take short walks down Canyon Road, partly to escape the constant chatter of the nurse he referred to as his keeper. Soon these labored strolls were interrupted by greetings and brief conversations with the artists, musicians, writers, and craftsmen that made this such a unique section of the ancient city. Within two weeks, he was being invited into the galleries, studios and homes of wannabe R. C. Gormans, Tony Hillermans, and Ottmar Lieberts. These people weren't befriending Calmut Benton of Benton Enterprises. They had no knowledge of the business community. They simply enjoyed the company of Cal, this ailing old gentleman who seemed to be just now discovering the world around him.

For the first time in his life, he was listening to music. He was drawn to the soothing sounds of what he used to refer to as "New Age noise." A sculptor working in ceramic tile and molten glass invited him to sit under the elms and share coffee and ideas with her. He was learning what art and music were all about. He found himself looking forward to the mornings, the companionship, and newfound knowledge and joy they brought.

Christa Annuncia was the name she had chosen for herself when she began her new life. She had to begin again because the doctors and the judge told her she could not continue to live the way she had, and she reluctantly agreed that they were right. The drugs had burned large holes in her mind, holes that she occasionally fell through and got lost. Sometimes all she could do was sit and watch the morning glories as they opened to the dawning sun. In her old life, she wouldn't have thought twice before stealing clothing or jewelry from a store, separating lonely men from their wallets and credit cards, working scams and schemes without a conscience. It was while in prison that she learned about art. She enjoyed it, was driven by it. When she wasn't practicing her work with clay, she was studying about it. The penitentiary held a "Festival of Inmate Arts and Crafts." She sold over two hundred dollars worth of clay birds. This was a lot of money for an inmate to have. In the subterranean economy of prison life it can even be dangerous.

That night was when they came back. The voices inside her mind came again. Several of them told her to spend the money on the cocaine they so desperately needed. They told her that if she didn't feed them, they would leave her and she'd be all alone. The voice of the young girl she might once have been begged her, "Don't let them do this to us again." Then the little girl retreated to the far corner of her mind and sat hugging her knees and sobbing.

In the darkness of her cell, the clay figures she had crafted also spoke to her. They often did this. Sometimes they would keep her awake all night. This time it was the little dove that cooed softly in her ear, "I will never leave you. Tomorrow take me with you, and WE will talk to the chaplain."

This made the other voices angry. They all began talking at once. Soon they began to shout, argue and fight. She hid under her cot, but couldn't get away from them. The voices were in her hair, so she grabbed it and pulled it out in tangled handfuls. She pounded her head on the floor until finally all the voices drowned in the pool of blood and pain. Now all was silent. Silent, except for the dove who stayed with her through the night, cooing gently, with its wings spread over her to protect and comfort.

It was the prison psychiatrist, working with the chaplain, who got her transferred to the psych ward. There, the therapy chased the voices away, but everywhere she went she carried the clay dove. After all, it was now her only friend. It would talk to her when no one else had time. It told her she didn't need the other voices. They weren't real friends. She found that she could hear her own voice, and that others could hear her voice through her sculptures. Sometimes, when there was no other light than the night light imprisoned in its wire and glass cage on the ceiling, the clay dove would fly up to that light and show her what she needed to make the next day. She taught Christa to work clay, rocks and chips of tile into molten glass to make beauty for the minds of others. All of her work carried the theme of peace, a theme she so desperately sought for herself, and found so elusive.

Christa liked this old man with an eye patch whose footsteps were accompanied by the distinctive tap of a cane. This cane wasn't needed to support his body, but it did give comfort and confidence to his mind. She began to set special works out on the table under the tree, so that they could discuss them with their morning coffee. Great periods of delicious indecision preceded her clothing selection every morning. It was fun to prepare for this visitor. As nervous as a schoolgirl, she would wait for him behind the doorway that led to the small backyard.

When he appeared at the corner by Carlos Nacos' studio, she would run inside and pour the coffee. Then she would bring it to the table steaming hot, just the way Cal liked it. She had even gone downtown to purchase perfume and makeup. A trip to Estelle's transformed the unkempt stringy hair into soft waves. She sat up in her bed talking to the dove about how it would feel when he ran his fingers through the new hair. The dove told her to sleep but she was afraid that would muss the hair and damage the waves. All the men she had known in her entire life marched through one of the holes in her mind and were gone forever.

Each morning, as he rounded the corner and waved to Carlos, Calmut would straighten his shoulders and appear to gain an inch or two in height. His breathing would become deeper, his step livelier as he approached the beckoning wall covered with bright blue morning glories. He would smile and rehearse his greeting. He knew nothing of her past, in fact, wasn't the least bit concerned about it. However, he did find himself very becoming interested in her future. That was what made him smile. He hadn't been in the habit of smiling and greeting people as he walked by, but he liked it. He was even getting good at it. At first he tried to maintain his dignity, assume the pose and posture of his position in the community, but these people didn't know who he was, nor did they care. Now he understood that it didn't matter. The smile mattered. He was beginning to like artist type people, this one in particular.

As days formed links in the chain of time, Calmut found himself spending more and more of his hours with Christa. For the past two decades he had known many women, had bought the companionship he needed, paid well to satisfy the lust that drove him. Here was a women that didn't know he had money, yet she was obviously eager to share time with him. Now, he was even helping her with the molten glass, would chip the ceramic tiles for her. He, Calmut Benton, sweating over the intense heat of the horno oven she used to melt the glass. Calmut

Benton doing something that wasn't going to turn a profit. They had even started to walk the hillsides looking for stones, potsherds and gnarled pieces of wood that she could use to create birds, angels, Santos and crucifixes. His strength was returning much faster that the doctors had anticipated, but he was a different man now. He would help her make the little pocket angels from wood chips and flakes of obsidian. These they would take to the Palace of the Governors in the afternoon, and sell them to the tourists and Californios. It was fun. That's it. Cal Benton was having fun.

He spent less and less time with his business, and more and more time with his life. He gained his strength while the lawyers and accountants struggled to hold onto a crumbling empire. Then the summons came. Title court has the jurisdiction over property claims and deeds, as well as water rights. There is no jury, only a judge. Calmut couldn't understand how Marquita could claim his property, but the fight was gone from him. His staff assumed that this was a way the family whore could create trouble for the Bentons, and perhaps get a substantial out of court settlement too. It was doubtful that any Spanish land grant claim would be honored at this late date, especially since the United States Government was a co-defendant. He knew he was an old man who had waited too long to experience real life. He made a fateful decision to let Landreth and his lawyers fight this one. He was too busy making a series of glass birds.

Don Aragon had moved into his sister's apartment with Marquita. Sis disapproved, but held her tongue because she loved her brother, and felt that Marquita was good for him. She was convinced he saw himself as El Cid, while the rest of the world knew he was Don Quixote, but it was his business if he wanted to tilt windmills and make a fool of himself.

The Land Grant Foundation orchestrated the filing. They felt that timing was the key. They didn't want Calmut to be too strong.

They knew Derritt was under the care of a psychiatrist in a residential facility. Brandy was still missing, despite an nationwide search. Landreth had achieved his goal. He was now in control of Benton Enterprises, and was ready to crumble under the heavy work load. They felt that the Benton tiger had been seriously wounded and wanted to strike before it healed. The claim against the federal government was more tenuous, but this was an election year and it was felt that the politicians would want this settled as quickly and quietly as possible. They were prepared to lease the acreage back to the Bureau of Land Management for a nominal fee. Don Aragon was certain that a deal could be worked out with the Secretary of the Interior. His greatest concern was that without the missing transfer deeds, they had a weak case on the Benton property and the ghost town where the looneys were playing ecology games.

The hot afternoon sun beat down on the courthouse in Santa Fe. Landreth shivered from the cold air conditioning, as he entered the door to the judge's chambers. He had dealt with Judge Sorenson before. He was a tough, by the book adjudicator; but Landreth knew everybody had a price. The discussion was brief. The offer of stock in Benton Oil, a private corporation, was of no interest to the good judge. The suggestion that child pornography might be one of the judge's favorite pastimes brought the expected outrage.

"Of course it isn't true." Landreth calmly responded. "All you have to do is prove that to the public after it hits the evening news with all the details at eleven."

The judge pointed toward the door. His face was livid. The blood vessels on his neck and forehead appeared ready to burst. He could not speak. He dared not speak.

Landreth smiled as he walked to the phone booth and dialed the number for KOB TV's Action News Hotline. He couldn't contain the chuckles as he went through the parking garage to the judge's dark blue

Olds Cutlass. He looked carefully up and down the rows of cars. He studied the stairway and the elevator to see if anyone was watching while he struggled with the plastic gloves. Finally, he unlocked the door with his dealer's electronic master key. He quickly spread the contents of his brief case on the back seat, glossy magazines showing some of Denmark's finest quality kiddie porn and assorted photos. Then, just for good measure he added two small plastic bags of cocaine.

Unfortunately for Landreth, he failed to look up. If he had, he might have seen the security camera that dutifully recorded his every move in living color, timed and dated.

Chapter Twenty-one

Two days later, Landreth's attorneys posted his bail and soon after that a court date was set for his trial on breaking and entering, attempted defamation of character, and attempted blackmail. The Land Grant Foundation noted with a certain amount of glee the news of Landreth's troubles with the law. The case of Marquita Lopez vs Benton Enterprises and the United States of America began the next day. All the evidence was presented within the first few days. The trail of ownership was traced from original Spanish land grants through legally recorded deeds to Marquita's antecedents. There were only two holes in the paper path. One concerned the disputed ownership of a small portion of national forest land that had resulted from surveying errors. The other was an important document was the deed transfer that had an official US documentary stamp on it. This would verify recognition of the binding transfer by the territorial government. Without it, the status quo would have to remain in effect.

Larry arranged a meeting between Belinda, Ben, Marquita and Don. It was agreed that they would all gather at the waterfall at about seven that evening. Over the phone Larry read Belinda's poem to Marquita. She was confused. Surely these people understood that her suit would give her ownership of the entire valley. Her rights superseded Ben's. Why would this women write her a poem? Nobody had ever written her a poem. She didn't really understand poetry, but knew this was an honor. Don Aragon suggested that she offer to let them lease the valley at one dollar per year, in return for the deeds, the same offer they were making to the BLM.

Her mind saw images of Ernesto, of them playing in the old buildings, bathing in the water tank, making love in the grotto behind the waterfall. She didn't want to let this part of her past go. Yet, she knew that Belinda was a very sensitive person. That poem didn't have to be written; Belinda had done that for her.

Don Aragon was planning the negotiations that he would control in order to get these papers. He suspected blackmail or a scam might be in the offing. Belinda was anxious to meet the Marquita that belonged to the box of memories she carried under her arm. Ben was apprehensive. He wasn't good at people contact. If Marquita had suffered as much at the hands of the Benton's as Larry had said, then she deserved the title to these lands. His concern was for the people who had put every ounce of their hope into Oblivion. He was forming a plan. His goal was to turn over ownership of the community to her, with the promise that it would continue the way it was. He wanted the experiments to continue, the multitude of ideas planted there to have an opportunity to grow, the community to prosper in the universal tolerance that made Oblivion a welcoming oasis.

Ben, Belinda and Larry arrived early at the waterfall. The long shadows of rocks and junipers gave tiger stripes to the uneven landscape. Cholla fingers reaching up to cradle the sunlight and cast dappled patterns of shade across the grass and sandstone, creating color combinations that fascinated Ben. As an artist, he knew that shadow is a reflection, but in this clear New Mexico sunlight, for the first time he made an artistic discovery. Shadow was traditionally portrayed as a matter of black and white, but in reality it was chromatically altered, but full of color. He was mentally blending watercolors into a background for the determined cactus at his feet. "Perhaps the shadows of our minds are not cast in black and gray either." He spoke more to himself than his companions.

Belinda was studying the sky through pillars of sandstone and thinking lines about "a limitless ocean of light framed by our eye's ability to see, mind's ability to comprehend, and the soul's ability to experience." She saw the weathered rocks casting shadows ten times their size and wrote the line in her mind, "People, in their season, like these ancient rocks, cast shadows larger than life. We are capable of deeds far greater than we are, if the illumination isn't blotted out by strife."

Larry was watching the two figures walking toward them from the stream bed. He noted their apprehensive steps, and wove a story around their need to be here, and their fear of a situation they might not be able to control. Through the years of watching and reporting the actions of the human animal, he knew that control was one of the most elusive of humanity's needs. He thought of the Bentons. How control was the ineffective shield for the insecurities and fears they all possessed. The old Indian had said once, "the drive for control makes each of us our own worst enemy, when we seek to control others. This can become such a heavy burden that we can only walk downhill. But, when we learn to control ourselves, we have a walking stick that will help us to climb the great mountains." Larry had followed the progress of the trial. He knew that their case depended on the papers Belinda held in the wooden box. He was curious to see how the fear of losing would control their meeting. As a reporter he was a spectator, but because this was Oblivion, somehow, he was forced into the role of participant as well.

Don Aragon had the boldness and daring of a super athlete in his arena, the courtroom. Here, in the desert, he felt the old insecurities climbing out of the storage closet of his mind. They were like snakes slithering through his consciousness, wrapping themselves around his pillars of confidence and leaving crushed bodies behind. As he tried to help Marquita over the rough ground, his polished black loafers slipped on the loose stones, and sweat beaded on his forehead. His armpits were soaked, and great rings of moisture shouted to the world how nervous he was. He hated the desert. He only tolerated the outdoors from the security of a comfortable hiking trail, and very little of that. He studied the ground, fearful of rattlers, scorpions, spiders and insects. Scurrying lizards sent shivers down his back. He would rather face an angry judge

210

than be eye to eye with a banded gecko. The constant squawking of the birds was an annoying distraction. His grand plans of a "power confrontation" were evaporating with the sweat that was drying to salt crystals on his designer shirt.

Marquita stepped lightly over the rocks, as the gleeful audacity of youth reclaimed her spirit. She found delight in the darting of the little creatures of the desert, in the smells of the juniper and wildflowers. She even caught a glimpse of a coyote beneath the saltbush. An owl opened its sleepy eyes as they passed a twisted old juniper. These joys couldn't mask for long the reality of the scars on her face, the puffy bruises, the healing wounds that made her feel insecure. Her beauty had carried her through life thus far, but now that was gone.

Even after the artful scalpel of talented surgeons, she knew she would never be attractive again. Her thoughts bounced back and forth between the meeting with people she didn't know for a purpose she couldn't comprehend, and the wheezing knight in shining armor at her side. As is often the case with love, she didn't see his fear of the desert. She felt the wet palms as she took his hand to lead him over the rocks of the arroyo, but she saw the dynamic defender waving his ball point scepter at the judge. She also saw the youthful Ernesto. As they paused to kiss, she could feel Ernesto's body pressed tightly against hers. She could smell the expensive cologne, but her memory held tightly to the Old Spice a boy had borrowed from his father.

Her adult reading was limited to romance novels, and everyone she met became a character from one of them. This was the way she dealt with people. She turned them into fictional characters. The Bentons had been pirates, plundering and raping, Don Aragon was a crusading knight, Ernesto was the lusty athlete with a beautiful body. She didn't know the people she could see across the stream bed, so she couldn't assign them roles.

211

Their steps slowed as self doubt became a heavy load for both of them. Don Aragon needed the structure of the courtroom, the rules of conduct, the legal jargon, the comfort of his organized notes and procedures. He forced his mind to turn the sandstone ledge at the base of the waterfall into a bench. The cascading water became the judge. Now he was ready.

Marquita could feel the last of her confidence draining away through the healing wounds beneath her eyes and under her jaw. Unwanted tears flowed down her cheeks. She took a deep breath, and flashed pictures of Landreth and Derritt in front of her. She saw them as pirates on a desert island. Mutineers had them in chains, bound helpless to the rocks, as snakes and wolves gathered around them. She pictured them on the cover of a romance novel, "Deserving Revenge." She saw Don Aragon dueling with them, and could see them both fall to his sword. Now, she was ready to face these people from Oblivion.

Ben and Belinda waded out into the shallow stream to meet them halfway. Ben extended his hand in friendship, while Belinda handed Marquita the wooden chest. As she took the box into her hands, Belinda gave her a hug.

"Welcome to Oblivion," Ben said with a smile that confused the lawyer. This was supposed to be a confrontation. "We have some Sandia Vineyards wine and fresh horno baked bread." Ben was leading them to the blanket and picnic basket. "The fruit was grown in Oblivion, and the cheese was even made here."

Larry was busy getting photos of this historic meeting. As they neared his position by the blanket, he activated the mini-recorder in his briefcase. He knew he was someday going to write the history of this community.

Belinda kept her arm around Marquita as they crossed the stream. There was so much warmth and caring, that Marquita became instantly comfortable with Ben and Belinda. Almost instantly she became overwhelmed with a sense of belonging, a sense of coming home. All the apprehension was gone.

As Larry poured the wine and served the meal, Belinda and Marquita went through the contents of the chest. It was curious that it was the photos that she examined first. She told stories about each of them, described her family, even shared some of the adventures she and Ernesto had in the old ghost town. She giggled with Belinda over some whispered comments about the water tank.

Finally the documents that held the future of Oblivion in their faded signatures were brought into the afternoon light. The lawyer had forgotten that he was supposed to be negotiating with an enemy. He had expected to have to offer a set of threats and bribes, battle for control of the situation. Instead, they were handing him what Marquita needed the most. Ben was reassured by Marquita's obvious love of the town. He was both intrigued and pleased that Belinda and Marquita were visiting like good friends separated by long years. Marquita was beginning to grasp what Oblivion was about. Without thinking, she hadn't assigned these people roles in a romance novel. She was dealing with reality.

Ben and Don Aragon chatted easily about the Benton family, and how the land grant hearing was progressing. Ben was waiting for an opportunity to offer them the community, with the terms he had envisioned. Don was so intrigued by the welcome they had received and the enthusiasm Ben had for the people and ideas that Oblivion had attracted, that he was eager to offer them the deal he had proposed to Marquita. If there could be this much good and love coming from this old town, he wanted to do nothing to interfere

As the sun began its final retreat before the advancing moon, they all began the trek back to Oblivion. Don didn't even notice that his fears and apprehension about the desert were gone. He stepped lightly and listened intently to each of the evening sounds. He even picked a daisy and tucked it behind Marquita's ear. She smiled and kissed him

213

lightly. As she approached the edge of Oblivion, Ernesto shouted something in her mind. She pictured him standing in a doorway. Then she saw herself closing the door and locking it. She gave Don a warm hug and another kiss.

They walked past the solar collectors and towers built to harvest the light. They listened to the calm whirr of the windmills, as they turned the ever present breeze into electricity. They toured Lake Hope with the last rays of the sun. Marquita was intrigued with the floating gardens that covered the lake. Introductions were made as they walked through the town, and finally entered the church. There, many of the people had gathered to discuss the day. The children were going over field notes with several of the environmentalists that were working on field studies. The Chavez brothers were discussing a pumping system with Dr. Carson, who had organized the lake project. Rita Alverez and her husband Pietro were talking with some children about the way to tell the difference between several of the grapes they were growing. Luis was having a problem with one of his sheep, and was getting advice from several other residents. The old Indian was sitting up by the altar talking with a small group while he tapped slowly on the drum.

Marquita was drawn to him. As she moved toward the front of the church, she passed the niches that held the Santos. She could remember a youth and herself playing with the wooden carvings as children. Her mind pictured the youth with Don Aragon's face. Her face reddened when she recalled one afternoon in their early teens, as they were discovering each other in new ways. She remembered turning each of the Santos around to face the wall, so they couldn't see what was happening.

The old Indian smiled and motioned for her to sit down beside him. "Welcome to Oblivion, Marquita. We've been expecting you."

She didn't know how he knew her name. No introductions had been made.

214

"I was just about to tell a story. Would you and your friends care to join us?" Without waiting for an answer, he stood and took the flute from the bag. As he walked toward the door, many followed. Marquita took Don Aragon's hand as they passed, and he joined them. His scepticism fell prey to the warmth of a lover's smile.

There was a small fire beside the old stable-garage. Several people were already there, playing guitars and singing ballads in Spanish. The old Indian put away his flute as he seated himself before the flames. The night chill had driven many of those present to seek the warmth of their jackets.

"Come closer," he said softly as he motioned them toward the fire. Marquita and Don were certain that he spoke to them. His eyes seemed to gaze deeply into theirs, so deeply that he could see their hearts. Don Aragon felt uncomfortable in this strange old man's presence.

"Come close, and warm your hands." There was a pause. His soft tapping of the drum joined the cords of the guitar. "Come still closer, and warm your hearts."

They did as he had invited. They watched the flames dancing, they felt the warmth of the flames and the warmth of their love. Marquita also felt a power beyond that, an energy that stimulated her soul as it soothed her body. Don's feet stopped hurting; Marquita's jaw lost its pain in a smile. Still Don felt naked, exposed and inferior before this wretched old faker, this sideshow relic.

"Shhhhhhh. Listen to the voice of the fire."

They all directed their ears as to the comforting rustle of the flames, punctuated by the crackle of the pitch as it exploded in the pinon logs. The blending of the fire sounds was almost a symphony.

"Do you see the lessons of the fire?"

The New Mexico twilight is but a momentary interlude between the cycle of light and darkness, between the day's warmth and the night's chill. As they gazed into the flames, the sun died.

Instinctively, they moved closer to the heat of the flames. Still, no response was made.

The old Indian smiled as he reached into the flames, "There is the comfort of warmth here, and the security of light." He paused for a moment, his hand suspended in the flames. "But look. If I pull one of these branches out, its flame fades." The stick in his hand had a flame dancing on the end of it. As he held it aloft, the fire withered into a glowing coal. This again faded into gray ashes and black charcoal. "Do you see that the fire is more than the total of the flames from each stick?"

Don Aragon was expecting some sideshow trick and pulled his mind back away from the thoughts of all the others. Marquita was trying to understand. Other thoughts than hers seemed to be entering her mind to help, but she didn't know what to do with them, so they went away.

"Oblivion is like that. If each of us is alone, we would be like the tiny fire, easily defeated by the world around it. But," With these words he reintroduced the twig to the community of flames, "But, when the individual sticks are joined together we light the whole street. We warm everyone's hands."

He leaned back to let them breathe in the words of his lesson. While he waited, he tapped the drum. The flames danced to his beat.

"When we all gather together in our village it is like the branches all burning together. Each stick makes a contribution to the fire. Each flame is the work of that twig."

Marquita interrupted, "I see, and the flame of the fire is far greater than the total flames of each branch. Is that what you are telling us?"

He smiled at her willingness to participate. Don Aragon was embarrassed that she had fallen for such a corny parlor trick and glanced around to see what the shaman or charlatan was going to try to sell to them.

216

"True. Each piece adds to the fire. Now I ask you another question. Which is more important? Is it the grass and flakes of bark that were the first ignited sparks of the idea of the fire? Or is it the twigs that nurtured the flames? Or, perhaps you might conclude that the heaviest logs that sustain the inferno are the most significant?"

They wrestled with this and each of those assembled formed ideas of their own, but none was willing to risk the embarrassment of answering wrongly.

"Is the log able to cast more than shade without the spark of ideas and dreams?

They all agreed that the answer was, "no."

"What does the twig nurture without the log?

"I see what you are saying. "Marquita was caught up in the flow of his words and lessons. "Each of us has a place in the community, a job, a contribution to make. By doing what each of us can, by working together, all survive and thrive." She was proud of her ability to voice these thoughts before a group of strangers.

After these last words were spoken, the Old Indian buttoned the denim jacket and picked up the flute. He silently turned and walked into the night. The soft peaceful notes faded into the distance, to be replaced with the yelp and howl of a coyote. Those gathered discussed the story as they returned to their homes. The crisp coolness of the desert night, illuminated by a full moon and billions of stars was an awesome sight to Marquita and Don. Ben and Belinda took special delight in it as well. It was the kind of a night that forced lovers to hold each other close and share the warmth of kisses, with the suggestion of more.

The pain from a broken jaw had made romance difficult for Marquita, but tonight her longing matched Don Aragon's desire. In a whispered conversation, it was agreed that they would spend the night in Oblivion. Ben and Belinda had thought at first that separate accommodations would be in order for the client and her attorney, but as the evening progressed, it became obvious that some privacy together might be more appropriate.

Larry stood by the fire and watched as Ben and Belinda walked hand in hand down the street. He watched Marquita and Don embrace and kiss with uninhibited passion. His shoulders drooped as he made his way to his car. An almost overwhelming sadness washed over him. It was going to be a long, lonely drive back to Albuquerque.   The four sat in Ben's studio chatting and laughing for over an hour, before Belinda asked where Larry had gone. Ben, for the first time, realized that Larry was alone, and lonely. He had done so much for the four of them, arranging for the publishing of their book, an exhibit of his art at the Jonson Gallery, delivering the deeds to Marquita. They had even neglected to include him in their conversation. They had forced him to be a spectator again. Ben knew that to be a spectator to some one else's love is cruel. He vowed to seek a solution. He would talk with Courtney about this.

Belinda missed Larry's intellectual input. If he'd been here, he could have answered many of their questions, provided insight, made a whole out of the fragments of ideas, friends and facts. She missed his calm confidence, his sad eyes and easy smile, his graying hair and purposeful stride.

Don Aragon felt awkward in the home of an artist and poet. He could not study Ben's art with a trained eye. He understood nothing of the artist's use of color, depth, intensity or tone. Many of the messages were beyond him. Ben could sense this, and knew that for most people art is a foreign language. The attorney did study the variety of works, and instinctively knew that this reflected the work of a gifted talent. Marquita began to read some of Belinda's poetry, but gave up as Belinda delivered a reading to them.

It was while she was reading "Song of Time" that Don spotted the guitar in the corner. Ben had borrowed it, because he wanted to have the children draw the instrument during one of their art classes.

Don picked it up without thinking, and began to softly work the strings so they would release their magic.

His agile fingers picked up the cadence of Belinda's words and the "Song of Time" was set to music. The words and music went well together, so well that Marquita began to hum. As Belinda read the last lines of her poem, Marquita mated them with the music and sang them. She took the poem from Belinda's hand and sang the entire piece. Her voice was softly melodic. The healing jaw limited her range, but gave subtle strength to every note. Her voice made love with the voice of the strings. Don Aragon and Marquita discovered new talent in each other. His playing had a bittersweet memory. His brother, Julio, had been a student at UNM, and had studied classical guitar and dreamed of a music career. Then, in the service of a cause he could not understand, he lost his life in a jungle war. For several years, Don had worked and studied the instrument. He enjoyed music. He liked its structure, its order. To him, music was math. His father suffered greatly from the loss of Julio, and talked his younger son into pursuing law as a career. Music was a constant reminder of the loss; a wound neither father or brother could come to terms with. At first, Don missed the music; but law was order, rules, almost a math. He followed his parent's wishes and became a very good lawyer, fighting for hopeless causes, battling injustice in the courtroom, and crusading for the rights of his people. The wisdom of their control over his life was evident in the pending decision that would make him both rich and famous.

Tonight, however, he felt again his youth, his joy in a life of freedom that music could grant. This was the first he had held the instrument in years. He could feel the warmth of the wood as he caressed it. The sensual vibrations of the strings as they came alive to the touch of his fingers aroused other feelings deep within his being. It was the sense of wholeness, of purpose that one feels in those rare moments when they are in harmony with their destiny. Ben could do nothing other than draw the picture of life. Belinda was content only when she could write the words of life. Don Aragon, in one of those flashes of insight that can change ones entire existence, understood that he must play the music of life.

Marquita finished her song with new found strength. The voice that, in its youth, had sung of joy, was free again. There was an intense exhilaration that quickened her breathing, freed her mind, and fulfilled her soul. The voice that had been stilled since the afternoon of the rape in the cave, had finally been liberated. She felt within her soul a goodness that had been suffocated by shame. The burden of a guilt that should not have been hers was lifted by hands she could not see, and her voice proclaimed her victory. Joy returned with the inner sense that her mission was to sing the song of life.

Fresh fruit, wine and cheese were shared, as well as the passion for creativity that these four possessed. In this small circle, this bond of friendship, they could each speak freely of the profound mystery, and the almost orgasmic excitement of producing beauty. Ben speculated that the talent sleeps deep within everyone, waiting for the awakening dawn. Don argued that while everyone can be moved by music, only a few dare to let themselves be musicians.

Belinda was the one that proposed a theory, "I think we are all born with some talent. As children, don't we all sing and dance and beat on drums and delight in fists full of crayons?"

Marquita, laughed, "Yes, until we color outside the lines, until we spell words wrong, until we are shamed by notes that are missed."

"That's just the point," Ben added. "We all think we can sing, and dance, draw and write, play our music with the beat of a drum or the plink of piano keys. Then we are told we can't color outside the lines, we can't put our own words in a song, we can't create our own tunes. The adults convince the children they can't sing, can't draw, can't even play baseball well enough."

"Yes," Belinda almost shouted, "We convince children they can labor, but they can't create. So we market people to sing for them, do

220

their art, play their music, even play their games for them. We force our society to live by somebody else's melody, to be spectators to our own lives and wonder why our personal harmony is so elusive."

Ben continued, "As artists, and we are all artists, we have an obligation to show society the power each human being has within his or her soul to make each life a work of art, a beautiful song, an existence filled with meaning. That my friends," he lifted the wine glass high in a toast, "is what Oblivion is all about." Then, as he swallowed the last of the beverage, he began to think of what he had just said. He realized that he could not be content just painting anymore. He had to be in Oblivion to be in Harmony. This was both a disturbing and a liberating revelation. It is sometimes disturbing to come face to face with your destiny, and realize there's no place to hide.

They all slept late. The heady thrill of new-found friendships, rediscovered talents, well spent passions, and a brief sense of harmony let them all rest well. They probably would have slept much longer, if it hadn't been for the arrival of a motorcycle.

Chapter Twenty-two

Emilio Franco saw himself swooping into town with the roar of a heavy Harley. In reality, it was more the sputtering sounds of mechanical farts and the wheezing of an asthmatic engine that brought Ben to the door. The vision of a middle aged man with love beads, sandals, a straggly beard and sweatband was not the most welcoming way to wake from a night of joy. A short black cape fluttered in the breeze. It had a green tree painted on it, the same shade as the helmet that was tied to the top of the bundles of leaflets that formed a tenuous backrest for this self proclaimed super hero.

"Take me to your leader." He said as he struggled to separate his body from the machine.

Ben extended his hand in greeting, to what he feared was a refugee from a psycho ward.

"I have an important message for the mayor of this community."

"We don't have a mayor. I'm Ben. I own Oblivion." He was ready to go into an explanation of how he had won the former ghost town, but his visitor interrupted.

"Halt! Halt! Stop that this instant!" He shouted, racing toward Carlos who was coming up the street munching on a stalk of celery. "Cease and desist. In the name of the Cosmic Order and the Organic Laws of Nature, I command you to release that poor wretched celery."

Carlos held the vegetable at arms length and turned it in his hand, trying to see what was wrong with it.

"You fiend. I, I am Emilio Franco, Defender of Botanical Rights, Crusader for vegetable justice." He pulled the belt from his pants and lashed out at Carlos. "Don't you understand? Plants have rights, too."

"Are you crazy, Man?" Carlos queried as he seized the belt in his hand and stared Emilio in the eye.

222

"They told me my mission would not be easy, that I would meet with failure and ridicule, that the guilty would mock and persecute me. I am ready for this abuse. I am ready to shed blood for my cause, even if it must be my own."

In the fray, the stalk of celery had fallen to the ground. The caped crusader knelt and gently picked it up. He cradled it in his arms and murmured soothing sounds to it. With a maniacal glare he turned to Ben. "How could you let this atrocity happen in your town? I thought you grasped the environmental needs of nature."

Ben had, in the past few months, encountered a wide variety of people with causes, some logical, some rather exotic, but nothing like this. In truth, he enjoyed meeting with some of the fringe element of the environmental movement, because they approached their life with passion. He could understand the reverence for life of the tree huggers. He understood the animal rights people, and viewed their cause with a sympathetic soul. The crystal people were seeking answers in beauty, and that in itself was a form of art. The peaceniks, those hoping for an end to violence were made welcome in Oblivion. Those constructively working toward alternative energy sources, more harmonic life styles, and a broader concept of education were valuable additions to the community.

Those who entered Oblivion with hatred, were filled with negative thoughts, would take up the sword rather than the pen or the spade, were out of harmony and never remained long. There was no need for violence in this community. There was no time for it. It was much more important to be for something, than to be against anything.

Emilio Franco at first amused Ben, but the attack with the belt caused some alarm. He did as he had done with every visitor to Oblivion. He invited Emilio to speak to the community at the nightly gathering in the church. It was a matter of principle with Ben. Every idea should be heard, with an open mind, then judged fairly.

"Good decisions can be made if we inform ourselves, question intelligently, listen carefully, and discuss openly," Ben offered in an attempt to sooth the rage within this fanatic.

"No!" He shouted. "I will not set foot inside a church. They have ripped the children from the arms of their mothers to make the bread and wine. Don't you understand how wrong that is? Can't you see that plants are living beings? Don't you care that they have feelings, too?"

Carlos entered the conversation. "It is a way of nature that one life feeds another. Doesn't the rabbit eat the grass, then the coyote eats the rabbit. Then in the coyote's death, the grass is fed again. Don' you think life is a cycle?"

He gave a loud anguished cry, "Aughhh! The ignorance of the damned." With that he untied the bundle of leaflets from his bike and thrust one at Ben and Carlos.

"This explains the rights of plants to exist in their natural role as the giver of oxygen, healer of the soil, caster of shade."

"What do you eat?" Carlos asked, keeping a wary eye on the belt griped tightly in Emilio's hand.

"This tells you all about the proper diet for all humanity. Dairy products contain almost all the nutrients you need. Milk and cheese, these are ideal foods. Fallen fruit can also be harvested, but only after the child has naturally left the protective branches of the parent plant. But care must be taken to preserve the seeds and plant them where they can grow. Don't you see how simple it is?"

He gave them no opportunity to respond. Without another word, he turned and walked down the street handing leaflets to anyone he met. He then started throwing them in the air. Several children came running after him, shouting at him to stop littering, as they gathered the papers in their arms.

Emilio walked through the gardens, wept at the sight of Inez' herbs drying on the porch, cursed the scientists working with the

224

artificial islands of crops on the lake, and scolded the children who were tending a plot of vegetables. He muttered to himself about the ignorance and cruelty of all people, everywhere. The residents tried to be courteous but he berated them and screamed about their disgusting consumption of body parts ripped from living beings. A carpenter sawing a piece of wood for a door frame retreated under his barrage of curses about being a tree butcher, building a house of bones.

He had wandered through the town until, exhausted by the horrors he had seen, he sought shelter and respite under the ancient cottonwood. The scream could be heard from one end of Oblivion to the other. There sat Courtney, holding a bouquet of flowers, while she took a dainty bite of a fresh squash blossom.

Emilio was genuinely horrified. "How could you do such a thing?" He seized the flowers from her and caressed them. "Isn't it bad enough to eat the life giving leaves of a lettuce plant, or the sustaining roots of a carrot? Must you commit unpardonable mutilations, and consume the sex organs of these gentle plants as well?"

Courtney stood, assumed her most benign smile, and studied the figure before her. "Do you understand nothing of the system, the role each of us plays? Why do you curse me for gathering my natural beauty around me? Do you also curse the larva of the butterfly that consumed the pubescent buds before their fulfilment?"

Emilio stepped back to assess his opponent. "That caterpillar is a part of nature."

"And you are not?" she interrupted.

She took him by the hand and led him into the arroyo behind them. She pointed to the intricate spider web that had been spun between the branches of a juniper and a rock. "See that web?"

He nodded, unsure what was coming next.

"Think of this as a symbol. We are all a part of the web of life woven by the Great Mystery." She look deeply into his eyes. He felt an intense power emanating from her. She spoke as if she were a part

225

of the Great Mystery itself. "In this blanket of nature," she spread her arms to encompass the landscape of the valley, "woven of leaves and petals, hair and feathers, fins and scales, is a beauty of function and purpose. It is up to you whether you wish to be a thread in the fabric of life, or a piece of lint."

He forced his eyes to look away from this lady, "You know nothing of nature. It is our duty to defend it, yet we defile and destroy these lovely plants."

The anger rose in her throat, and she struggled for control. Those who knew the true nature of Courtney were well aware of her ability to be forceful, to exert great power. The wind rose behind them, and pulled the sand into the whirling dervish of a dust devil. While Courtney smiled, it swept over Emilio, knocking him to the ground.

When he stood, she was gone. He dusted himself off and marched through the gathered crowd.

The old Indian came around the corner of the library and greeted the humiliated crusader.

"Here. I have just what you need." He handed the eco-crusader a small leather pouch.

Emilio opened it, and puzzled over the pale yellow dust inside. "What is this?"

"Corn pollen. A pinch is tossed to the rising sun each morning, as a prayer to help you find your way to harmony."

"Aughhh." Was all he uttered as he threw the pouch to the ground and ran toward his cycle.

The old Indian laughed, "It's good for your rheumatism too."

As he struggled to get his mechanical steed in motion, Oblivion's residents sought to sooth his troubled soul with kind words and small gifts. Someone began to play a guitar. A quiet young lady possessed of a subtle beauty began to dance. She took his hand and drew him away from the smoking cycle, into the midst of the impromptu fiesta.

226

"This is the day we celebrate God's gift of the flowers," she said as she drew him into the rhythm of the dance. "We honor the beauty by surrounding ourselves with it." She took a rose from someone's hand and tucked it into his sweatband. Another was offered, and it was placed in the chains of his beads. "It is the custom of our people to thank each plant for its gifts of color and fragrance. Then we water, tend, and care for them." She took a thermos from the hand of one of the assembling crowd, poured the contents on an aster with its cushion of lavender blossoms. She then returned her attention to Emilio, "Don't you see? We nurture the plants and they nurture us. This is what the scientists call a symbiotic relationship, but I think we instinctively know that it is the way of all life."

He started to say something, but it was difficult to put words together while he was watching her swaying hips.

"All life is a symbiotic relationship, because all life depends on each other. This town is like that, too. If a community of people is to thrive, each citizen must play a part. Life has no time for spectators." She paused and looked into his eyes. Her smile melted the crusader. She hugged him as they continued to sway to the music. "You, however, are not a spectator. You are a dynamic leader, and even if you are a little misguided, you are driven by a zeal that few know. Won't you stay and share your ideas with us tonight?"

Her eyes were difficult to refuse. She and Emilio wandered through the town. This time, handshakes replaced invectives. Emilio felt a great emptiness within him being filled. He was accustomed to harshness, cruel insults, ridicule of himself and his ideas. Several times people asked him questions about his cause. They were willing to sit and discuss his ideas, far more willing than he had been. He met Dirty Maria, and felt an instant bond with her. Perhaps it was because, before Oblivion, she had been ridiculed for her bulk, her sometimes questionable ideas about education, her failure to adhere to fashion dictates. They were both crusaders, out of step with their times. Not only did they march to a different drummer, as Maria had said on several occasions, "I am the different drummer."

The dancer left Maria and Emilio to discuss their respective causes. She was convinced that it was love at first sight for both of them. What a perfect couple they made, an aging hippie and an obese chronic student, both driven by Quixotically noble causes. To make life more interesting for them both, the Great Mystery had made Maria a vegetarian.

Serena was the name of the dark haired dancer turned matchmaker. She had come to Oblivion from, no one knew where. In the several months she had been a part of the community, she had helped every one with their tasks, but remained shy. Ben had met her, but spoken only two or three times with her. She was an elusive mystery to them all.

Today, she was the reason the old Indian had come down from the canyon rim where he had been spending most of his summer. He smiled a greeting and complimented her on the way she handled Mr. Emilio Franco. Then they sought the afternoon shade of the cottonwoods, while he explained the project he had in mind and expressed the hope that she would become a part of it.

She was flattered that he had thought of her, but felt she was neither qualified nor good enough to tackle such a mission. She enumerated on her fingers others that would be better suited for the challenge. Of course, in the end she was following him up the steep trail away from Oblivion.

The top of the canyon rim was barren, but the small stone shelter had cactus and other desert flowers growing around it. Courtney met them at the doorway of the structure with a knowing smile.

"She's in here," the old Indian said as he led Serena by the hand into the small room. A window provided all the light there was, but the light fell across the sleeping face of a woman perhaps thirty years of age.

"Brandy has been recovering from a confrontation with her brothers. Her leg was badly broken, as were several ribs. Our medicine," he gestured from Courtney to himself, "has healed her body. She is well enough now for you to work with her spirit. She needs to know your gentleness.

With that Courtney and the old Indian left the two alone in the building.

Serena sat before Brandy, unsure what it was she was to do. Outside the window grew a cholla cactus, its many arms bearing both the fruit of earlier blossoms and the lavender-purple flowers of today. Brandy stretched and opened her eyes. Serena smiled, unsure of her mission, but sensing the depression and fear that so totally controlled the lady on the cot.

Brandy saw the stranger and drew herself into a fetal position with her arms wrapped around her head. A low whimper was all that escaped her lips. Serena put a gentle hand on her shoulder. Brandy shivered and cringed at the touch. The old Indian began to play the flute somewhere in the distance. The wind made the cholla branch dance before the window. Serena carefully plucked one of the flowers from the plant and held it in front of Brandy.

"This is for you." The voice was calm, soothing, filled with compassion.

Brandy peeked out from under her arms and studied the waxen petals. The sun shone through their translucence to cast a lavender shadow across her face and arm. She almost smiled.

"I'm a friend you don't know yet." The voice was almost lyrical. Serena reached out to take Brandy's hand. She placed the flower in her hand and smiled. You don't know it yet but you have many friends in Oblivion.

For the first time in several months, Brandy spoke. "I have no friends. I have no family." She spoke as the depression in her head dictated. She knew she must not feel any joy; pleasure was only the

229

avenue to more pain. Her mind was fighting to keep the smile from forming on her lips. She felt shame at abandoning her father, humiliation at the hands of her brothers, loss from the burning of the estate, confusion from her isolation. Yet, the depression that gripped her so tightly was being unraveled by the gentle touch of the flower in the palm of her hand.

The notes from the flute spoke of safety, the soft petals of the cactus blossom told her that even within the harshest spines beauty can grow. Serena was telling her that life was like the cactus. The thorns of life provide the shelter for the beauty it holds. She couldn't follow the words. Her mind twisted them around, dismembered and reassembled the sounds, but the way they were spoken was comforting. Serena took her hand and helped her to her feet.

They walked to the doorway and looked out on the barren mesa. The sun felt warm, and its light was a welcoming invitation to something new. Her mind fought with her soul; told it terrible, horrible lies. Serena led her into the sunshine, one cautious step at a time. There was pain in Brandy's legs, it still hurt her to breathe, but the light carried it all away. They sat on a rock and studied the earth and the sky before them. Serena pointed to the beauty of the clouds, soft pillows in the endless blueness. It was Brandy who saw the cactus wren flit from branch to branch in the cholla. A smile escaped her when she heard the chirp of fledglings and saw the nest. The lizard that was sunning itself was comfortable with their presence. The barrenness of the landscape now seemed to teem with life. Wild morning glories held their bright white and pink flowers up for her to see. The magenta blossoms of the desert four-o'clocks formed a mound behind her. The lavender flowers of the rabbit-thorn were contrasted with their red berries and silvery leaves. Serena pointed out the small flowers of a desert phlox and the tiny yellow blossoms and thread-like leaves of the Indian tea. Not far away from them were several yucca with their seeds stalks providing sustenance for assorted birds and insects. A roadrunner raced past them, several ravens called from behind the ancient stone shelter, and a hummingbird visited first a penstemon then one of the Indian paintbrush.

Brandy's soul was smiling; in time, her mind would have to do likewise. Serena began to tell her stories about the spiders, animals, and plants they saw. The flute music was replaced with the steady beat of the drum. Serena stood and took Brandy by the hands, slowly leading her in the movements of the dance.

Suddenly, tears streamed down Brandy's face. Inconsolable sobs made her body tremble. She crumbled to the ground. Serena knelt next to her. Brandy began to pour out all the pain and misery that had been the poison within her.

Serena held her hand as they walked through the mists of time. They saw many shadows of her past. It was unfortunate that the dark events always block the sustaining rays of the good from our vision. Through the clouds, she saw her brothers and relived her life back to a troubled childhood, filled with criticism and correction, with no room for compassion or love. They stood beside the bed and watched her mother die again. She clutched Serena's hands as they witnessed the parade of young men that her father forbid her to date because they weren't worthy. The women visiting her father and brothers was a second parade. She lamented the lack of love and caring that pervaded her life. She shed many tears over the loneliness that filled her being, and left her so hungry for someone to talk to, thirsting for anyone who would listen.

They returned through a fog that evaporated once they were back on the canyon rim. A chipmunk cautiously approached Brandy, sniffed her hand, then sat up, staring at her. She reached out and touched it gently on the head. It didn't run. Rather, it placed its tiny paw on her ankle. Her smile was broad and she felt the warmth of it deep inside.

She understood that her inner joy was at the departure of the demons that had controlled her for so many years. With unsteady steps, she followed Serena to the edge of the canyon rim. They looked down on the community of Oblivion.

After several minutes of silence, she turned to Serena, "What is that place? I was there once, but that seems so long ago, so far away."

Chapter Twenty-three

Brandy's recovery wasn't swift. Depression cannot be cured by one friendly smile. It is mortal battle, warfare with the demons of one's own mind and body. For Brandy to welcome the sunrise, she had to slay the monster that told her she had always been the failure of her family. To smile at the baby wrens, she killed the fiendish sense of hopelessness. The most fearsome foe was loneliness, for it wasn't an enemy she could destroy herself. The first journey off the canyon rim was to the mission at Chimayo. The parked by the little gift shop and sat silently studying the centuries old chapel. The sand colored structure itself was small. The weathered wooden gates were framed by massive ancient junipers. It seemed to belong to the landscape, to be a natural part of the New Mexico hill country. Serena spoke reverently of the healings that had taken place within these walls.

Brandy wasn't into religious experiences. In years past, she had ridiculed the so-called miracles, mocked the lines of pilgrims on their journey of faith to this holy spot. Still, on this day, as they stood in the doorway, she felt a heavy weight lifted from her mind. As she sifted the healing soil through her fingers and listened to Serena's prayers she felt something inside her gaining strength. She couldn't identify it or put a name to it, but she felt a sense of comfort and peace that she had never known before.

As the days turned to weeks and summer began to age, Brandy gained some small victories. The old Indian spent long evenings playing the flute, and talking with her about how harmony was possible for her when she could focus on others as well as herself. Serena greeted her mornings with a smile and lessons in Spanish. Calmut had forbidden his children to study other languages, and wouldn't even permit guests to speak anything other than English in his house. In his mind that was un-American. Now, she was enjoying the sense of defiant independence as much as the insight gained by acquiring a second language. She missed her father, and in a way she couldn't explain, she even missed her brothers.

One evening the old Indian told her she missed her childhood, then, with the flute, he took her back to her youth. She was crying because Derritt and Landreth had hanged her teddy bear. When she wouldn't stop screaming at them, they tore it apart and threw the head at her. Daddy was scolding her from the window of his office. Now he was coming toward her, his face red his hand raised. He pulled a ten dollar bill from his pocket and, as he slapped her face with his left hand tossed the money on the ground in front of her. "Go get yourself another damn bear," he told the five year old girl. Chi was the one that wrapped comforting arms around her and carried her into the house speaking soothing words in a language she couldn't understand.

In the next visit to her youth she was sixteen. She smiled at herself in the frilly white and blue dress nervously waiting for Bo Belsky to arrive and escort her to the homecoming dance. She watched over the shoulder of her teenaged self as he drove up to the house. She relived the horror of her brothers teasing him as he got out of his aging Chevy. She tried to shout and stop them from doing what she knew was going to happen.

The old Indian placed his hand on her shoulder and whispered to her, "You cannot change what has been, but you can change what will be. You have the power to change all the pasts yet to come. History does not repeat itself, but we relive it, over and over again in our minds, until we learn enough of its lessons to face tomorrow. What lessons are you learning now?"

Brandy the teen was humiliated and shamed by the events that followed. Today's Brandy was angry. Her rage increased as Landreth taunted the youth about his intentions regarding his kid sister. Then it all happened so quickly. Derritt stepped in front of the boy to block his path to the house. Bo started to step around him. Derritt grabbed his

234

shirt and tore it as he pushed him into the side of his Chevy. Bo swung with his right arm and knocked Derritt to the ground. Landreth seized his arms from behind while Derritt regained his feet. Then the beating began. The brothers pounded on his chest and abdomen until Bo crumbled into a heap beside his car. Derritt stripped the moaning youth naked, laughed as he pointed at his genitals, and, as he pulled him to his feet, spat in his face and shouted, "You ain't got the balls to stud Brandy." Landreth had opened the car door and Bo was scurrying to gain the security of his vehicle. Derritt aimed a kick at his groin but caught the car door instead. As Bo made his hasty and humiliating retreat the brothers threw rocks at the car. Then they gathered Bo's cloths and buried them in the manure piled behind the stable.

Other visits to childhood followed, at each of these her feelings of shame and failure were replaced with anger and the gradual growth of a feeling that she could influence events in her life. The old Indian would tell her often about the symbiotic relationship between the past and the future; how the blanket of one's life is woven of many fibers, of many colors. Over a campfire one evening he told her how everyone she meets moves the shuttle across the warp of her life blanket, as she weaves a thread into theirs. "We are, literally the product of everyone we meet." After many such journeys, she thought she understood. When she closed her eyes and opened her mind, she could see her blanket. She could see that it was only begun. There was a border of dark colors, but spots of brightness were beginning to show. She was pleased that there was much of her life blanket to go.

It was at the time of the cicada's song that a plan was made. Serena worked with Brandy's hair. Sitting in the warm morning sun Brandy delighted in the way Serena gracefully moved around her, combing and curling to make waves. When she looked in the mirror the rays gave a glow to her hair that matched the radiance of her face. When Brandy looked at herself now she felt beautiful. She smiled, not at her appearance reflected in the mirror, not at Serena. She smiled at the world. That afternoon Serena and Brandy went into Santa Fe to shop for clothes. They laughed over lunch at the Coyote Cafe, walked through the Georgia O'Keeffe museum, and stood silently in the Chapel of Loretto. Brandy felt uncomfortable wearing a dress, but Serena had insisted. She had watched the way Serena wore her clothes, and the way she walked. She had wished she was as beautiful; now she felt she was.

They reached Oblivion after the orange glow of sunset had surrendered to the glittering myriad of stars that make New Mexico's night sky such a wondrous sight. The old Indian had told her some of the stories of the sky people, and she remembered from her childhood the Greek myths of the constellations. There was a special feeling that now came over her as she studied the beauty of these stars. It was a sense of personal smallness linked to the inner knowledge that she was only one part of something vast and great. There was comfort in this understanding that she couldn't explain. She knew she couldn't fathom this great mystery, but, she also knew she didn't have to, and that is a great wisdom.

Tonight, as they approached the gathering of people in the street at the center of the town, she heard the music. It was a joyful blend of guitars and other instruments cheerfully blending country, rock and Tejano. Dr. Taggertt played a fiddle while Chad struggled with a saxophone, and Frog added the tones of a harmonica. Carlos raced to keep up with his accordion, but the effort was often in vain. This was the joy of music; not perfect notes by professionals, but people having fun as participants. Domingo Chavez was on the drums, and he was doing reasonably well.

As Brandy passed under the streetlight, shadows accentuated the classic form of her cheeks and illuminated her petite figure. Her appearance was so different that, at first, no one recognized her. The brightly colored dress Serena had helped her select now made her feel good about herself. No, it was more than good, she felt alive! She liked

236

the sensation of the long skirt brushing against her ankles. She drew her shoulders back and began to sway to the cheerful melody. Her hair glistened, as her smile captured Domingo's attention.

He whistled. Brandy had never been whistled at before, not once, in her entire life. Domingo left his drums, reached for her hand, led her into the throng of couples dancing in the street. They danced, shared a cold glass of watermelon juice, talked, then danced some more. She enjoyed taking an active part in her life, in the lives of others. There was sensuous joy in simply living life rather than vainly attempting to control it. Tonight she was living. Tonight she felt free, accepted by these people who should have hated her and her family. As the evening turned into night she began to understand that there was so much happening in Oblivion that there was no opportunity for anger to fester, no time for the hate to become a cancer that could destroy individuals, communities, even nations.

The residents of Oblivion knew who Brandy was, they also knew about both Landreth and Derritt. Larry had told them that Cal was making great progress in his recovery. They were all courteous enough to avoid mentioning her family, her past, or anything that would have been painful. When she was ready to talk about her family they would be ready to listen but this was not the night. Tonight was song and dance, friendship and celebration. Brandy's return from the healing solitude of the mesa was a journey they could all understand. That, after all was one of the elements that made Oblivion such a success. Everyone there was experiencing a second chance at life. The failures, the misfits, the flawed, the square pegs, the dreamers, the different drummers, in Oblivion were all now successful at life. They were all weaving bright colors into their blanket; and they were making certain that their shuttle pass on the blankets of others was colorful as well.

Brandy was overwhelmed at her acceptance; everyone was able to share in her victory and this made it even greater. Joy shared is multiplied geometrically.

Larry had brought some papers to Ben and Belinda. Editorial notes on the Oblivion books, a proposal for a series of posters, and a date for Ben's one man show at Jonson Gallery were the legitimate reasons for his visit this night. But they weren't the real reason he had made the long journey from Albuquerque. Several times in the past few weeks he had seen a woman of such serene grace and beauty that her walk was a dance of life. Her long dark hair was always adorned with a flower. She seemed so shy and quiet, so delicate. He had only found the courage to make his decision that afternoon. On the lengthy drive from Albuquerque he rehearsed the things he would say to this lady possessed of such delicate charm.

Larry's life too had known tragedy, pain and heartache. He had seen friends killed in the war protests of the Sixties. As a reporter he saw the horror of the drug wars. He had also invested his soul in a love that left and took his heart with her. He was drawn to this woman not by her beauty, but by her gentleness.

He walked into the gaiety with a smile on his face and practiced words on his lips. He searched for her in vain. Finally, he wandered away from the crowd and sought the comfort of the old cottonwoods. He sat and watched the lake. There was great and subtle beauty in the way the moon had been broken into thousands of pieces on the rippled surface of the water.

Larry refused to dwell on his loneliness. Instead, he softly dictated into his pocket recorder more impressions of the scientific and social progress being made in this experimental city. Somehow, these literary exercises didn't satisfy his longings tonight. Concentration was difficult. Pictures of Ben and Belinda, Marquita and Don Aragon, Chad and Frog kept flashing through his mind. Most of all he could see the hazy image of the shy and gentle lady he couldn't find. This quest of the heart could not be denied, neither in the dreams of sleep nor in the visions of wakefulness.

Serena was surprised when Domingo and Brandy danced with each other. The Chavez brothers had been among the most vocal detractors of the Benton family. In her mind though, Brandy was no longer a Benton. She wasn't even certain that the family existed any more. Serena wondered if this was a part of some plan, a destiny she couldn't begin to comprehend. Whatever it was she knew that there was a force there she could neither influence nor control, even if she were so inclined. She was pleased that this little town was big enough to open its arms to someone whose family had wronged it so. She was happy for Brandy. But, she was sad for herself. She understood that her work, the task the old Indian had given her was now complete.

The isolation that had been her companion for most of her confused life was back. In this crowd of happy people, she realized she was again only on the edge, perhaps too sensitive to be loved. Her feet continued to move with the music, even as the distance softened the vibrance. She was drawn toward the calm, comforting sound of wind weaving its way through the cottonwood leaves. The multitude of reflections floating on the lake gave her a melancholy pleasure. She was almost to the trees when she thought she heard a voice. Her feet were driven forward by cautious curiosity.

The shadowed form under the tree seemed to be engaged in a conversation with himself. Serena strained to hear the words, while she told herself to respect this man's privacy. His voice sounded only faintly familiar. As she inched closer, her foot snapped a twig. Larry turned. His neatly trimmed beard reflected the moonlight, giving him the appearance of gentle ruggedness. She sensed an aura of sadness about him. Something within her cried to reach out and take this man's hand, wash away his burden with her smile, salve his soul with her touch. She felt the need to look into his eyes, see into his soul, and comfort his being.

He studied her movements as she approached him. The pale gossamer folds of her dress clearly defined her feminine form. Her movements were poetry in the moonlight. Her face cast a radiance that began with her soft lips and ended deep within her seductive eyes. Her body swayed to its own rhythm as she neared him. Even in the moonlight, she could read the sadness in his eyes, bringing tears to the corners of hers. One escaped to caress her cheek as it glistened in the moonlight.

He stood and took her hand in his. "Beautiful evening," he fumbled with the words, forgetting completely the practiced sentences he had intended to utter to her. He gently wiped the tear from her face. They both smiled, both unsure what to do next, both fearing their feelings.

She reacted in the only way she knew how. She took both of his hands in hers, and began to move with the distant music.

Larry didn't dance, but he easily followed the poetry of her body. As they waltzed around the lake, it was to the silent music of their souls. When they paused to watch as the moonbeams made a dappled path across the lake to their feet he explained the scientific and technological experiments that could make Oblivion the world's best chance for a better future. A future where work would not poison our souls, consumption exhaust our resources, and pollution destroy our world.

She pondered the effects such changes would have on the people, "If we can free ourselves from the instincts of competition, greed, and suspicion, how will our lives be filled, our days occupied?"

"We have controlled other instincts and redirected drives in answer to social and environmental demands. As an example, I suspect that the instinct for war is not as strong as the instinct for peace. Yet . . ."

"True," Serena responded as she clutched his hand tightly, "harmony is the goal of all the world's great religions, and peace the dream of all truly great people."

"Are harmony and peace synonymous.?"

240

"Don't you feel that they have to be? How can one have inner peace if his, or her, life isn't in harmony?"

Larry studied the ripples on the Lake Hope, each carrying a tiny bit of the light from the distant moon. "Aren't we talking about societies? The problem of peace is compounded when you view people in their collective role as a society, village, state, or nation."

"No. Don't you see?" Serena was excited about the ideas, so thrilled with the opportunity to converse, to say some of the things that had been on her mind for so long, just waiting for the right person with whom to share them, someone who might understand. "Don't you see? When you gather people together, you increase the potential for peace. Isn't a bouquet more beautiful than the individual flowers that dot the garden or hillside? When you are dealing with life, the whole is truly greater than the sum of its parts; Oblivion is vase holding a bouquet of people, as is any village or city."

Larry was silent for a long moment as he contemplated her comments. "But there are so many different personalities. How can they all live in harmony.?"

"What is harmony? Isn't it the combination of different sounds of different pitches, from a variety of instruments or voices, combined together to produce a melody.?"

"Well, yes."

"How could we possibly have harmony if all the notes were the same? The music comes from the differences, not all sounds being alike. The harmony of a community must be the same. It is the diversity that makes the delightful music of life." She startled herself that she was arguing with this man she hardly knew, but it felt right to do so.

They sat and watched the floating islands in the lake, listened to the blend of nature's night sounds and the music of Oblivion. Larry took her hand in his. She relaxed and leaned her head onto his shoulder. At some inner level, they both knew that loneliness was a part of

241

yesterday. Still, neither was willing to contemplate their tomorrows. It was the moments of now that were to be savored.

"Peace is, it could be argued, the natural state of humanity, not war. If we were to trace each culture's history, I'm certain that periods of peace vastly out weigh the periods of conflict. As a reporter, I understand that the norm doesn't make the headlines or the history books. We see on the evening news the one child who was a problem in school, not the thousands who weren't; the one person that holds up a bank, not the thousands of folks that every day do their work, think their thoughts, sing their songs." Larry was still contemplating the ability of Oblivion's harmony to sustain itself.

"I have seen Brandy, spent time with her. I even think I understand a little of what it was that made her so bitter, made her brothers so aggressive and avaricious. It is a drive within us all to be 'well thought of,' to force peer respect. So much of childhood is spent teaching negatives. Even after we are adults, most of the rules we establish, the laws we subject ourselves to, are negative, not positive. Since it is impossible for the spirit to obey all these sets of rules, we all feel like failures." Without realizing it, she had begun to softly stroke his beard with her hand.

"If we each contain within us a spark of something divine," Larry's arm was now wrapped around her. He was holding her tighter, feeling the warmth of her body, inhaling the sweet perfume of her presence, "we ought to be able to replace competition with cooperation, greed with generosity, conflict with peace, hate with love."

"It has to be a transformation within each individual. It can't come from another set of rules. It is the goodness that lives within us all, like the butterfly in its chrysalis, just waiting for its moment to break free."

They continued to discuss the potential of the human animal and the human spirit, the need for universal goals where all can focus their energy collectively. "Perhaps we have an instinctive need for a common

242

enemy," Larry suggested, "It can be a positive battle against ignorance, disease, pollution; or it can be a self-destructive war against people who don't think like us, wear different clothes, speak a different language, or call God by a different name."

Serena thought about this for some time before responding, "Isn't it better to have a common goal than a common enemy? Haven't many of the great accomplishments of humanity been the result of concentrated effort toward a universal objective?"

Larry pondered this for a few seconds, while his mind drew forth images of the pyramids, great cathedrals, the development of the polio vaccine, and the landing of a man on the moon, the formation of the world's great religions, the careers of the great thinkers, the lasting art and the meaningful words. They continued their discussion as yesterday turned into tomorrow. They fell asleep in each others arms, and both slept well with the new found comfort of belonging.

Chapter Twenty-four

Emilio Franko was involved in animated discussion with Chad, Frog and Inez. He had been extolling the virtues of "the fallen harvest." He explained that his mother taught him, as a small child, that gathering the apples, pears and peaches that had fallen was not stealing. They were a gift from the tree.

Inez suggested that his madre was referring to stealing from the person that owned the trees, not the trees themselves.

"How can mankind be so vain as to think it can own a tree. Plants can't be slaves, forced to do your bidding!" He was standing again, waving his arms, working himself into a frenzy.

Chad added fuel to Emilio's flames, "The tree might not have even been there without the people that planted it, cared for it, pruned it . . ." At that he was interrupted.

Emilio was livid as he grabbed Chad by the arms and began to shake him. "No more evil device has ever been created by the cruel mind of man than the pruning shears. A tool whose only purpose is to wound, maim and destroy, to bring insufferable pain and suffering to peaceful plants, all in the name of beauty or productivity! How can you dare even think such a thing?"

Frog was fearful that the radical crusader was going to hurt Chad, so she tried to reason with him. "If we don't prune out the damaged and errant branches . . ." But she also was interrupted.

"Nature prunes!" He almost screamed. A crowd was beginning to form around them. "Frost, insects and fungus all play a part." He was breathing hard, his face was red, and the words were coming with difficulty. "We . . . the people are the violators. . . .We upset the natural order. . . . We are the interlopers. . . . We are the evil that . . ."

The strong voice came from the darkness. "Emilio, by your irrational acts of terrorism, you have damaged my cause, perhaps even cost us entire species. Why is it?" Courtney stepped out of the shadows. A small owl blinked at them from her shoulder. In her hair was a wreath of wildflowers, like jewels in a crown. "Why is it that you think it is right to destroy logging equipment to defend a tree? Burn a cannery to win rights for a tomato plant? Steal a chile roaster, and deny a farmer needed income for his family? How can you justify bankrupting a farmer by filling tractor gas tanks with dirt and water, stealing parts and cutting hydraulic lines?"

He raised his fist and started to speak, but was interrupted before he could form the words.

"We are all seeds well sown as much as the sower. We are also as much a harvest as we are the harvester. Humanity only needs to find its place in the harmony of the natural world." She turned and pointed toward the homes in Oblivion. "Is this any more unnatural than the nest of the wren or cities of ants? You are neither better nor worse than the rest of the life on this planet, you are merely a part of it. Accept that, and work from there. If we can learn from all life there is still time to heal both ourselves and the earth."

Emilio stood straight and tall to face this challenge, "You know nothing of glory of nature, or the degradation of humanity." He was going to say more but never got the opportunity.

Courtney's anger was swift to surface and terrible to behold. The rattlesnakes appeared at his feet, the scorpions began to crawl over his boots, while a swarm of mosquitoes descended on his face and arms. "I am NATURE!" Her words were spoken so softly that they echoed through his head, amplified by the terror he was feeling.

Her arms spread to encompass the entire valley. "The goal is for the human animal to accept a harmonious position within this natural world, to cease and desist the battle with nature and learn how to accept your share of responsibility for the future. This can happen only when we use knowledge and reason to create cooperation and understanding. It isn't enough to be against something. You have to create acceptable

245

alternatives." She was now speaking to the entire crowd. "Don't you see what these people are doing here? You can't achieve their goals with terrorism."

Emilio was experiencing his own terror as the scorpions scurried over his boots and up the legs of his jeans, the incessant buzzing around his head, and the deadly rattling at his feet. He cried, "Please, take them away."

The wind moaned and drew all eyes to the treetops. In the silence that followed, Emilio cautiously looked down. He saw the bare sand where the diamondbacks had been; the buzzing of the insects was gone, and he no longer felt the footsteps of scorpions on his legs. He stepped back and collapsed into an exhausted heap. Ben watched from the edge of the crowd, puzzled by the power Courtney possessed, puzzled by the obvious fact that she used terror, even as she decried its use. In his mind, he was sketching a picture of Emilio, being held prisoner by branches of the trees he vainly defended. The trees, sheaves of wheat, bouquets of flowers and a basket of vegetables were all in vivid colors, while Emilio was in tones of gray. This would symbolize his separation from the real world, his unwillingness, or inability, to accept a part in the natural world.

Marquita forced herself awake; by sheer mental effort, she separated herself from the dream world. In her sleep, she kept returning to the cabin where Landreth had beaten her, to the bedroom where Derritt had used and abused her. When the mind is freed from the grasp of wakefulness, it can travel the many paths of time, both into the future and back into the past. Marquita was sustained by the anger, the hatred that she felt toward the Bentons. Her mind journeyed back to those cataclysmic events, to fuel the flames of this hatred. This night she cried out when Landreth's fist struck her face, but she awoke in Don Aragon's arms. His soft shoulder made a comfortable pillow, while she traveled the short distance to wakefulness.

When the tears stopped, he poured her a glass of Sandia Shadows wine. They sat on the bed talking long, about how the Benton family would be brought to its knees when the judge validated the land grant. Don had begun the land grant challenge with little hope of success. He did it to bring attention to what he felt was a wrong that cried for redress. Now, after finding all the pieces of the puzzle, he felt that victory was a reality within their grasp. His greatest weapon came after using an Anglo friend, acting as a Benton attorney, to gain more than the public documents from Monty Themaine at the Office of Archives and Historical Documents. He had presented to the judge copies of contracts, mineral and water rights deeds that had been removed from the archives. There was also a thank you note from Landreth, complimenting Monty on a job well done. Monty saved and carefully filed everything.

Don Aragon's victory was at hand, yet it was secondary to the feelings he had for the lady whose head now rested on his lap as they discussed a future on a restored "estancia." He spoke of the mountains she would own, while his hands roamed the soft peaks of her breasts. Her fingers explored the hair on his chest, as she talked of the rangeland and grazing cattle. The nightmares of brutal lust faded into her personal oblivion, to be replaced with desire for the man whose body was now so ready for hers. They embraced, kissed and shared the special joy of lovers. Don Aragon was possessed by an almost fanatical confidence in the outcome of the land grant hearing. He had arranged deals with the US Department of Interior that could well become a landmark decision. The strange little town of Oblivion would be no problem. Those people were so confused and focused on their radical dreams that they weren't even appearing before the judge. He was confident he had slain the dragon called the Benton Empire. During their love making he fantasized himself a valiant knight wielding a powerful sword.

Marquita was not as confident. She didn't understand the legal process. She only knew that the Bentons, in her experience, had never lost. They weren't as easy a foe as her lover thought. She tried to caution him, but it was difficult for her mind to concentrate on dusty old papers while her body was anticipating a closer delight.

She found comfort in her dreams that night, not from the lover whose arms held her so tightly, but from the inner knowledge that she had vindicated her abuelo. Don Aragon dreamt of himself as "el Patron." In his vision he replaced Calmut Benton as the most powerful man in San Miguel County. The only step that remained was to marry this little senorita asleep in his arms. She was his ticket to success.

Landreth's attempts to make some of the documents disappear had backfired. He contacted several of his friends in the state legislature to demand Monty Themaine's firing. This would happen, but it would be a victory in name only.. His pending trial on his attack on Judge Sorenson was a popular subject for discussion on talk radio. The newspapers were gleefully charting the daily decline in the Benton empire, while the evening news was, tabloid like, following every step Derritt and Landreth made. They broadcast pictures of Brandy, who had been missing for months, with the offer of a bounty for information on where she was now. NPR's Bob Edwards had done an in-depth series on the history of the old Spanish land grants, complete with his Marquita Lopez interview, the only one she had granted.

In the wake of this tidal wave of publicity, Landreth was finding himself friendless and almost pennyless. His influence had evaporated. He was now powerless to bribe or threaten. His last hope was to use some of the knowledge he had acquired about the governor and several of the cabinet members. He knew blackmail was a dangerous weapon. He would have to use it carefully. He was also feeling the pressure of running the family's empire. There was labor unrest; questions were being raised about the timber leases; the BLM had called for a review of the rangeland leases; and there were claims against the Benton water rights contracts. He hated the rangers that patrolled his timber tracts, charting stumpage, hassling him about the logging trails he had cut. Now, there were charges that he had crossed his boundary lines and cut timber on land he didn't control. When his trial came up in October, he feared he would have to spend some time behind bars; but he already felt that he was a prisoner, and he blamed every one but himself. The more he lashed out at the press, the more often his picture was in the news. The more people he threatened, the fewer friends he had. The Benton empire was crumbling. His debts were becoming insurmountable. In desperation, he called Marquita. The threat that she wouldn't live to enjoy the victory was on tape. He was behind bars the next time he heard his words.

Calmut was getting stronger as the asters replaced the desert four-o-clocks, and the aspen leaves began to turn from green to gold. He went with Christa to the State Fair in Albuquerque. Together they sampled the wines at the Bernallio wineries, drove to the crest of Sandia Mountain, bought tacky souvenirs, then spent the Labor Day weekend back in Santa Fe. They were a part of the crowd that watched the raising of the gigantic effigy, Zorzoba, also called "Old Man Gloom.". This was a tradition started by an artist who came from Philadelphia to Santa Fe in 1920 to die. Will Shuster had tuberculosis. In 1926 his health restored, he created Zorzoba. The huge paper mache figure represented all the troubles that plagued each of those present. At sundown, everyone gathered in the plaza as the effigy was ignited. The flames consumed all the discomfort, sorrows, and sins of those present. As the brilliant flames reduced the great looming figure to ashes, Calmut felt a change deep within himself. When he thought about it later, he described it as a warm, comfortable sense of freedom. He had never stood in a crowd like this before. Now, here he was, shoulder to shoulder with thousands of people he didn't know, smelling their sweat;

being forced to move to their music and feel their joy. Everyone was a stranger, yet they were shaking his hand, sharing smiles, exchanging greetings in languages and dialects he recognized, but did not understand in this festive confusion.

Christa seized him in her arms, and gave him a great kiss as the mass of humanity began to move in time to the Mariachi band. They worked their way to the concession booths at the edge of the plaza. As they shared a beer and platter of nachos, Calmut found himself shouting joyfully, seeking hands to shake, making momentary friends and permanent memories. For the first time in his life, he was not standing at a distance, but was a part of the festivities, one of the people. He no longer felt a need to control, but he was now strong enough that he wouldn't be controlled, either. This old man, defeated and almost destroyed by his heart, drained the can of beer, seized his woman by the hand, and with an exuberance that he had never known before, danced her into the evening.

He didn't go back to his apartment that night. When the Zorzoba festival began to break up, they retreated to her house on Canyon Road, in the company of about a dozen new found friends. Over wine and nachos con queso they discussed art, music and poverty. Spanglish was the dominant language, and Calmut found that he could easily comprehend the flow of conversation. He even tentatively employed a few words in Spanish. The blending of languages was like a seasoning of fine herbs on a great but otherwise bland meal. None of those present recognized Cal as Calmut Benton. As wine flowed and the comfort level increased, jokes were made about the demise of the once powerful family. They all laughed at the video of Landreth at the judge's car. It had appeared on almost every newscast for weeks, while each newscaster gave his or her twist to the scandal. Calmut fell silent when they talked about the fire that consumed his home. Several times it was compared to the flames of Zorzoba, and analogies were drawn, about the consumption of sin. Tears formed as they made jokes about

250

Derritt. The Chicano community despised this Benton the most, because he was the one who most visibly abused them. He used and raped their daughters, fought with their sons, evicted their grandparents, and worked the men to death in the mines. Vulgar laughter filled the room when it was suggested that they should have removed another part of his anatomy instead of his hands.

Christa was the only one who noticed the pain on Cal's face. Immediately, she stood and told the guests Cal was not well; it was time to leave. While they found the door, she led the old man to her bed. He had known such joy earlier that evening, as he shared the festival with these people. Now, it was not anger that returned the lines of age to his face. It was shame that put the weight back in his heart, brought the burden back onto his shoulders.

The clay dove on the dresser told her to light a candle and say a prayer. She was so fearful that this man was going to leave her, was going to die. She knelt before the candle, put her very soul into the plea she made to God. Cal fell asleep listening to her, a vision of her silhouetted in the candle's glow remained in his mind to comfort him while he slept.

The dove told her to undress him and bathe away the pain and sorrow that had somehow returned to plague him. She selected her softest washcloth and towel, filled the basin with warm water, splashed some rose scented perfume in it, and returned to the bedroom. Carefully, she rolled him over and unbuttoned his shirt. She was fascinated with the gray hair that covered his chest; her hands gently patted over his heart. The warm moist cloth washed over his face and neck. She gently held his arms as she washed the burden from his shoulders and hands.

He smiled at her as she sat on the edge of the bed. In the candlelight, she appeared almost angelic to him. He felt so weak, so tired. She unbuckled his belt and began to unzip his jeans. A wave of embarrassment overwhelmed her. She had never seen his nakedness.

251

Theirs had been a pure and chaste relationship, although she had felt the heat of his body against her on several occasions.

His hand raised to stop her, but he lowered it again. Her hair brushed his face as she leaned down and kissed his chest, giving her warmth to his heart. His mind had opened its photo album to the picture of Derritt as he threw the paperweight at him. With this image in his mind, he heard again the raucous laughter of the evening's guests. Her hair brushing against his body erased these heavy thoughts while his mind prayed for peace.

She carefully pulled the jeans from his body and washed his legs. For one who had been as ill as he had been, his legs were still firm and strong. She cleansed his feet, rubbing the ankles and soles. The dove told her this was an act of humble love. She questioned the dove about this, and it assured her that she was in love.

The clay bird laughed and cooed at her foolishness. "How could you not know you are in love?"

She kissed his feet. Then, after a long pause while she sought the courage, she grasped the band of his underwear with her fingers. The dove cooed from the dresser again, "It's all right. He loves you as well."

She gently pulled the shorts down from his groin, freeing his manhood. She had known many men, known them in many ways. "Why am I as shy as some silly schoolgirl?" she asked the dove.

It flew over and landed on Calmut's chest. "You've never been in love before. You are afraid of the future. You have known the intensity of lust, now it's your turn to know the comfort of love."

She squeezed the excess water from the cloth, releasing a wave of the rose perfume. "What will he think of me when he finds out who I am?"

"He knows who you are. What you fear is that he will not be able to accept who you were." The dove spoke, as it gingerly stepped down from his chest to his abdomen. "You don't know who he was

252

either, but you love what he is now. Isn't that what's important?" With that, it flew up onto her shoulder and rubbed its head against her ear.

She pressed the washcloth to her lips, then closed her eyes as her hands gently sought their objective. He smiled at her touch. With the soft rubbing of the towel, he reached up and put his arms around her shoulders, and pulled her down on top of him. The embrace found its companion, the kiss. The kiss became passionate. As he unbuttoned her blouse, she heard the dove, "It is good." Then she saw it turn its head to give them privacy.

At three o'clock that afternoon final arguments were heard. Judge Sorenson would take two more days before he handed down the decision that was already firm in his mind.

Part Three

Belinda's Dream

But I, being poor have only my dreams;
I have spread my dreams under your feet;
Tread softly, for you tread on my dreams.
W. B. Yeats, *The Cloths of Heaven*

"As the day's hours shorten,
and the nights turn from cool to cold,
as the trees' wardrobe changes
from green to shades of rust and gold,
as summer becomes autumn in the great circle of time,
then, from within each of us,
instinctive restlessness will climb."
Belinda

Chapter Twenty-five

Belinda wrote as she sat by the small evening fire on the mesa top that gave her a poet's eye view of the canyon that now held all her hopes and dreams. She watched the flames dance and cast shadows in the long red rays of the setting sun. Word followed word as she felt the increasing chill in the air. Lines of poetry compared the flow of the seasons in life to the seasonings a great chef might use in a fine meal. The central word was *season*, a word she defined as change. On a personal level, she knew she was not the same person on this September evening, as she had been last winter in St. Louis, or that first day this spring when she met Ben and Oblivion, or even the summer months that just passed. When she paused to contemplate the progress that Oblivion had seen, she envisioned a beautiful flower opening to the sun. How much change there had been in these few short months, these seasons; how much change there had been in her. How well seasoned she had been by life.

As this autumnal season of the harvest approached, she worried about the pending land grant decision. She was concerned about the latent threat from the Bentons. Ben was the focus of many of her concerns. He was an artist, trapped by fate in the role of "el Patron." He felt the increasing pressure daily. Duties stole his time, robbed him of the opportunity and ability to create. She also worried about her identity. It was all good and fine to say she had escaped a past that wasn't acceptable, but she didn't feel that she had replaced it with anything tenable. She watched the daily activity of Oblivion's thinkers and doers, and all she could do was write a few pretty words. This was the harvest season; and in her mind, her crop was meager, the yield insufficient.

She felt the slow rhythmic drum beats, before she actually heard them. They seemed to be coming from the flames. Their sound comforted and warmed her, because she knew the old Indian was near. She had grown to love this mysterious old man and his strange way of appearing when she needed to talk with him. He wasn't sitting by the fire when she glanced up toward the horizon, toward the last red rays of the falling sun. He was there, smiling his benign grandfatherly smile, when she looked back at the flames.

His fingers tapped lightly on the drum, soothing, so soothing, almost hypnotic in the repetition of comforting tones. It was a primitive, yet ageless, music that was felt inside the head, not absorbed by the ears. It was also felt in the heart, for it was music for both the mind and the soul. She closed her eyes to let her mind concentrate on the music.

"If you close your eyes you can't see the flames," he spoke so softly, so in time with the drumbeats, that it seemed he, too, was addressing her heart, not her ears. "Come closer to the fire, and let the flames share their warmth with you."

He continued to speak as he tapped the drum. "I will ask you a question."

She nodded and inched closer while he paused.

"Which is the greater reality?" He was pointing to the long wavering shadows of the flames. "The warm flame is alive. It moves, gives light and warmth. We have made friends with the fire, but we respect it for what it is. You released the fire that was trapped within the sticks and branches. Could this be the genie in the bottle spoken of by our Arabian brothers?" He chuckled at her puzzled look.

"Did not this flame grant you three wishes?"

"What do you mean, old man?"

"These flames gave you warmth, did they not?"

Belinda nodded her head in affirmation.

"Is that not a cup of coffee and a potato warming in the coals of this fire?"

Again she agreed.

"And, the flames give you light, and in the light is security. You are comforted by the light because you can see what is there." He pointed out into the increasing darkness.

"Then the lamp of the genie was an oil lamp used for light?"

"Perhaps." He looked at the sun, rapidly losing its grip on the canyon wall. Then he gazed beyond the flames to the shadows that danced on the sand and rocks of the mesa top. "But what of these? Are the shadows a part of the flame? Is your shadow a part of you?"

She struggled to understand what he meant. "A shadow is the interruption of light rays. When the sun meets the flames, the flames cast their shadows."

"You have not answered my question."

256

She felt embarrassed by her ignorance. Images flashed into her mind of a school girl being called upon by Mrs. Evans to give the class answers she didn't know. "I guess a shadow must be real. Isn't it a part of the flame? Isn't my shadow a part of me?"

The palm of his hand pounded rapidly on the taut hide of the drum. "Bueno! You do understand. All of us have a shadow. This is a reality. I ask you now another question." When do you see your shadow?"

"When I stand in the light?"

"Exactly. When we live in a world filled with the darkness of ignorance, the depression of hopelessness, or the poison of hate, we don't cast shadows because we are our shadows. This is the other reality of us. Belinda, understand that no one is perfect. No one is without the shadows. The question is whether we lead our shadows, or if we become shadows themselves."

His hand silenced the drum and he pointed to the place where the flame's shadows had danced. "Look at what has happened."

Belinda saw that the fire no longer cast a shadow of itself. Rather, its light increased so that it provided illumination to all that surrounded it. In turn, it made the rocks and grass cast shadows of their own.

"The Great Mystery gives us the sun that we might see, and that we might be illuminated. This light is in the form of knowledge, hope, and love. You are like the sticks you gathered to build the fire. You contain within you flames that can grant the three wishes to others. This is good. You, and all the people of your village, Oblivion, are a part of the Great Mystery. So are the people of villages all over the earth. So are the bird people, the fish people, the grasses, the trees. All life is a part of the Great Mystery. We can all learn from each other. We are all called, in different ways, to share our gifts."

Belinda interrupted, "If this is true, then why is there so little peace in the world? Why do people like Derritt and Landreth and

Calmut Benton do such violent and hurtful things? Why is there greed and glory in the warring of nations and the pillaging of corporate competition?"

He again tapped the drum softly, the tempo slower now. "Because, while we all seek harmony, few know how to achieve it. Because we all cast shadows, and some are lead by them"

"But, old man, don't we only cast shadows when there is light?"

"Eureka, to quote an old friend of mine. The shadows of our bodies contain the shadows of our souls. This is the dark side that all of us possess. This is where anger, greed and fear live. We are not aware of their nature until we are aware of our own. This is the illumination of knowledge, hope and love. These are the great lights of our existence. These are the gifts from the Great Mystery."

Belinda studied the face of the old Indian. Searching for understanding, for clues. "If we all have these gifts, again I ask you, why are so many people unhappy?"

"When you give a child a toy as a gift, he or she doesn't always play with it. Sometimes it is neglected, sometimes it is broken, even discarded. So it is with these gifts of light from the Great Mystery. When the gifts are discarded, then the shadow of us is larger than the light of us. We are not built of purity and joy, only potential."

He set the drum aside and took the flute from his bag. As he wet his lips, he smiled at her. "Think on what we have said. Put it into the beautiful words you craft so well. Do this so others will understand. Know also that many are not ready to hear what you will be saying. Don't let this stay you from speaking to those who are."

Her mind followed the sound of the flute as it wound its way down from the mesa top. Belinda gathered her back pack, pulled a flaming pine branch from the fire, and put the rest of the flames to rest. Then, with torch in hand, she descended toward her home.

These September days had added to the burdens Ben already carried. He had come to the disturbing realization that many of the environmentalists that visited Oblivion were so negative. They seemed to view humanity as an entity outside of the natural world. Some, like Emilio, considered people the enemy. Others were less radical, but self-righteous and sanctimonious in their role as savior. The business community that toured the experimental village were of the opinion that the natural world, the mountains, valleys and lakes, were nothing more than raw material for their industry. They viewed people as a market to be developed. A surprising number of the farmers who came to see first hand the experimental agriculture projects were firm in their conviction that nature was a foe to be vanquished. They were agrarian soldiers engaged in mortal combat.

Courtney had witnessed his growing frustration with these assorted interest groups and suggested that he express this ire in a painting. Ben had never used his art as self therapy before and wasn't certain that this was an appropriate use of his talent. Still he knew the poison of stress and internal fury. He had felt the pain of the monster within. The work only increased his inwardly directed hostility, increased the agony he felt.

"Why," Ben cried as he splashed the dark acrylics on the Masonite board, "Why, can't they understand that nature views humankind as only a part of its own, not something apart." The painting was a massive work showing two hands brandishing a shovel and a hoe at each other while a storm cloud looms overhead. Trees, plants, animals and birds were juxtaposed with litter, smokestacks and dead fish. There was a sense of foreboding in the work. Ben's frustration and anger were evident in the slashing brush strokes and the clash of shades. Detail was non-existent.

Ben stood back from the work. He was furious with himself, with his inability to concentrate on detail, to express beauty. He was holding a sketch of what he had intended to create. As the rage seethed

259

within him, he crumpled it in his hand and threw it at the work before him. It stuck on the not yet dry paint. He had seen dimensional art before and thought that it lacked merit, yet it seemed to work on this piece of eco-art. Soon he was gluing pieces of twig, leaves, dried flowers and grasses, a dried and desiccated fish, some random bones, a cigarette pack, crumpled beer cans, a disposable razor, plastic bags, and an empty oil can. Over the painting of a shovel and hoe were now glued real tools. These extended beyond the limits of the frame to add another dimension to the work.

By the time he was finished, he was exhausted. His anger was spent. He still disliked this, his latest creation, but he lacked the energy to change, or even destroy it. The afternoon sun struck the assorted dimensional materials and cast myriads of shadow lines across the massive four by eight foot sheet of art. The sometimes subtle, sometimes blatant shades of shadow gave greater depth. In the brilliant light of the New Mexico sky, it took on an intensity greater than Ben had imagined.

"Almost a sculpture,' Courtney said as she studied it from the corner of the building. "You must have had a lot of anger to express, to have done something like this."

Ben started to apologize but she stopped him in mid-sentence. "I wasn't being critical. It's so dramatic. It is a visual image of what I've been trying to say." She paused for a few seconds before she continued, being careful not to offend. "It is a negative statement. What if you made it the first of a massive series? It could take us on an artistic journey from today's reality, to a positive future where humanity is accepting its place in the real world, my world."

It was impossible to say "NO" to Courtney, even though this wasn't something Ben wanted to do. This was the first commission work Ben had ever done. To work on commission requires more than creative artistic talent. It takes discipline. It takes art out of the realm of personal expression and makes it work. To some, this is a

260

prostitution of their talent; to others, it is the supreme artistic challenge. For Ben, it was another stress.

Courtney made suggestions about subject matter, but Ben heard demand. She asked if he could, through the series, gradually lighten the shades, bring the colors from somber to joyful. He kicked over the small table that held his paints and threw his brushes as far as he could. Then, as she walked away he sat and clutched the pain, holding it inside.

Chapter Twenty-six

Christa was so excited she could hardly wait for Cal's arrival this morning. She stood at the arched doorway to the walled garden. When she saw his figure in the distance, she wanted to race to greet him and tell him about the place she had just learned existed. Instead, she retreated to the kitchen and prepared the coffee and the tray of cookies she had baked early that morning. As she wiped the dew from the patio chairs, she wondered if he owned a car, then she thought to herself, "Never mind. I have enough money to rent one." While she didn't have a driver's license, she did think she could drive, at least as far as this wonderful place she had heard about.

He stood more erect; his shoulders were thrown back. Steps quickened as he approached the bright sunflowers that peered over the adobe wall to welcome him, while the blue morning glories smiled at his appearance. The red rose bushes he had helped her plant at the gate were now a mass of color in the brisk morning air. Yesterday he had decided that it was time to explain to Christa that he was Calmut Benton, but he had come to a decision this morning that she could probably not love someone with his background. He felt much better after he decided to keep his identity a secret. Then, before he had left his apartment this morning, the phone rang. His ultimate weapon had dealt him what should have been a mortal blow. Instead, it was a sense of liberation that he received the news.

"The Lopez land grant claim was upheld," his lawyer's voice intoned with the most sorrowful of tones. After a long pause, the voice added only, "I'm sorry. We did the best we could under the circumstances. I'll start work immediately on an appeal."

In a way, Cal knew this would be the outcome. Somehow it didn't matter. He was experiencing more happiness making glass birds than he had ever known from a good business deal. In many ways he was relieved to be freed of these responsibilities. He could now court this lady in earnest. He had brought enough cash to take her to dinner. Just now he decided he wouldn't go back to his apartment tonight. In a few short sentences he told his attorney not to pursue the appeal; rather, to begin work on the liquidation of his holdings. His terse order was to set up a trust fund for him and Brandy, if she were ever found. Lastly he insisted that Marquita Lopez be treated with respect and integrity. He mentioned neither of his sons.

She watched him pause at the gate and select just the perfect rose bud. With great care he opened his pocket knife and cut the stem, just above a leaf facing out so the next bud would grow that way. She had taught him this, and was pleased that he had remembered. This morning in the clear crisp Santa Fe air, he was absolutely handsome. The black eye patch made him look so distinguished, so cultured. His clothes gave the appearance of quality. She guessed he shopped at Goodwill or the Salvation Army. Many of her friends clothed their entire families that way. It puzzled her that he seemed to know little about art, even less about literature. Still, she was pleased that he was so eager to help, so willing to learn about the message each piece of her work carried. He seemed to be genuinely excited when they toured the local galleries, when he came face to face with new ideas, new people.

She knew he had a past he didn't want to talk about, and that was perfectly all right with her. She lived with the fear that he would discover hers and walk out of her life. The clay dove had told her he wouldn't do that, but it still worried her. She would spend long hours at night, while the dove slept, writing down all the things about her past that she wished hadn't happened. She would then feed them to the fireplace flames, one page at a time. She would watch as each piece of paper, filled with its regrets, it shame, its dishonor, would make a flash of light and cast a shadow across the hearth. She feared that the shadows would become the ghosts of her past, even after she had removed them from her memory and destroyed them. She feared her past as much as she anticipated her future.

They greeted each other with a warm embrace that held the potential of becoming passionate. They shared the coffee and cookies while they watched the iridescent glitter of the sun as it danced on the dewdrops that covered the leaves and flowers of her small yard. Cal was consuming this beauty with an eye just now awakening to what Christa referred to as "God's art."

"Do you drive.?" She broke his reverie, shattered the magic of the moment with her question.

"Yes?" He spoke it as a question, in truth he was asking why.

"I'll rent a car and we can go visit this place I heard about yesterday." She was excited and he liked the see the sparkle in her eyes and the broad arch of her smile when she had an idea.

He reached across the table and took her hand in his. "Where would you like to go, Precious?"

There's this place that some artist owns and they are doing all kinds of new things in the town. A couple of young women had been in town a while back and they visited the same hair dresser I went to yesterday. Estella was telling me about them and this place." She leaned over the table and gave him a kiss, making certain that her breast brushed across his hand in the process. "They called the town a strange name, but I can't remember what it was."

This request was like a knife in his chest. He couldn't go there. They all knew who he was. She would find out, and tell him she never wanted to see him again.

She read the shock on his face, but had no idea what had disturbed him so. "Don't worry. I have enough money saved up to rent a car. If you don't want to drive, I think I can do it."

He leaned back in his chair and started to laugh. "You're talking about a place called Oblivion, aren't you?"

"Yes! That's it." She was pleased that he knew about this apparently dynamic community.

"I don't think I'm very welcome there."

"Oh, it isn't like those trendy artist colonies. This place is supposed to have a lot of poor folks like us living there."

This brought more laughter. Finally he slapped his hand on the table, "You don't know who I am. You just don't have any idea." He paused while he wrestled with the decision, whether to tell her or not. Finally, he blurted out, "Look, I'm Calmut Benton. Up until this morning I ran half of San Miguel County. I spent a lifetime abusing the land and using the people. There I said it." With this revelation he rose to leave.

She grabbed his arm and almost screamed, "Who the hell cares who Calmut Benton was? You're Cal, and I love you."

He stopped, turned and took her in his arms. "You don't know about the Bentons?"

"I heard about them being in some trouble with the law, but most of the folks I know have had a run in or two." She was leading him back to the table. "I've done time myself. Yesterday don't matter. It's tomorrow that we're meant for." Her arms were wrapped around him as she began to sob. "Please don't leave."

They talked the rest of the morning, had a delightful lunch at Tito's, then walked together to his apartment. He held the door for her as she entered his deep blue Lincoln. Within minutes they were off to Oblivion.

Ben had struggled with the massive panels of dimensional art that were supposed to show the way toward a brighter tomorrow. He had used over thirty sheets of building board to get the twelve paintings right. Still, he wasn't certain he had the message that Courtney desired. It was difficult to paint someone else's dreams. He had moved from dark warnings of air, water and land poisoned beyond nature's ability to repair it, to panels in warmer, lighter tones that spoke of hope for the future, harmony with all creatures, the potential consequences of lasting peace.

The one the he liked the best began with soldiers marching. Guns and spent shells were held in place with epoxy cement. The dismembered bodies of several mannequins were being trampled under foot. Gradually, as the center of the painting was reached by this army, guns were replaced by peace symbols and loaves of bread. Mannequin babies were being fed. Books, plants and candles were being distributed to all. Drab camouflage uniforms were replaced with brightly colored clothing, as if humanity was through hiding and ready to claim its place in the sun.

Another began as a desert of litter and garbage, asphalt and an old tire. Gradually the litter was joined by bright wildflowers and green vines. Finally, a verdant forest grew out of recyclable trash, including leaves and aluminum cans.

Belinda had studied these while they were works in progress, but made few comments on them. She knew that this was a difficult work for Ben. His art usually gave him contentment and a sense of fulfillment, but these did not. While he worked on them, he was withdrawn, attended the town meetings fewer and fewer evenings. His appetite waned and he lost weight. Their love making became less frequent and less satisfying to them both. This was the first time she resented his art.

For Ben, the stress was not only from doing the art, but also from the continuing parade of interruptions. While Oblivion hadn't actually become a tourist destination, the number of educators, environmentalists, business managers, writers, political figures and dreamers roaming the town continued to grow. The flood of salespeople sometimes threatened to engulf the town, and each one of them had to talk to Ben. Each visitor felt obliged to chat, usually to offer advice, make suggestions or try to sell something. The residents of Oblivion

266

proudly introduced each guest to Ben, many introducing him as "el Patron." He was also troubled by the fact that UNM wanted him to enter the social world of Albuquerque's fine arts scene. Ben had not walked the arroyos, climbed the canyon wall, visited the other towns that dotted the New Mexico landscape, for weeks. He was feeling more and more restless, trapped, angry.

Courtney had watched his work and understood the pressure he was under, but chose not to intervene. Now she could see the anger growing like a cancer within his mind. Today, Courtney was going to help. Carlos had offered assistance as Ben move the last of the four by eight foot panels from beside the house to the open space by the cottonwoods. Now they sat in the shade studying the art in silence. Carlos had emptied his Coors, Ben had barely touched his.

"Man, you gotta get away from this for awhile." Carlos finally spoke.

"I can't. I can't. They won't let me." Ben snapped in response.

Courtney approached from behind, humming softly. She knew she was the focus of his anger, but not the sole cause. She removed the can of beer from his hand and replaced it with a bouquet of flowers. "These are magnificent." She spoke in soft tones as her arms spread to encompass the panels.

Ben's only response was a polite smile; a smile that was turned into a grimace by the pain in his stomach. This time it was so bad he doubled over, a captive of the agony inside him.

Carlos carried him back to the comfort and security of his home. Belinda was in tears. Courtney tried to comfort her while he moaned with the pain.

Within minutes, the old Indian was at the doorway. Without a word he approached the bed, took Ben's hand in his, and began a soft chant. He pulled a small bundle of dried herbs, juniper and white sage from his leather bag and motioned for Carlos to light them. Soon the fragrant smoke was floating through the room. He took a small tablet from an old medicine tin and helped Ben to a sitting position, so that he could swallow it.

"Zantac. Good medicine." He said mocking the way Indians speak in the movies. "The sage smoke relaxes the stress of the mind, while the drug soothes the anger that lives in his tummy." He then put his flute to his lips and began to make soft music that calmed the troubled soul.

Courtney made some tea for Belinda. After a few sips, she was beginning to relax. She leaned back in the chair, held Ben's hand in hers and slept. The fears about Ben were buried under a blanket of snow in her mind. She was walking along a trail that was pure white, overwhelmingly white. The only contrast was the brilliant blue of the sky. It was silent, unbelievably silent, soul soothing and peaceful. Ben was also dreaming. He could see himself sitting under a cottonwood that in summer would be a shade giving canopy of green. Now it was leafless, but each branch was graced with the soft cotton-like comforter of snow. He saw himself sitting under this tree, watching each snowflake as it floated and danced toward its destiny. He could feel the cold purity of the flakes as they struck his face, as they melted on his fingertips. He marveled at the bright colors reflected in each minute arm of each crystal, iridescent rainbows that glittered all around him. He relaxed within the solitude, the total silence, the overwhelming peace.

In Belinda's dream, she was still on a journey. In the dream she understood that all life is a journey, a journey of discovery, and found comfort in that knowledge. She was enthralled with the overwhelming beauty, and from the falling snowflakes she composed a poem. Then a wave of sadness swept over her like a cold wind. There was no one with whom to share the beauty.

"How long has this pain been inside him?" The Indian asked.

Carlos could only shrug his shoulders. He'd had no idea his friend was hurting until now.

Courtney started to tell the old man she hoped that the panels hadn't caused this, but he waved his hand to silence her.

"You often ask far more than you should, but I think we are all guilty of causing his pain. Carlos, you are his friend, and yet you did not even know the anger was building inside him, devouring him."

Several others had entered to either satisfy their curiosity or share the burden.

The old Indian now stood and started pointing his finger, "You constantly interrupted his work, mostly to seek praise for your own endeavors. You constantly pushed him to seek the fame of his artistic career, when his interest was only in the creative part of it. You never let him escape from the issue of Oblivion's need for money. You always demanded more of his time to teach, to speak. Belinda even added to his burden, by her insecurities."

Apologies were spoken, "We didn't know." " I thought I was helping." " Isn't that his job?"

"All these demands and interruptions turned into anger. When Derritt became angry, he lashed out at everyone else. When the demons of anger found Ben, he couldn't lash out at others. He held them inside himself and fed them from his own flesh, his own soul." The old Indian was beginning to show anger himself as he continued, "All Ben wants to be is an artist. All he *can* be is an artist. All *we* can do is let him be what he is. Isn't that what he has tried to do for all of you?"

There was some muttering and some feelings of shame and guilt. Visitors started to wander out of the home into the street. There they spoke in small groups. They all loved Ben, cared for him, felt a loyalty to him. Now, they all wanted to help him.

The snowflake were falling softly, gently on Belinda. They melted on her cheeks and joined with the tears. This dream Belinda began to shiver. She kept walking, but the snow was now deeper and the journey became more difficult. The gentle snow became a blizzard. She lost direction.

269

Ben was enthralled with the beauty of each snowflake as it fell, but then they began to fall faster and faster. The unique beauty of each flake became overwhelming, so awesome that it became a frightful sight. His hands became cold; his fingers were numb. A fear grabbed his heart that he would never be able to paint again. Then, the greater realization spawned the greatest fear of all. Even if he did paint, who would see it? "Is there art if there is no audience?" He asked himself, breaking the silence.

The old Indian turned his attention to the drum and beat in time to Ben's heart. He chanted the peace chant, while his mind joined Ben and Belinda in their dreams. He found Belinda wandering, lost in the swirling snow, gripped by the icy fingers of loneliness, struggling under the burden of empty accomplishment. She didn't see him, but she felt her feet being turned in a new direction. The storm didn't lessen but, in some way, she was strengthened.

Ben sat, struggling to capture impressions on his sketchpad, but the snowfall turned the paper to pulp, while the cold turned his sensitive fingers into uncontrollable bundles of pain. His tears joined the snow on the wasted pages. He was crumbling under the weight of his twin terrors. He tasted the bitter fruit of failure and the agony of loneliness. The old Indian, with unseen hands, pulled the pad from Ben's frozen fingers and flung it into the driving snow storm. He pulled the artist to his feet and directed his steps.

The old Indian smiled as these two dream people walked through their snowtime to find each other. Belinda saw the dark cloud of a shape approaching her through the great waves of snow. She could hear within her soul a drumbeat, a heartbeat. Ben looked up from his misery and saw what looked like a shadow walking toward him. He called to this shadow and in that instant the blizzard halted and the sun shined down on them both. They stumbled as they ran toward each other. They embraced, cold lips joined to make warm kisses. Their feet didn't

270

touch the snow now, as they almost floated over the peaceful, pure whiteness to the waterfall and grotto behind.

They didn't notice the footprints that preceded their journey to this magical place. The old man had hurried ahead to prepare a fire and warm the grotto for them. He pulled heavy blankets and thick comforters from his small leather bag to prepare a warm bed for them. Next he set a rock ledge as a table; covering it with wine, sweet cakes and fruits long out of season. There was ice at the edges of the waterfall. These splashes of water, frozen in time, became rainbows of color in the cold afternoon sunshine. As they entered the small cavern, he disappeared through the waterfall and again sat beside Ben's bed. Belinda and her lover remained in their dreamtime. Smiles crossed and re-crossed their faces for the rest of the afternoon.

Courtney brought several bouquets of flowers into the room. Carlos and Domingo lit candles and said prayers. Others brought gifts, tokens of their love and concern, physical evidence of heartfelt apologies, and sincere concern.

Chapter Twenty-seven

It was late afternoon before the dark blue Lincoln turned at the sign that still pointed toward Oblivion with weathered letters on aged wood. Cal was forced to stop the car because of an old Indian sitting in the middle of the road smoking a pipe. When he blew the horn, the old man's only response was a polite wave and warm smile. Finally, Cal and Christa got out of the car and stood before the Indian. Cal started to ask him to move, but the seated figure raised his hand to silence them, then motioned for them to join him on the dusty road. Without questioning, they both did as they had been directed.

A perfect smoke ring escaped from the bowl of the pipe, and the old Indian's lips formed a broad smile. "I've been working on this." He gestured toward the rising donut of smoke. "Think I'm getting pretty good at it, too." To prove the point, he puffed again on the pipe and released another ring of smoke.

Cal started to speak, but another wave of the hand silenced him again.

"I know you want to get to Oblivion. You're curious and want to know what your old friend has been up to while this fine lady was healing your soul."

Christa gave an embarrassed smile and started to ask what old friend, fearing there might be another woman. She, too, was waved to silence. He put the flute to his lips and began a joyful tune that sounded somewhat like Vivaldi. This gradually blended into something more Medieval. Finally, without realizing when the transitions took place, Christa realized she was listening to purely Native American flute music while Cal was hearing more of the new age music he had discovered only this summer.

"Your friend needs your help, Cal." He finally spoke as he set the musical instrument aside and began the work of relighting the pipe.

Finally, Cal could no longer restrain himself. "Who are you?"

"A friend of yours," he responded, then directed a smile toward Christa. "A friend of yours, as well." He gave up on the pipe and set it aside. "Do you remember when you were nearly dead with heartache in the hospital, and Ben brought you a picture, and Belinda delivered a bag full of cards and bouquets of flowers. Wouldn't it take a friend to do that?"

Cal had to nod in agreement. Christa wanted to know who Belinda was.

"Oblivion is filled with folks who have been wounded by life, folks who never had a chance before, the people sociologists call the disenchanted and the disenfranchised. Folks that society thought were failures or hopeless dreamers."

He was trying to tell them something, but Christa interrupted. "That sure sounds like me." She smiled at the possibility of acceptance in this strange community, then she thought of Cal. He had been a big success, but he had felt big failures too. She was afraid he might be right, that he wouldn't be as comfortable here as she would be.

"Ben is very ill. You need to know that you are not here by accident or whim. You were brought here by the Great Mystery. You can literally save Ben's life." He started to stand, then added, "By the way, he will appreciate the gift you brought for him. It is great art, filled with meaning and made by your hands." With that, he was on his way down the hillside. He disappeared into the junipers while they watched.

"What gift is he talking about? What's this Great Mystery?" Cal asked as he opened the car door for her.

"Who is he?" Christa asked. None of the questions were answered.

Cal was reluctant to go the rest of the way. This was a journey through difficult emotional terrain. He knew he couldn't do this without her at his side. They drove the rest of the way in silence. Cal couldn't force himself to look over the hillside toward the remains of his homestead. He couldn't live in the past, and he was unsure of the future. All he really understood at this point in his life was that he loved Christa, and, somehow, that was enough.

News of the judge's decision had rippled through Oblivion. It was a double blow to the residents. First Ben was ill, now the future of the town was again in question. The community's fear was becoming hysteria. People meeting on the streets could speak of nothing but the direst of consequences. Twice during the afternoon rumors had flown through the community that Ben had died. Some were linking the decision to Ben's health. The sense of helplessness and hopelessness that is always the burden of those who have known poverty, those for whom the American dream was more of a nightmare, became a soul crushing weight. Some wept, while others searched for a target. The Bentons became the enemy again. Now Marquita was cursed as well. Fear is a hungry beast, and today it was prowling the streets of Oblivion.

Camille had been drawn to this little community by the stories she had heard, stories about people who would know nothing of the power she possessed. She was a French speaking Haitian refuge. Her husband had been one of Papa Doc's Tonton Macoutes, the dreaded militia of terror. He was also a hougan, a priest of the dark petros, the spirits of fear. Camille herself was a mambo or priestess. While her role in the fear filled culture of Voodoo had retreated into her past, she still retained the materials of her black arts. It was something she had never mentioned to any of the friendly folks of Oblivion. Her past was something to be guarded and protected until it was needed. She kept her

274

secrets locked in the closet of the little frame house she now called home. The most important was an old, stained, leather bound book that her mother had given her. In a culture where fear rules, a book of spells, hexes and curses is a valuable weapon.

Now, for the first time since she had escaped the horror of the revolution, she felt the need to consult this text of darkness. In preparation, she practiced the incantations and inhaled the incense. Then, after she had gathered the materials she would need, she drank the potions that put her in a trance. Then the dark spirits, the loa petros, entered her. She surrendered to their power and ceased to be Camille. From an old shirt, she created an effigy of Marquita. She carefully tied the ribbon around the doll's waist, the piece of ribbon that had fallen from Marquita's hair that night she first visited Oblivion, the night she sang. Then, she made one to represent Calmut Benton. For the Voodoo to work she needed something of his. She would go on this quest to save her new village, to keep herself safe. The petros that seized her mind told her to gather cactus spines to serve as needles. By late afternoon she was ready and could wait no longer for the security of nightfall. The petros were impatient. She pushed pieces of cardboard into her windows to make the room dark and lit her candles.

Serena sat alone on the far side of the lake. She had placed her crystals on the scarf that she had spread on the grass. After sitting and contemplating the judge's decree and Ben's illness for what seemed like a long time, she tried to pray. Visions of shame kept her mind from concentrating. Hers was guilt, not from what she had done, but from the sin she had contemplated, the dreams she had while sleeping against Larry's side. Finally, she removed her clothes and bathed in the cold purifying water of the lake. The sun dried her body while she tried to force the angry sounds from Oblivion away from her consciousness, while she tried to make her mind as clean as her body. Finally, she was ready to pray again. First, she breathed the deep rhythmic breaths that would let her know her place in the universe. She pulled thoughts together that would make her worthy of the request she was going to make to God. She focused on the amethyst that captured the sun and splashed rays of lavender glow across the scarf and over her lap. This was her candle. She still felt so unworthy. What right did she have to petition God? After the uncountable number of times she had failed, failed to help when others needed her, failed to think the thoughts and do the deeds that would make her worthy, failed to keep the unclean thoughts from her mind. Yet she wasn't asking for herself; she had never prayed for herself. It was for all these wonderful but frightened people that she was asking help, seeking comfort.

She held the crystal up to the sun. The glow bathed her face, illuminated her soul. Softly she began to sing the song from her childhood that had given her so much comfort.

"Jesus loves me. This I know." Into these words she wove the thoughts of her prayer. She asked God to restore the peace that had been so much a part of Oblivion, the hope that had nourished it and the dreams that gave it purpose. She prayed that Ben be comforted and healed. She prayed for Marquita, that she might be granted the wisdom to make the right decisions. She prayed for the Bentons. She understood that the judge's ruling destroyed their empire, that they lost all that was important to them. She asked for strength for Brandy. Throughout these heartfelt prayers, images of Larry intruded into her thoughts. She didn't understand that this was her prayer unspoken. She knew she wasn't worthy enough to pray for herself. These images of the bearded writer interrupting her prayers were proof to her that she was undeserving, unfit to seek the comfort of God. The tears formed.

The scientists and engineers were no less fearful than the campesinos. Dr. Taggertt was almost in a state of panic. They sought comfort in knowing, their information coming from the telephone, but even with the hundreds of calls being made few answers were found. Inez had been kneeling before the Santo and candles of her personal

276

altar all afternoon, fingers plying the beads of her Rosary as her lips repeated over and over the "Our Fathers, Hail Marys, and Glory be's." She paused only to light more candles. Her old legs ached from kneeling, and her back reminded her of her age with its pain, but she knew this was good. The pain was her mark of passion in the prayers. One's life could be measured by the pains it knew. The stumps of the candle were flickering as she continued "Hail Mary, full of grace; the Lord is with you; blessed are you among women, and blessed is the fruit of your womb, Jesus. Holy Mary, Mother of God, pray for us sinners, now and at the hour of our death, Amen."

Chi, Chan Ton and Lau were sitting in the back of Chan Ton's shop facing the small Buddha. Theirs was a silent meditation. They focused inward to know themselves, then sought to know their place in the community, in the universe. They united their souls in the quest for peace. In the middle of their prayers, they could hear the growing anger in the voices on the street. Fear and unknowing were turning these fine people into a mob. Chi, feeling the call to act, rose from the group and silently retreated. On the street, she saw groups gathering to feed the rumors. Some were saying that Marquita had sold the entire land grant to Calmut and his sons. There was talk of conspiracy, that Brandy had been sent into their midst as a spy, that the power companies felt threatened and wanted to put an end to the solar projects, that Ben had died, that he had been murdered. Beer cans and wine bottles were beginning to litter the street, as others sought comfort by communicating with these liquid spirits.

Camille uttered her spells as the cactus spines were prepared. She smiled because she knew how to deal with these threats to her new home. She was a mambo; she would be their Tonton Macoute. The others would go out in the streets and shout their fear and anger. She alone knew the forces to call upon. Potions were prepared by her hands, guided by the spirits of fear, the evil that possessed her.. She stood and selected just the right knife. She pulled on her shoes and left the security of her darkened house in search of a goat and a chicken. Sacrifices had to be made to the great one, and she was the only one that seemed to understood this. She alone could call on these forces.

Serena continued her prayers, continued them through the tears that streamed down her cheeks and made great wet patches on her white blouse. She wept at her failure to keep her prayers pure, she wept at her inability to keep Larry's face from her thoughts, she wept for the people of Oblivion. The children were seeking their comfort at the lake's edge when they saw her. Children understand fear in their parents, although they can't comprehend the cause. They had left the street and the growing confusion there, because they were frightened by what their parents were becoming. To hear Serena singing the songs they knew, was a comfort and they gathered around her, joining in her words.

The solar towers and great shining dishes seemed to glow in the late afternoon sun, while hundreds of windmills spun in the ever present canyon breezes. The once crumbling buildings of the former ghost town were now bright painted homes, all trimmed with green plants, flowers and trees. Lake Hope was most puzzling to Cal. Here was a medium sized body of water with islands of green floating on it. Strange plastic arches spread like giant wings over these raft gardens. He wanted to know more about this. He had no idea that something like this was happening in what had been his backyard. Christa saw the people gathered in the street and knew an instinctive fear.

The first person Cal encountered when he entered Oblivion was Dirty Maria. She gave him directions to Ben's house, but warned him that the community didn't trust him. Over a hundred angry fearful people watched as Cal climbed out of his car and opened the door for Christa. Shock waves of murmurs radiated down the street.

"Why would he appear here, on this day of all days?" One of the men said as he threw the beer can against the side of Cal's car.

"Why is he here on the day of Marquita's victory?" another asked, as the man they hated knock on the door of Ben's house.

278

"It was all a trick. That Marquita is his whore!" one of the women shouted. "It was all a trick to get our town!"

Courtney answered his knock on the door and invited him in with a smile. Ben was sitting on the edge of his bed; the pain had retreated after this attack. A broad smile crossed his tired face as the adversaries shook hands. Belinda was pleased to see that Cal was doing so well, but she was curious about the red haired woman at his side.

The four stood facing each other for a long moment, no one spoke, then without thinking, Cal embraced both Ben and Belinda. Then he turned and introduced them to Christa. Christa reached into the enormous handbag she carried, and removed a glass and tile sculpture they had worked on several days before. As she held it out to Ben, it captured the rays of the afternoon sun from the window. It was a tree formed of molten glass from green wine bottles they had found along the Canyon Road in Santa Fe. On this tree were chips of ceramic tile fruit in assorted colors. A dove, carved from pure white glass, was landing on the top of the tree. As she handed it to Ben and Belinda she titled it. "We called this *Abundant Peace*. It's for you."

Ben understood the artistic expression contained within this work, but he was most taken with the fact that Cal had created art, then shared it with him. He looked around the room for a suitable gift and realized that all his energy had been spent on those damned panels. All he had to offer was a small drawing of Brandy and Domingo, done weeks ago. It was only a preliminary sketch he had done one evening when they were dancing in the street. Belinda had written a rough draft of a love poem on the margins. Cal wept. For months he hadn't known whether she was alive or dead. Now here she was, dancing, happy. Christa couldn't understand, but was caught up in the emotions of the moment. Tears formed in her eyes.

It was in the middle of the emotional moment, that the noise began outside. First was the shouting and cursing. It sounded like Dirty Maria screaming, "Let him go! God damn you! Don't hurt him!"

The mob that had gathered outside Ben and Belinda's home assumed the shouting came from within the house and stormed the door to save Ben from the evil intentions of Cal. Others gathered around his car and rolled it over in the street. Later no one admitted setting the fire, but within minutes the dark blue Lincoln was ablaze. Those who had entered the house seized Cal and dragged him into the street. These weren't professionally bad people, so once they had him surrounded in the dust and smoke of late afternoon, they couldn't decide what to do with him. Ben, Belinda and Christa shouted at the mob but could not be heard, or would not be heeded.

While everyone was shouting and no one was listening Courtney stepped out into the bright afternoon sun and raised her arms, waving them in a circular motion. The cloud formed so quickly and darkened the sun so completely that everyone fell silent.

"Now that I have your attention," Courtney began, "I must ask you to welcome this gentleman into Oblivion as a friend. He came bearing gifts for Ben. The lightening flashed between the crowd and the burning car. The deluge fell only on the flames, but the thunder redirected the fear that dwelled within them all.

Into this confusion ran Camille clutching the baby goat to her chest as she tried to escape the wrath of Dirty Maria, whose bulk was amazingly capable of keeping pace with the fleeing thief. Courtney pointed to the ground in front of Camille, and a tangle of vines appeared. Camille saw them but couldn't stop. The goat squirmed free as she fell. The vines disappeared as Maria seized her by the hair. Later many of those present couldn't remember seeing the vines, but they all remembered the dove that landed on Camille's head and cooed at Maria as she prepared to strike. Maria's fist halted in mid-air. Then she extended her hand to help the thief to her feet. They shouted at each other in angry French. Then Camille, shaken by the events, retreated to her darkened house. On the way, she stooped to pick up the pen that had fallen from Cal's pocket.

One of the women in the street pointed toward the retreating Camille and whispered, "Cuidado, es una bruha, una mal bruha."

It was Chi that was playing the flute they heard. The angry voices quieted as she approached. This little old lady, back bent with age, was dancing to the cheerful tune as she reached the mob. One by one, they began to follow her. She paused at the steps of the old church to wait for the reluctant to catch up with those already assembled. From inside they could hear the soft reassuringly steady beat of a drum.

As some walked past Cal they spat on him. One woman, unable to contain her anger, threw a half empty can of beer at him, splashing the contents on his shirt. He understood their hatred, and rather than returning their anger, he felt only guilt and intense sadness. He looked to Ben and Belinda for guidance. Belinda took him by the arm while Ben went inside to get a clean shirt and jacket for the old man.

Christa had climbed inside one of the holes in her mind and refused to come out. She continued to sit on the doorstep and stare at the flame consumed vehicle. After changing his clothes in the middle of the street, Cal went over to Christa. He removed the clay dove from her purse and placed it in her hands.

Ben, Belinda and Cal could no longer resist the music of Chi's flute. As they all turned to walk away, the dove flapped its wings, and flew inside her mind. It quickly found the hole where she sought refuge and spoke to her. It explained that this was a ripple in the ocean of time. That long ago Cal had thrown a big rock into the water and the wave had just now caught up with him. It also tried to tell her that Cal had been washed by this wave of anger, that his past had been cleansed, that he was now free of it, and was an even better person now. The dove fluttered before her, leading her out of the hole in her mind, helping her to her feet, guiding her to freedom from her hiding place. Then it raced with her as she ran to catch up with this strange man she loved so deeply.

Chapter Twenty-eight

Don Aragon had been overwhelmed with the decision. He really was a knight in shining armor, a knight that had slain the dragon. The news media was eager to interview Marquita and her attorney. He gloried in the media attention. Before he was out of the courthouse, he had hired an old friend as their press secretary. Alicia would arrange the best interviews, get them on the most popular talk shows, get him the most lucrative print coverage. He was in his glory as he stood before the reporters on the courthouse steps, his arms around both Marquita and Alicia.

Marquita was also overwhelmed by the decision and the attention. She was still trying to comprehend the meaning of it all. If they were leasing the national forest back to the US government for one dollar a year, were giving Oblivion the same deal, and the Benton estate was only a few charred timbers and a bankrupt empire, what had she gained? Had she done this only for revenge? She didn't want to go through all these interviews, she didn't want to be on the evening news. She knew she should be supremely happy at this moment, but she wasn't. Her life wasn't following a plot from a romance novel. She didn't feel victorious. She didn't feel joyful. If anything, at this point in time, she felt confused.

This newly hired press secretary joined them on their drive back to the hotel in Santa Fe. Don began to list the developers and investors they should contact. He dominated the conversation with ambitious plans for ranches, tourist destinations, upscale retirement communities, golf courses, hunting/fishing lodges and movie sets. It was agreed that Alicia would prepare a biographical summary of Marquita, and her "rags to riches" story as a part of an official press release package that would begin the media victory tour and investment promotion. At dinner, the questioning began. They roamed through her childhood. Alicia made notes about a drunken abusive father. Hints were dropped about a deranged grandfather who may have sexually assaulted her. Although Marquita had said nothing that would imply such a thing, and knew it wasn't true, it would appear in the official press release. She described the joyful times she had as a child, helping her padre with the garden, caring for the goats and cow, helping her madre with the cooking and canning. She relaxed a little more as she spoke of the fun she had in the old ghost town. The press release spoke of a child so overworked by her lazy parents that her only escape was the drunken orgies held in a ghost town.

Marquita was both insulted and humiliated when Alicia asked, "Could you describe for me just what it was like, being the Benton family whore?" She refused to discuss this. Her stomach churned and rebelled against the degrading questions. She excused herself and sought refuge in the restroom. While she was gone, Don Aragon provided details about Marquita and the Bentons that had been shared as a confidence between lovers. It was agreed that he would provide her with more details after they got back to the hotel.

Marquita instinctively distrusted this "press secretary." She felt uncomfortable with the tone of the questions. The way she talked down to the newly decreed largest land owner in the state of New Mexico was insulting. She was also bothered by the fact that, as the dinner progressed, she seemed to be sitting closer and closer to Don. In some strange way, she couldn't quite understand, she was feeling more shame from her association with Don Aragon than with her former role as mistress to the Bentons. She knew what she had been to them. With Don, questions were beginning to form in the corners of her mind. Questions she didn't want to deal with on what was supposed to be the day of her greatest victory.

She had fulfilled her Abuelo's dream. She had restored the land grant. Now, she wasn't certain what that meant, and she was beginning to wonder just what the costs would be. She wished again that she could simply sit and talk with the poet she had met in Oblivion. In the cubicled privacy of the restroom, she again took the poem from her purse and read it. She knew the girl described in these words was really her, not the miserable creature being created by this Alicia. Tears began to fall on the paper. Tears that wouldn't stop. Her mind sought refuge in the past. Abuela took her hand and led her up the hillside to gather pinon nuts, the seeds of the pinon pine. She felt great comfort in this late autumn walk, the harvest not only of the natural bounty of food, but the bounty of beauty and peace as well. She thanked her grandmother for the gift of this journey into the hill country, as she returned to the reality of a restaurant bathroom. She dried her tears and returned the poem to her purse.

Reluctantly she returned to the table where Alicia was engaged in close conversation with Marquita's knight in shining armor. She was telling herself this was a foolish jealousy, when Alicia leaned forward and kissed Don on the cheek, brushing her breast against his arm, a motion that released the top button to expose more of her body than Marquita thought was appropriate. When she was seated again at the table, awaiting a dessert she couldn't eat, she suggested that Alicia might want to button her blouse.

Alicia flirted with the idea of asking Don to button it for her, but instead, fumbled with it enough to draw his attention. She then leaned over and whispered to Marquita, "But of course, you being a professional, you understand very well the value of buttons on a blouse. Don't you?"

Don spent the rest of the evening discussing in detail how HE had built the case. How HE had challenged the mighty Bentons. How HE had used the judge to get the results he wanted. How HE fought the greatest legal battle of the century and won the glorious victory. How HE had vanquished not only the Bentons, but the pitiful Indians and the bumbling government of the United States as well. How HE would turn

284

this into the richest piece of property in the world. Alicia stroked every word he spoke, fed his ego at the turn of every sentence, responded to each of his courtroom exploits with increasing awe, with surrender in her wide dark eyes.

After they had left Alicia at her room on the third floor and reached the privacy of their room on the fourth, he held Marquita in his arms and kissed her passionately. This was a passion that wasn't reciprocated. As she sat on the edge of the bed, he noticed the scars on her face, the cheekbones that were now slightly uneven, the ears that had become an imperfect match because of the beating, the puffiness around the eyes, the look of sadness that hung over her like a veil. Mentally he was comparing her with the beauty and willingness of Alicia. He was dismayed that she seemed not to appreciate what he had done for her. He was dismayed by the obvious intellectual shortcomings. Her mind clearly lacked the agility to soar with his grand ideas. His mind conjured up images of Alicia, smiling, understanding how great his accomplishments had been, respecting him for his skill in the legal arena, his position as "un gran hombre." He couldn't understand how his client, his lover could possibly withhold her body from him, how she could deny him, after what he had done for her. He understood the invitation of Alicia's loose button and contrasted that to the tightly collared tuxedo shirt Marquita wore. "Don't you understand what I have done for you?" He was genuinely hurt.

"Do I own the farms on the other side of the canyon rim? The farms where I grew up, where my friends lived?"

"Yes, you do." He hoped it was beginning to register with her the magnitude of the gift he had given her.

"What will happen to them?" She was staring into his eyes, earnestly seeking answers. "Those people have generations buried in the cemetery at San Lorenzo. You are talking about a recreation area with vacation villas. I don't think we should do that. I don't think we can do that."

"Don't you understand? This is the way owning property is going to make you rich. Who cares about a handful of old farmers." He could see the pained look of disbelief in her eyes and hastened to add, "If that bothers you, we can give them an all expense paid ticket to their favorite nursing home. Hell, you can even give the kids a scholarship, if that would make you feel better."

He put his arms around her but she only shivered. As he stood, he cursed her ingratitude. She watched as he straightened his tie. She tried to speak as he opened the door, but no words would form in her mind. He slammed the door, and moments later she could hear the elevator. She knew he was going to Alicia's room. She rolled over on the bed and wept. She retreated into her tears, into the sleep that her exhaustion drew over her like a soft warm blanket.

Alicia had prepared well. The lighting was subdued, the passion of flamenco guitars was seductively audible. The brandies had been carefully selected to accompany the caramelized cakes and rich fruited custards she knew were another of Don Aragon's weaknesses. She was waiting when the soft rapping came at the door. Her deep purple lounging gown had no inconvenient buttons, only a sash tied loosely at the waist.

When Don Aragon returned to Marquita's room hours later it was empty.

She had read this romance novel before and knew the plot well. She understood her role now. After all, she owned the property. She had the final say, not some bitch with a tape recorder, not some bastard of a lawyer who had used her so many different ways. It wasn't difficult for her to find a friend in the Chicano community of Santa Fe willing to drive her to Oblivion. She felt this need to meet with Belinda again. She felt a bond with this poet. She read and re-read the poem by flashlight as they bounced along the back roads of New Mexico's hill country. When they stopped for gas in Las Vegas, she saw the headline in the Albuquerque Journal, *Benton Mistress Gets Revenge*. The article

286

began with retelling of the great legal maneuvering by attorney Don Aragon, then related events from Marquita's past that she had only shared with Don Aragon, and when they weren't sufficiently sordid there were pure fabrications. It wasn't until the continuation of the article on page seven that the Land Grant Foundation was mentioned. The last paragraph pondered the effect on the farmers, the pueblo, the water rights, and the experimental community of Oblivion.

Chapter Twenty-nine

Cal had aged terribly in the less than thirty minutes of mindless confusion. The old Indian took him by the hand and led him to the chair by the altar, beside the clay bowl that held a small fire of pinon and juniper needles. Cal was stooped, spent and trembling as he walked up the center aisle past the people who had attacked him. Now, the wisps of smoke seemed to relax him. In some way he didn't understand, he felt that he was being prepared for something. Chi continued to play the flute, while the old Indian poured some sweet hot coffee into a small cup and handed it to Cal. Words were spoken that none of those present could hear. Next, an apple was removed from the Indian's leather bag. He fumbled with his Swiss army knife for several moments, before cutting a slice of the fruit and handing it to Cal. While Cal slowly consumed a piece of the apple, the Indian sat on the floor in front of him and wiped away the spit and dust from his shoes. He removed his sweatband and dipped it in the basin of water that sat on the floor beside them. With this moist cloth, he washed Cal's face and hands.

As he applied the cleansing fabric, Cal's shoulders straightened. Lines left his face, as if years had been erased. As he squeezed water from the cloth onto Cal's head, the hair seemed to darken. When the old Indian stepped back, the only lines left on the elder Benton's face were those built from the faint smile that he now wore. While the Indian retied his sweatband, the bell began to ring. Two children started to giggle as they fled from the rope, but the Old Indian only smiled, motioning for them to continue.

Serena heard the music of the bell, and led the children that had found security with her to its source. She ushered the children inside, but held back herself. Knowing how impure her heart was, she felt unworthy to enter this holy place. She sat in the dust at the edge of the steps, trying to catch the words and sounds that escaped the white walls.

Inez heard the call of the bell and knew she must heed it. She struggled to her feet and snuffed the candle stumps. The rosary was carefully folded into its velvet pouch and tucked into her pocket. Her legs ached, walking was difficult, even with her cane. She was the last one to approach the building. When saw Serena sitting as an outcast at the doorway the old lady reached down and offered her hand to the young lady in tears.

"Won't you join me?" Inez asked as her eyes made the short journey from Serena to the open door.

"I'm not good enough to enter such a place." Serena could not look Inez in the face. Rather, she bowed her head in humility.

"Mi hermosa, none of us are good enough. That's why churches exist. Now please, help this old lady up these steps."

"It seems that the children have called us together." The old Indian spoke with a smile, while Serena asked a couple to sit closer together so that room could be made for Inez. When the old lady was comfortable, Serena retreated to the back wall and sat on the floor.

The scent of juniper smoke floated throughout the structure, calming all those present. It was combined with the pinon, to give hope for the future.

He sat on the chair and pulled a small box turtle from his bag. He held it up for all to see. "I found it walking down the road that leads to Oblivion. Look. Here are scars," he pointed to a frayed edge of the shell. "Perhaps Coyote thought Turtle was dinner. But gave up. Why?"

Those gathered were still calming their anger and the fear that had spawned it. They only shrugged their shoulders.

He continued, "not because Turtle was more ferocious than Coyote, but because he was more patient. He knew that if he waited, this too would pass. Is this not the way of turtles?"

All nodded in agreement.

"When the long droughts come, as we know they always will, does Turtle panic and fear the worst?" He paused, but none were willing to contribute. "No. Of course not. He relies on his inner storehouse of nourishment, his inner strength to help him survive. Is this not the way of a turtle?"

Again, all nodded agreement.

"When the sun falls below the western mountains, does the turtle give up, thinking the sun will never return?"

The children were willing to give answers, where the adults feared humiliation. They all waved their hands and shouted, "No."

"Then is Turtle smarter that we are?"

Again the children didn't hesitate with their enthusiastic answer, "No."

"Then, if Turtle is patient enough to survive Coyote, is confident that he can withstand the drought, and has sufficient faith to believe the sun will return; and if we are smarter than a turtle, why are we so fearful today?"

He put the turtle on the floor. It looked around for less than a minute before it began its slow but determined march toward the door, oblivious to the people watching it.

"See. He goes about his job. His job is being a turtle. He is comfortable with his ability to be a turtle and concerns himself little with you. Perhaps we should be more like this turtle. Now, again I ask you, why was there such fear in our street only minutes ago?"

Through the mutterings and murmurs he detected the fear that was fed by rumors, by expectation of the most dire consequences.

"Perhaps this is a test from the Great Mystery." He spoke while beginning to tap lightly on the drum. It was a soothing rhythm that enhanced the waning juniper smoke. "If this was a test, how well do you think you did?" He stared at faces, one after another.

Some shook their heads, others hung them in shame.

"Let's try another test. Perhaps we can do better on this one." He continued to beat on the drum while handing a bundle of papers to Chi. She began to pass them out to everyone there.

Gasps and looks of fear and confusion formed on the faces of all present. It was a page full of math questions, dozens of questions, all in small print. Some were simple addition and subtraction, others were division, percentages, fractions, simple equations. Monetary signs and metric symbols were in evidence, as were scientific notations and Navajo words.

Everyone stared at the page, immobilized by the overwhelming size of the test. Then one of the children started to laugh. Then another. While their parents stood shocked by the magnitude of the test, these children remembered the lessons from Dirty Maria. They were looking at the individual problems.

The old Indian chuckled himself, amused by the anguish of the assembly. "How can you all be so dismayed by a simple piece of paper? How will your life change if you fail to answer a single question? What if you trample this paper underfoot and walk away? What will happen?"

He was further amused by their silence. "What if we all look at the first question?" He held his hands to conceal all but one problem. It was $140 - 139 = ?$

Several cautious hands were soon raised. Someone in the back said, "Isn't the answer 1?"

Another chided this courageous volunteer, "That's too easy. There's got to be a trick."

"Si, la respuesta es uno." one of the ladies in the front row confirmed after she had rewritten it on the back of the paper, just to be sure.

"Let's look at question number 17." It read five quarters minus fifteen pennies and one dime = how many dollars?

Laughter rippled through the building as they began to discover that this answer also was '1.'

Finally it became apparent that all the questions were answered with the numeral '1.'

"Some things do not change from childhood. When you were a child and the teacher gave you a math test, you saw the test and were overwhelmed by it. You didn't see each individual problem, most of which you could solve. You saw the entire test and were so immobilized by fear that you started to blame the teacher for your failure before you even tried. Is this not so?"

Embarrassed murmurs confirmed this statement.

He then continued, "Life itself is like a math test. Every rising sun brings with it a test for each one of us. Is this not so?"

Some nodded in agreement.

"I know that the news of this day is cause for concern, but think on this. Did we not welcome the Great Mystery with a thanks for the rising sun this morning?" He paused to let them reflect, then continued, "Will that same sun not rise again tomorrow?"

They could do nothing but agree.

"Because of a piece of paper signed by some judge you have never met, you are fearful. Is there a single blade of grass changed today by his decision? It the sun shining less brightly? Did you look at the whole test rather than each problem?"

Chi came to the altar and put her hand on Cal's shoulder. "We are fearing the one among us who has lost the most. Look at each of the problems on your test."

The old Indian was pleased with Chi's intervention. She offered the explanation. "If we look at each question, we will find that the answer is '1.' This is the way it is with life. We can usually manage one question at a time. The answer is always within us. Within each of us is the spirit of the Great Mystery. If we will listen to this part of us, then we will be as wise as the turtle, and we will make good choices.

292

If we make our decisions by listening to our fears and our ignorance we panic and run like foolish sheep.

Because we live within a community, we also have the comfort of knowing that when the problem is too great, others are here to help. Today, Cal needs our help. Today, Ben needs our help. Who in this community will extend a hand in friendship?"

Ben was in some ways offended by the suggestion that he needed help, but he knew it was true. The pain in his stomach was again telling him something was wrong. Still, he was the first to stand and offer his friendship to the transformed Calmut Benton.

It was easy for the good people of Oblivion to come forward and embrace Ben, to shower him with love and petition for him in their prayers, because they felt dependent on him. Many worried that something would happen to him. If Ben weren't there, how would Oblivion function?

Whether he could comprehend his role in this town or not, they did. He was *el Patron*. He was their leader. True he didn't father every new idea, he didn't approve or disapprove every action, he wasn't the source of financial security, he never corrected errant activity. His role was symbolic. He represented stability, hope, what was good in Oblivion. Through his art, they all saw the best in themselves. He helped them face the future with a sense of adventure. By his example, he showed them how to be individuals, unified in their goals. But, a leader must be strong. In the strange art he had done on the sheets of building board, they didn't see hope, they saw weakness in Ben, they saw his shadow. This is what they feared, that their leader could no longer lead. Ben, falling ill after completing art that appeared to all to be negative and depressing, on the same day the law literally stripped away his ownership of their town was cause for despair. The shadows held within each of them grew larger and briefly gained control of the good that lived inside them all. The shadow side of the community was roaming the street.

What they all failed to understand, scientists, farmers, carpenters, bakers, shopkeepers, all of them, was that Ben was not suited to the role of leadership. This was an accidental role that was eroding his talent, wasting away his health.

Cal had a lifelong tradition of managing, leading, making decisions. This summer he had tasted the creative life, and enjoyed it. The fact that he was a leader was what made the people fear him, distrust him. He envied Ben's talent, perception, insight, and, even though he wasn't ready to admit it, Ben's position of leadership in the community.

Camille watched from the window as the fools that lived in Oblivion gradually came forward to shake hands with the demon in their midst. The old Indian pulled apple after apple from his bag and handed them to Chi. She cut them into quarters and sat these on the altar. As each person came forward, Cal handed them a slice of the fruit.

The old Indian took Ben aside to explain what was happening. "It is important for people to share food. This is traditionally the first step in building a sense of community. It's also the best way to welcome a new member to the community."

Ben agreed, remembering the first day he and Belinda had spent in Oblivion. The image of the fiesta the night the first loads of people came into the town flashed into his mind.

The old man offered Ben a cup of tea, "A tea, to sooth your angry stomach."

Ben sipped the dark colored drink. He still felt the fangs gnawing at his insides. The waves of pain had exhausted him as much as the waves of misspent emotion on the street. He sought the chair, but missed and slumped to the floor.

A benign smile escaped the Indian's lips as he cushioned Ben's head with his leather bag and turned his attention toward Cal. Those gathered were beginning to feel more comfortable with their adversary's presence. Several were actively engaged in conversation. Cal began

294

asking questions about the solar collectors, about the terraced gardens that covered the walls of several of the buildings, about the rooftop gardens, about the strangely shaped windmills that dotted the landscape. Oblivion's residents were eager to respond. The answers fascinated Cal. He quickly grasped the significance for the future of what these pioneers were doing here.. As the gathering began its disintegration, several of the men invited Cal to join them in a little fishing at the lake. No one had ever asked him to go fishing with them before. He eagerly accepted.

"Swallow this before you go to the lake." The old Indian handed Cal a small glass vile that contained an aromatic liquid. "It will help to keep you from harm." He explained.

Cal held the little bottle while he studied the strange old man. Finally he asked, "From what harm?"

"As each of us has a shadow side, so does a community. We must protect ourselves from this, while we work to bring these shadows into the light. Please drink this. Many here need you. You owe it to them to maintain your health."

"These people don't need me," he said as he put the tiny bottle to his lips. Chad was excitedly explaining how the ecosystem of the lake had been so carefully constructed and how well the concepts of aqua-farming and aqua-botanics were working.

Christa and Belinda helped the Indian carry Ben back to his house. The drugged sleep was the complete rest that Ben needed. He would awake refreshed and renewed. He would see the answers he needed in his dreams.

Camille was thwarted at every turn as she sought a chicken and goat for her sacrifice. This was a part of the ritual. It was necessary for the spell to work. Finally, in the darkness she was able to seize one of Inez's chickens. Wrapped in the fold of her dress to keep it quiet as she ran through the shadows back to her house. In the wavering light of the candles, with the aroma of the pungent incense, while she chanted the incantation, she severed the unfortunate chicken's head and drained the blood into a bowl. She split the carcass open and removed the warm still throbbing heart. She put the heart in the bowl of blood and put it to her lips. She drank deeply of the warm salty liquid. Then she washed her hands in the blood.

The effigy of Calmut Benton was taken from its place in front of her candles. She tied his pen to the doll, then placed the chicken's heart on its chest. She pinned it in place with a cactus spine. The blood was smeared over the four corners of the table with lines painted toward the center where the doll rested. Then the book of curses was opened and propped against the candles so she could read the dark words. The verses were repeated over and over as she selected one of the cactus spines and dipped it in the blood. With all the hate she could call forth from the darkest regions of her mind, she raised the spine into the air and drove it through the heart and deep into the doll. Again and again she did this. The frenzy of hate was so great that when the last spine was used, she fell to the floor, completely spent.

Cal had never had as much fun as he was having with these fine gentlemen, two Hispanics and this strange fella named Chad. They smoked cigars, drank a beer or two, and talked late into the night. They spoke of fish and solar energy, of good women and ecosystems, they enjoyed the present as the shared stories of the past and hopes for the future. They all came to respect each other as friends, as compadres. Cal even caught several of the lake trout that had been stocked there by the aquaculturists. He never felt better. It was a glorious night for him. When they broke up the fishing party at about two in the morning, he returned to Ben and Belinda's home and related the events with enthusiasm. Ben had been carried to the sofa in his studio. There he would continue to sleep until late the next morning.

Finally it was suggested that Cal and Christa could sleep in his bed. Belinda wrapped herself in a quilt on the floor beside Ben in the studio. Cal and Christa both had a sense of belonging, a feeling of

296

fulfillment, a feeling that they had come home. This euphoria powered their love making and gave them both great joy. When they awoke late the next morning, they both wanted to explore this place called Oblivion.

It wasn't until late that afternoon that Inez complained of a missing chicken and, accompanied by Dirty Maria, pounded on the door of the house Camille had claimed. Finally, when there was no response, they opened one of the windows and pushed the cardboard out of the way. The horror of what they saw made them both sick. The candles had all burned away, leaving black waxy scars and the ashes of what had been a book on the old battered dresser. The blood stained doll lay on the table with dozens of pins holding some sort of animal flesh to its chest. A dead and disemboweled chicken was on the floor next to the body of Camille. The medical examiner told them later that the cause of her death was a heart attack. The old Indian knew she had died from an overdose of fear.

Chapter Thirty

Marquita was comparing the lines in Belinda's poem with the vicious words that robbed all the joy of her victory. Belinda had described her parents as hard working people living in poverty. Images of love, faith, a closeness to the soil, were all a part of the poet's picture. These impressions of a culture, new to Belinda, were imperfect but respectful. Alicia shared Marquita's heritage, yet demeaned it. As they drove through Juniper Crossing, Marquita felt the need to change her destination. She asked Roberto to take the road that led to the remains of the Benton estate. As they traversed the long driveway, they could see, looming ahead, the charred timbers and piles of stonework standing black against the night sky. It brought to her mind the skeleton of a great dinosaur. She knew it was a way of life that was extinct, a great beast that had fallen from the weight of its own excesses.

She stood beside the car for several minutes before it registered with her that she owned this as well. Accompanied by overwhelming sadness, she walked to the timbers that marked the entrance hall. Looters had picked the body of this beast clean. It only remained now for nature to reclaim her own, to cover the scars with vines, heal the wounds with wind and sand. Tears flowed from her memory as her mind saw Derritt and Landreth, felt their brutality, lived again the humiliation. Her mind could see Cal sharing a drink with her before he took her by the hand and led her up the stairs. He had used her as well, but, at least, he treated her as a fellow human being.

For the first time she realized Cal had suffered the greatest loss of them all. He lost his family, his home, his empire and his identity as a powerful member of the business community, all at the same time he lost his health. She knew her scars would remain, but at least she could look forward to a life of normal activity and vigor. Cal had lost an eye and suffered heart attacks because of Derritt's viciousness. Some of the tears were for him.

She was trying to picture the house and out buildings as they had been before the fire. She forced her mind to walk through each room. Perhaps Alicia was right. All she had ever been, all she would ever be, is the Benton whore. Her mind was telling her that what Alicia described was reality. Belinda's poem was the romance novel she wished she could live. Maybe she wasn't suited to own this much property, control this many people. Maybe she did need Don Aragon to handle the business of the reinstated Lopez land grant. Still, managing the land as a business had failed for the Bentons. Perhaps she needed to do something else.

It was now almost three a.m. As she returned to the car, she knew she had to visit the home of her parents next. She had spent her childhood in the small community of farms that clustered around the Chapel of San Lorenzo. This was, at one time in the distant past, a gathering place for the faithful. This was before the twentieth century brought its paved roads, electricity and new jobs. Eventually power lines were run as far as the chapel. Several of the farmers also tapped into this as a symbol of the prosperity they found so elusive. Marquita's family could not afford electricity, telephones, indoor plumbing or running water. It had been difficult for her to understand, as a child, how there could be such poverty less than half a mile from the great Benton ranch house. Then, she blamed her parents. Now, she could understand that there is more than one kind of poverty.

She had reluctantly attended the funeral of her father in the chill of a late October morning. It had been so long ago. At nineteen, she had been little more than a child. Her mother had struggled alone with the house and little garden plot until, five years later, she too was gathered up in the harvest season by the father of time. She had died as Father Andy gave her the last rites, in the same bed where she had given birth to three children.

Now, someone she didn't even know was living in this house, tending the garden, drinking the water from the well. Even in the darkness of night she could see the ristras, the strings of drying chiles, hanging along the porch. The trees at the side of the house were loaded with apples ready for the harvest. The fruit reflected the moonlight, giving the appearance of Christmas lights strung through their branches. She could see the cabbages and vines bending under the late season tomatoes, where the garden had always been. The names of the people might be different, but in this culture, little else changed.

It had been a long time since she had seen her parents, a longer time still since she had visited the chapel. From where the car sat, she could see it in the distance, silhouetted against the clouds forming in the night sky. She wanted to go to this sanctuary and beg God's forgiveness. She wanted to walk into the cemetery and beg for the understanding and forgiveness that only parents can give. After all, she had deserted them in their old age, abandoned their love, to live a life of carnal sin in the Benton household. She asked herself if there was any way they could they understand, accept, or forgive what she had done.

This night, she also felt a need to go to the place where Abuelo's body rested, and tell his soul that he had been right. She had fulfilled his quest. In her troubled mind, her grandfather was the only one she hadn't failed.

Roberto was reluctant to visit a graveyard in the middle of the night, but this lady in the backseat was the biggest landowner he had ever met. This made her rich, powerful, someone to be obeyed. Whatever she asked, would be done. He parked outside the gate, but lacked the courage to accompany her inside the adobe and stone walls. She paused at her parent's graves and pulled the weeds from the markers. The names were almost weathered away.

300

"Does one's place in the memories of others fade as quickly as the paint on the markers?" she spoke aloud. She missed her madre y padre so much. Through the tears she could see Daddy roasting the chiles, could smell their pungent aroma. With each breath now, she was inhaling the fragrance of the bread and pies baking in Mama's kitchen. "NO!" She shouted to the night sky. "You were nothing like the people Alicia showed the world in her press release. You were kind and loving. We made a good family. Didn't we?"

True, her father drank, her mother lived in a world of superstition, but they still loved their children and mourned deeply, and forever, the death of her brother and sister.

She knelt and apologized for deserting them in their old age, for not understanding their sorrow and suffering, for not joining in their joys. Her tears watered the weeds that, in their own way gave proof of a life everlasting. She vowed to them that she would honor them by caring for all those left on these farms, those she had turned her back on years ago.

Next, she went to the corner of the walled cemetery, where, under the pinon, her grandfather had found his eternal rest. She talked for a long time with her abuelo. She told him all about the trial, the vindication of his dream, the fulfillment of the quest that had brought him so much ridicule. She was talking to him about the strange community that had grown where the ghost town once was, when the figure approached She didn't see the dark form that seemed to emerge from the shrubbery by the wall.

Roberto was watching from the security of his car as this apparition approached Marquita.

He wanted to shout a warning. He also wanted to start the engine and get the hell out of there. Instead, all he could do was make the sign of the cross and continue to watch, in breathless silence.

"Your grandfather was a good man." The old Indian spoke softly as he placed his hand on her shoulder. "He had great dreams. He had a vision. His greatness came not from the dream, but from the courage he showed by not abandoning it when it seemed hopeless, and others laughed."

Marquita was startled at the touch, but was comforted by the soft words. Her mind saw Father Andy, although she knew that his soul had made its journey to heaven years ago. If this was his ghost, perhaps it was here to take her. The thought didn't frighten her, or even cause dismay. In the presence of this figure, she felt strangely at peace.

He took her hand and helped her to her feet. "You are a good person, too. You have seen much of what is not beautiful in this world. You have known pain, suffering and humiliation. These all have given you wisdom others do not possess. It is now time for you to sing your song."

She fell to her knees again as she held tightly to his hand. "Forgive me Father, for I have sinned." She began her confession. She gave voice to all the burdens of her soul. Her mind was confused, but it had been years since she had sat on the hard dark bench, stared at the candle and told Father Andy the sins of childhood. Now, it was true, she spoke with more understanding. But this only compounded the guilt. She confessed her failure as a daughter to comfort her parents. She confessed her failure to honor the rites of the Church. She begged forgiveness for turning her back on the people of her community. She told him she knew there could be no penance great enough to pay for her sins of the flesh. She told him of her career as a prostitute, and how she had whored after money. "There can be no atonement for these sins. I am doomed."

He knelt beside her and wrapped his arms around her. Her tears soaked the shoulder of his flannel shirt. She still saw the bald head of Father Andy and found comfort in the folds of his dark robe.

He raised his ancient hand, and with a gentle finger traced the lines of the scars across her face.

"For those of your faith, the price of forgiveness was paid long ago. Think on this though." He placed a hand on each shoulder, "Has the sin not been its own penance?"

"Am I dying?" She finally asked.

A comfortable laugh was the first response. This was quickly followed by, "Quite the opposite. You, my child, are just beginning to live."

Questions were forming in her mind, but she couldn't put the words together to give them voice.

He stood, helped her to her feet, faced again the resting place of her grandfather. "What you do with your victory will determine how well you honor him, and the Great Mystery."

It was no longer Father Andy beside her. It was a smelly old Indian. She clenched her fists and closed her eyes in fear. A short prayer escaped her lips.. When she opened her eyes, she was alone.

Her steps quickened as she sought the security of the car, as she retreated from this place of the dead, from this conversation. Before she buckled the seatbelt, the car was in motion. The more she thought about the visitor, the more confident she was of her ability to do the right thing. In the neglected cemetery of the old church of San Lorenzo, Marquita had buried her past. The mile and a half to Oblivion was a time of discovery for Marquita. She found comfort in the great solar collectors, black against the night sky, the welcoming arms of the cottonwoods by the lake, the steeple of the community's church, the variety of home styles, each an experimental look into the future.

Roberto stopped his chevy beside the charred remains of another car, laying upside down like a dead turtle. Marquita stood in the middle of the dark, dusty street. Now that she was here, she had no idea where to go, or what she was to do.

She handed Roberto a hundred dollar bill, and thanked him for the ride. He wasted no time retreating from this strange place, from this night of dead buildings, ghosts and a community that looked too different for his mind to accept.

She watched the rolls of dust that followed the car's retreat, then she stood alone. Even the silence was comforting. It let her mind roam freely through the valleys of before and the mountains of tomorrow. For the first time in her life, she owned property and controlled lives. Standing in the dark street of Oblivion she finally realized the magnitude of the court's decision, and it humbled her. She shivered in the cold night air. She hadn't thought of where she would go once she got here. She had left Santa Fe to escape something she couldn't cope with, but now that she was in Oblivion, she was thinking about a future that she couldn't yet comprehend.

She walked up the street, paused and sat in the doorway of the old jail for awhile. The pre-dawn breezes increased the chill. She stood and reached for the latch on the door to the jail, but decided the past was the only prison she could deal with tonight. The jail could provide no warmth for body or soul. She studied the church across the street, wondering if its door was locked. Finally, she decided to try it. After all, she did own Oblivion. The door opened easily, almost as an invitation. As her footsteps echoed across the wooden floor, she thought she could smell coffee. The aroma drew her to the front of the structure, past the altar. Then, the soothing tones of a flute joined the fresh warm fragrance. The door of the vestry was open. A soft light joined the sound and smell as all the senses awakened to the approaching dawn.

She paused at the door, then cautiously looked inside. The light came from a candle sitting on the table beside the coffee maker. a plate of Danish, cheese, apple and berry, was also on the table. Sitting cross legged on the floor sat the same old Indian she had seen at the cemetery. He was playing the flute so softly that she wasn't certain whether she was hearing it or dreaming it.

Without turning he spoke. "You must be cold and hungry after your journey. I made some coffee for you. I couldn't remember which flavor rolls you preferred, so I got the three choices they had. Help yourself." Then, as an afterthought, he added, "There's a blanket hanging over the chair. It will also give you comfort and warmth."

She poured her coffee, then thought better of it and offered him the first cup. He smiled at her thoughtfulness. The soft old blanket did indeed provide comfort. She was just starting to eat the Danish when he stood and looked at his watch.

"It's almost dawn." He spoke with of a sound of urgency in his voice, as he removed the small leather pouch from his neck. "Would you care to join me at the door for of a moment or two?"

They stood watching as the first hints of the sun's arrival crept over the canyon's east rim. He opened the bag and removed of a pinch of the yellow powder it contained. Then he handed the bag to her, motioning for her to do the same. She didn't understand but followed his lead and also removed a small bit of the dust.

"As the first rays reach us, and the morning sun rests from its climb, we offer this corn pollen, to nourish it and say thanks. It is always a good thing, don't you think, to start the day by giving something away and being thankful for the opportunity to enjoy one more day?"

Much of her life she had dreaded the advent of each morning, feared the hours of each day. Now, she truly felt there was something to look forward to, joy to be anticipated, work to be accomplished. She started to thank him for the great insight.

"I know what you are thinking." He interrupted her before she could speak. "They are good thoughts. Now, let's have some more of that coffee and, if you don't mind, I think I'll have one of these apple pastries."

They talked long about Oblivion, people's dreams and their fears, how some truths are universal, even when they are known by different

305

names. As the coffee pot was drained, they began to discuss the problem of evil.

"Why do people do bad things?" she asked as her mind opened its trunk of past deeds, bringing to a new light the sins she had buried last night. Her mind was now looking beyond what she had done to see that Derritt, Landreth and Calmut were also guilty of sins. "Look at the Bentons. Their violence, deceit and greed have affected the lives of so many."

"It is true. In the ripple effect of our actions, people we don't know, people still unborn are either beneficiaries or victims of every move we make. We even influence the flowers that bloom and the bird's song."

"That's kinda what this place is about, isn't it?" She was trying to understand.

"As much evil can be done by not acting as is done by committing the evil deeds. Many mourn the death of species, complain about poison in the air, cast blame for fouled water, but if they do nothing more than point fingers they are as guilty. Here we are trying to lead by example. Out of Oblivion we hope to create a future where humanity learns again how to assume its place as a part of nature, not its enemy. In the process of learning this, hopefully, we will also learn how to live in harmony with ourselves. But we still have a long way to go."

"It seems like this is a peaceful community."

"There was great evil in our midst yesterday. It was the sort of evil that is born of fear and hate. When we do not understand something, our ignorance makes us act out of fear. Fear always expects the worst, and then fulfills its own prophecy. We cannot condemn these good people for their lack of knowledge. But while they sought only to defend, another chose to destroy. She came to us from a way of life that did not have room for the peace and harmony that we seek here. She didn't understand that, in the light of the sun, we can all be brothers and

306

sisters. She destroyed herself because she chose to combat the power of love with the weakness of hate."

"Why did Derritt do such terrible things? Why did Landreth try to kill me?" She paused for of a moment, trying to find the answers to her own questions. "Is it the work of the devil?"

He smiled, pleased that she was willing, and capable, in the art of dialogue. She had always demeaned her intellect because of a lack of education. Now it was obvious, that in the school of life, she had gained the wisdom to know that she had to seek the answers. "The Great Mystery gives us the strength of gentleness, arms us all with compassion. The devil, as you call it, is a tempter, and a horse trader. It offers what we don't need at a price we can ill afford. The price paid by those who embrace evil, are the gifts of the Great Mystery. Isn't it curious that we are so willing to trade love for pleasure, compassion for possession, or gentleness for power? Think on this. Do not our shadows purchase what was already ours?"

She still did not understand.

"Understanding doesn't come in a cloudburst, accompanied by thunder and lightening. Understanding comes as a gentle rain that first sprouts the seed and then, in its own time, creates the flower." He stood, gathered the dishes and washed them.

As she dried the plates and mugs, he continued to talk to her about all the good that was possible when people worked together, with each other and with the natural community. He spoke to her of the global nest, how the Great Mystery gives us all great gifts. He told her, "Peace is a universal goal that can only be achieved if we first accept the gift of inner peace, then we can share this most valuable of possessions.."

She pondered these words, but true comprehension eluded her.

" Now, if you will excuse me, I have much work to do."

She watched as he walked out the door, her mind caught up in the swirling mist of thoughts and ideas, concepts she was having difficulty

307

grasping. She folded the blanket and placed it over the back of the chair, extinguished the candle, and followed his steps to the street. She had more questions to ask. He was nowhere to be seen.

Ben dreamed well in his drugged sleep. He had taken great journeys in time, both forward and back. The vision he possessed as an artist had returned. He had glimpsed what he must do yet, and insight had been given on how it was to be achieved. He saw himself illuminating a dark forest with glowing paintings, paintings that showed love, peace, humanity as a part of nature. All existence was a wheel, turning freely in time. This new art would show the beauty of form and the joy of life. He knew that never again could he show the anger that had filled the great panels. In his dreams he destroyed them. He now understood that they were the catharsis, they were the agonized screams of a creative soul being reborn, being again set free.

In these visions he was no longer "el Patron" of Oblivion, but he had now a greater responsibility. That was to use his gifts to illustrate the possibility, the potential of a universal harmony. His awakening was accompanied by an awareness. All his life he had felt like a failure. He had no money, no great accomplishments, no one cared what he said or did. Then, he owned an entire community, and discovered that possession can be a great weight on the soul.

He savored the sweet flavors of success with his art. He was honored with shows at a major university gallery, prints of his work hung on the walls of many homes. He had illustrated two books. Then he saw his talent fall to anger, as he discovered that the size of his paintings was no substitute for talent lost.

He wallowed in his anonymity until he owned Oblivion, now he understood that fame often comes with a price tag that must be paid for with time. He hadn't longed for power and control. Yet, he had wanted people to seek his permission, or at the least, his opinions. Now he was sought out by every visitor possessing an idea or product to sell. Before he owned Oblivion, he possessed the freedom, and the time, to create. He was now forced to the realization that those who control are the most controlled, that in many ways the price of power is freedom.

He had spent a lifetime in his personal oblivion, now he owned the community that gave form to the word. This morning he grappled with several great truths. First, he had not sought to be the owner of this town. He now grasped the truth that he was a part of some one else's dream. He was a catalyst, and little more.

The second truth that confronted him this morning was that he was no longer the owner, Marquita Lopez was. He wanted to talk to her about protecting all the good people living here. He felt a drive to plead with her for the continuation of the environmental experiments and projects. He had to make her understand that Oblivion was a successful community because it was a wholesome blend of people and ideas. This must continue.

The last truth that he dealt with, he wrapped himself in, like a warm blanket. He had been drawn to Belinda from the first moment on the hillside overlooking the town, at a time when it was as empty as his life had been. He now understood that it was her love that had sustained him through his difficult summer. He took great delight and comfort in the simple truth that love is the greatest gift, that there is something profoundly sacred, something most beautiful, something overwhelmingly good in it. He wanted to talk with the old Indian about this. He had to know more about this many faceted gem called love. He wanted to devote his life to Belinda. "The understanding of love, after all, requires a lifetime of experience," he told himself as he struggled with the conflict between leading, managing, creating and loving.

As he approached the church, he saw Marquita coming down the steps and called to her. She was unsure how he would accept her ownership of Oblivion. She didn't want him to feel that he had lost it. She was eager to make him understand that she didn't want to do anything to interfere with what was happening here. She didn't want to usurp his position, even though she had no idea yet what her role would be.

He grasped her hand awkwardly, as he welcomed her to Oblivion. Then she hugged him, and gave him a kiss on the cheek. After an uncomfortable silence, he thanked her profusely for setting him free. This thoroughly confused her, but she was pleased by this display of genuine acceptance and friendship. She started to ask him questions about the town, the people, the projects. While he tried to explain the many methods they used to capture the power in the sun and the wind, she was looking at the gardens around the school, laughing at the chickens on the rooftops, delighting in the vitality and comfort she instinctively felt in Oblivion. When they walked past the old pump and water trough, she giggled and Ben blushed, but neither spoke a word about it. The feelings came from two different memories.

Several of the townspeople were already at the lake, some to get in an hour of fishing before the day's labors commenced, others were monitoring the mineral level of the lake, or harvesting food and flowers from the floating islands. Because these islands were covered with plastic vapor collectors, warmth was concentrated there, greatly extending the growing season. It was hoped that these semi-greenhouses could be sufficiently energy efficient to grow plants throughout the winter.

Marquita paused to chat with a couple preparing to take their small boat out into the waters of this new lake. She was much better at understanding the people of Oblivion than the science that was happening here. She was little interested in the explanations he offered of the solar towers and the array of solar collectors flashing their reflections of the dawn back toward the sky. He tried to explain the work of a botanist who was trying to replicate the efficiency of a green leaf in solar collection. She was more interested in the story of Emilio Franco, who was now devoting all his energies toward support and funding for this project. He was firm in the conviction that if humanity

310

could harness the power contained in the cell of a leaf, the power to convert the sun's energy into the food for the world, the lives of millions of plants could be saved.

She stood and studied the huge panels of art that sat in the shade of the cottonwoods. Finally, she had to admit that she couldn't understand them. Pointing to several features, she said they looked angry, full of fear. She liked the one of the soldiers becoming peaceful, and speculated on whether any of the Bentons could ever be comfortable enough with themselves to feed little children. They walked out of the town to the gardens under the solar collectors. She paused to chat with the people tending their plots. She helped them with their late season harvest, and listened intently while they explained to her how the soil had been coated with a product made from vegetable oil and old newspapers. Because of this mulch evaporation was slowed and insects discouraged. This required less than a third of the water an open field would use. Another showed her a waffle garden patterned after a technique developed centuries ago by the Zuni people to conserve water in an arid climate. She was intrigued by raised beds with a honeycomb of cells where each plant was growing in its own space. The scientist explained to her that with this intensive gardening system impoverished people everywhere could raise healthy food for their survival.

They proudly showed her the unusual plants that were part of another experiment. Seeds of Change, an environmental seed company concerned with bio-diversity, had supplied many of the species they were growing. Marquita was intrigued that these elderly gardeners were so excited about the new plants they were growing. She tried to picture her parents tending such a plot, then it dawned on her. She could do it. This is what she could do to serve this community. She could help to grow its food. She began to sing softly a song from her Hispanic youth. She felt happiness and contentment in Oblivion's sunshine.

Chapter Thirty-one

Belinda was awakened by the purring of the half grown kitten, comfortably curled in a ball at her side. Sunbeam stretched, licked its paws and rubbed its head against her arm. While sleeping, the image of a poem had come to her. Often her ideas were born in dreams. On rare occasions she would even speak key lines in her sleep. Ben wrote these down, and they become the seeds of new poems and essays.

This morning she struggled with the lines of a poem that had begun in her dreamtime. She was trying to draw the analogy of personal oblivion, with this community that bore the name. As is often the case with writers, the words refused to flow. She could smell the delightful aroma of Don Francisco's Vanilla Nut coffee, and hoped that might provide her with enough inspiration to find the right words. Ben, as usual, had made a pot of coffee before he left for his morning walk. Belinda poured herself a cup, then sat at the studio desk to write. Sunbeam curled up beside the mug of coffee, consuming its warmth as Belinda consumed the liquid.

The word *oblivion* was defined in Belinda's mind as "forgotten, mentally withdrawn, insignificant, obscure, in a state of limbo." She could see how these definitions applied to the community Ben had first shown her. She could see how it was a term that applied to the past of virtually everyone that now resided here, but it didn't define the community now. The lines of this poem that formed under her pen portrayed the people here as pioneers, people who possessed the courage to change their lives rather than give up, people who knew they weren't perfect, but were willing to use their flaws as stepping stones on the pathway to something better. The name Oblivion didn't seem to fit.

Other lines looked at the experiments being conducted in each home. She wrote of the courage of these people who had not retreated into the mythological comfort of some idealized past. They were boldly seeking the unclaimed and yet to be created future. Perhaps, she thought, the adversity and the faults within each of us make this a community of caring and courage. Even more, the name Oblivion, didn't seem to fit.

Next, lines explored how curiosity and the thirst for knowledge spread over these people like warm sunshine. Lines spoke of Dr. Taggertt learning how to grow herbs from Inez; how Chad and Frog listened intently to the stories and traditions of the Hispanic and Indian past in New Mexico. This was all knowledge that was not to be forgotten. By learning these things, everyone was constantly changing, forever growing. Definitely now, Belinda questioned the appropriateness of the name Oblivion.

Sunbeam yawned, stretched and stood. In the process, the young cat knocked a book over onto Belinda's words. It was a dictionary. She decided to open it and check her understanding of the word that was giving her so much trouble.

oblivion 1. The state of being forgotten, as by the public. 2. The state of forgetting or being mentally withdrawn. 3. Official disregard or overlooking of offenses; pardon; amnesty.

"That's it!" She shouted, as she hugged the purring cat.

Words flowed so swiftly from her mind now that her fingers could not keep pace. This was where one's past with all its failures, mistakes, problems, sin, faults, missed opportunities and wrong moves could be overlooked These flaws could be disregarded because they were universally accepted and shared. Even more important was the fact that, rather than looking back, instead of wallowing in the secure misery of the past, these people had pardoned themselves, and in the process gained their personal freedom, their ability to visualize a future. Yes! There was no better name for this rag-tag collection of misfits, social cripples, geniuses, and outcasts than Oblivion. This was their place of healing, their haven, their amnesty, their home, their future.

It was a powerful poem, with lines short and sometimes blunt. It spoke of everyone's need to seek oblivion. It explained that Oblivion was a state of mind, a comfortable village to be found within each one of us, wherever we are, whenever we are ready.

While she was refilling the coffee cup, Cal and Christa dressed and left the bedroom to seek their hostess. Cal saw the poem lying on the desk. He could not help but read it. He was still holding the pages when Belinda returned.

"It's as though you were speaking to me," he said, then offered an apology for reading something for which no invitation had been given.

Christa was looking over his shoulder, trying to follow the penciled flow of words. "I wish these people didn't hate me. I know I deserve it, but . . ." He looked so sad, yet, under the stubble of a beard and the tussled gray hair, there was a vitality that Belinda had not noticed before.

Christa nodded her head in agreement, although she had no idea why Cal had caused such rage the day before. Her red hair begged for a brush, but it also framed, with reckless abandon, the love that was in her eyes when she glanced at Cal. They had only the clothes from yesterday, and these were wrinkled and smelled of sweat from the heat of the day and the stress of the afternoon. Their suitcase was destroyed when the people of Oblivion burned Cal's Lincoln. Belinda led them to the kitchen, poured them coffee and served them some of Mama Rosa's apple pie. While they ate, she put together a change of clothes for each of them. Cal was a little thinner than Ben, but the shirt and pants would fit, even if they were baggy. Christa was taller and heavier than Belinda, but the sweatsuit she had been wearing the first day she met Ben should be comfortable and warm enough to defend against the morning chill.

After sharing the pot of coffee and discussing the people of Oblivion, Belinda offered to give them a tour of the village. They were

314

both eager to see more of Oblivion, as soon as they showered and dressed. She smiled and suggested that they shower together. Blushing, she admitted that she and Ben had a long history of bathing together. After all, in the desert one must conserve water whenever possible. She even told them the story of the water trough on her first day in Oblivion.

Cal and Christa were not yet accustomed to shared nudity. They were both delightfully uncomfortable as they stepped under the warm water. They giggled like children as they soaped each other's hair and body. Neither had made love in a shower before, but both delighted in the experience. Belinda smiled as she contemplated the reason the water was running so long. She wouldn't tell them that their words and laughter were audible through the wall. It pleased Belinda that these two were able to find joy in each other. She wished they could become a part of Oblivion.

The walk through the town began at the school. Cal wasn't accustomed to children, but they were eager to show him and Christa what they were doing. Within minutes he was on his hands and knees looking at the different species of ants and other insects that occupied the playground. The kids were battling for the opportunity to explain the role each of the creatures played in the world under their feet, the mini-environment that was an insect's world. They explained that the ants aerated the soil, stored food for the winter ahead, could carry many times their own weight, raised farms of aphids that they milked, and had farmers and soldiers and workers. They went on and on, delightfully sharing their knowledge.

One little girl pulled him down closer to the soil and pointed to a small cocoon fastened to a cluster of grass. His eye patch concerned her. If he couldn't see well, he wouldn't understand her story about this little moth that would break free of the cocoon next spring. She handed him a magnifying glass.

"Why, thank you." He was overwhelmed by this act of kindness and concern from a small child. A picture of Brandy at this age flashed into his mind. It was accompanied by a twinge of sadness. The little girl was concerned about the frown that claimed his face for a moment. He saw this and quickly added, "I assure you, I can see better today with one eye than I could last year with two."

She didn't understand, but accepted the return of the smile as an invitation to continue her story.

Dirty Maria was cordial, but distant. She remembered the threats and violence that the Bentons had brought to the community. She wasn't certain why Cal was here. Emilio recognized him as a man of wealth and power. Without waiting for an invitation, he began an explanation of the Organization for the Rights of Plants, and the research he was promoting on the synthetic production of botanical starches and sugars. He even suggested that a check for $100,000 would be appropriate. Belinda tried to calm the crusader, but Cal finally put an end to his plea by reminding him that he had just lost everything he owned the day before, and was now looking for a place to live.

Cal marveled at the varied means by which energy was harvested from the sun and the wind. Belinda explained that with less than half the collectors in place, they were already producing three times the energy Oblivion was consuming. This surplus energy was sold to Mountain States Electric. She was proud of the fact that every resident got a check every month, instead of a bill from the electric company. The agriculture on a micro scale also intrigued him. He recalled the joy he felt helping Christa with the roses and flowers that filled her yard in Santa Fe. He talked with Inez and her husband about the herbs they were growing. Juan took Cal aside and suggested several herbs that might help a man of his age be a bit more vigorous. They all laughed when Christa interrupted to tell them that he was vigorous enough already.

Christa asked why so many of the homes looked so strange, with terraced earth walls, rooftop gardens, solar panels, pipes and

316

barrels, solar ovens, and underground matrixes to harvest the run off from the infrequent rains. Belinda explained that many different building materials and insulations were being tried. Each home was an experiment of one sort or another. Cal was fascinated with what was being done here. He had envisioned a community composed of potheads, winos and moonbeams. What he saw today was science, research, hard working people, creative energy and more ideas than he could comprehend.

He asked Belinda about the row of machinery that lined the wall of the old garage. Porfirio and his partner explained that all garbage had a secondary use. All organic matter was shredded and composted, then used to enrich the desert soil. Aluminum was compressed into blocks and sold, as was all cardboard. Plastics were sorted by type and melted down in several of the ovens in the row of machinery. Some of this plastic was then molded into 2 x 4's for construction. The small facility that produced this synthetic building material also provided income to the community while it utilized only solar energy in the process.

The mini Bessemer oven was used to melt down aluminum cans, scrap iron, and other metals. These ingots were then sold to cover the cost of recycling them. Cal quickly grasped the profitability of this recycling project that provided industry with a necessary raw material and saved acres of landfill space. He could relate this to mining, only it was considerably more efficient and environmentally sound.

The remaining garbage was compressed into blocks that were used as fuel in the small smelting ovens. Christa spied the bins of glass and bottles and immediately formed mental images of art work that could be done, sculpture that could speak to the world about what Oblivion was doing.

Porfirio was eager to explain that even the human waste was recycled. He explained the experimental solar toilets that cooked the waste to kill any bacteria, dried it and turned it into pellets that were sold to golf courses as fertilizer. At every turn Cal was confronted with exciting new ways of doing things and solving problems. By the time they got to the lake with its floating islands, his mind could handle no more.

He turned to Belinda, "How does Ben possibly manage all this?"

She then explained, that was why Ben was suffering from an ulcer, why the stress had almost destroyed his ability to be the artist she knew he was. She led them to the set of panels he had done for Courtney. Cal and Christa viewed them from different perspectives. She was a self educated artist who understood the message Ben was trying to convey. She also understood the flaws, artistic shortcomings, the elements that made these all failures as art. Cal could see in these the same messages that were in his wolf painting. These were warnings, but they lacked any resemblance to the quality of art he knew Ben could produce.

An idea was forming in Belinda's mind as she watched Cal's reactions to each of the elements of Oblivion. "Perhaps this can be his pardon, his amnesty, his new beginning as well," she whispered to herself as the circle was being completed and they again approached the school.

Several of the children eagerly grabbed them by the hand and led them into the community museum that was a part of Dirty Maria's school. These enthusiastic students were leading them by the hand toward a new exhibit. They were putting together a "Wall of Geology" and a major find had been placed there this morning.

"It's a fossilized mud crack." One of the girls proudly exclaimed. "We found it down by the mouth of the canyon." Another child was so excited he couldn't stand still.

On the pedestal was a large piece of rock that indeed was an ancient mud crack, formed when a puddle had dried in the sun millennia ago. Cal sat on the floor in the midst of the children and removed a piece of gold ore from his pocket. He had carried it as a good luck token for years. Belinda and Christa stood at the side and smiled as the old man with an eye patch told story after story about the valley, ranching in the old days, mining machinery and harvesting timber on the Zia Reservation land, how foolish it was to spend a lifetime searching for gold. He was handing the kids the gold ore, as a contribution to their museum, when Ben and Marquita entered.

Marquita saw Cal sitting cross legged on the floor surrounded by children, just like an Indian storyteller. He was doing just what she had pondered, when she looked at Ben's painting. He was feeding the children. He wasn't feeding their bodies, but he was feeding their minds. Marquita began to weep.

Belinda took Ben's hand and whispered that she wanted to talk to him. They left the building and strolled down the street. She described her poem and the new found discovery of Oblivion's meaning. She expressed her concern for his health, then told him she had a possible solution. First, she reminded him again of oblivion's definition. Then she described Cal's reaction to each of the proto-type projects, how he was comfortable communicating with the people, and how most of them were becoming comfortable with him. Like a lawyer would present a case before the jury, she listed Cal's losses, how Oblivion was amnesty for everyone here, how he possessed skill and talent Ben did not. How Ben could be free to be an artist if he didn't have the obligations of the community.

"I know Cal would make a perfect town manager for Oblivion. But, Belinda, it is no longer my decision. I no longer own this town. Marquita does." Even if he viewed the lifting of this responsibility with a sense of relief, there was still a hint of sorrow at the loss of influence.

Belinda returned to the school just in time to see Marquita, with hesitant steps, approach Cal. She extend her hand to help Cal up from the floor. There was an awkward handshake, as each wrestled with insecurities. They were both unsure of the other. Embarrassed, Cal introduced Marquita and Christa. There was, at first, a definite discomfort, but as they walked past Belinda, Cal had a lady on each arm. Belinda hurried to join them and pulled Marquita aside for a few seconds. There were whispers and nods, then smiles, as they came to some sort of agreement.

Belinda was turning to Cal when Christa pointed to a building that was, as yet, unoccupied. It had been, in its long career, an assayer's lab and doctor's office. During the town's heyday it was the even the home and workplace of a popular "lady of the evening." Now it was reduced to eroded adobe walls protecting stacks of the materials needed to build more solar collectors. Crista could see the adobe walls repaired and a studio at the back that looked out over the lake and mountains beyond. She could close her eyes and see yellow sunflowers, blue morning glories and red roses in the front yard. There would be no fence or wall around the yard because all would be welcome.

While Christa was walking toward the vision of a home of their own, Marquita and Cal were sitting on one of the school benches charting the future of Oblivion. Cal stood and they shook hands. He seemed to walk taller, with a sense of purpose as he joined Christa at the ruins from which her dreams would grow. Marquita watched them and smiled. Then she began to sing a song she remembered her mother singing to her father as they sat on the porch after a long day's labors. It was a song of joy and thankfulness that the ordeals of the day were over, that they could now relax. She walked over to Mama Rosa's to help her make the crust for some more apple pies.

Cal nodded his head in disbelief. He was overwhelmed with the fact that these people were accepting him, not for what he had been, but for what he was now. Oblivion would be his new beginning as well. He hugged Christa, then they started to plan their new home and their new life.

Ben had set off on a personal journey. He stopped at the jail, seized an axe from the tools stored there, and, with determined steps, marched toward the cottonwoods. Great primal screams accompanied each blow of the axe. Each of the panels was quickly reduced to splinters, until he got to the one titled "The March." He raised the tool to strike the first blow, but the dove landed on the edge of it and spread its wings to protect the painting, and its message of peace.

"Don't you think that one ought to be spared?" Courtney spoke from behind him.

His need to escape from these dark works of his own hand had been satisfied. He tried to explain to her that he could not create images of hate, anger and despair when the world was in such great need of hope and promise.

"Many say the rose is cursed by its thorns. Ben, you understand that it is the thorn that is blessed with the rose."

The old Indian sat with Belinda and watched Ben in his act of destruction. She wanted to run to Ben, to comfort him, but the old sage held her back.

"Nature is not only a cute bunny. It is also a hungry lion and a waiting vulture. The mother of nature knows anger with her joy, death with her birth, the music of life with the wisdom of time." He was silent for a brief moment of eternity, then took the small drum from his leather bag and began to tap out the rhythm of life, the heart beat of the soul.

Belinda was seeing Ben in slow motion, engaged in a ballet of destruction. He was sending to another oblivion the symbols of hate, greed, ignorance, cruelty, suffering, intolerance, violence, war, destruction, selfishness and fear. He left only the transformation of destruction into compassion. The words of this journey were forming in her mind.

"The lesson most difficult to learn is that there are many answers to each question." He pointed to a row of asters, in their autumn glory, crowned with a multitude of flowers in a myriad of colors. "Each flower speaks to the sun in its own voice, and is beautiful. Is the white aster more truly an aster than the blue?"

She smiled with the comprehension. "Of course not. They are all asters, they are all from the same seed."

"Good. Now, is the garden more beautiful than the asters alone?" He waved his arm to include the sunflowers, goldenrod, saltbush, winterfat and apache plume.

"The garden is far more beautiful in its variety, in the way colors and forms contrast and compliment, than any single blossom could be."

He smiled again and plucked a single flower from the thousands of asters within his reach. "Is there not a glory in this single bloom that you do not see in the beauty of the garden?"

She nodded, but was puzzled by this contradiction.

"The wonder of humanity begins with the beauty within each single individual. Until that individual bud becomes a blossom of peace and love, the garden cannot be a thing of beauty. Ben is, at this moment, cleansing his soul. His art will be his blossom. Your words will be your fair flower. Do you think it was some accident that the two of you met in the oblivion of your lives, that now you will spend the rest of your lives in Oblivion?"

She watched him as he put the bag over his shoulder, then his flute to his lips. "Who are you?" She finally found the courage to ask.

"I am known only as the old Indian, for to name me would be to limit me. Someday, you will understand my mystery. I am more than now, I am more than before, and I am more than what will be. I give great gifts, and they are wasted. But, I am patient, because I understand that so much of what we do is learning about ourselves, and what is within us. That is the most fearful, for we don't want to know what we are. This is foolish, for all are part of the great mystery; that makes each one of us so wonderful, so precious. I am what you need for me to be. Speak of me only as the father of time, and know that you are never without me."

Every ending is only another beginning.
Ben

Epilogue

Oblivion is not utopia. Happiness is not the constant companion of everyone living here, although it is a frequent visitor. The majority of the environmental projects survived the journey from dream to reality. Other communities are gradually adopting the lifestyle of these pioneers. The great conflict between "People and nature" has been replaced, in many parts of the world, by a truce. The impact of global warming and the environmental consequences we still can't comprehend, and many still refuse to accept, will force everyone to begin to think in new directions. Oblivion may well be our destiny. It will take generations before we will truly understand what Courtney tries to tell us about being a part of nature, not something apart, not the enemy. But the good news is that, as a need for cooperation replaces the artificial drive of competition, everyday people are seeking and finding their personal harmony. This has not, as yet, brought a peace universal, but perhaps we are getting closer.

Belinda has continued to blossom as she applies the talent she had been given, the gift of words. Her verses continue to speak of hope, optimism, the value of every person, the confidence that, "We can do this, we can know that" is a universal talent. This faith in the future and acceptance of personal growth, nurtured within the comfort of a cooperative community, will make her the best read, and most loved poet of this new millennium. All the proceeds from her words have been channeled into foundations and organizations that provide comfort to the troubled, alleviate fear, abolish conflict, and promote universal peace.

Ben is becoming more reclusive as fame again pursues him. His

323

art continues to reflect his private journey toward understanding. He uses a variety of mediums to convey messages of harmony within ourselves, within our communities, and with nature. The majority of his work continues to be of an environmental nature. His overriding message is that we are each a single cell in the global organism. "Whether we like it or not, we are participants, not spectators in this thing called life," he said during a rare interview. He guards his time and often seeks solitude to create. He is pleased that his art has been used to spread environmental messages and fund many projects. He seems happy, but has periods when he is moody, almost depressed. Perhaps this is the nature of an artist, or the rhythm or the creative spirit.

Cal is doing a great job managing the multitude of projects that keep Oblivion in a constant state of change. He has become a champion and spokesman for what he refers to as "cooperative ecology." He background has given him the ability to defend Oblivion and its people against the never ending onslaught of those who would take advantage of this community of dreamers, activists and survivors. He is, for the first time in his life, a truly happy warrior.

Christa is gaining considerable respect and renown for her sculptures, all carrying the message of peace. She continues her personal journey. As more and more of her past falls through the holes in her mind and is lost forever, she focuses more and more on her new life. The dove continues to talk to her, but she now spends a good deal of time visiting with the other folks in the community, sharing stories and learning about life.

Would that all those in this story of a unique community were experiencing joyful and productive lives filled with peace and harmony. Unfortunately, such is not the case. Derritt is showing slow progress, as he continues to experience periods of intense rage and uncontrollable hatred. Landreth will probable be released within the next year. He has already made claims about his father's sanity, in an attempt to gain control of the modest trust fund that's all that survives of the Benton empire. There does seem to be a growing storm, with father against son.

Brandy had spent several weeks in Oblivion, but disappeared just days before Cal and Christa first visited the community. No one has seen her since and there has been no communication from her, either. This is a weight on Cal's mind. The worst is feared because there have been no withdrawals from her bank account since her disappearance. She had been struggling to understand what Oblivion was about, but many of the residents say she remained apart, and, in some ways, aloof. Perhaps she has much healing to do before she can truly return.

Marquita still hasn't come to terms with the magnitude of what she owns. She has worked hard to help the farmers in the valley of her childhood, and has relied on Cal to manage her other properties, as well as Oblivion. She has worked closely with the scientists and environmentalists to make certain that there would be trees, flowers, clean air and water for future generations. She wears her scars as if they were badges and financially supports many causes that oppose violence. She still spends much of her time assisting folks with their gardens in Oblivion, occasionally helping Mama Rosa with the pies, digging garlic and stringing chile ristras with the campesinos in the valley. She shows no interest in assuming any role in the management of her vast holdings. She still struggles with the demons of her past as nightmares all too often haunt her dreamtime. Landreth's release weights heavy on her mind. Her spoken regret is that she now has little time to read her romance novels.

Larry Scott resigned his teaching position at the University of New Mexico, and left the Albuquerque Journal to take up residence in Oblivion. He began to write *Oblivion's Chronicle* as an accurate account of its creation as a proto-type community, but soon realized that he would require something in the form of a novel if he was to say some of the things he needed to voice. He loves the enigmatic and sensitive

Serena so deeply. Their love is one of almost mythical purity, a union of mind and soul, but they shared the passion of ideas, never the passion of their bodies. She was the primary reason he moved to Oblivion. In the first winter, on one of those dark days when guilt was devouring her, she walked out into a swirling snow and simply disappeared. She had been plagued by waves of guilt about something in her past that she never shared. Shame, about the physical attraction she felt for Larry, had again overwhelmed her. Sins of omission troubled her mind as she counted her failures to do all she could have done to help many of the people she encountered. Their images haunted her nighttime hours as transgressions real and imagined became a burden too great for her soul. She danced less and less, finding her only joy in humble service to others, and thoughts shared with Larry.

Most of the residents assume she has died in the snowstorm. Larry clings to the voice within him that insists she lives. He is writing *Child of Oblivion*, a novel about Serena, and has now devoted his life to making his fiction come true. It has become his quest to find her.

The end of this story is only the beginning of Oblivion. Thank you, kind reader, for taking the time to share the first step in this journey. I wish you peace. hb

Non-fiction:

Gardens for the Senses, Gardening as Therapy, an introduction to the field of horticultural therapy by Hank Bruce $14.95

Garden Projects for Horticultural Therapy Programs, by Hank Bruce and Tomi Jill Folk $18.95

Garden Projects for the Classroom, by Hank Bruce and Tomi Jill Folk a guide for the integration of diverse subject disciplines in the garden
$25.95

Global Gardening, by Hank Bruce & Tomi Jill Folk, explores the causes and how we can all be a part of the solution to global hunger $23.95

The Courage to Create: A Writer's Workbook, by Hank Bruce $15.95

The Family Caregiver's Journal: A Guide to Facing the Terminal Illness of a Loved One, by Hank Bruce& Tomi Jill Folk $14.95

Que Tips: A Stage Management Handbook for High School Theatre, By Elizabeth D. Ward $15.95

Visits with the Storyteller, Stories from a Native American elder that deal with a wide range of subjects from corn husk dolls to merry-go-rounds, blankets to cracked pots. Retold by Tomi Jill Folk $19.95

Fiction:

Oblivion, An artist and a poet bring new life to a New Mexico ghost town and in the process develop an eco-friendly community $19.95

Inspired by His Music: A Tribute to John Denver's Vision, 15 short stories dealing with peace, the environment, hunger, refugees, love and eagles, all inspired by the work of John Denver $19.95

About the author

Hank Bruce is a writer, horticultural therapist, hunger activist, teacher and speaker. He is the former president of the Florida Chapter of the American Horticultural Therapy Association. Hank has conducted research on the use of plants, flowers and gardening activities as therapeutic tools with stroke and Alzheimer's patients, and the value of gardening activities in the treatment of victims of domestic violence and substance abuse.

In April 2007 he was awarded the Lifetime Achievement Award by the Florida Chapter of the American Horticultural Therapy Association and in 2001 he was given the Humanitarian of the Year Award by the American Horticultural Therapy Association.

He has also done research on micro-intensive vegetable gardening systems that are adaptable for use by gardeners with limitations, and for those living where there is limited water, space, soil or other resources. He is the program director of a non-profit food security organization, Hunger Grow Away, and his proceeds from sale of this book will be donated to that organization to help support their work.